CW01497399

Spilling the beans

MANCHESTER
1824

Manchester University Press

Spilling the beans
*Eating, cooking, reading and writing
in British women's fiction,
1770–1830*

Sarah Moss

Manchester University Press

Manchester and New York

*distributed in the United States exclusively
by Palgrave Macmillan*

Copyright © Sarah Moss 2009

The right of Sarah Moss to be identified as the author of this work has been asserted by her in accordance with the Copyright, Designs and Patents Act 1988.

Published by Manchester University Press
Oxford Road, Manchester M13 9NR, UK
and Room 400, 175 Fifth Avenue, New York, NY 10010, USA
www.manchesteruniversitypress.co.uk

Distributed in the United States exclusively by
Palgrave Macmillan, 175 Fifth Avenue,
New York, NY 10010, USA

Distributed in Canada exclusively by
UBC Press, University of British Columbia, 2029 West Mall,
Vancouver, BC, Canada V6T 1Z2

British Library Cataloguing-in-Publication Data is available

Library of Congress Cataloging-in-Publication Data is available

ISBN 978 0 7190 8644 1 paperback

First published by Manchester University Press in hardback 2009

This paperback edition first published 2011

The publisher has no responsibility for the persistence or accuracy of URLs for any external or third-party internet websites referred to in this book, and does not guarantee that any content on such websites is, or will remain, accurate or appropriate.

Printed by Lightning Source

Contents

Acknowledgements   *Page* vi

Introduction   1

1 Eating her words
   The politics of commensality in Frances Burney's
   fiction and letters   44

2 The maternal aliment
   Feeding daughters in the works of
   Mary Wollstonecraft   82

3 The bill of fare
   The politics of food in Maria Edgeworth's
   children's fiction   122

4 Eating for Britain
   Food, family and national identity in
   Susan Ferrier's fiction   160

Afterword   191

Bibliography   193

Index   202

Acknowledgements

I began work on this book as the Randall McIver Research Fellow at Lady Margaret Hall, Oxford, and I thank the trustees and the fellows for their support. In Oxford, Lucy Newlyn offered useful advice on my earliest ideas, and the Women's History Group gave me a friendly forum for thinking aloud. Rebecca Park helped me refine my ideas about gender and consumption from a perspective new to a literary critic as well as offering invaluable fellowship in the early days of combining motherhood and scholarship.

This book's greatest and most pleasurable debts were acquired in the School of English at the University of Kent. I cannot adequately thank Jennie Batchelor for her endless generosity with her time, which is short, and her expertise, which is great. Rod Edmond provided support which made me feel able to combine new professional and domestic commitments with ongoing research, and Scarlett Thomas, Jennie Batchelor and David Stirrup in particular provided an environment of sociable scholarship in which anything is possible. Nicki Humble, Sinead Mooney, Debbie Lee, Alec Badenoch and the students on my Food and Literature courses have helped to shape my ideas. I am particularly grateful to everyone at Manchester University Press for good humour combined with intellectual thoroughness.

I would like to thank Mary Eminson for showing me that it is possible and useful to apply one's intelligence to what happens at the table, and my parents for abundant opportunities to do so. I thank Anthony Maude, without whose support this kind of productivity would be unthinkable, and Max and Tobias, whose intellectual curiosity is a constant inspiration. This book is for them, and in loving memory of Irene Gummersall and her opportunities, missed and taken.

Introduction

Love and hunger, I reflected, meet at a woman's breast.[1]
— Sigmund Freud, *The Interpretation of Dreams*

[T]he power of population is infinitely greater than the power in the earth to produce subsistence for man.[2]
— Thomas Malthus, *An Essay on the Principle of Population*

I began with the idea that there are, essentially, two ways in which we might understand food in literary texts. The first, for the last century informed by psychoanalysis, sees food as a manifestation of love, a confirmation (which may be self-administered) that the eater is deserving. Eating, in this reading, is a way of both constructing and imagining a 'subjectivity' that has become steadily more problematic over the last thirty years of literary theory.[3] It is in this tradition that recent scholarship on Romanticism and food has tended to work, attending to the bodies in the poems of Wordsworth, Keats, Byron and Shelley in ways shaped by psychoanalysis and deconstruction.[4] The second, developed from social contract theories of

1 Sigmund Freud, *The Interpretation of Dreams,* in *The Standard Edition of the Complete Psychological Works of Sigmund Freud* (trans. James Strachey *et al.*), vol. iv (London: Hogarth Press, 1958), p. 204.
2 Thomas Malthus, *An Essay on the Principle of Population* (Harmondsworth: Penguin, 1985), p. 71.
3 See in particular Jacques Derrida, '"Il faut bien manger" ou le calcul du sujet', in *Points de suspension: entretiens* (Paris: Editions Galilée, 1992).
4 See Timothy Morton (ed.), *Cultures of Taste/Theories of Appetite: Eating Romanticism* (New York and Basingstoke: Palgrave Macmillan, 2004), and Denise Gigante, *Taste: A literary history* (Newhaven: Yale University Press, 2005).

the eighteenth century via Karl Marx, understands food as a basis of economics, the fundamental reason why people labour, and in this tradition we might find recent historicist work on 'consumption' that is, interestingly, rarely literal.[5]

Like all the best binary oppositions, of course, this neat alignment of Freud/Marx, deconstruction/historicism, Romanticism/long eighteenth century, opens up on closer inspection. In *The Interpretation of Dreams*, Freud recounts a dream of his own, in which 'tired and hungry after a journey ... the major vital needs began to announce their presence in my sleep':

> *I went into a kitchen in search of some pudding. Three women were standing in it; one of them was the hostess of the inn and was twisting something about in her hand, as though she was making Knödel [dumplings]. She answered that I must wait until she was ready ...*
>
> When I began analysing this dream, I thought quite unexpectedly of the first novel I ever read ... The hero went mad and kept calling out the names of the three women who had brought the greatest happiness and sorrow into his life. One of these names was Pelagie ... In connection with the three women I thought of the three Fates who spin the destiny of man, and I knew that one of the women – the inn-hostess in the dream – was the mother who gives life and furthermore (as in my own case) gives the living creature its first nourishment. Love and hunger, I reflected, meet at a woman's breast.[6]

Freud goes on to associate the movement his mother made rubbing her hands together to shape Knödel (dumplings) with the movement she made to produce by friction 'the blackish scales of epidermis ... as a proof that we were made of earth'. The professor who taught Freud about the epidermis had had his work plagiarised by a man called Knodl. The dream-work connects Knodl the man with Knödel the dumpling and Pelagie the fictional heroine with the actual villainy of plagiarism. But Freud's analysis connects the pleasures of reading with the gratification of eating, and women's manufacture of food with the dust to which we shall all return. The woman's body makes milk, and her hands make food, in exactly the same way as they make dead bodies. 'Giving life', as we know,

5 See particularly Elizabeth Kowaleski Wallace, *Consuming Subjects: Women, Shopping and Business in the Eighteenth Century* (New York: Columbia University Press, 1997); and Harriet Guest, *Small Change: Women, Learning, Patriotism, 1750–1810* (Chicago: University of Chicago Press, 2000).

6 Freud, 'On the Material and Sources of Dreams', in *Interpretation of Dreams, Standard Works*, vol. iv, p. 204.

is also 'giving death'. So far, so Kristevan. But Freud, who often discusses wet-nurses and mothers as if they were interchangeable, elsewhere remarks that the breast is to the baby as an inn is to a (male) adult. From the perspective of recent work on gender and economic productivity in the late eighteenth century, it clear that part of what is repressed in the announcement that 'love and hunger meet at a woman's breast' is the economic. The inn-hostess, like the wet-nurse, does not 'give' life but 'sells' it. In some cases, it is not love, or not only love, and hunger that meet at the breast. Money is there too.

And yet the 'opposite' approach to the meanings of food also contains its own contradiction. In *Two Treatises of Government*, John Locke sets out eating as the basis of work and ownership of food as the model for all other, subsequent, kinds of ownership. Food, here, is money rather than love, even if, as Locke implies, the presence of raw material is the sign of divine love for humanity. Locke writes,

> Though the earth, and all inferior creatures, be common to all men, yet every man has a property in his own person: this no body has any right to but himself. The labour of his body, and the work of his hands, we may say, are properly his ...
>
> He that is nourished by the acorns he picked up under an oak, or the apples he gathered from the trees in the wood, has certainly appropriated them to himself. Nobody can deny but that the nourishment is his. I ask then, when did they begin to be his? when he digested? or when he eat? or when he boiled? or when he brought them home? or when he picked them up? and it is plain, if the first gathering made them not his, nothing else could.[7]

Consumption, here, seems to be a form of production. Eating makes property. Paul Youngquist comments in his essay on 'Romantic Dietetics' that for Locke, 'Eating is the epitome of human agency both because it requires work and because that work is transformative ... The agency of eating transforms common matter into personal property, giving all men a property in their own person.'[8] The act of incorporation is indeed the basis of ownership here, but it is not in fact eating but 'gathering' that constitutes the legitimate taking of possession. One can, as Locke goes on to explain, feed another person. 'Children or servants' may share in 'the meat, which their master or father had provided for them', but 'Though the water

7 John Locke, *Two Treatises of Government*, ed. C. B. McPherson (Indianapolis and Cambridge: Hackett Publishing, 1980), p. 237.
8 Paul Youngquist, 'Romantic Dietetics', in Morton (ed.), *Cultures of Taste*, p. 241.

running in the fountain be every one's, yet who can doubt, but that in the pitcher is his only who drew it out?' It is not the 'agency of eating' (or drinking) that is transformative here, but the agency of foraging.

It is important that this is 'foraging' and not 'harvesting'. The examples Locke uses are noticeably 'raw' (to borrow from another discourse about food and its formations). Acorns, apples, in section 26 'The fruit or venison which nourishes the *wild Indian*, who knows no enclosure', in section 30 'what fish anyone catches in the ocean, that great and still remaining common of mankind' and 'the hare that any one is hunting'; these are ingredients, not food. It is also interesting that this politics of entitlement is limited by shelf life, for Locke, like modern British law, defines 'enjoyment' in relation to use rather than pleasure. 'As much as anyone can make use of to any advantage of life before it spoils, so much he may by his labour fix a property in.' The advantage of money is that it does not 'go off' before its time. '*A little piece of yellow metal*, which would keep without wasting or decay' allows the individual to accumulate surplus without the criminality of 'rotted fruit' and 'putrified venison' removed from the common pot and wasted, and cooking is what links the two:

> for it is not barely the plough-man's pains, the reaper's and thresher's toil, and the baker's sweat, is to be counted into the bread we eat; the labour of those who broke the oxen, who digged and wrought the iron and stones, who felled and framed the timber employed about the plough, mill, oven, or any other utensils, which are a vast number, requisite to this corn, from its being seed to be sown to its being made bread, must all be charged on account of the labour, and received as an effect of that: nature and the earth furnished only the most worthless materials, as in themselves.[9]

This is cooking as an (apparently ungendered) economic activity, the exact opposite of the work of love done by Freud's inn-keeper and his mother. Food here is a commodity, or perhaps *the* commodity, but if it is the basis of all economics it is nonetheless grounded in need and greed. Eating may be the foundation of private property, but it is also a daily reinscription of dependence.

'Thing theory', which considers the ways in which literary texts imagine or admit the subjectivities of 'objects', might seem to offer a bridge between these ideas of objects as abjected subjects and

9 Locke, *Two Treatises*, p. 324.

objects as transferable value, but the point about the study of food in literature is that it demonstrates the limits of these metaphors. Barbara Benedict writes in 'The Spirit of Things',

> Things and ghosts seem opposite: the first all material form, the second all immaterial spirit. Both things and ghosts, however, lie on the margins of form and formlessness, materiality and meaning: things metaphorically connote the soulless body, ghosts the bodiless soul, and both express the problem of finding selfhood in the nexus of spirit and form.[10]

Benedict continues to offer a fascinating account of eighteenth-century stories of ghosts and poltergeists, but the relation of food to such formulations is vexed. Food does not 'connote the soulless body'; it is the precondition of the body and therefore of consciousness. Food 'keeps body and soul together', holds the mind that thinks and the body that works, and most importantly, writes, in the endlessly questionable relationship to which we are endlessly devoted. Ghosts do not, so far as I know, eat (although Benedict gives some interesting accounts of ghosts that throw food and spill drinks), but the initial presence of humans – subjects, consciousnesses, however we wish to define or challenge them – is conditional upon food. It is not a 'thing' in the sense that the locks of hair, lapdogs, diamonds and books discussed in *The Secret Life of Things* are things, because food is not an option, although at the same time it is more of a 'thing' than air or water because of its infinitely variable, and endlessly meaningful, forms.

One cannot either claim to 'read food' in the way that scholars of eighteenth and nineteenth century material culture are 'reading' jewellery, pockets, hats and wallpaper, or even in the way that a few literary critics have 'read' the coffee house, the tea service and polemic demanding a boycott of sugar.[11] Jewellery and wallpaper

10 Barbara M. Benedict, 'The Spirit of Things', in Mark Blackwell (ed.), *The Secret Life of Things: Animals, Objects and It-Narratives in Eighteenth-Century England* (Lewisburg: Bucknell University Press, 2007), p. 19.

11 See, for example, Jennie Batchelor and Cora Kaplan (eds), *Women and Material Culture, 1660–1830* (Basingstoke: Palgrave Macmillan, 2007); Kowaleski-Wallace, *Consuming Subjects*; Charlotte Sussman, *Consuming Anxieties: Consumer Protest, Gender and British Slavery, 1713–1833* (Stanford: Stanford University Press, 2000); Maxine Berg and Helen Clifford (eds), *Consumers and Luxury: Consumer Culture in Europe 1650–1850* (Manchester: Manchester University Press, 1999); Maxine Berg, *Luxury and Pleasure in Eighteenth-Century Britain* (Oxford: Oxford University Press, 2005); Lorna Weatherill, *Consumer Behaviour and Material Culture in Britain, 1660–1760* (London: Routledge, 1988); and Amanda Vickery, *The Gentleman's Daughter: Women's Lives in Georgian England* (Newhaven: Yale University Press, 1998).

are still here (still there?), and china, glass and silver survive and can be rearranged on the table with reasonable confidence thanks to the guides to table-setting in contemporary cookbooks, which are also still here. Pockets survive, albeit hidden in walls, but food 'goes off' in one way or another, its energies passed on to other forms of production. Reconstructive cooking is not like setting eighteenth-century tables with eighteenth-century tableware in eighteenth-century rooms in accordance with descriptions of eighteenth-century meals. Not only are the ingredients different in both quantifiable and inconceivable ways, but – as the burgeoning scholarship on cookbooks is beginning to explore – recipes, like other forms of conduct literature, are not transparent documents.[12] As we see with the lavish cookbooks of twenty-first century Britain, sometimes the consumption of recipes replaces cooking (as, later, I will suggest that the consumption of Romantic-era pregnancy and breastfeeding handbooks might replace the actual performance of these activities). Food, then, even when it appears in non-fiction prose, is not material culture. We cannot read food because, like the past, it is not there.

The 'disappearance' of food may be one of the reasons why the sophisticated scholarly literature on consumption so rarely turns towards consumption's most basic and frequent form. There is some work on food in modern fiction, especially in relation to ethnicity and post-colonialism and more on food in film, but even the scholarship on the body in eighteenth- and nineteenth-century literature more or less ignores food and what people do with it.[13] From Mary Douglas and Baron Isherwood's *The World of Goods* onwards, interdisciplinary studies of consumption and consumerism concentrate on the roles of shopping (for consumer durables), fashion, gift-giving, architecture, landscape and interior design in the formation of post-Renaissance identities, but the universal daily purchase, cultivation, preparation, ingestion and digestion of food seems to repel such nuanced analysis. Until the work of Timothy Morton and Denise Gigante, eighteenth- and nineteenth-century food had

---

12 See Nicola Humble, *Culinary Pleasures: Cook Books and the Transformation of British Food* (London: Faber, 2005); Sherrie Innes, *Dinner Roles: American Women and Culinary Culture* (Iowa City: University of Iowa Press, 2001); and Anne Bower (ed.) *Recipes for Reading: Community Cookbooks, Stories, Histories* (Amherst, Mass.: University of Massachusetts Press, 1997).

13 See Sarah Sceats, *Food, Consumption and the Body in Contemporary Women's Fiction* (Cambridge: Cambridge University Press, 2000); and Anna Krugovoy Silver, *Victorian Literature and the Anorexic Body* (Cambridge: Cambridge University Press, 2002).

been left to historians, and studies here are detailed and fascinating, especially since Gilly Lehmann's *The British Housewife: Cookery Books, Cooking and Society in 18ᵗʰ-century Britain*.[14] Lehmann's work in particular reminds us that all food participates in culture and that cooking is an art form (and therefore in some sense readable, or at least open to interpretation), as well as the means by which people convert what grows into energy. Roy Strong writes compellingly about dining habits and table manners in *Feast: A History of Grand Eating*, and Rebecca Spang's work on gastronomy and restaurants transforms our understanding of cuisine and French national identity in the eighteenth and nineteenth centuries.[15] Food historians have lots of friends, but *Spilling the Beans* is not about food history. I am interested in how food works in writing, in the challenges and complexities of the relationships between food and text. Elspeth Probyn suggests in *Carnal Appetites: FoodSexIdentities* that we have been 'reading' sex and money as culturally constituted aspects of identity for a long time, and we might now – against the background of our own culture's burgeoning obsession with food in all its stages – turn to the table.[16] I hope to bring some of these interpretative strategies to bear on eating, not eating, cooking, shopping and, last but by no means least, becoming food in novels.

Like money, then, food is an object. Like sex, it is a process. And unlike the objects of 'thing theory' and 'material culture studies', food is always in process, being grown, harvested, stored, cooked, served, eaten, digested and then either expended (in physical, intellectual or reproductive labour) or excreted. We perform with food as we perform with other objects; studies of cooking, eating and identity are legion. But the difference is that we cannot perform without it, and food, like life itself, changes second by second whether anyone is watching (representing, interpreting) or not. Food is power in material form, both physical power to move a pen and political power to maintain social inequality. It represents love and money

---

14 Gilly Lehmann, *The British Housewife: Cookery Books, Cooking and Society in 18th-century Britain* (Totnes: Prospect Books, 2003). See also Sandra Sherman, '"The Whole Art and Mystery of Cooking": What Cookbooks Taught Readers in the Eighteenth Century', *Eighteenth-Century Life*, 28:1 (2004), 115–35.

15 Roy Strong, *Feast: A History of Grand Eating* (London: Jonathan Cape, 2002); and Rebecca Spang, *The Invention of the Restaurant: Paris and Modern Gastronomic Culture* (Cambridge, Mass.: Harvard University Press, 2000).

16 Elspeth Probyn, *Carnal Appetites: FoodSexIdentities* (London: Routledge, 2000).

and it becomes ordure. There are specific, and timely, challenges to literary theory here. Timothy Morton writes in the conclusion of *Cultures of Taste/Theories of Appetite*:

> Nevertheless, while historicism uses the 'real' as a rhetorical supplement that enriches its analytical observations, post-structuralist work in psycho-analysis and deconstruction posits the real as inaccessible, visible as a gap or an inert presence. Diet studies need what Theodore Adorno meant by negative dialectics: the encounter of thought with what it is not – non-identity.[17]

I do not claim to offer such 'negative dialectics' in what follows, but I hope to remain mindful of the challenge.

The apple and the garden

I begin, then, as books on women's eating and its consequences will, with a man, a woman, an apple and a garden:

> Thursday. Before we had quite finished Breakfast Calvert's man brought horses for Wm. We had a deal to do to shave – pens to make – poems to put in order for writing, to settle the dress pack up & c & The man came before the pens were made & he was obliged to leave me with only two – Since he has left me (at ½ past 11) it is now 2 I have been putting the Drawers into order, laid by his clothes which we had thrown here & there & everywhere, filed two months newspapers & got my dinner 2 boiled Eggs & 2 apple tarts ... I transplanted some snowdrops – The Bees are busy – Wm has a rich bright day – It was hard frost in the night – The Robins are singing sweetly – Now for my walk. I will be busy, I will look well & be well when he comes back to me. O the Darling! here is one of his bitten apples! I can hardly find in my heart to throw it into the fire. I must wash myself, then off.[18]

There is something hauntingly 'real' in this writing-to-the-moment, something about the way the text conjures the poet's scattered clothes, the boiled eggs, the birdsong, the apple, reminiscent of the strange immediacy of John Clare. These things are no more or less than themselves, the domestic clutter of a moment charged and even iconic for modern readers. Students who have read William Wordsworth's poems and are presented with Dorothy's journals

17 Timothy Morton, 'Let Them Eat Romanticism: Materialism, Ideology and Diet Studies', in Morton (ed.), *Cultures of Taste*, p. 258.
18 Dorothy Wordsworth, *The Grasmere Journals*, ed. Pamela Woof (Oxford: Oxford University Press, 1991), p. 74.

often greet her writing with indignation, feeling that this is the 'real thing', the authentic antecedent concealed beneath the slippery rhymes and reasons of Romantic poetics, and there is something about the jerky prose and housework that make this writing seem the opposite of the poetic magic wrought by the 1805 *Prelude* or the 'Ode on Intimations of Immortality'. Poetic liberties of the sort that usually engage professional Romanticists seem to exist in a different sphere from the record that 'We had Mr Clarkson's turkey for dinner, the night before we had broiled the gizzard & some mutton & made a nice piece of cookery for Wm's supper.'[19] This seems qualitatively different from, and perhaps less interesting than, William carving Mary Hutchinson's name into the stone at the foot of the lake and the strawberry blossom in the rock described on the next page.

And yet even Romantic poets must eat. The existence of their writing tells us that they did eat, for on this most basic level the economics of production and consumption apply to the most exquisite ode. The precondition of writing – much less climbing Snowdon or swimming the Hellespont – is a body, and bodies are contingent upon eating, but at the same time it is clear that food in writing is not the same as food for writing. The reason Wordsworth's apple core provokes tears is because it is a sign of presence that has outlasted its eater. Half-eaten food is at the very least a pledge of immediate return, but in this case it is matter out of place, giving the wrong meaning. The poet is gone and so it is his sister's housewifely duty to tidy up the detritus of presence. There is a poetics of memory and mourning here that is inseparable from the materiality of the apple, burning partly in the poet's body and partly on his hearth as he travels away, thinking, writing, walking. Paul Youngquist writes of Wordsworth's turn to his sister in 'Tintern Abbey', 'This strange materializing of memory is the poem's equivalent of waste, the remainder of digestion unassimilable to the being it sustains. Dorothy incarnates a materiality irreducible to the proper body and incommensurable with the private subject.'[20] The apple is also 'waste', and it is from this position of feminine materiality that this book begins.

The texts I study here live for the most part in parallel to Romanticism. These women novelists of the Romantic era speak from and to positions in which corporeality, domesticity and economics figure very differently from the poets studied by other writers on food in

19 Wordsworth, *Grasmere Journals*, p. 58.
20 Youngquist, 'Romantic Dietetics', p. 251.

this era. The novels show the female body, and in a different way the female mind, to be inescapably implicated in a cycle of production and consumption that offers considerable opportunities for the fulfilment of moral and economic potential. For Frances Burney as for Virginia Woolf, the feeding of the female body is inseparable from the productivity of the feminine mind. For Mary Wollstonecraft, good mothering, which includes good writing, depends upon good eating, which means constant surveillance of potentially disordered appetites. For Maria Edgeworth, the proper management of domestic resources merges with the economic functionality which is the basis of upward social mobility, while Susan Ferrier shows how the national identities of the early nineteenth century are concocted in the kitchen and affirmed at the table. Other texts would, and I hope will, produce other narratives, but these four show some of the ways in which food complicates existing discussions of material culture, things, identity and the body in Romantic-era women's fiction.

While it emerges throughout this book that 'real' food is both inaccessible and qualitatively different from textual food, and while it is not clear to me that any kind of culinary re-enactment is constructive in reading fiction, it remains worth noting some of the distinctive Romantic-era foodways which fiction complicates. The most obvious, and the one which exerts the greatest tacit influence on the texts studied here, is that this is an era in which many people went hungry much of the time, and deaths from starvation, while far from common, were an occasional result of destitution. Literary criticism, particularly where it is concerned with children's literature, sometimes assumes that instabilities in food supplies or employment were sufficient to tip large numbers of the poorest British people into starvation.[21] The evidence from food and agricultural history suggests that this is not so. Even in the Highlands and Islands of Scotland in the closing decades of the eighteenth century, when the impossibility of sustaining rapidly expanding populations on poor land provided most of the rationale for the Clearances, although mortality rates rose during the hardest winters and epidemics were more frequent and caused more deaths than at other times, very few people died of malnutrition.[22] In both history (Peterloo) and fiction (*The Wanderer*), the prospect of imminent

21 See Bruno Bettelheim, *The Uses of Enchantment: The Meaning and Importance of Fairy Tales* (Harmondsworth: Penguin, 1978).
22 See Eric Richards, *The Highland Clearances* (Edinburgh: Birlinn, 2005).

starvation is always greeted with an outrage that confirms its rarity. To be short of food is to suffer an insult rather than to endure a fact of life, however poor the sufferer. Amartya Sen demonstrated in the 1980s that, 'Starvation is the characteristic of some people not *having* enough food to eat. It is not characteristic of there *being* not enough food to eat.'[23] This certainty comes over clearly in late eighteenth-century fiction, especially in the repeated trope of the child who pauses on the way into a cake shop to spend his pocket money and either gives the money to a beggar child or buys bread for that child. The idea of 'charity' as a means of feeding those who would other-wise go hungry makes it clear that the problem is entitlement rather than shortage of supply. No one needs to starve because there is not enough food, and the sense that the cake of the few is purchased by the bread of the many is common from Versailles to Edgeworths-town. Eighteenth-century food, like oil today, is political because everybody needs it and some people have more than they need. There is a sense, played out at the tables of Romantic-era novels as well as in the Place de la République, that quantities are limited so that one person's gluttony ensures another person's starvation. It is the logic that, in another age, connects the unfinished fish fingers on the British child's plate to the generic (and politically dubious) 'starving children in Africa', and it is powerful.

As the founding texts of social anthropology tell us, the rituals of dinner work in the context of these anxieties about hunger to share out what is available in a way that reinforces the politics of entitle-ment.[24] People come to the table (or its cultural equivalent) to share food, but unless the table is an altar and the meal is Communion, they will leave with varying quantities of varying foodstuffs in their stomachs. The variables responsible for these differences are enor-mous and are not, for the most part, addressed in my project here. Certain foods are reserved for certain people – for instance, expensive foods for powerful and dominant individuals – but other examples are purées for babies or milk for young children. Some diners may have ideological reasons for rejecting, for example, meat, alcohol or sugar, and mere personal preference, albeit always culturally

---

23 Amartya Sen, *Poverty and Famines: An Essay on Entitlement and Deprivation* (Oxford: Oxford University Press, revised edn, 1982), p. 1.
24 See, for example, Margaret Mead (ed.), *Cultural Patterns and Technical Change* (New York: UNESCO, 1955); Claude Levi-Strauss, *The Origin of Table Manners: Introduction to a Science of Mythology*, vol. 3 (London: Jonathan Cape, 1978); Mary Douglas, *Implicit Meanings: Essays in Anthropology* (London: Routledge and Kegan Paul, 1975).

inflected, directs choices and behaviours in ways that may or may not be interpreted as politicised. Some people come late to the table, perhaps because the meal is breakfast and they have stayed in bed, perhaps because they were awake in the night – studying, keeping secret appointments or too unhappy to sleep – or perhaps because they are lazy. Some people leave the table early, usually women and usually because they are upset. Sometimes food is spilt (on account of bad servants, probably because the lady of the house is a bad manager, or a nervous hostess, in which case the reader probably knows what she is nervous about). It is, perhaps, in the reading of these rituals and (mis)behaviours that the study of food in literature is most obviously exciting, and the concept of commensality, coming together around the table, may have nearly as much to offer literary critics as it does to social anthropologists.

The foodways of the Romantic era make the theatre of the table particularly rich. Gilly Lehmann's chapter, 'The Eighteenth Century at Table' provides a detailed and thorough account of changing dining habits; what follows is based largely upon her work and is meant to sketch the basis of later observations about dining and social codes. Readers of eighteenth-century fiction know the charged atmosphere surrounding the timing of meals. Dinner began – and indeed for some people remains – as a midday meal. By the 1750s, dinners among the elite in London were served around 4 p.m., with an informal supper usually composed of left-overs from dinner provided before bedtime. Working people and those outside London dined earlier, but there is a continuum between status and dining hour, so that even in the provinces and among the middling sort, formal and celebratory meals took place later than ordinary dinners. By the 1820s, the gentry were dining at 8 and 9 p.m., which made supper redundant except at the end of a ball or late party in the early hours of the morning, and created a vacancy which was filled by what became 'lunch'. Breakfast was stable throughout the period as a collation of breads and hot drinks served around 10 a.m., although in many houses it was not a formal meal and remained available until the last person had risen and eaten.

The comedic potential of this changing timetable is fully exploited by contemporary fiction. In Jane Austen's unfinished novel *The Watsons*, 'as Nanny at five minutes before three, was beginning to bustle into the parlour with the Tray and the Knife-Case, she was suddenly called to the front door, by the sound of as smart a rap as the end of a riding-whip could give'.[25] It is Lord Osbourne and Tom Musgrave, who stay, 'disregard[ing] every symptom, however positive, of the nearness of that Meal', until Elizabeth tells the servant to 'take up the Fowls' and apologises for 'what early hours we keep'. Tom Musgrave begins a later call by telling his hostesses that 'he was going home to an 8 o' clock dinner'.[26] Characters attempt to prove social superiority by expecting dinner when their hosts are preparing supper (usually instead demonstrating idle and luxurious habits), and heroines, like Burney's Cecilia, evince virtue by looking for breakfast hours before it is served.

Earlier in the eighteenth century, precedence determined by social status had dominated customs of dining, dictating not only the order in which diners entered the dining room but where they sat and what foods they were served. Women, arranged by rank, sat at one end of the table and men at the other. By the 1770s, men and women were sitting together, all food on the table was in principle intended for all diners, and guests as well as the host and hostess expected to carve. Gilly Lehmann reads these changes as signalling 'the shift in eighteenth century table manners from the formal to the sociable', but, as with most forms of elite sociability, it was achieved by excluding the lower orders from the table.[27] The air of democratic commensality becomes fashionable at roughly the same time as the servants' hall, and novels of the period suggest that precedence continues to be a matter of concern, although usually in proving the petty arrogance of those who think about it. When Elizabeth Bennet's sister Lydia returns to Longbourne after Wickham has been forced to marry her, Elizabeth leaves the room in disgust,

> till she heard them passing through the hall to the dining parlour. She then joined them soon enough to see Lydia, with anxious parade, walk up to her mother's right hand, and hear her say to her eldest sister: 'Ah, Jane, I take your place now, and you must go lower, because I am a married woman.'[28]

This vignette also suggests how coercive commensality can be. However strong her feelings, Elizabeth must rejoin the family as they move to the table, and this more or less compulsory sociability sets the scene for a sequence of interactions under pressure.

25 Jane Austen, 'The Watsons', in *Northanger Abbey, Lady Susan, The Watsons and Sanditon*, ed. John Davie (Oxford: Oxford University Press, 1990), p. 304.
26 Austen, *Watsons*, p. 312.
27 Lehmann, *British Housewife*, p. 357.
28 Jane Austen, *Pride and Prejudice* (Oxford: Oxford University Press, 1990), p. 272.

At the table, *service à la française* meant that social interaction and eating were co-dependent. In *service à la française*, which was gradually replaced by *service à la Russe* over the course of the nineteenth century, a dinner consisted of one or two courses, sometimes followed by a dessert, and all the food in each course was arranged on the table for diners to help each other. As the many table plans in eighteenth- and nineteenth-century cookbooks make clear, the progression from savoury to sweet foods came later, and between the 1770s and the 1830s each course would consist of two or three joints of meat accompanied by smaller dishes of fish, vegetables, sweet and savoury puddings, tarts, jellies and creams. It is not obvious to the modern reader that there is any principle separating first-course dishes from second-course dishes.[29] All the component parts of what we would now recognise as 'a meal' appear on the table together, and where only one course was offered – which did not necessarily mean that there was either less food or fewer dishes than when there were two – the hostess might tell guests, 'You see your dinner.' Away from cities with confectioners' shops, dessert often consisted of fresh and dried fruits and nuts, although some cookbooks recommend the making of more complicated sweets as recreational cooking for ladies of leisure. Confectioners would provide ice creams and the ornate creations of marzipan and spun sugar which link medieval visual games and jokes with food to modern wedding and Christmas cakes. Dessert was for display and play, and marked formal and high-status occasions. It often appears in novels as the sign of conspicuous consumption divorced from either need or productivity, nutritionally redundant eating of the sort that continues to generate anxiety.

The presence of all the food on the table without servants to hand it around meant that diners controlled each other's access to dinner. In some situations diners could help themselves to dishes within reach and ask their companions to pass foods from further away (the truly unassuming heroine contents herself with whatever happens to be at hand), and in others, according to some of the conduct books, neighbours should help each other to what they could reach and wait to be offered anything else. Men are counselled against giving women quantities suggesting that they believe the lady to have a gross appetite. John Trusler, ostensibly writing for socially mobile young men in 1791, advises,

---

29 For a much more detailed analysis, see Lehmann, *British Housewife*, p. 330.

As eating a great deal is deemed indelicate in a lady; (for her character should rather be divine than sensual) it will be ill manners to help her to a large slice of meat at once, or fill her plate too full. When you have served her with meat, she should be asked what kind of vegetables she likes, and the gentleman sitting next the dish that holds those vegetables, should be requested to help her.[30]

Whoever carves – women at the beginning of this period and men by the end – should consult each recipient's preferences ('Do you run or fly?' the carver asks, serving chicken in Susan Ferrier's *Inheritance* and offering a worrying but widespread conflation of eater and eaten). What actually happened at the table, what Gilly Lehmann calls 'eating on the ground', is of course beyond investigation, but taken together, conduct manuals, cookbooks, letters, journals and fiction suggest that the rules of engagement at the table were widely variable and honoured as much in the breach as in the observance, offering endless potential for absurdity and disruption.

Poisoning minds: eating/reading, cooking/writing

Now, if in the intervals of leisure you can with relish repair to books, you need never be at a loss … After being disgusted with the nauseous or the meagre diet, served up in most companies, where low scandal, or mere town-talk, supply the place of urbanity and sense; how rich and regaling will she find that repast which her library is always ready to furnish.

There she will not fail of meeting with food of every different flavour, whether of lighter or more solid substance, agreeable to her present inclination; at the same time that nothing is forced upon her, and she is left at liberty, not only to vary the entertainment as often and as much as she pleases, but also to rise from it whenever she will.[31]

Rarely have young women been so benignly invited to partake of the fruits of knowledge. James Fordyce's notorious sermons do not usually encourage his readers to enjoy 'liberty' or pay attention to their 'present inclinations', much less to take control of 'entertainments'. But reading here figures as a safe form of both eating and socialising, a nourishing alternative to the revolting and dangerous world beyond the text. Fordyce shows a tacit understanding of the politics of the table. As we will see, in both fiction and autobiographical writing young women do not order meals (and if they do,

30 John Trusler, *The Honours of the Table* (London: 1791), p. 7.
31 James Fordyce, *Sermons to Young Ladies* (Edinburgh: rev. edn 1775) vol. 2, pp. 78–9.

they consult the inclinations of a parent-figure and not themselves), frequently have food and drink 'forced upon them' and are certainly not free to rise from the table at will. So Fordyce is fantasising here on his readers' behalf a private or even secret meal, a time and space to attend to their own appetites in a way that is not otherwise culturally sanctioned (especially by Fordyce). There is something of the serpent in his invitation – sit down and eat; it's safe; there will be no consequences. Conduct books and medical advice literature castigate women who regale themselves with rich food, and this invitation to do so even in a displaced form is unusual. Much as modern women are invited to use as cosmetics foodstuffs deemed too 'fattening' or pleasurable to eat, Fordyce's readers are offered a banquet of forbidden fruit.[32] The point is that it is a banquet of Fordyce's preparing. His sermons were frequently anthologised in 'Readers' for girls and young women, which claimed to offer precisely the convenient package of 'Historians, Philosophers, Orators and Poets, the best of every class' that he advocates. There are no novels on this table. Fordyce feeds his readers an improving and salutary diet, reliant on the belief that young women, if not other people, are what they read.

It is not exaggerating much to say that nearly all images or accounts of women's reading in this period use eating as a metaphor for the consumption of text. Charlotte Sussman, commenting on the prevalence of this analogy, argues that, 'The writer's need to differentiate good reading from bad reading, just as luxurious food is differentiated from wholesome food, signals not a refusal of consumer culture, but rather the necessity for discrimination in all object choices, especially for women.'[33] I hope to show that there is a closer connection between reading and eating in this era, that women are what they read in the same way as they are what they eat.

The idea that women eat knowledge goes back, of course, to Eve, and some Romantic-era writers draw on the traditional image of female consumption (of food and text) as voracious and beyond control. Maria and Richard Lovell Edgeworth suggest in *Practical Education* that women should not read novels because 'Pink appears pale to the eye that is used to scarlet, and common food is insipid to

32 For a more sustained analysis of Fordyce and reading, see Jacqueline Pearson, *Women's Reading in England 1750–1835: A Dangerous Recreation* (Cambridge: Cambridge University Press, 1999).
33 Sussman, *Consuming Anxieties*, p. 11.

the taste that has been vitiated by high art.'[34] Fiction makes readers take the fallen woman's scarlet for the young girl's pink, which is like taking strong flavours for 'common food'. Rather as computer games are now seen to accustom the young to extreme violence, so novels accustom their readers to too much colour, making us discontent with daily life. Mary Brunton's preface to *Self-Control*, addressing the always awkward issue of the novel which presents novel-reading as an immoral habit, displays involved assumptions about women as producers and consumers of fiction:

> This little tale was begun at first merely for my own amusement. It is published that I may reconcile my conscience to the time which it has employed, by making it in some degree useful. Let not the term so implied provoke a smile! If my work is read, its uses to the author are obvious. Nor is a work of fiction necessarily unprofitable to readers. When the vitiated appetite refuses its proper food, the alternative may be administered in a sweetmeat. It may be imprudent to confess the presence of the medicine, lest the sickly palate, thus warned, turn from it in loathing. But I rely in this instance on the word of the philosopher, who avers that 'young ladies never read prefaces'; and I am not without hope, that with you [Joanna Baillie, to whom the book is dedicated], and with all who form exceptions to this rule, the avowal of a useful purpose may be an inducement to tolerate what otherwise might be thought unworthy of regard.[35]

So, publication works to assuage guilt about time spent writing, presumably, since the 'uses to the author are obvious', because time spent in a way that generates income is not a source of guilt in the way that time spent generating unsold text would be. The primary purpose of publishing *Self-Control* is economic (and therefore moral) justification for writing. However, those who read the book (it is unclear whether there is any distinction between readers and buyers here) will not necessarily be without profit of their own, although the appetites of those who buy fiction are by definition 'vitiated'. *Self-Control*, Brunton claims, has a moral worth which is not only different from but in conflict with its economic value, since buyers of fiction are so debased that they would refuse to invest in a novel known to have a moral effect. Brunton presents a marketplace in which morality cancels out novels. But since sick appetites cannot stomach paratextual material, the debauched will rush on to ingest a story they do not know to be salutary, while the virtuous will embark

---

34 Maria Edgeworth and Richard Lovell Edgeworth, *Practical Education* (London: J. Johnson, 1801), p. 3.
35 Mary Brunton, *Self-Control*, ed. Sara Maitland (London: Pandora, 1986), pp. v–vi.

on it only once assured that in fact this text's morality cancels out its ficticity. The nature of the novel, its novel-ness, is equated to sweetness, but the writer here imagines herself as healer as well as cook. To write is to produce a saleable commodity and also to make food, for good or ill. Reading is both buying, completing the economic act of writing, and eating. These activities are so closely bound together here that it is hard confidently to distinguish metaphor from ostensibly factual statement. The book is obviously not a sweetmeat but the 'uses to the author' of being read are not as obvious as she suggests, and the resulting tangle of money, text and food in relation to women's economic, textual and bodily acts of consumption and production is one to which *Spilling the Beans* will return again and again.

I concentrate here on women's writing because of the ubiquity of such tangles in late eighteenth- and early nineteenth-century writing for and about women, and where I have discussed writing by men it is concerned with women's eating and its effects on their production of babies and milk. I would go so far as to say that it is never really possible in relation to the writers I discuss to separate literary from culinary production. If the woman writer is not preparing nourishment or poison for the (woman) reader's mind, it is because she is bringing up children on the purest and most salutary stories. Women, in these terms, cannot read without eating any more than they can write without either cooking or breastfeeding. We are what we read, and in this context Brunton's association of sweetness with feminine vice bears investigation, for it is common in this period as in others.

The disgust provoked by women's appetites nearly always focuses on sweet foods, from Mary Wollstonecraft's diatribes against aristocratic women to the hectoring tones of pregnancy handbooks (I will suggest later that this step is not as large as readers have tended to believe). Modern versions of this scolding and revulsion tend to revolve around dismay at the fat bodies that are perceived to result from imbalanced or disorderly eating, but I have found only two Romantic-era warnings against women's increased size as a result of excessive consumption. In both cases the expression of the concern contributes to and derives from the speaker's characterisation as irredeemably shallow and obsessed by appearances. Even female characters whose eating exceeds the norm or the ideal are not described as unusually large, and in fact, as Pat Rogers observes in the one critical essay on this subject, there is little concern with the volume of women's eating unless, through poverty or emotional distress, they are courting starvation.[36] It is what women eat that matters, rather than how much, to the extent that gourmet grazing is a sure sign of moral inadequacy while eating generous quantities of plain food (itself a loaded term) often betokens a healthy mind in a healthy body. There are very few fat women in late eighteenth- and early nineteenth-century women's fiction and little explicit anxiety about fatness or weight gain, but the qualities of women's food attract endless excitement and censure. Since, as we are already beginning to see, narratives about women's consumption are also always narratives about women's production or failure to produce, anxiety centres around the perception that disorderly eating is both the sign and the cause of moral and economic dysfunction.

These specific connections between diet and moral fall are implicit in most Romantic-era fiction, especially that written for children and young people in which sexual appetites are displaced onto food. Those who cannot assert a virtuous mind to control physical longing are almost as despicable at board as in bed, but the longings are gender-specific. Depraved men indulge themselves with strong flavours that are hard to obtain or complex to prepare. Lynmere in Burney's *Camilla* insists on offending the ladies by eating cheese, claims to have sent for Stilton from Leipzig, and threatens his uncle's servants when they cannot produce shrimps and oysters on demand. The gluttonous Dr Grant in *Mansfield Park* scorns fruit, but on three occasions abuses his wife because changes in the weather mean that poultry cannot be kept as long, or needs to hang longer, than she had planned, so that his appetite cannot be immediately gratified. The gluttons in Susan Ferrier's work also are disruptive because they abuse positions of power or authority to demand food that is not local, not seasonal or requires arcane techniques of preparation. Again, disorderly eating is only partly an issue of quantity. The principal effect of excessive male appetites in women's fiction is to disrupt the domestic economy, making it difficult for women – at whatever social level – to go about their daily business.

Women's and children's greed is different, and is often presented with disconcertingly intense disgust. There are a few female characters whose offence is to eat like men, such as Harriot Freke in

---

36 Pat Rogers, 'Fat Is a Fictional Issue: The Novel and the Rise of Weight-Watching', in Marie Mulvey Roberts and Roy Porter (eds), *Literature and Medicine During the Eighteenth Century*, Wellcome Institute Series in the History of Medicine (London: Routledge, 1993).

Belinda, but usually women who eat badly do so in the same way as children, eating sweets and cakes and eating them in secret. The terrible revulsion with which this kind of eating is described seems disproportionate. Perhaps part of the outrage arises from an implicit connection between secret snacking and masturbation, both private forms of bodily self-gratification that seem to work against regulated ways of consuming and (re)producing. One could here posit a connection between Wollstonecraft's infamous denunciation of the 'nastiness' that takes place when girls share beds and women sleep and dress in close proximity to each other and the vitriol she expends on female gourmets, for in both cases physical pleasure is divorced from functionality, from 'usefulness'. This may offer some interpretation of otherwise gratuitous distress at children's eating, as in Martha Sherwood's horrifying but popular *History of Little Henry and His Bearer* (1809).[37]

Little Henry is brought up by his Indian 'bearer' after his father is 'killed attacking a mud fort belonging to a *Zemeendar*' and his mother dies. A neighbour takes him in, but she is 'one of those fine ladies who will give their money […] for the relief of distress, but have no idea how it is possible for anyone to give all his goods to feed the poor and yet want charity'.[38] Henry is left entirely to the care of the servants, who let him 'eat *bazar* sweetmeats' and teach him that 'the God to whom his mamma prayed at Dinapore was no better than the Gods of wood, and stone, and clay, which his *bearer* worshipped'. We are told that 'Henry was moreover taught by the servants many things, which a little boy should not know.'[39] The text of course can offer no detail about these things, but it seems reasonable to imagine some sexual content, and it is interesting that the provision of sweetmeats, idolatry and knowledge about sex are apparently equivalent errors in child rearing. When Henry is five, 'the daughter of a worthy clergyman in England' comes to stay and sets him on the road to redemption. She makes 'the little boy understand that eternal death, or everlasting punishment, is the consequence of sin', and she compels him to memorise some alarming biblical verses. After a year and a half, she must go home, and while she packs she questions him 'concerning the things she [has] taught

---

37 Martha Sherwood, 'The History of Little Henry and His Bearer', in Robert Bator and Jonathan Cott (eds), *Masterworks of Children's Literature*, vol. 4 (New York: Stonehill Publishing, 1984).

38 Sherwood, 'Little Henry', p. 442.

39 Sherwood, 'Little Henry', p. 443.

him'. He answers perfectly, but she withholds praise 'lest he should become proud' and asks instead about Henry's conviction that God would bring about his redemption: '[He will] make me a new creature and I shall be purified as he is pure.' I quote the reply at length because the jumble of different offences is much of the point:

> Before I knew the Lord Jesus Christ, I used to think of nothing but naughty things. I loved myself more than any body else. I loved eating fruit and sweetmeats; and was so greedy of them, that I would have told a hundred lies, I do think, for one mouthful of them. Then I was passionate and proud. I used to be so pleased when anybody bowed to me and said, 'Sahib.' And you cannot think how cruel I was to all kinds of little creatures I could get hold of … But now I do think my heart is beginning to change a little, I mean a very little, for I gave all my last sweetmeats to the matre's boy.[40]

A note glosses 'matre' as 'a sweeper: a person of low caste, who eats every thing'. There is a colonial discourse here about eating like a 'native', in which the child at risk of assimilation by sweet-eating (and, implicitly, worse) is redeemed by abstention, and it is interesting that Sherman feels no need to be explicit about these associations. The connection between 'bad' food and subaltern identity is apparently too obvious for words. I have dwelt on this obscure text because it provides an unusually concise example of the way eating and appetite interact with politics and morality in the didactic fiction (which is nearly all fiction) of this period. The equation of godlessness, naughty thoughts and sweets is striking, and even through the lens of modern anxieties about sugar and selfhood the absolute correlation between loving oneself and loving to eat fruit and sweetmeats seems to demand investigation. There is clearly something very bad about fruit and sweets, but the nature and source of the badness at first appear obscure. Few of the writers I will discuss here show any explicit concern about slavery in relation to sugar, although the relationship between the vogue for sensibility and a sugar boycott has been convincingly discussed elsewhere.[41] In any case the anti-slavery campaigns would have no bearing on fruit, which is invariably included in the horror of sweetness. In this case, the 'sweetmeats' – the term seems to cover all sweet foods that are not baked and do not require a spoon – are of markedly local provenance anyway. There is no suggestion here, or in most other

40 Sherwood, 'Little Henry', p. 449.
41 See Sussman, *Consuming Anxieties,* and also Timothy Morton, *The Poetics of Spice: Romantic Consumerism and the Exotic* (Cambridge: Cambridge University Press, 2000).

similar castigations of sweet-eaters, that sweetness does long-term damage to health.

Part of the explanation of Sherwood's disgust is perhaps offered in the second part of this extract. Eating sweets is like taking pleasure in the servility of the natives, which is also like taking pleasure in cruelty to animals. It seems to be part of an ideological package which mimics the identity and behaviour of the colonial and domestic master. From Mr B in *Pamela* to John Reed in *Jane Eyre*, men who abuse positions of power over other people enjoy torturing animals, and it is not difficult to relate this generic master-figure to the colonial Sahib and indeed to the West Indian plantation owner, which would suggest that Henry's turn away from sugar and towards Christ is also a turn from colonial ideology. Interestingly, in women's fiction, the fool who spends most of her time lying on the sofa eating sweetmeats and reading light fiction is usually surrounded by lapdogs on which she lavishes the attention she denies her children.[42] In both cases there is a misapprehension of the true status and meaning of animals which is part of both the master's and the fool's failures in humanity (humanity being itself in this context a literary construct which must be played out through interaction). Sweetness does form part of this package in Romantic-era fiction, but why it does so is less clear, and most of the compelling analysis offered by Sidney Mintz is based on later developments.[43] Sugar is always exotic, whether produced by slavery or in '*bazar* sweetmeats', and fruit, although local, is not usually far from the tree of knowledge. I am not convinced that these are adequate explanations for the horror and desire that surge around sweetness in the text I explore here.

These equations between sweetness, badness and the abuse of power are made repeatedly in Romantic-era writing for children. Dorothy Kilner's *Life and Perambulations of a Mouse* uses cake almost as the substance of affection. We first meet the exemplary Master George, 'a young gentleman, about ten years of age', when he stops on his way to school to see his nurse: 'I am come to bring you a slice of cake, which my grandpapa gave me yesterday.'[44] Betty, the

42 See Markman Ellis, 'Suffering Things: Lapdogs, Slaves and Counter-Sensibility', pp. 92–117, in Blackwell (ed.), *The Secret Life of Things*.
43 Sidney Mintz, *Sweetness and Power: The Place of Sugar in Modern History* (Harmondsworth: Penguin, 1985).
44 Dorothy Kilner, 'The Life and Perambulation of a Mouse', in Robert Bator and Jonathan Cott (eds), *Masterworks of Children's Literature*, vol. 3 (New York: Stonehill Publishing, 1983), p. 238.

nurse, refuses the cake ('for though I am poor, I am honest'), and she prefers a happy life on a peasant diet to the indulgences of the rich. George puts the cake in her cupboard and runs away, and when Betty finds it she exclaims, 'Bless his heart! I do think he is the sweetest child that ever was born. You may laugh at me for saying so; but I am sure I should have thought the same if I had *not* nursed him myself.'[45] Children, like breastfeeding women, enact love with food, and the disturbing transferability of qualities between children and the food they give to others is found across the genre. Feeding his cake to the woman who nursed him, George himself becomes 'sweet', as if it were himself that he is offering for her consumption. She fed him with the sweetness of her body (the economics of wet-nursing are partially suppressed here), and now, in giving her cake, he also gives her the sweetness of himself. As Julie Kipp remarks in another context, 'The wet nurse utilized her body to turn a profit (she turned body into bread, so to speak).'[46] But the return of cake for milk (milk which is also love) complicates this reading. The cake, it is worth noting, has been given to George by his grandfather, and in its transferability and apparent physical and semiotic stability – it does not go stale and carries the same meaning between grandfather, grandchild, nursling and nurse – it exhibits, like the wet-nurse's milk, the qualities of currency. This slippage between eater and eaten shows in an unusually literal way how subjectivity itself is produced and consumed within fiction, mirroring the writer's production and the reader's consumption in the literary marketplace. Such transactions characterise children's fiction in this period, and – as Chapters 2 and 3 will show – dominate the children's writing of Wollstonecraft and Edgeworth.

As this analysis suggests, the equation between the consumption of food and the production of morality appears most starkly in relation to pregnancy, breastfeeding and prostitution, the states in which it is most obvious that women's bodies are economically active in a way that men's cannot be. There is now a body, so to speak, of scholarship on maternity and reproduction in late eighteenth- and early nineteenth-century fiction and culture, but as with the scholarship on consumption, critics tend to concentrate on the metaphysics and gender politics of mothering. I will turn in Chapter 2 to the baser discourses of pregnancy and breastfeeding handbooks, where

45 Kilner, 'Mouse', p. 239.
46 Julie Kipp, *Romanticism, Maternity and the Body Politic* (Cambridge: Cambridge University Press, 2003), p. 106.

the female body can appear as a unit of production inconveniently attached to an appetite. (Readers familiar with modern pregnancy advice literature may note similarities.) If women in eighteenth-century literature are eaten as much as they eat, then breastfeeding mothers and nurses provide a particularly stark image of women's place in this jungle of consumerism.

Children's greed is in many ways similar to women's greed. Some writers, notably Mary Wollstonecraft, conflate the woman who eats with the child who has not learnt not to eat, insisting that appetite infantilises women and that women who enjoy food confirm a widespread view of women as 'merely sensual creatures'. But writing for adult women can develop connections between eating, sexuality and reproduction in ways that remain powerfully implicit in children's literature. Good eating is usually Malthusian, meeting hunger generated in honest toil so that the eater can go on labouring. Bad eating is libidinal, undertaken, sometimes compulsively, for pleasures which relate more to the mouth than the stomach. This kind of oral self-pleasing typifies certain kinds of anti-hero, but it is particularly worrying in relation to women's eating, perhaps implying the recreational waste of reproductive potential.

It is generally true that greedier women in these novels are more sexual women, that one kind of appetite offers an accurate measure of the other, but there are refinements and contradictions that help to codify the moral hierarchy of ingredients. As I will show in Chapters 2 and 3, the woman who snacks secretly on pastries and sweetmeats is invariably enslaved to appetite and beyond redemption, but someone who eats plenty of porridge or vegetables usually does so in cheerful recognition of her status as a labourer. This is probably the context in which to read Jonas Hanway's provisions for the Magdalen house, in which penitent prostitutes would receive generous quantities of 'bread, with water-gruel, milk, milk-porridge, bread with butter, or cheese'.[47] Hanway suggests the diet is 'rather to be worse than better, than they may expect when they return into the world', but the prescribed quantities are generous and the range no worse than monotonous.[48] However one might judge the rest of the scheme, Hanway's dietary regime is salutary rather than

---

47 Jonas Hanway, *A Plan for Establishing a Charity-House or Charity-Houses, for the Reception of Repenting Prostitutes, to Be Called the Magdalen Charity* (London: 1758) p. 26. I thank Jennie Batchelor for drawing my attention to this text.

48 Hanway, *Charity-House*, p. 23.

punitive. The way to the erring woman's heart is not through her stomach; the diet is not calculated to remind its adherents of the pleasures of the flesh, but nor will anyone go hungry. The fantasy of eating divorced from ideology represented by this plan is one much cherished by those who write with suspicion about physical pleasure; from Wollstonecraft to Edgeworth, the authors of didactic fiction continue – against all evidence – to invoke the moral diet, finely calculated to meet all physical need without arousing any emotion at all. Food is not like that. If women cannot read without eating, nor can they eat without being read. Food's relation to material culture is complicated, but eating is always a political act.

As I have already implied, the politics of eating are particularly evident in relation to meat, where eating or rejecting either inscribes or interrogates fundamental assumptions about selfhood, humanity and the world. Very little Romantic-era fiction explicitly promotes vegetarianism, but there are constant connections between meat and the bodies of women and children which imply profound ambivalence about the meanings of meat, especially in the more or less colonial fictions of Edgeworth and Ferrier. It is interesting that awareness of these connections never leads to abstention from meat on principle, as if the pragmatics of the kitchen demand that women and children digest what they are encouraged to identify as equivalents of their own subjectivities. The children's stories, fashionable in the earlier part of this period, which use animals as protagonists, work on the basis that children's relationships with animals both mimic and prefigure adults' relationships with children. Inevitably, this model makes meat-eating particularly hard to negotiate, for if animals are to children as children are to adults, the Swiftian possibilities which are never far from fairy tale cast a worrying shadow across these stories of domestic sensibility. Charles and Mary Lamb's 1809 *Tales of Mrs Leicester's School* subscribes to this connection between belief in the subjectivity of animals and moral sensibility.[49] In Chapter 2, seven-year-old Louisa Manners recounts a visit to her grandmamma in the country which is also a first encounter with the moral lessons of the natural world. She learns that it is wrong to take birds' eggs because 'the little birds would not sing any more, if their eggs were taken away from them', but that a hen is 'a hospitable

49 Charles and Mary Lamb, 'Tales of Mrs Leicester's School', in Robert Bator and Jonathan Cott (eds), *Masterworks of Children's Literature*, vol. 4 (New York: Stonehill Publishing, 1984).

bird', which 'always laid more eggs than she wanted, on purpose to give her mistress to make puddings and cakes with'.[50]

This solution is even less convincing in Sarah Trimmer's *Fabulous Histories, or, The History of the Robins*.[51] To quote from the introduction, this is 'a series of FABLES, intended to convey a moral instruction' in which 'the sentiments and affections of a good Father and Mother, and a Family of Children, are *supposed* to be possessed by a *Nest of Red-Breasts*'. Two children, Frederick and Harriet Benson, watch the family of robins and put out food which the parents take to the nestlings. One morning, 'fatigued with a very long walk the evening before', the children get up late, rush down to 'demand the collection of crumbs' the cook keeps for them and then run across the breakfast room and open the window without greeting their mother. She reminds them that, 'It is customary for little boys and girls to pay their respects to their papas and mammas every morning' and, moreover,

> You depend as much on your papa and me, for every thing you want, as these little birds do on you: nay, more so, for they could supply their own wants, by seeking food in other places; but children can do nothing towards their support: therefore it is particularly requisite, that they should be dutiful and respectful to those, whose tenderness and care are constantly exerted for their benefit.[52]

The implication is that children have more to fear from parents than robins do from children, which is worrying in the context of the Malthusian justification for eating fish which follows. Mrs Benson takes Harriet and Frederick for a day out at a neighbouring farm, where they see a fishpond. The farmers' children are forbidden to use fishing rods on the grounds that it 'hardens the heart and leads to idleness', but the fish are sometimes netted. Harriet asks, 'Pray, mamma,' [...], 'is it right to catch fish?' and is told,

> Man has dominion over the fish, as well as over beasts and fowls, and many of them are excellent food for mankind; and the astonishing increase of them shews that they are designed to be so; for were all that are spawned to grow to full size, there would soon be more than our ponds, or even the

---

50 Lamb, 'Mrs Leicester', p. 291.
51 Sarah Trimmer, 'Fabulous Histories, or, the History of the Robins', in Robert Bator and Jonathan Cott (eds) *Masterworks of Children's Literature*, vol. 3 (New York: Stonehill Publishing, 1983).
52 Trimmer, 'Robins', p. 280.

sea itself would hold, and they would be starved; therefore there are the same reasons for feeding on them as on poultry, but we should be very careful to dispatch them as quickly as possible.[53]

So, the same text which condemns Eve's temptation authorises meat-eating, and the Malthusian argument against famine relief is also an argument for the consumption of meat. Sensibility requires one to subscribe to the fiction of animal subjectivity while sense requires the consumption of meat, even in full awareness that children and animals are in the same political if not ontological category. The problem is that children, in relation to children's literature, are by definition readers, so that the child is simultaneously constituted as the reading subject and the edible object. The reader consumes the fictional subjectivity of animals (by reading) at the same time as being adjured both to consume animals by eating them and to recognise her own potential edibility. The ability to read, it seems, does not place the reader outside the category of food.

A similar argument is made to similar effect in relation to adult women in Jane West's *Letters to a Young Lady*. Showing how men's power over women is reflected in human dominion over animals, authorised by both Genesis and 'natural theology', West asserts a proto-Darwinian basis for eating meat:

> Some few years ago, our souls were harrowed up by pathetic narratives of the sufferings of hares, partridges, fishes, horses and reptiles; and man was abused for tyranny, in destroying his fellow-animals, and for gluttony in devouring the joint tenants of this sublunary sphere. At last, some sapient discoverer perceived that many of these much-pitied beings actually subsisted by destroying some other species; and then the benevolent feelings of a good many children were exercised in rescuing 'captive mice' and 'benetted flies' at the hazard of starving cats and spiders ... there was manifest danger not only of our becoming a nation of Brahmins, but that eating would be cried down as an act of cruelty, since it is impossible to cultivate the ground, or produce vegetables, without annihilating many harmless worlds ... I must rejoice in the popularity of such a work as 'Natural Theology'; in which the ridiculous refinements of extreme susceptibility are admirably corrected, by those just sentiments which an enlarged mind is sure to inculcate after it has contemplated the whole works of God.[54]

---

53 Trimmer, 'Robins', p. 331.
54 Jane West, *Letters to a Young Lady* (London: Longman, Hurst, Rees, Orme and Brown, 1811) vol. 2, pp. 397–8.

West's arguments for women's acceptance of subjugation are entirely pragmatic. Her objection to Wollstonecraft's *Vindication of the Rights of Woman* is not that it is morally wrong but that it advocates 'a course of action which cannot but make its followers unhappy'. (West might be said to have a point here.) The basis on which she requires women to suffer and be still is not that her readers are incapable of better things but that men 'certainly do expect that the smile of complacency should always illumine the countenances of their female companions, whenever it is not suspended by sympathy for them'.[55] Once again, the reason for eating meat (and implicitly consuming the subjectivity of other beings) is not that it is moral but that it reinforces a world order we must learn to accept. All of this seems to anticipate Carol Adams' argument that, 'Eating animals acts as a mirror and representation of patriarchal values. Meat-eating is the reinscription of male power at every meal.'[56]

It is not surprising in this context that the other politically and morally charged food in this hierarchy is fruit. Fruit is often related to Eve's apple but, particularly in the 1790s, may be the bounty nature offers to rich and poor alike. Miltonic fruit is very different from Rousseauvian fruit, and much depends on the means of production as well as the mode of consumption. This becomes particularly clear in novels which trace a harlot's progress, where connections – or coincidences – between what a women eats and how she uses her body are writ large.

Amelia Opie's anti-Wollstonecraftian fiction, *Adeline Mowbray, or, the Mother and Daughter*, depends upon and exemplifies these gustatory moral codes.[57] Adeline is betrayed by her mother and then by a sequence of lovers, and in each case her virtue and their treachery are evinced by food. Adeline's mother devotes herself to 'fatal and unproductive studies', neglecting her daughter and 'her venerable parents'. Obsessively formulating plans for a perfect education for Adeline, Editha fails to spend any time with her daughter, but it is in the management of Adeline's diet that her mother reveals her real unfitness:

55 West, *Letters*, vol. 2, p. 83.
56 Carol J. Adams, *The Sexual Politics of Meat: A Feminist-Vegetarian Critical Theory* (New York: Continuum, 1998), p. 187.
57 Amelia Opie, *Adeline Mowbray, or, the Mother and Daughter*, ed. Shelley King and John B. Pierce (Oxford: Oxford University Press, 1999).

At one time Mrs Mowbray had studied herself into great nicety with regard to the diet of her daughter; but, as she herself was too much used to the indulgencies of the palate to be able to set her in reality an example of temperance, she dined in appearance with Adeline at one o' clock on pudding without butter, and potatoes without salt; but while the child was taking her afternoon's walk, her own table was covered with viands fitted for the appetite of opulence.

Unfortunately, however, the servants conceived that the daughter as well as the mother had a right to regale clandestinely; and the little Adeline used to eat for her supper, with a charge not to tell her Mamma, some of the good things set by from Mrs Mowbray's dinner.[58]

Mrs Mowbray betrays herself by her greed, and the emphasis on clandestine regaling is significant. The problem is not with the food itself but with the way it is eaten, as we see when Mrs Mowbray finds out what has been happening, when 'though usually tenacious of her opinions, she in this case profited by the lesson of experience'. It is interesting that food forms the exception to Mrs Mowbray's stubborn blindness to the consequences of her inadequate mothering. When Adeline falls, it is important that readers continue to believe in her underlying but misguided virtue, and perhaps this one successful lesson is essential to that virtue. Having learnt to manage her appetite, it is possible to believe that, despite appearances, Adeline can also manage her sexuality. Mrs Mowbray's solution to the clandestine regaling is that, 'Adeline, her appetites regulated by a proper exertion of parental authority, was allowed to sit at the well-furnished table of her mother, and was precluded, by a judicious and open indulgence, from wishing for a secret and improper one ... Would that Mrs Mowbray had always been equally judicious!' The only other success in Adeline's education is that her grandmother teaches her 'them there sort of things that women commonly know' in which, 'stimulated by the ambition of being useful' Adeline shows such aptitude that 'even the department of making pastry was now given up to Adeline' and in due course, 'Adeline soon thought it right to assume the entire management of the family.'[59] Virtue is shown by utility, and specifically by the appropriate management of food.

This connection between moral worth and domestic economy is complicated by the pineapple scene for which the novel is best

58 *Adeline Mowbray*, p. 6.
59 *Adeline Mowbray*, p. 9.

known. Following her mother's second marriage, Adeline has eloped with Glenmurray, a radical writer who has ideological objections to marriage. Glenmurray is dying of consumption and Adeline has placed herself outside polite society by living with him outside marriage, and they are running out of money. With three guineas left for a week's expenses, Adeline strolls through the town and pauses to buy grapes, 'knowing how welcome fruit was to the feverish palate of Glenmurray'.[60] She sees a pineapple on the counter and 'felt a strong wish to carry it home as a more welcome present' but it costs two guineas, 'a sum which she could not think herself justified in expending'. When she tells Glenmurray about it, he rejects the grapes and 'was continually talking of pineapples, and in a way that showed how strongly his diseased appetite wished to enjoy the gratification of eating one'.[61] At last she tells him that she has borrowed money and could buy the pineapple, 'and he, who in health was remarkable for self-denial and temperance, scrupled not, overcome by the influence of the fever which consumed him, to gratify his palate at a rate the most extravagant'. Adeline 'proceeded to a shop to sell her lace veil, the only ornament she had retained, and that not from vanity, but because it concealed from the eye of curiosity the sorrow marked on her countenance'.[62] There is already an odd table of equivalence developing here, in which Glenmurray's 'diseased appetite' takes away the veil that Adeline uses to protect herself from the public gaze, a gaze which turns in her direction mostly because of her sexual activity outside marriage. Her lover's appetite consumes her privacy, forcing Adeline bare-faced onto the streets in a way that thins the line between how she is seen (as a prostitute) and who she 'is' (the heroine).

These equivalences appear in a very different light when, on the way to the fruiterer, Adeline encounters a man being dragged to jail from the arms of his wife, 'a young mulatto woman, the picture of sickness and despair', while their son, the 'Tawny Boy', 'was crying bitterly, and hiding his face in the poor woman's apron'. The man owes six guineas to a grudging creditor, who will not take less than half that sum immediately. Adeline agonises, torn between empathy for the wife of the sick man dunned by creditors and the conviction that it is her duty to gratify Glenmurray's final wishes. The circumstantial equivalence of the man's life and the pineapple, each to be

60 *Adeline Mowbray*, p. 135.
61 *Adeline Mowbray*, p. 136.
62 *Adeline Mowbray*, p. 136.

obtained for three guineas, is spelt out with disconcerting clarity:

> 'But were Glenmurray here, he would give up his own indulgence, I am
> sure, to save the lives of, probably, two fellow-creatures,' thought Adeline;
> 'and he would not forgive me if I were to sacrifice such an opportunity to
> the sole gratification of his palate.' – But then again, Glenmurray eagerly
> expecting her with the promised treat, so gratifying to the feverish taste
> of sickness, seemed to appear before her, and she turned away: but the
> eyes of the mulatto, who had heard her words, and had hung on them
> breathless with expectation, followed her with a look of such sad reproach
> for the disappointment which she had occasioned her, and the little boy
> looked up so wistfully in her face, crying, 'Poor fader, and poor mammy!'
> that Adeline could not withstand the force of the appeal.[63]

Having sold the last sign of her status and forfeited the now
unmerited appearance of a lady, Adeline buys William's freedom
at the price of Glenmurray's indulgence. It is important that these
things happen at the same time, for the sale of the veil marks a
station along the way of the harlot's progress. Well dressed and
expensively veiled, Adeline looked like what the reader knew her
to be despite her ill-advised liaison with Glenmurray, but without
her veil and with Glenmurray's death imminent, she becomes
and resembles an abandoned woman. This is the point at which
the novel's marketing of fictional subjectivity becomes essential. If
readers do not subscribe to Adeline's essential virtue, which is now
not only independent of but in conflict with her behaviour and
circumstances, then the novel must fail. It is in our consumption of
subjectivity that *Adeline Mowbray* succeeds, and it is in Glenmurray's consumption of the heroine's identity that Adeline Mowbray
begins to fail. Opie is emphatic about the triviality of Glenmurray's
desire for 'indulgence' and 'a treat' in comparison to the health and
freedom of the young family, so that readers identify with Adeline's
sense of duty and begin to understand Glenmurray as a predator,
particularly when his initial response to the story of the three
guineas is accusatory: 'So then, to the relief of strangers you sacri-
ficed the gratification of the man whom you love, and deprived him
of the only pleasure he may live to enjoy!'[64] Glenmurray, living with
Adeline outside marriage, consumes her. Like food, women are of
little value second-hand.

---

63 *Adeline Mowbray*, pp. 138–9.
64 *Adeline Mowbray*, p. 140.

A final example from this novel shows how much the harlot's progress is a narrative of consumption. Glenmurray's cousin Berrendale, whom Adeline marries after Glenmurray's death, finds after six months of marriage that the household bills are too high. Adeline, 'assiduous to anticipate her husband's wishes', has 'contrived so many dainties for his table, which she cooked with her own hands' that they have lived happily together. Berrendale 'remonstrates very seriously' with Adeline, who promises to 'please [his] appetite at less expense', adding: 'a little suffices me, and I care not how plain that food is'. The substitution of the cook for the cooked is telling here; it is Adeline herself who hopes to please his appetite:

> 'Still, I think I have seen you eat with a most excellent appetite,' said Berrendale, with a very significant expression.
>
> Adeline, shocked at the manner more than at the words, replied in a faltering voice, 'As a proof of my being in health, no doubt you rejoiced in the sight.'
>
> 'Certainly; but a less robust health would suit our finances better.'[65]

Adeline is pregnant at this time, and it is this interchange in which, for the first time, 'the sordid selfishness of his character was at once unveiled to her view'. She rises the next morning, resolved that 'her appetite should never again, if possible, force a reproach from the lips of her husband', and henceforth, 'whatever she provided for the table, except for the simplest fare, should be for Berrendale alone'. She hopes this will shame him into sharing, but 'busy in the gratification of his own appetite, he never observed whether any other persons ate or not, except when by eating they curtailed his share of good things'. It is left to Savanna to spend her own money in order to 'tempt [Adeline's] weak appetite with some pleasant but expensive sweetmeats'.[66]

The point here is that Adeline's past negates her entitlement. Usually, as I will show in Chapter 2, (re)production gives women some, highly contested, right to consume, but because of Adeline's fallen status Berrendale has no respect for her and she cannot appeal to a wider community. In marrying her he has saved her from an inevitable fall into prostitution. She owes him everything and he owes her nothing, not even enough to eat while she carries his child. Adeline has become the eaten and not the eater. She dies

---

65 *Adeline Mowbray*, p. 181.
66 *Adeline Mowbray*, p. 183.

a few months later of a 'decline', during which nothing can tempt her appetite, with 'sunken features' and a 'wasted form' that horrify her attendants. The fallen woman's diet declines dramatically with each man who courts her favours, her body physically depleted by the men who consume her substance.

It is not coincidence that Opie's chosen fruit here is a pineapple.[67] Suspicion of luxury and the exotic – categories that are rarely separated in relation to food – runs through eighteenth- and nineteenth-century food writing. Maxine Berg argues that the traditional identification of 'elite luxuries' with French manufacture and 'ordinary commodities' with British in the eighteenth century is a fallacy perpetrated by mid-twentieth century historiography, showing that, 'Fashion and luxury imports from Europe, especially France and Asia, had high political and cultural profiles, though they made little showing in the national accounts.'[68] Nevertheless, it is the cultural profile that is of interest here, and there is a strong sense that dietary distinctiveness is necessary to the formation and maintenance of national and regional identities. This becomes particularly important in Scottish and Anglo-Irish fiction at the beginning of the nineteenth century, but the conviction that nations as well as individuals are what they eat is writ large in less engaging ways throughout the eighteenth century. The 1757 polemic against luxury, *The Tryal of Lady Allurea Luxury*, studied in much of the recent scholarship on luxury, conflates luxury and foreignness in relentlessly gastronomic terms.[69] The play's opening line is, 'Is not the prisoner a foreigner?', followed by the swearing in of a jury which includes Sir Oliver Roastbeef and William Strongbeer. An early witness, Lord Good-Mind, describes the consequences of his wife's intimacy with Lady Allurea:

> In a few Days, my Lord, my old English hospitable Table was covered with nothing but Frenchified disguised Dishes ... My Chairs were all converted into Couches; my strong Beer and roast Beef were sent to the Dog-Boy ... All my old faithful Servants discharged, to make room for French Cooks, Madamoselles, and powdered Pickpockets, Burgundy and

67 For a detailed discussion of possible significances of pineapples in this context, see H. Carol, 'The Story of the Pineapple: Sentimental Abolitionism and Moral Motherhood in Amelia Opie's *Adeline Mowbray*' in *Studies in the Novel*, 30:3 (1998), 355–72.
68 Berg, *Luxury and Pleasure*, pp. 92–3.
69 Anon, *The Tryal of Lady Allurea Luxury* (London: F. Noble, 1757).
70 *Allurea Luxury*, pp. 12–14.

> Champaign the only Liquors fit to be seen at a Lord's Table; and nothing produced in our own Climate bearable.[70]

The Lord Mayor later testifies to Lady Allurea's recent control of the menu at 'City-Feasts':

> the Consequence of which has been that we have had nothing to eat, fit for an Englishman to put in his stomach. High-seasoned Ragouts and masqueraded Poisons have been substituted in the place of honest roast Beef and Plumb-Pudding, and the noble Bacon Chine and Turkey. But the City of London is determined, for the Time to come, to assert the Dignity of their Ancestors Food; and to let the World see, they will be no more Slaves to a French Cook, than to a French Tyrant.[71]

The political power of cuisine is well established in this period. Hannah Glasse famously rails against 'the blind folly of this age, that they would rather be imposed on by a French booby, than give encouragement to a good English cook!'[72] Chapter 3 of her cookbook is entitled, 'Read this Chapter, and you will find how expensive a French cook's sauce is', and she concludes the first recipe in this section ('The French way of dressing partridges'): 'This dish I do not recommend; for I think it an odd jumble of trash; by that time the cullis, the essence of ham, and all other ingredients are reckoned, the partridges will come to a fine penny. But such receipts as this is what you have in most books of cookery yet printed.'[73] Elizabeth Raffald writes anxiously in the preface to *The Experienced English Housekeeper*, 'though I have given some of my Dishes French Names, as they are only known by those Names, yet they will not be found very Expensive, nor add Compositions but as plain as the Nature of the Dish will admit of'.[74] Written in 1729, but still in print and going into the eighteenth edition fifty years later, Mrs E. Smith's *Compleat Housewife* concurs with many contemporaries in the ambivalent offering of,

> Directions generally for dressing after the best, most natural and wholesome Manner, such Provisions as are the Product of our own Country; and in such a Manner as is most agreeable to English Palates; saving that I have

71 *Allurea Luxury*, p. 19.
72 Hannah Glasse, *The Art of Cookery Made Plain and Easy* (London: printed for the author, 1774), p. 4.
73 Glasse, pp. 103–4.
74 Elizabeth Raffald, *The Experienced English House-Keeper* (Manchester: printed for the author, 1769), p. ii.

so far temporized, as, since we have, to our Disgrace, so fondly admired the French Tongue, French Modes and also French Messes, to present you now and then with such Receipts of the French Cookery as I think may not be disagreeable to English Palates.[75]

The use of food to mark tribal and regional identities is universal – a crucial part of the definition of 'foreigners' is usually 'people who eat things we don't eat' – and there is a growing literature on food and post-colonial identities. Julie Kipp suggests in relation to these cookbooks that, 'The domestic home-maker functioned in cookery books of the period ... as the "unacknowledged legislator" of a society increasingly defining itself through the food it consumed, and increasingly wary of the choices it thereby confronted.'[76] There is nothing very novel or surprising about this eighteenth-century investment in the idea of English food for English bodies making up the English nation, except that in fact these cookbooks all participate in the trend they decry, offering traditionally French recipes and methods more or less adapted to English – or sometimes British – ingredients, technologies and habits (although the regional nature of French and, to a lesser extent, English cuisine undermines all such easy categorisation along the lines of national boundaries). As the Lord Mayor's inclusion of turkey, a post-Columbian import to Europe, and plum pudding, always made with raisins and nutmeg, often also with mace, ginger and cinnamon, sometimes with almonds, orange peel and other dried fruits, implies, much of the food regarded as intrinsically English and intrinsic to Englishness was in fact merely well-naturalised; Joan Thirsk's study of food in early modern England finds imported fruits and spices widespread in the fourteenth century.[77] To say that there has never been a pure or authentic English cuisine is not to set a historical truth against a discursive fiction, but to suggest that food is always a highly contested means of expressing the amorphous concept of national identity. Like nationhood itself, national cuisine exists only by interaction. I offer a close reading of some of these interactions in relation to Romantic-era Scottish women's fiction, where anxieties about gender and consumption overlap and interact with concerns about sovereignty and empire, in Chapter 4.

---

75 Mrs E. Smith, *The Compleat Housewife, or Accomplish'd Gentlewoman's Companion*, (London: printed for the author, 15th edn, 1758), p. iv.
76 Kipp, *Romanticism*, p. 102.
77 Joan Thirsk, *Food in Early Modern England* (London: Hambledon Continuum, 2006).

National identity, then, is played out at the table, where individuals eat, and in some ways individuals' eating mimics the national incorporation of foreign commodities and gives rise to similar anxieties. The conservative fantasy of English bodies sustained on authentic, culturally pure 'English food' is no more probable than the self-starving woman's fantasy of living without ingesting foreign matter. In both cases the rejection of food – or the fantasised rejection of food, since, as Morag Sweeney points out, 'the aim of anorexia is not death, but living with a complete physical integrity maintained through the absence of desire' – is an attempt to retain an impossible purity.[78]

Anorexia nervosa was first identified by William Gull and Charles Lasègue in Paris in the 1860s and 1870s, and I am not suggesting that Romantic-era starving women were anorexics *avant la lettre*. Histories of eating disorders usually begin in the mid-nineteenth century with discussion of Sarah Jacob, the Welsh 'fasting girl' who died of starvation under the gaze of a medical team assembled to investigate media excitement over her miraculous survival without food.[79] Those who write on self-starvation acknowledge a continuum linking the holy fasts of medieval Christianity to the situation of the Victorian anorexic, but, apart from scholarly speculation about self-starving individuals such as George Cheyne, Byron and, to a far lesser extent, Frances Burney, there is no study of eighteenth-century eating disorders.[80] It is not part of my project here to fill this gap in any thorough or synthetic way, but it is obvious that what Lilian Furst and Peter Graham have called 'disorderly eating' took place, and was recognised to take place, throughout this period.[81]

78 Morag Sweeney, *Anorexic Bodies: A Feminist and Sociological Perspective on Anorexia Nervosa* (London: Routledge, 1993), p. 208.
79 For a detailed account of Sarah Jacob's story, see Sian Busby, *A Wonderful Little Girl: Starving for Fame* (London: Short Books, 2004).
80 See Anita Guerrini, *Obesity and Depression in the Enlightenment: The Life and Times of George Cheyne* (Oklahoma, University of Oklahoma Press, 2000); Helen King, *The Disease of Virgins: Green-Sickness, Chlorosis and the Problems of Puberty* London: Routledge, 2003); Caroline Walker Bynum, *Holy Feast and Holy Fast: The Religious Significance of Food to Medieval Women* (Berkeley: University of California Press, 1987); Joan Jacobs Brumberg, *Fasting Girls: The Emergence of Anorexia Nervosa as a Modern Disease* (Cambridge, Mass.: Harvard University Press, 1988); Krugovoy Silver, *Anorexic Body*; Nancy A. Gutierrez, *Shall She Famish Then? Female Food Refusal in Early Modern England* (London: Ashgate, 2003); Leslie Heywood, *Dedication to Culture: The Anorexic Aesthetic in Modern Culture* (Berkeley: University of California Press, 1997).
81 Lilian R. Furst and Peter W. Graham (eds.), *Disorderly Eaters: Texts in Self-Empowerment* (Philadelphia: Pennsylvania State University Press, 1992).

The most cursory scan shows Henry Thrale, George Cheyne and Samuel Johnson gorging themselves into sickness, Frances Burney and Byron writing obsessively about self-imposed dietary restriction, Dorothy Wordsworth weighing herself and reporting the results to her friends with triumph or dismay. The more detailed reading of letters and journals shows size, if not usually weight, and eating as matters of widespread concern and occasional self-destruction. Burney reports the death of her acquaintance Sophy Pitches from 'fasting and pining' or 'Quack Med'cines to prevent growing fat, or perhaps to repress Appetite', and Wollstonecraft rails against the cult of debility for undermining women's health for the sake of aesthetic fragility.[82] Just as it is hard to find fat women in British fiction before Dickens, it is hard to find women who starve themselves in order to be thin (despite the obvious case of Burney, discussed in Chapter 1). Nevertheless, not eating is at least as inevitably significant as eating.

Anxieties about national and personal identities in this context come together in Mary Brunton's *Self-Control*, a novel which, as we have already seen, imagines itself in consistently gustatory terms. Laura Montreville, the heroine, has grown up in an isolated Highland village, supported by her affectionate Scottish father and abused by her bad-tempered aristocratic English mother. This is one of several Scottish novels of this period in which the heroine recognises her absolute obligation to honour and obey a father whose fallibility becomes increasingly apparent (the parallels with the national situation are obvious). Laura's mother dies, and when her father learns that the annuity arranged for Laura in the case of his death is based on a flawed deed, she accompanies him to London to reason with the bankers. Captain Montreville is keen that Laura agree to marry Colonel Hargrave, and Laura feels unable to tell him that Hargrave has tried to seduce her lest this trigger a duel in which she might lose her father. In London, the bankers prove recalcitrant, partly because Laura spurns their advances, and Montreville becomes ill. De Courcy, a family friend who also falls in love with Laura, secretly pays half the rent on a pleasant house for them during Montreville's convalescence. But De Courcy has to leave town and Montreville is slow to recover, and when Laura discovers how much she owes her landlady she understands that, 'The poverty, whose approach she had so long contemplated with

---

82 See Frances Burney, *The Early Journals and Letters of Frances Burney*, ed. Lars E. Troide (Oxford: Clarendon Press, 1998), vol. 3, pp. 332–3.

a fearful eye, had now suddenly overtaken her.' She determines to conceal their poverty from her father, for 'Weakened both in body and in mind, how would he endure the privations that attend on real penury?'[83]

At this point, Laura's practical dilemma mirrors her social difficulties. She cannot encourage De Courcy, whom she admires, because she believes herself sullied by Hargrave's attempt on her virtue. She cannot contravene the will of her father, and will not tell him how Hargrave has offended, so she remains under pressure from her sick father to marry a man whom she knows to be a libertine. Now, she cannot accept financial support from Hargrave, because it would compromise her yet further, or from De Courcy, because she cannot marry him. She cannot raise a loan against her father's income because he believes himself to be dying. She will not sell anything from their house because it would upset her father, apart from taking too long, and her only way of earning money is by painting, which will also take too long. She turns to 'Him who hath supplied me in yet more urgent want … who hath fed my soul with angel's food' and determines that, 'Could she but hope to obtain a subsistence for her father, she would labour night and day, deprive herself of recreation, of rest, even of daily food, rather than wound his heart, by an acquaintance with poverty.'[84] Furthermore, 'since his pride is hurt by the labours of his child', she will do all this in secret.

Despite the vocabulary of 'labouring', this undertaking sets Laura's endeavours apart from the economy of production and consumption that defines conventional work. In a parody of feminine virtue, she intends to produce without consuming, or even to produce by not consuming, in order to 'obtain a subsistence for her father'. This fantasy of feeding her father by denying herself, by the wasting – or expenditure – of her own body, works in several ways. It is as if her father is her baby, nourished on her blood and milk. There is also a gesture towards the consumption of the body of Christ, but this is most obviously a self-destructive parody of her father's impossible demands on Laura. Her father is eating away at her integrity in nagging her to marry Hargrave out of filial obedience while also requiring her to nurse himself as if he were a child, and in this context Laura's self-starvation begins to look like a

83 Brunton, *Self-Control*, p. 138.
84 Brunton, *Self-Control*, p. 140.

savage protest. Maud Ellmann writes that, 'the act of self-starvation can achieve the status of a hunger strike only through a declaration of intention'.[85] There are here, arguably, a sequence of such declarations. Laura turns to work on her portfolio

> till the hour of dinner arrived. She then went to summon her father from his chamber to the eating-room. 'This day,' thought she, 'I must share in his precarious substance – another I shall be more provident. And is this then, perhaps, our last social meal?'[86]

Montreville makes a gloomy meal and then, 'After spending a few silent hours without effort towards employment or recreation, he retired for the night; and Laura experienced a sensation of relief, as, shutting herself away into her apartment, she prepared to resume her labours.' It is as if this divorce *a mensa* is an economic merging of identities. They will no longer eat together, but he will consume without producing, 'without effort towards employment', and she, 'prepared to resume her labours', will produce without consuming. Laura 'continued to work till her candle expired in the socket; and then threw herself on the bed to rise again with the first blush of dawn'. She is like the virtuous woman of Proverbs 31 whose 'candle goeth not out by night' but who 'riseth also while it is yet night' except that nobody 'gives her the fruits of her hands'. 'Hastily swallowing a few mouthfuls of dry bread, she continued her drawing, until her father rang for his chocolate.'[87] Chocolate, still at this stage a drink and not a solid, is a rare luxury usually consumed by the middling sort only at weddings. The repeated contrasts hammer home the injustice of Laura's deprivation in the name of the father.

The currency of self-starvation in the overlapping economies of morality and labour which characterise Romantic-era women's fiction is elaborated in the following pages. On her way to humble herself by asking a rich relative for money, Laura meets a beggar. She remembers that she cannot give him money, but takes him home to 'bestow on the old man the humble fare which she had before destined to supply her own wants for the day, glad to purchase by a longer fast the right to feed the hungry'. She scolds herself for being unable to 'ask without pain' for the charity she can 'offer to

85 Maud Ellmann, *The Hunger Artist: Starving, Writing and Imprisonment* (London: Virago, 1993) p. 19.
86 Brunton, *Self-Control*, p. 140.
87 Brunton, *Self-Control*, p. 141.

him with ease, and even with pleasure', but cannot convince herself
that she and he are 'made of ... the same frail, sinful, perishable
dust'.[88] The explicit transaction here is arresting; Laura uses her self-
inflicted hunger to buy 'the right to feed the hungry', which on the
one hand is the right to be good but on the other is the right to align
oneself with those who have a surplus against those who do not
have enough. Laura's hunger, then, because it is elective, buys her
both moral and social status, and more of it buys more status. When
she returns home after a day of adventures which includes being
harassed by Hargrave,

> Montreville returned to his chamber; and there Laura ordered his small
> but delicate repast to be served, excusing herself from partaking of it, by
> saying that she could dine more conveniently in the parlour. Having in
> the morning bestowed on the beggar the meagre fare that should have
> supplied her own wants, she employed the time of her father's meal, in
> the labour that was to purchase him another; pondering meanwhile on
> the probability that he would again enter on the discussion of Hargrave's
> pretensions.[89]

Again the vocabulary of commerce expresses the dynamics of self-
starvation. The time her father expends in eating, Laura employs
in labour to purchase more food, so that, in the familiar metaphor,
time itself is a commodity that can be earned and exchanged for
food. Laura's wants go unsupplied because she has spent her bread
on status and is now spending the mealtime on production for
her father even while she contemplates his unwitting, or perhaps
witless, persecution of her.

Laura's hunger reaches its inevitable conclusion in similarly
revealing terms. Hargrave, in a *tête-à-tête* to which Laura has been
compelled by her father, threatens that if she persists in refusing
him he will 'turn to the bought smile of harlots, forget [her] in
the haunts of riot, or in the grave of a suicide'. She is firm: 'everlasting were my cause of repentance, should I wilfully do wrong' so,
'frantickly straining her to his breast, he rushed out of the room',
and 'the wretched Laura found refuge from her misery in long and
deep insensibility'.[90] Montreville responds to the cries of the servant
who finds Laura, and 'The unfeeling landlady immediately expressed
her opinion that Miss Montreville had died of famine, declaring that

88 Brunton, *Self-Control*, p. 145.
89 Brunton, *Self-Control*, p. 158.
90 Brunton, *Self-Control*, p. 183.

she had long feared as much.'The servant confirms the probability of this, adding that 'many a long night has she sat up toiling when the poorest creature was asleep', and 'all the storm, from which his dutiful child so well had sheltered him' bursts on Montreville.

> 'Oh Laura,' he cried, clasping her lifeless form, 'my only comfort – my good – my gentle – my blameless child, has thou nourished thy father with thy life! Oh why didst thou not let me die!' Then laying his cheek to hers, 'Oh she is cold – cold as clay,' he cried, and the old man wrung his hands, and sobbed like an infant.[91]

The strain is too much; Montreville ruptures a blood-vessel, sinks 'down by the side of his senseless child' and is 'conveyed to bed without hope of life'. He survives long enough only for Laura to recover and receive his final blessing.

Laura has 'nourished her father with her life' and, in doing so, returned him to a state of infancy. Self-starvation, here as in *Adeline Mowbray*, is a way of inverting the dominant/powerless dyad, as the hungry woman proves her moral and economic value. As many feminist writers on eating disorders point out, self-starvation is a protest which only reinscribes the hierarchy in the end, since the protester finishes either dead or eating. *Self-Control*, a novel notorious for the wildly melodramatic ending foreshadowed in the extravagance of this scene, in fact offers here a fantasy in which the oppressive man is overcome by his daughter's self-starvation. In an oddly satisfying variant of the childish fantasy of dying so that the grown-ups are sorry, Laura not only gets to hear how upset everyone is by her death but also finds that her self-denial has killed her father. She starves for him and he dies, a neat but disconcerting realisation of the fantasy of self-destructive protest.

I have dwelt on this novel at such length partly because it offers a typical context for women's disordered eating in the Romantic era. The vocabulary of economic productivity is used to justify or condemn a woman's eating, while her behaviour at the table works to express the fine balance between sense and sensibility required of the viable and moral fictional heroine. Letters and memoirs often display anxiety about their female authors' control of appetite and body shape, but in fiction these concerns mark vain and trivial minds. What matters most about food in the women's fiction of the late eighteenth and early nineteenth centuries is its function in rela-

91 Brunton, *Self-Control*, p. 183.

tion to productivity, be that biological (babies and milk), manual (goods and services) or intellectual (writing). The texts I study here play endlessly with the idea that food is a precondition of fiction (no writing without eating), that reading is food, or poison, for the mind (no reading without eating), and that writing, which depends on eating, is therefore an intellectual form of cooking. Novels may look like junk food, 'trash' for 'vitiated appetites', but there is a pill in the jam. Since readers are what they eat and writers feed readers with the fruits of their bodies, writing can figure as breastfeeding as well as cooking. The analogy is particularly clear in the context of the contemporary emphasis on maternal breastfeeding to save elite babies from the characteristics of labouring-class wet-nurses, which would be passed on in the milk as immorality and false ideology would be passed on in novels. Eating and reading, cooking and writing, are inseparable in the women's writing of the Romantic era. To be a woman is to produce. Production necessitates consumption, and therefore women must consume, but to consume beyond what is needful for production is to heed the serpent in the garden and fall into the sins which characterise and even define the aristocracy in these novels. The late eighteenth century displays an awareness we have now lost that Eve's sin is not eating *per se* but eating for reasons which have nothing to do with need. Hunger is not (morally) dangerous in these novels – if anything, it is a guarantee of virtue since it proves that one has produced before seeking to consume – but appetite marks the fallen or falling woman. Most of the novels I read here include the figure of the older woman who has come through the tribulations of youth and acts as a mentor to the temporarily or permanently motherless heroine. All of these characterisations reference Proverbs 31, which, quoted more fully than in relation to Laura Montreville's daily routines, says it all:

> Who can find a virtuous woman? For her price is far above rubies.
> The heart of her husband doth safely trust in her, so that he shall have no
>   need of spoil.
> She will do him good and not evil all the days of her life.
> She seeketh wool and flax, and worketh willingly with her hands.
> She is like the merchants' ships; she bringeth her food from afar.
> She riseth also while it is yet night, and giveth meat to her household, and
>   a portion to her maidens.
> She considereth a field, and buyeth it: with the fruit of her hands she
>   planteth a vineyard.
> She girdeth her loins with strength and strengtheneth her arms.

She perceiveth that her merchandise is good: her candle goeth not out by
  night.
She layeth her hands to the spindle, and her hands hold the distaff.
She stretcheth out her hand to the poor; yea, she reacheth forth her hands
  to the needy.
She is not afraid of the snow for her household: for all her household are
  clothed with scarlet.
She maketh herself coverings of tapestry; her clothing is silk and purple.
Her husband is known in the gates, when he sitteth among the elders of
  the land.
She maketh fine linen, and selleth it; and delivereth girdles unto the
  merchant.
Strength and honour are her clothing; and she shall rejoice in time to
  come.
She openeth her mouth with wisdom; and in her tongue is the law of
  kindness.
She looketh well to the ways of her household, and eateth not the bread of
  idleness.
Her children arise up, and call her blessed; her husband also, and he praiseth
  her.
Many daughters have done virtuously, but thou excellest them all.
Favour is deceitful, and beauty is vain: but a woman that feareth the Lord,
  she shall be praised.
Give her of the fruit of her hands; and let her own works praise her in the
  gates.

These verses ring so loudly through the women's fiction of the
Romantic era because virtue and economic productivity are woven
together like warp and weft. Virtue is worth more than rubies, but
as the proverb proceeds there is a sense that the writer is comparing
like with like in that image. Woman's goodness inheres in what she
makes and sells, in how she manages material resources. A great
deal of scholarly work in the last decade has explored women's
economic activity in late eighteenth-century life and literature; what
I hope to do here is to show how the economies of the body and the
literary marketplace come together in the unstable currency of food.

1

Eating her words
The politics of commensality in Frances Burney's fiction and letters

My Heart beat so quick against my stays, that I almost panted with extreme agitation, at the dread either of hearing some cruel criticism, or of being betrayed: & I munched my Biscuit as if I had not Eaten for a fortnight …
… I could sit still no longer; there was some thing so awkward; so uncommon, so strange in my then situation, that I wished myself 100 miles off; – & indeed, I had almost Choaked myself with the Biscuit, for I could not for my life *swallow* it, – & so, before I could consider the embarrassment of *returning* I got up, &, as Mr Lort went to the Table to look for Evelina, I left the Room. – & was forced to call for Water, to wash down the Biscuit which stuck in my Throat.[1]

—Frances Burney

Until *The Wanderer*, there is not much food in Burney's fiction, but there are many tables. Until Juliet, her heroines rarely eat, and certainly rarely eat anything in particular, any specified foodstuff rather than 'breakfast' or 'supper', but they come dutifully to the table three or four times a day, and at periods of crisis flee it in distress almost as frequently. There is no simple meaning or function of the dining table in Burney's first three novels – it is where people perform their chosen or enforced roles, endure prosecution or attempt defence and display authentic or assumed status – but there is minimal sense of the table as a place of comfort or pleasure. In Burney's fiction, commensality, coming together around the table, is about social coercion and the enforcement of rules and obligations on reluctant individuals. Power, in Burney's fiction (and perhaps also in her letters), can be measured by the consistency of feeling

1 Burney, *Early Journals*, vol. 3, pp. 113–14.

in private and at the table. The owner of the table – usually but not always the head of the family – is the only member of the household whose identity between meals is precisely the same as his role at the table, the only person who might move with pleasure and equanimity between the closet and the dining room. For everyone else, to varying extents and in varying ways, commensality is sinister and mealtimes are a fight for survival in more ways than one.

My opening quotation, from Burney's account of a supper during Hester Thrale's house party of August 1778, offers a powerful example of the plight of the dissenting individual at the table. *Evelina* was at the height of its popularity, but Burney had not acknowledged her authorship except to her immediate family, through whom the secret had leaked to the Thrales and Johnson. Burney was living in fear of discovery, and she dreaded occasions like these on which conversation turned towards her book and her continuing happiness depended on her ability to simulate indifference. Burney, in this account, is far too anxious to make speech part of her performance of disinterest and is forced back into trying to mime a negative, to 'act normal'. Since, as Maud Ellmann reminds us, eating and speaking are alternatives (in etiquette, but also in fact in practice, however messy), Burney's biscuit displaces anything she might say, whether an admission or acknowledgement of authorship or an attempt to deceive the minority around the table who would not know that she is lying.[2] This displacement does nothing to postpone, much less resolve, the problem. 'Munching' instead of talking displaces the meanings of speech onto eating, and in this instance Burney's eating is more honest than her intended meanings. The attempt to 'act normal' fails because, in Burney's formulation of this episode, it is at least as hard to eat a lie as it would be to pronounce it. Deceiving by putting things into one's mouth turns out to be as difficult as deceiving by what comes out. The Thrales' table has become a kind of literary courtroom, and Burney is eating on oath, deploying and/or betrayed by the slippery relationship between writing, eating and speech.

This image of the table as the place of (coded) interrogation and coercion is a good place to begin to think about food in Burney's work, both fictional and epistolary, but the meanings of the table

2 Ellmann, *Hunger Artist*, p. 17.

are not stable across her oeuvre, and I will be particularly interested here in the differences between commensality in the early
letters, where Burney invariably represents herself as the sufferer at
someone else's table, performing for and defending herself against
the rest of the coterie and/or the family, and in the (much) later
letters where the table is her own and the spotlight is firmly trained
on her son and particularly on her son's plate. The implications of
food and commensality also change enormously between *Evelina*
and *The Wanderer*, in ways that both parallel and contradict Burney's
epistolary concerns.

One of the most obvious disjunctions between the fiction and
the letters seems to be that, except in *The Wanderer*, to which I
will return, cooking is entirely absent from the novels. Burney is
concerned only with women whose identities depend so fully on
not getting their hands dirty that the issue never arises, however
desperate their actual circumstances. Juliet is, exceptionally, forced
to witness food preparation when fear and indigence oblige her to
accept the hospitality of working families, but even she, the most
degraded of Burney's heroines, never contemplates a situation in
which she might find herself cooking her own meals, much less
preparing food for anyone else, and none of the others sets foot in
a kitchen. In all the scenes where shops form a backdrop or a foreground for the heroine's performance of her moral status and all the
episodes organised by shopping, none of the commodities at issue
are edible. Burney's heroines buy everything from ball gowns to
needles and books to seats in a carriage and beds at an inn, but they
do not get hungry while they are doing it and they display no more
awareness of the provenance of food than of babies. Meals appear
on the table at times that indicate the hostess's actual or desired
social standing, are served in ways that encode the social status and
marital prospects of the assembled company and eaten or, more
usually, not eaten in representation of the diners' emotional states.
Ingredients and flavours are almost never mentioned, being no more
relevant to the drama at hand than the colour of the curtains in the
morning room Evelina must leave because her distress is better
suited to the bedroom. Characters who violate this convention (of
which there are so many that interest in food becomes a shorthand
for moral failure) unwittingly disclose irredeemable inferiority of
every sort.

Recent critical works on Burney have emphasised the thin veneer
of 'manners' through which violence in various forms is constantly

bursting, and in these analyses the body frequently articulates what the mind and the pen may not say. Julia Epstein writes that, 'Burney and her heroines experience social oppression with and through their bodies',[3] and in Burney's accounts of the table we see that part of that oppression is that the body cannot shut up. People must eat, and eating – both what is eaten and how it is eaten – can always be interpreted. But, as Burney's early letters disclose, starving is as easily and relentlessly readable as eating. For the first three heroines much more than for Burney herself, the problematic imperative is only in part that of eating. Commensality figures as an (inseparable) form of trauma, an absolute obligation to violate all inclination and feeling several times a day. Like it or not (and it is almost invariably not), Evelina, Cecilia and Camilla must appear at the table and behave themselves – enact themselves – several times a day, and the form of this behaviour includes eating as well as serving food and disciplining the body at the table. If, as Barbara Zonitch and Joanne Cutting-Grey contend, the Burneyan body enacts what the mouth cannot pronounce, it seems that eating forms an unavoidable connection between the silent body and the disembodied voice.[4] If, as Burney's writing suggests, eating and reading, writing and cooking, are in some sense equivalent ways in which the body is tied to the market, then self-starvation and writing to Nobody may be seen as equivalent fantasies of self-sufficiency which are similarly self-negating. The self-starver's ambition to live without food has qualities in common with the secret writer's fantasy of writing without readers, for in both cases there is an impossible desire to produce without either consuming or being consumed. The writer, after all, no more exists without readers than without food; this is where textuality and corporeality intersect. Writing read by nobody is as much an oxymoron as life without food.

It is interesting, in this context, that Burney's letters and journals display a strikingly minute interest in who eats what and why. She gives precise accounts of Johnson making an exception to consume a mutton pie, Sophia Streatfield being chased across the Thrales' orchard by other guests bearing the children's lunch (leg of lamb and apple pie) and her own steadfast rejection of supper

3 Julia Epstein, *The Iron Pen: Frances Burney and the Politics of Women's Writing* (Bristol: Bristol Classical Press, 1989), p. 33.
4 See Barbara Zonitch, *Familiar Violence: Gender and Social Upheaval in the Novels of Frances Burney* (Newark: University of Delaware Press, 1997); Joanne Cutting-Gray, *Woman as 'Nobody' and the Novels of Fanny Burney* (Gainsville: University of Florida Press, 1992).

(water, toast and biscuits, 'all there is any chance of Eating after our late & great Dinners'). Perhaps different rules apply to fiction, but in Burney's records of her late teens and early twenties, eating is at least as important as writing, especially during her first forays into independent socialising. I would like to consider the role of eating in Burney's performance and reporting of her public, authorial persona, moving on to contrast this detailed reportage of mouthfuls and recipes with her fictional heroines' unremitting lack of interest in sustenance or gastronomy. 'She don't care what she eats; she cares for nothing but books, and such kind of things,' Indiana tells Clermont of Eugenia, thereby revealing her own triviality and Eugenia's moral and intellectual superiority.[5] Burney, staying at Streatham Park, recounts excitedly, 'we have not once missed a pine apple since I came, & therefore you may imagine their abundance besides Grapes, melons, peaches, nectarines, & Ices.'[6]

Streatham Park, August 1778

In August 1778, Hester Thrale invited Dr Johnson to stay with her in Streatham in order to meet Frances Burney, who had recently published *Evelina* and not yet publicly acknowledged her authorship. The Thrales had a large household, of which Samuel Johnson was a semi-permanent member, and a succession of guests and houseparties interrupted only by Hester Thrale's annual confinements. Mary Hyde writes in *The Thrales of Streatham Park* that, 'Streatham Park was liberty hall, and only at meal times were guests obliged to meet and join in the 'flash' of conversation',[7] but Burney's letters show that food and socialising were more complicated than that. In much late eighteenth-century fiction, mealtimes are intensified by being the only regular occasion for mixed sex socialising, but at Streatham Park they were also the only time when the writers, readers and critics who usually stayed there were obliged to interact. Meals were a source of tension also because Henry Thrale habitually ate and drank until he was ill in defiance of repeated medical advice that he was eating himself into an early grave. Burney's great

---

5 Frances Burney, *Camilla*, ed. Edward A. Bloom and Lillian D. Bloom (Oxford: Oxford University Press, 1972), p. 579.

6 *Early Journals*, vol. 3, p. 126.

7 Mary Hyde, *The Thrales of Streatham Park* (Cambridge, Mass.: Harvard University Press, 1977), p. 184.

interest in mealtimes during her visits to Streatham may reflect these pressures as much as it portrays her own concerns, but it is at least clear that she seized upon the vocabulary of eating and self-representation offered in this house of gustatory unease. There is no account of Johnson's experience of the visit, but Burney's, in a long letter to her sister, reflects her (and perhaps Johnson's) complex attitude to food:

> Mrs. Thrale introduced me to him, & he took his place. We had a Noble Dinner, & a most elegant & delicious Desert. Dr. Johnson, in the middle of Dinner, asked Mrs. Thrale what was in some little pies that were near him? 'Mutton, answered she, so I don't ask you to Eat any, because I know you despise it.'
>
> 'No, Madam, no; cried he, I despise *nothing* in its way that is good of its sort: – but I am too proud now to Eat of it; – sitting by Miss Burney makes me very proud to Day!'[8]

Burney's developing relationship with Johnson, at least in her epistolary account, continues to centre as much on food as on writing, and Johnson goes on teasing her about the relationship between eating and literary status. The joke that mutton pies are unworthy of the author of *Evelina* gives place to a less hilarious concern about eating, language and the young female novelist, a concern which seems to dominate all her visits to Streatham Park. My project here is to begin to unravel some of these complicated and often destructive connections between eating, speaking and feminine celebrity.

Johnson knew a little about the domestic habits of the Burneys because of his friendship with Frances's father, the musicologist Charles Burney, and so when it became obvious to Hester Thrale that Frances would sooner starve than make demands of her hostess, she took Johnson's word rather than Frances's about what she wanted to eat:

> At night Mrs Thrale asked if I would have any thing? I answered *no*: but Dr Johnson said 'yes; – she is used, Madam, to suppers; – she would like an Egg or two, & a few slices of Ham, – or a *Rasher*, – a Rasher, I believe, would please her better.'
>
> How ridiculous! however, nothing could persuade Mrs Thrale not to have the Cloath laid: & Dr Johnson was so facetious, that he challenged Mr Thrale to get Drunk! ...
>
> I Eat nothing, that they might not again use such a Ceremony with

8 Burney, *Early Journals*, vol. 3, p. 74.

me. Indeed their late Dinners forbid suppers; especially as Dr Johnson
made me Eat cake at Tea, for he held it till I took it, with an odd, or absent
complaisance.[9]

This image of Johnson trying – and, interestingly, in the end, failing
– to embarrass Burney into eating cake and bacon and eggs that
she does not want, apparently for his own amusement, is curious
given her usual absolute docility towards her famous collection of
father figures. In one sense perhaps Johnson's joviality creates a
carnival atmosphere in which Burney feels able to reject supper as
she was unable to reject cake in the more public and serious setting
of afternoon tea in the drawing room, but his interest in feeding her
at all attracts attention and may serve to establish the importance
of public eating in Burney's introduction to the literary elite. The
sequel to this episode, over breakfast the following morning, is also
revealing, as Johnson answers Mrs Thrale's hope that he slept well,
'Why no, Madam, no ... I could not sleep at all; – there I lay, restless
& uneasy, & thinking all the Time of Miss Burney! – Perhaps I have
offended her, thought I, perhaps she is angry; – I have seen her but
once, & I talked to her of a *Rasher*! – Were You angry?' Burney denies
anger, and Johnson continues, 'I have been endeavouring to find
some excuse ... so, as I could not sleep, I got up, & looked for some
authority for the word, – & I find, Madam, it is used by Dryden: in
one of his Prologues ... So you must not mind me, Madam, – I say
strange things, but I mean no harm.'[10] Johnson's apology is mostly
a joke, as Burney realises after a moment ('I was almost afraid he
thought I was *really* Ideot enough to have taken him seriously ... '),
but it wouldn't be funny without an underlying point and the point,
I think, is that it is slightly indelicate to anatomise a young lady's
food in general and that 'rasher' in particular is a somewhat vulgar
word. (Although Johnson's dictionary, defining it as 'a thin slice of
bacon' and citing examples from Dryden, *The Merchant of Venice*
and William King, does nothing to clarify this). What I would like
to emphasis here is the sense that food words themselves can, even
in a joke, offend against the rubrics of class and gender. As Burney's
frequent deletions of adjectives referring to the taste rather than the
appearance of food attest, the lexis of cooking and eating can seem
almost as dangerously embodied as the sizzling rashers and fat little

---

9 Burney, *Early Journals*, vol. 3, p. 87.
10 Burney, *Early Journals*, vol. 3, p. 89.

pies themselves. In this context, it is no wonder Burney rejected this vocabulary in her published fiction. In her letters, it is explicitly countered by reiterations of her own thinness and abstinence.

Many of Burney's descriptions of social occasions during these first years of popularity include disingenuous descriptions of men telling her that she is alarmingly thin and apparently trying to starve to death. It is clear that her appetite and 'shape' were a major preoccupation of her adolescence and early adulthood. If one resists the temptation to offer a retrospective diagnosis of anorexia nervosa, then it becomes possible to think about Burney's own very knowing constructions of the meanings of her desire not to eat and pleasure in thinness. As she repeatedly points out, most of these men are interested in her body, and feel entitled to comment on it, only because she has written and published a successful novel. I would like to avoid straightforwardly equating a woman's body with her text, an unnecessarily gendered manoeuvre that negates exactly the disembodied qualities of writing that Burney plays with in her self-representations. Rather, what seems interesting here is the negotiation of celebrity, Burney's awareness that she is being watched as she would not have been without *Evelina* and that the relationship between her physical presence at a gathering and her authorial presence in a book is not self-evident. The very presence of an audience, imaginary or otherwise, turns her social interactions into something of a performance, a quality heightened by Burney's extraordinarily detailed accounts of meetings and conversations, which, in the end, offer a self-representation (the letters) of a self-conscious (at the table) performance of herself (as a celebrated author). Burney plays endlessly with and between the spaces between these portrayals, and it is often the metaphor of words-as-food that returns us to the final literary quality of all of this. Morag Sweeney writes that, 'anorexic women transform the categories through which female experience is created in an attempt to resolve at the level of the body the contradictory demands of individuality and femininity.'[11] Disregarding for the moment Sweeney's apparently transhistorical understanding of 'anorexia', it is clear that eating and not eating simultaneously internalise and announce the eater's stance in relation to her companions' expectations. The body is used to represent and create itself at the same time, under the scrutiny of fellow diners. It can seem hard to imagine an act in which it is more the

11 Sweeney, *Anorexic Bodies*, p. 239.

case that 'identity is the effect of performance, and not vice versa',[12] and yet the important point, from which it is easy to be distracted by Burney's informal and detailed epistolary style, is that Burney is not only eating knowingly – which may or may not be the case – but also writing knowingly. This is performance masquerading as performativity.

Burney's consciousness, and manipulation, of the merging of identity and performance is sometimes disconcerting. An early example of this is her account of the traveller Richard Twiss's supper at the Burney home in Queen Square in March 1774. Twiss distressed Burney by being 'pleased to make Confession that he had left [Naples] in disgrace.' Typically, she combines dismay at being subjected to improper conversation with powerful scorn for masculine pride: 'these sort of avowals immediately imply a love affair, & wear a strong air of Vanity.' While one guest, Mrs Young, tries to divert Twiss from further details, another, Dr Shepherd, seems unaware of the conversational quicksand at the feet of this mixed gathering and asks the questions Twiss is hoping for. Mrs Young's diversions, according to Burney, 'shewed as much too much quickness, as the Doctor did too much dullness.'[13] Twiss turns to Burney, 'You know what a *Ragazza* is, Ma'am? ... A *Signorina?*' I stammered out something like niether yes or no, because the Question rather frightened me, lest he should conclude that in understanding *that*, I knew much *more* ... ' Charles Burney rescues Frances from this awkward position in which admitting enough knowledge to understand the story will reveal unmaidenly information but denying it will result in improper explanation (and thus unmaidenly information), but Twiss's scrutiny seems relentless:

> When supper was removed, Mr Twiss again attacked me in Italian –
> 'Credo che e innamorata, perche non mangiate –' [I believe you are in love, that's why you don't eat –]
> 'O no! answered I, – but I seldom Eat much supper.'
> 'E il Lingua d'Amore –' continued he, & added that it became *una bella Bocca* –' [It is the language of love ... a beautiful mouth.]
> 'And it had best be confined to such!' answered I.[14]

Burney is tart in rejecting both Twiss's compliment and his reading of her rejection of the meal that provides the focus for

12 Vikki Bell (ed), *Performativity and Belonging* (London: Sage Publications, 1999), p. 3.
13 Burney, *Early Journals*, vol. 2, p. 15.
14 Burney, *Early Journals*, vol. 2, p. 17.

their meeting. Italian is one of the languages in which 'tongue', *lingua*, also means 'language', so Twiss is punningly articulating the assumption that women use their mouths to communicate as clearly by eating as by speaking. As in Burney's account of her choking on a biscuit, Twiss suggests that Burney's consumption or rejection of food articulate her contribution to the discussion more clearly than her speech or silence. Having previously put her in a position where there is nothing she can say, exemplifying potential difficulties of mixed socialising and thus of meal-times for unmarried women, he proceeds to interpret her other decision to hold her tongue. It is easy to understand Burney's resentment here, for whether she speaks or is silent, eats or does not, she will be understood to announce her knowledge of and interest in sexuality. There is no escaping performance at Burney's table, no position available in which the quantity she eats speaks only of her physical requirements at that moment, and it is hard to know how straightforwardly to read her suggestion that this should be possible. Full or empty of air or food, the beautiful mouth bespeaks the body even as it fuels or starves it. Four years later, Burney's apparent (assumed?) impatience at this state of affairs seems to have given way to a certain collusion:

> Sunday morning, when I went into the Library, Mr Thrale called out, 'Why, Miss Burney, this will never do!'
> 'What, Sir?' cried I.
> 'Why You grow Thinner & Thinner! You have hardly any waist left already! What account can I give of you to Dr Burney?'
> 'Ay, well,' cried Mr Lort, drily, – she will be all spirit, & no substance, by & by, for she Eats nothing; – however, it will be all the better for the World, one way or other!'
> 'Yes, – cried Mr Seward, in a low voice, – I hope it will be all the better for our Comedy!' [15]

Burney has entered the library to join the late morning breakfast, and the 'comedy' is 'Streatham, A Farce', which Johnson had been joking that Burney should write. Seward is punning on the dual meaning of 'spirit' in the eighteenth century (spiritual/spirited) to joke that the less Burney eats, the closer she approaches complete physical dissolution, the wittier her writing should be. Part of the point of Lort's and Seward's remarks is that the important part of Burney, unusually, is her 'spirit', her extra-bodily identity, and not her 'substance'; her social identity is based on intellectual achievement

15 Burney, *Early Journals*, vol. 3, p. 122.

rather than on her 'shape'. It is hard to say if they are teasing Burney for apparently espousing this view, assuming that her self-starvation is based on her neglect of the bodily aspects of writing as well as of her physical needs, or whether the joke is that the author's body is disposable. The same trope appears from the mouth of Dr Delap:

> I did not, therefore, want a Friend at Table, for, as usual, he resumed his watchful attention & care of my plate, & his wondering & reiterated exclamations at the little I Eat, – telling me, however, that, with or without Eating, I knew how to make myself immortal! So, you find, he has not lost his gallantry.[16]

Again, the writer's immortality plays with the mortality of the eater and the more immediate mortality of the starving. The presence of the writer at the table – and Burney's insistence in her letters on being present at the (written) table as a writer whose life (*Life?*) depends on production rather than as a diner whose life depends on consumption – disrupts commensality by upsetting the symbolic equations between eating and reading, writing and cooking. It is as if the Burney we read in these letters insists that writing places her above eating, that the literary economy replaces rather than represents that of food, standing in for the miraculous nutrition of the holy fast. Unlike the other guests at Thrale's table, the writer of these letters is already immortal and her self-representations of her self-starvation thus highlight her professional success.

Burney elaborates her position in this and subsequent visits by retreating from the table altogether. She ambivalently praises Hester Thrale's kindness to her during periods of unspecified illness that required her to retire to her room. Every day there is 'a sumptuous dinner of three courses' and 'a superb desert', but Burney never describes herself eating and rarely mentions the flavour or texture of a dish. Instead, as she languishes upstairs, Hester Thrale comes up to tell her: 'Dr Delap said that you were the charmingest Girl in the World for a Girl who was so near being nothing, & they all agreed nobody ever had so little shape before, & that a Gust of Wind would blow you quite away.'[17] When she rejoins the party, Mr Blakeney presses her 'to Eat & Drink with much solemnity of kindness, – 'Why, Ma'lle, you Eat nothing! – it's all very fine, & delicate, & all that kind of thing, – but then you'll be no substance, – & so & so on, – & then we will lose you!' The letter to Susan is calculated to excite

anxiety about and interest in Frances's eating even as it recounts the
conquest of literary London, constituting in itself both the performance of self-starvation and the celebration of plenty. Writing about
her thinness and malnutrition is crucial to Burney's art of hunger,
although in doing so, she refrains from offering any readings of her
own body or even contradicting those of others. Maud Ellmann
writes in *The Hunger Artist* that,

> the drama of starvation unsettles the dichotomy between the fictive and
> the real, between the world of language and the world of violence. It is
> obvious, for instance, that any form of inanition eventually leads to death,
> and in this sense the mimed or fictional starvation of a hunger strike
> ultimately converges with the real privations that it imitates. More impor-
> tant, the starving body is itself a text, the living dossier of its discontents,
> for the injustices of power are encoded in the savage hieroglyphics of its
> sufferings.[18]

What is lacking in the letters is any sense of 'real privations' or
'the world of violence'. Burney ventriloquises the announcement of
her self-starvation, placing it in the mouths of mature men whose
interest in her body she then claims to resent. In recounting these
conversations she seems to efface herself, inhabiting her body no
more than the proverbial fly on the wall, although at other moments
her munching and choking are visceral enough. These changes
in narrative position between the satisfying onomatopoeia of
'munching' and the apparently omniscient narrator's rehearsal of
a description of her eating offered in her absence destabilise the
status of the starving body analysed by Ellmann. Burney's 'starving'
body cannot be a text because it does not speak, because it appears
to exist only in the echo-chamber of her letters. There are no 'savage
hieroglyphics' of its sufferings (if any) because it performs only in
others' mouths. There is no sense that the writer of these letters
inhabits the starving body she describes, no sense of what it might
feel like to be hungry and surrounded by pineapples, ice cream,
little mutton pies, biscuits and delicious dinners. While Burney
is clearly anxious to tell her sister that she is eating very little and
getting very thin, she is at least as anxious not to own her hunger
and emaciation. This clearly invites comparison with her horror of
acknowledging her own authorship, and Burney's attitude to both
shows a rather complicated need to be seen to act without accepting
her own agency. She performs both her hunger and her authorship,

18 Maud Ellmann, *Hunger Artist*, p. 17.

writing constantly about both, but at the same time denies them by speaking only through others, as if the representation of her hunger, her performance of not eating, matters more than her bodily experience of it.

As I have just illustrated, it is difficult to write about food and language without punning at every turn. To 'ventriloquise' is literally to speak from the stomach, although we would now understand it as akin to 'placing words in someone's mouth'. Burney's letters constantly exploit the vexed relationship between speech (and therefore language) and food, and writing and eating are literally and metaphorically connected throughout her letters. In the middle of this same visit to Streatham, she writes to Susan,

> My opportunities for writing grow less & less, & my materials more & more: – yet I am unwilling, for a thousand reasons, to give over my attempt, – & the first is, the Debt I owe my dearest Susan, who so kindly feeds me, whenever I am hungry, & she has abundance. But really, after Breakfast, I have scarce a moment I can spare all Day.[19]

Following the discussion of feeding and hunger, it is not immediately obvious that 'breakfast' here is a reference to chronology rather than nutrition. Burney's literal meaning is, of course, that before breakfast is the only time she has to write letters. After everyone has met for the first time at the table, their activities become public and it is difficult to arrange quiet and privacy for writing (the late eighteenth-century aristocratic breakfast came late in the morning for precisely this reason). But these sentences also read as if sharing and consuming breakfast exhausts Frances's nourishing capacities for the day so that there is nothing left with which she can feed Susan's hunger and thus pay her 'debt'. Particularly interesting here is the implicit distinction between the sisterly feeding on demand that characterises their private correspondence – Susan, like a good mother 'kindly feeds me, whenever I am hungry' – and the coercive schedule of commensality. The letter continues, 'I had the Honour of making Tea & Coffee for all this set, & upon my Word I was pretty well tired of it. But, since the first 2 Days, I have always made Tea, & now I am also the *Break fast woman*. I am by no means passionately fond of the Task, but I am very glad to do any thing that is a sort of relief to Mrs T.'[20] Again, supplying others with food is draining and

19 Burney, *Early Journals*, vol. 3, p. 104.
20 Burney, *Early Journals*, vol. 3, p.126.

obviously resented, an echo of Burney's rather ungracious assertion that her main reason for writing to her sister is to pay off a debt for which she is really too busy. Burney, here, is the child who needs to be fed, and it is not reasonable to demand that she feed others, either privately or at the table. Feeding, like reading, is not reciprocal, and perhaps there is a nascent sense here that writing is a form of production which replaces the obligation to feed others and even brings its own entitlement to consume. Although there is still no account of Burney's own experience of hunger, of basic needs unmet, a very strong sense that writing letters, making tea and serving breakfast are more or less identically depleting begins to emerge.

This is both supported and complicated by Burney's first meeting with Mr Seward on the first day of this August visit to Streatham. The Thrales have gone to dress for dinner, leaving Frances in the library with 'a new Translation of Cicero's Laelius' when Mr Seward comes in. She writes 'I instantly put away my Book, because I dreaded being thought studious & affected. He offered his service to find any thing for me, & then, in the same Breath, ran on to speak of the Book with which I had, myself, *favoured the World!*' Burney is 'astonished and provoked' that he knows of her authorship and the praise continues. She goes on,

> I doubt not but he expected my thanks! – but I only stammered out something of my surprise to find the affair so spread, & then, with the coldest gravity, I seated myself, & looked another way.
>
> It could not be very difficult for him, now, to perceive that he had wholly mistaken his Game, & that my Greediness for praise was by no means so gluttonous as to make me swallow it when so ill Cooked; but I fancy he imagined I should, of course, be delighted to hear my own Book mentioned with Compliments, & so he concluded I should, with much eagerness, Enter upon the subject.[21]

Again, words figure as sustenance, and it seems that Burney is at least as much offended at being thought to have an appetite as she is at being known as a writer. It is an odd metamorphosis in which praising *Evelina* is accusing the emaciated author of gluttony, but this is the logical conclusion of Burney's elision of disordered eating and anonymous publication. Seward's appreciation of *Evelina* is experienced as just as intrusive as Mr Lort's, Mr Thrale's and Dr Johnson's comments on Burney's thinness, but in both cases

---

21 Burney, *Early Journals*, vol. 3, p. 72.

Burney is quick to immortalise the 'insults' in letters which she later prepared for publication. It is as if acknowledging authorship is acknowledging appetite, as if there is, in her reading, little difference between claiming her novel and inhabiting her body, and of course both can be related to the commodification of feminine identity. When Burney ventriloquises Seward as 'perceiving that he had mistaken his Game', she may be imagining him playing a game in praising her (either the courtship game men play with women or his own social game of insincerity) or it may be that she is the game, a hunted object of pursuit to be consumed the moment she acknowledges greediness. But she is not greedy and is not, therefore, available for consumption, either as a writer or as a young woman. These vexed, and presumably vexing, connections between talking about writing and eating arise again when Mr Lort, ignorant of Burney's authorship, asks Johnson and Hester Thrale why he is hearing so much about 'a Novel that runs about a good deal, called Evelina.' Burney, afraid of being criticised in public but secure in her anonymity, is able to go on eating: 'I munched my Biscuit as if I had not Eaten for a fortnight.' She records, 'I believe the whole party were in some little consternation', but, reasonably confident of not being 'betrayed', 'I am sure I had wickedness enough to enjoy the whole scene.'[22] However, when Lort hears Johnson and Mrs Thrale's praise and cries, 'if *Johnson* can read it, I shall get it with all speed!' he is referred to a copy 'on yonder table' and Frances's composure vanishes:

> I could sit still no longer; there was some thing so awkward; so uncommon, so strange in my then situation, that I wished myself 100 miles off; – & indeed, I had almost Choaked myself with the Biscuit, for I could not for my life swallow it, – & so, before I could consider the embarrassment of returning I got up, &, as Mr Lort went to the Table to look for Evelina, I left the Room. – & was forced to call for Water, to wash down the Biscuit which stuck in my Throat.[23]

It is this episode which leads to Burney's discovery that both Johnson and Mrs Thrale consider her physical revulsion at the prospect of acknowledged authorship to be either an affectation or 'an over-delicacy which may make [her] unhappy all [her] Life!' The private individual can cheerfully munch biscuits at moments of anxiety, but the moment she is threatened with a public persona it becomes so

22 Burney, *Early Journals*, vol. 3, p. 113.
23 Burney, *Early Journals*, vol. 3, p. 114.

impossible to eat that she cannot swallow the mouthful taken in the moment before the transition was made. It is easy to share Hester Thrale's irritation that Burney should 'write a Book, Print a Book, & have every Body Read & like [her] Book, – & then sneak in a Corner & disown it!', but for Burney at this stage there was an absolute incompatibility between eating and celebrity. As with the curtailed appetite and extreme thinness, the crucial issue is one of performance, about how to be a woman and a writer in public and particularly how to be a young woman and a writer before a watchful audience of fathers.

In later years, Burney's appetite and 'shape' occupy much less of her correspondence, to the point where she can recount with apparent gratitude a conversation with the King on his birthday in June 1792:

> He said I was grown quite fat since he had seen me, – & appealed to the Duke of York: – he protested my arm was half as big again as heretofore, & then he measured it with his spread thumbs & fore fingers – & the whole of his manner showed his perfect approbation of the step I had taken of presenting myself in the royal presence on this auspicious Day.[24]

The point here seems to be to assure the Burney family of the King's regard for the writer, and there is a sense of pride in the Royal awareness of Burney's changing shape. Her unhappiness can now be expressed away from the table.

It is after the birth of her son Alexander that Burney's heightened interest in food reappears. From the outset, when breastfeeding fails after two weeks, Alexander's body figures as the ground of battle between his mother and his illnesses, which are often personified and usually take the readily anthropomorphised form of worms. The first letter to Marianne Waddington after Alexander's birth explains:

> – my opening recovery was the most rapid I ever witnessed or heard of – but in a fortnight the poor thing had the Thrush – communicated it to my Breast – & in short – after torment upon torment, a Milk fever ensued – an abscess in the Breast followed – & till that broke, 4 Days ago, I suffered so as to make life – even My happy life – scarce my wish to preserve!
> [...] But – they have made me wean my Child! – O my Marianne! you who are so tender a Mother can need no words to say what that has cost me! But God be praised my Babe is well, & feeds, while he pines – adieu – & Heaven bless you![25]

24 Frances Burney, *The Journals and Letters of Frances Burney*, ed. Joyce Hemlow (Oxford: Clarendon Press, 1972) vol. 1, p. 188.
25 Burney, *Letters*, vol. 3, p. 94.

It is noticeable in this extract that there is no sense of the new mother's agency (except as a 'witness' and hearer). Alexander has 'the Thrush', he communicates it to the breast, the fever ensues, the abscess follows, Burney suffers. And then 'they' (the full context makes 'their' identity no clearer) make her wean the baby, the weaning costs her greatly and the baby is well, feeds and pines. The only time the writer is the subject of her own clause is when she 'suffers', and otherwise she is silent under repeated assault, dissociated (partly by capitalisation) from her malfunctioning breast and knowing that for her reader, the shared experience of breastfeeding makes words redundant in communicating the subjective experience of early weaning. Once again, narratives of bodily production and consumption seem to replace or encode what the subject is seething to say.

Alexander's body remains a site of conflict throughout his childhood, and there is constant anxiety that he does not eat enough and is too thin, and furthermore that Burney's attempts to feed him well enough to generate a good body are undermined, and the bodily economy that she controls disrupted, by 'his sworn and inveterate old enemies, the Worms'.[26] Alex's worms figure largely through twenty years of correspondence, gnawing him from within but more importantly consuming what Burney feeds him, diverting his precisely managed diet so that there is no end to her labours and anxieties. She writes to Dr Burney in July 1797 about Alexander's loss of appetite: it has 'frightened us out of all strict regimen for this once, except in withholding from him Butter', despite which 'he is thinner & thinner & every little rib, every little bone can be counted & seen'.[27] At the beginning of August, she is able to tell d'Arblay, 'our little Darling has given me this morning the only proof I require of his Well-doing, the only one I have sighed for of his improvement, by a return of natural appetite. His Breakfast has had almost no temptation but for hunger, and yet he has eat of it with almost heartiness … to Day every moment while his little Mouth was at work, I repeated to myself – If his Father did but see it!'[28] Again, this gives the impression of a hyperactive economy of consumption and the body. The three-year-old Alex gives his mother the proof of well-being that she requires, as if this rather abstract gift were something he could produce at will. The breakfast itself, again

26 Burney, *Letters*, vol. 5, p. 475.
27 Burney, *Letters*, vol. 3, p. 331.
28 Burney, *Letters*, vol. 3, pp. 335–6.

aided by Burney's old-fashioned approach to capitals, seems to wield – or decline to wield – power, and the working of the child's mouth seems independent of his subjectivity, a subjectivity which receives no attention whatsoever in this strangely limited catalogue of maternal concern. Burney often gives the impression that Alexander is of interest only as an eater, and she describes his eating as if it takes place in isolation. There is no table and no commensality in Burney's accounts of her son the consumer, but merely a rather desperate inventory of what goes in and comes out. In November 1801, she writes to d'Arblay that she is treating 'symptoms … of a wormy tendency' with 'red port wine, with a little salt dissolved in it' three times a day, declaring: 'I shall not rest from studying and attending him' until he is 'all I wish & hope to see him'.[29] Two days later, writing to her father, 'I now devote all my attentions to nourishing & fattening him & bracing him.' The worms guarantee failure to produce an acceptable son's body, which in turn guarantees an endless narrative of conflict over food.

Served in vain: the honours of the table in *Cecilia* and *Camilla*

For the heroines of Burney's first three novels, meals rarely involve eating anything in particular. *Cecilia* opens with Cecilia's parting breakfast visit to the Moncktons. There are detailed accounts of general and private conversation and precise analyses of behaviour and motivation, but all one learns about the meal is that, while foolish and flattering conversation rages around her, 'Cecilia, who was placed next to the lady of the house, quietly began her breakfast.'[30] Even as bankruptcy threatens the Harrels, 'Mrs Harrel could eat nothing; Cecilia, merely to avoid creating surprise in the servants, forebore following her example; but Mr Harrel eat much as usual [sic].'[31] *Camilla* is more explicit, and the heroine goes so far as 'to fill a plate from a dish'[32] and even to 'quit the room with her tea undrunk',[33] while the gluttonous Lynmere and the vulgar Mr

29 Burney, *Letters*, vol. 5, p. 25.
30 Frances Burney, *Cecilia*, ed. Peter Sabor and Margaret Anne Doody (Oxford: Oxford University Press, 1988) p. 12.
31 Burney, *Cecilia*, p. 383.
32 Burney, *Camilla*, p. 169.
33 Burney, *Camilla*, p. 181.

Dennel take every opportunity to source and analyse pleasant things to eat. Nevertheless, it is very rare for Camilla or Eugenia to acknowledge the existence of food as anything more specific than the stuff of life for the poor and the material of social ritual for everyone else. *Evelina*, written at the height of Burney's epistolary focus on food, offers the most extreme examples of this: Evelina is 'relieved by a summons to tea' from Madame Duval's conversation;[34] Lord Orville 'addressed himself wholly to me, till we were summoned to dinner';[35] Lady Louisa wants to 'take something' on arrival at an inn and is invited to 'take the air before dinner'. Although almost every social interaction takes place during a meal and all invitations involve the provision of food, Burney never describes anyone eating anything, nor even serving or arranging anything. This is commensality reduced to a pure, and strangely disembodied, form. In all the other novels, food is used to distinguish those of high moral status, who may consume meals at conventional intervals but neither eat nor mention specific foods, from lower beings who look forward to the next meal, hope for a particular dish at their preferred hour and join eagerly in discussions of 'the pleasures of the table'. The heroines evince distress by failing in the formulaic administration of meals, pouring too many cups of tea or putting too much food on a plate for a guest, as well as by leaving the table before the meal is over, but it is emphatically meals and not named comestibles that they reject. Food itself is unmentioned, perhaps unmentionable, and it may be that for good girls, commensality overwrites eating in Burney's fiction; the social implications of the table are overwhelmingly much more important than nutrition, much less pleasure. Less moral characters rejoice in the opposite interpretation, working on the understanding that social events are an excuse for good eating, preferably at someone else's expense. Oddly, in the context of Burney's letters, attention to particular things to eat is always a sign of moral bankruptcy.

Evelina is an exception to this in that there is only one conversation about food, and even that is explicitly bowdlerised. Evelina has been invited to dine by the snobbish Mrs Beaumont at Bristol Hotwells. Three young aristocrats, Lord Merton, Mr Coverley and Mr Lovel, are showing off to each other while Evelina is being snubbed for her uncertain origins:

34 Frances Burney, *Evelina*, ed. Margaret Anne Doody (Harmondsworth: Penguin, 1994), p. 135.
35 Burney, *Evelina*, p. 319.

the conversation turned wholly upon eating, a subject which was discussed with the utmost delight; and, had I not known they were men of
rank and fashion, I should have imagined that Lord Merton, Mr Lovel,
and Mr Coverley, had all been professed cooks; for they displayed so much
knowledge of sauces and made dishes, and of the various methods of
dressing the same things, that I am persuaded they must have given much
time, and much study, to make themselves such adepts in this art. It would
be very difficult to determine, whether they were most to be distinguished
as gluttons, or epicures, for they were, at once, dainty and voracious,
understood the right and the wrong of every dish, and alike emptied the
one and the other. I should have been quite sick of their remarks, had I not
been entertained by seeing that Lord Orville, who, I am sure, was equally
disgusted, not only read my sentiments, but, by his countenance, com-
municated to me his own.[36]

Unlike Burney's apparent transcriptions of conversations at
Streatham, Evelina's account of Merton, Lovel and Coverley's
discussion edits out the real focus of the conversation. Only the
generic 'sauces' and 'made dishes' (i.e., dishes combining several
major ingredients usually associated with French cuisine) reach
Evelina's page, and this is countered by the fastidious vagueness of
'several methods of dressing the same things', implying that even
the methods of cooking that form the organising principle of eighteenth-century cookbooks are too gross for words. This disgust comes
partly from Evelina's certainty that 'rank and fashion' (usually ambiguous terms in Burney) are betrayed by delight in food, although this
is complicated because gluttony characterises certain kinds of loose-
living masculine 'rank and fashion' throughout Burney's fiction. It
is, for her, an aristocratic vice which confusingly undermines claims
to aristocratic identity, sorting those who combine aristocratic birth
and sociability with true moral worth from those who regard their
status merely as the basis of pleasure. These men are demeaning
themselves by exploring the proper domain of the 'professed cook',
a term almost always reserved for the French or pseudo-French
male cooks who were becoming very fashionable in aristocratic,
usually metropolitan, households (female cooks were 'plain cooks' or
'good plain cooks'). The issue, then, seems to be about class rather
than gender; the problem is not that cooking is women's work
but that it is properly work and not leisure. The 'professed cook'
is not cooking for himself, and inasmuch as cooking is an art, his
cooking is art for art's sake. Merton, Lovel and Coverley's interest

36 Burney, *Evelina*, p. 320.

is that of the consumer; despite their apparent expertise, it is eating and not cooking to which they have devoted their time and study. Without any pretensions to productivity, the three rakes' investment in consumption knows no bounds, and Evelina and Orville's deep revulsion stems partly from this free-floating and menacing greed. The verbal transgression of class identities causes people to feel sick at dinner only partly because food words, for Burney, participate in the visceral power of the unmentionable substances themselves. The other source of horror here is the untrammeled and unlimited greed of aristocratic masculinity, which, divorced from any consciousness of the moral imperative to produce, constitutes a general but convincing threat.

Camilla and *Cecilia* deploy these linguistic energies to more noticeable effect. Because Cecilia lives as a guest until near the end of her progress, most of her observations of the preparation and consumption of food relate to the regulation of sociability. With her own involvement with food confined to the polite performance of breakfast, dinner, tea and supper at whatever hours her hosts choose to provide them, moving in a class above those in which a woman would be expected to take day-to-day responsibility for family meals, Cecilia is strangely free to observe without involvement Mrs Harrel's uncontrollable expenditure on the 'desert-table' and Mrs Belfield's insistence on 'cold meat from the cook shops' so that her son can live in luxury. For Cecilia herself, there are difficulties about presenting herself at the right hour for breakfast (her own virtuous habits lead her to expect it several hours earlier than either Mrs Harrel or Lady Delville order it to be served) and about being forced to await 'the moment of retiring' from the mixed company at dinner, but her eating seems to be a matter of social choreography rather than ingestion of energy, much less pleasure in the process. Even her charities, unlike Camilla's, focus on securing the long-term future of poor children rather than giving them food to meet their immediate needs. This disembodied stance foregrounds the moral dimensions of other people's eating, particularly in the conflicting but equally deluded expectations of the rival guardians.

The Harrels and Mr Briggs maintain opposing misunderstandings of the proper qualities of food, indicating the position implicitly occupied by Burney. For the Harrels, food has become divorced from its physiological meanings. They identify themselves so slavishly by conspicuous consumption that the only literal object of consumption, food, has been displaced by the ethics of fashionable consumerism. This is clear when Cecilia, 'tired, indeed, of dissipation, and shocked at the sight of unfeeling extravagance', visited her other guardians and discovered that they were even less congenial than the Harrels. Returning to Portman Square, she was stopped on her way to 'her own apartment' by Mrs Harrel, who 'begged she would come into the drawing room, where she promised her a most agreeable surprise':

> Cecilia, for an instant, imagined that some old acquaintance was just arrived out of the country; but, upon her entrance, she saw only Mr Harrel and some workmen, and found that the agreeable surprise was to proceed from the sight of an elegant Awning, prepared for one of the inner apartments, to be fixed over a long desert-table, which was to be ornamented with various devices of cut glass.
> 'Did you ever see anything so beautiful in your life?' cried Mrs Harrel; 'and when the table is covered with the coloured ices, and those sort of things, it will be as beautiful again'.[37]

Display replaces nutrition here, with coloured (rather than flavoured) ices complementing the appearance of the dessert service. Despite all her entertaining, this is the only time Mrs Harrel is seen to give any attention to what her guests are going to eat, and the moment is framed by her inappropriate excitement about home improvements. The point is not that 'an elegant Awning' is wrong *per se* (although in the Harrels' debt-ridden circumstances it is) but that Mrs Harrel's pleasure in such things has made her incapable of feeling any interest in or affection for old acquaintances from the country. Objects have replaced people, and food has become an object like any other. The Harrels have no sense of relative monetary values, 'buying' whatever they desire on credit without asking for prices, and thus no sense at all that underlying all this consumption is the reality that survival itself, in the form of food, has a price. Immediately after Mr Harrel's exhibition of her awning, Mr Harrel has the idea of 'running up a flight of steps, and a little light gallery here, and so making a little Orchestra'. He asks his interior designer, 'What would such a thing come to, Mr. Tomkins?':

> 'O, a trifle, sir,' answered Mr Tomkins, 'a mere nothing.'
> 'Well, then, give orders for it, and let it be done directly. I don't care how slight it is, but pray let it be very elegant. Won't it be a great addition, Miss Beverley?'[38]

37 Burney, *Cecilia*, p. 100.
38 Burney, *Cecilia*, p. 100.

Mr Harrel's satisfaction with the lack of numbers in Tomkins' reply can be seen as part of the same culpable misjudgement as his wife's greater pleasure in table decorations than in old friends. In both cases, the value system of money has come adrift from its anchor in the price of labour and the cost of food and become dysfunctional and chaotic. As Burney and Cecilia know, because of most people's need to work to eat, even the Harrels' budget cannot expand infinitely. It is not long before the builder interrupts a discussion of coloured lamps in 'fantastic forms' to insist loudly, 'Sir … it is of no use you employing me, if I can never get my money: All my workmen must be paid whether I am or no; and so, if I must needs speak to a lawyer, why there's no help for it.'[39] In the end, the workers' need to eat makes itself felt, eventually pushing Mr Harrel into a position where he chooses to kill himself rather than moderate his expenditure.

Nevertheless, Mr Briggs' views on food make it clear that it is equally improper to regard food merely as fuel for the working body. In common with most of the vulgar and offensive men in Burney, a significant proportion of Mr Briggs' conversation is devoted to food but, unlike the others, he is usually entirely committed to minimising cost and maximising 'value' (which we might understand, anachronistically, as 'calories'). With this in mind, Mr Briggs feeds his miserable child-servants on poor-quality porridge and accepts social invitations only if he will save more money by eating someone else's food than he will lose in getting to their house. If the Harrels have failed to understand that money, food and survival are directly related, Mr Briggs fails to understand that it is a relationship and not an equation. He treats food simply as a manifestation of the worst kind of expenditure, that without hope of return. Mr Briggs' greatest annoyance when he expects Cecilia to come and live with him and she goes to the Delvilles instead is that he bought special food for her:

> 'Did n't, did n't!' answered he, angrily, 'waited for you three days, dressed a breast o' mutton o' purpose; got in a lobster, and two crabs; all spoilt by keeping; stink already; weather quite muggy, forced to souse 'em in vinegar; one expense brings on another; never begin the like agen.'[40]

Crab and lobster were not the luxury goods in the eighteenth century that they are now, and at least in London were easy to

39 Burney, *Cecilia*, p. 104.
40 Burney, *Cecilia*, p. 452.

obtain and cheaper than butchers' meat (of which mutton was the cheapest). This is unusual expenditure for Mr Briggs, who usually seems to eschew protein altogether, but it is nothing more than a lower middle-class household might ordinarily expect. It is not his purchase which is exceptional but his treatment of and attitude to it; the biggest difference between money and the food for which Mr Briggs has reluctantly exchanged it is the corruptibility of food, and it is this that he graphically resents. There could be no place for rotting seafood in most polite fiction of this period and the word 'stink' is genuinely shocking, suddenly introducing decay and disgust into the Delvilles' opulent drawing room. Mr Briggs begins to pursue this theme energetically as a dispute with Mr Delville develops, referring to the ancestral Devilles from whom Mr Delville's aristocratic iden-tity derives as, 'a set of poor souls you won't let rest in their coffins; mere clay and dirt! fine things to be proud of! a parcel of old mouldy rubbish quite departed this life! raking up bones and dust, nobody knows for what! ought to be ashamed; who cares for dirty carcasses? nothing but carrion'.[41] Because of Mr Briggs' exclusive and miserly interest in money, deceased relatives and tainted food are similarly worthless, suggesting a collapse of consumer and consumed that strangely mirrors the Harrels' inability to imagine an identity apart from consumption. For Mr Briggs, food is merely fuel for the body which is valuable only and exactly inasmuch as it generates money, which means that he objects to it for exactly the reasons that the Harrels, who regard food entirely as adornment, enjoy it. Mr Briggs scorns the superfluity of food for pleasure while the Harrels take pleasure only in its superfluity. This is evident in Mr Briggs' account of the supper for which Mrs Harrel commissions the awning, which closely follows his complaint about the spoilt crabs:

> Invited me once to his house ... pretended to give a supper; all a mere bam; went without my dinner, and got nothing to eat; all glass and shew; victuals painted all manner o' colours; lighted up like a pastry-cook on twelfth-day; wanted something solid, and got a great lump of sweetmeat; found it cold as a stone, all froze in my mouth like ice; made me jump again, and brought the tears to my eyes; forced to spit it out; believe it was nothing but a snow-ball, just set up for shew, and covered over with a little sugar. Pretty way to spend money! never could rest till every farthing was gone; nothing left but his own fool's pate, and even that he could not hold together.[42]

41 Burney, *Cecilia*, p. 454.
42 Burney, *Cecilia*, p. 453.

Ice cream was one of the great discoveries of late eighteenth-century cuisine and, to quote Elizabeth David, 'quite a craze in fashionable London'.[43] The technology for making it still depended on an ice-house as well as access to uncontaminated milk and cream, which could not be taken for granted in London, so the nineteenth-century transition to street food was unthinkable, and ice cream remained an elite and high-tech novelty. Interestingly, in this context, it stayed firmly on the dessert table, as part of the display, and did not become the focus of gourmet attention, perhaps because sweet milky foods tend to be gendered as feminine and disdained by serious eaters. Although there was a strong aesthetic of food throughout the eighteenth-century day, a formal dessert was far more for show than for eating, and anyone accustomed to high society would have known that the bright colours and vertiginous towers of sweets, fruit and ice cream often owed their beauty to food colourings at best unpalatable (beetroot) and at worst toxic (copper). Although the inclusion of ice cream in such a display, particularly in a crowded room lit by candles, poses obvious difficulties, the challenge was probably a large part of the attraction for hostesses wishing to be spectacular, and freezing it solid would certainly be an obvious part of the solution. In some ways, then, Mr Briggs is exactly right. The Harrels' house is 'lit like a pastry-cook' to display their wares to best advantage, although the pastry-cook's reckoning of food and money is exactly what the Harrels are not able to do, and the miser's encounter with ice cream, a 'food' which, on this occasion, resists incorporation and is thus, in his reckoning, without function as well as conspicuous, highlights both misapprehensions. The Harrels do not understand that the poor must eat and Mr Briggs does not understand that there must be more to life than poverty and eating.

Spilling the beans: accidents at the table

Burney's interest in and deployment of violence in fiction has been explored at length, and I would like to argue that the trope of spilling represents a similar, if more coded, break in social mores. The incidents in *Camilla* and *Cecilia* are not droplets missing a cup or crumbs on the lap but tea cascading across the table and dishes overturned

43 Elizabeth David, *Harvest of the Cold Months: the Social History of Ice and Ices* (Harmondsworth, Penguin, 1994) p. 310.

on a scale barely envisaged by the most pessimistic of conduct book writers. Even those who feel the need to warn against nose-picking and adjusting underwear in public assume a basic ability to manipulate cutlery and crockery, suggesting that this is something more elemental than, or as well as, a lapse in table manners. The interaction between Camilla's distress at being accused of trying to win Edgar away from Indiana and her handling of food is reminiscent of Burney's behaviour at Streatham. Camilla is in the invidious and typically Burneyan position of knowing that her unselfconscious behaviour has been damagingly misinterpreted and that she must therefore make an effort to act innocent even although she is innocent. Like Burney herself, Camilla finds that the table is a dangerous place:

> Satisfied of the innocence of her intentions, she knew, not what alteration she could make in her behaviour; and, after various plans, concluded, that to make none would best manifest her freedom from self-reproach. At the summons therefore to dinner, she was the first to appear, eager to shew herself unmoved by the injustice of her accusers, and desirous to convince them she was fearless of examination.
>
> Yet, too much discomposed to talk in her usual manner, she seized upon a book till the party was seated. Answering then to the call of her uncle, with as easy an air as she could assume, she took her accustomed place by his side, and began, for mere employment, filling a plate from the dish which was nearest to her; which she gave to the footman, without any direction whither to carry, or enquiry if any body chose to eat it.
>
> It was taken round the table, and, though refused by all, she heaped up another plate, with the same diligence and speed as if it had been accepted.
>
> Edgar, who had been accidentally detained, only now entered, apologizing for being so late ... The moment he appeared, the deepest blushes covered her face; and an emotion so powerful beat in her breast, that the immediate impulse of her impetuous feelings, was to declare herself ill, and run out of the room.
>
> With this view she rose; but ashamed of her plan, seated herself the next moment, though she had first overturned her plate and a sauce-boat in the vehemence of her haste.
>
> This accident rather recovered than disconcerted her, by affording an unaffected occupation, in begging pardon of Sir Hugh, who was the chief sufferer, changing the napkins, and restoring the table to order.[44]

Camilla's acting works well enough here until the food appears. She can sustain her efforts to 'manifest her freedom from self-

---

44 Burney, *Camilla*, p. 169.

reproach', 'shew herself unmoved' and assume an easy air until, taking her place at the side of the master of the house, she undertakes the concomitant task of serving the meal (this is an informal version of service *à la Française*, in which the lady of the house fills the plates from dishes before her on the table and the servants hand them around). But the focus on acting normally betrays Camilla when it comes to the choreography of dinner; she plays her part, but she plays it in isolation, as if the filling of plates is to be done for its own sake and has nothing to do with other diners' articulation of their wishes, and this could be seen to reveal her own sense of alienation. Edgar's entry causes Camilla briefly to abandon the performance of normality, but the violence done to her feelings by her decision to resume the act is reflected in the overturned plate and sauce-boat. No Burney heroine would think of throwing plates, but emptying them on the table cloth (and the patriarchal uncle) seems to be a different matter.

There is another, similarly marked, kind of spilling at the first meal with Clermont Lynmere. Camilla has just refused Sir Sedley Clarendel and is upset because Edgar mistakenly believes her to have encouraged Clarendel's attentions. Eugenia is upset because Lynmere's scorn and distaste for her are evident and it is clear that the arranged marriage will never happen, while the oblivious Sir Hugh expects everyone to enjoy themselves, 'the breakfast having been spoilt this hour already'. Lynmere's gluttony immediately becomes apparent as the family assemble: 'Miss Margland made the tea, and young Lynmere instantly and almost voraciously began eating of everything that was upon the table.'[45] Silence is broken only by Sir Hugh's 'delight and loquacity joined to his pleasure in remarking the good old English appetite which his nephew had brought with him from foreign parts'. Camilla returns from turning down Sir Sedley at Mrs Arlbery's hoping to see Edgar, who is not there: 'her heart sunk, she felt sick, and would have glided out of the room, had not Sir Hugh, thinking her faint for want of her breakfast, begged Miss Margland to make her some fresh tea'.[46] When Sir Hugh tries to start a conversation by suggesting that those who can (Eugenia, Dr Orkbourne and, he presumes, Lynmere) trade Latin verses, Lynmere responds by spilling tea:

45 Burney, *Camilla*, p. 565.
46 Burney, *Camilla*, p. 566.

A verse of Horace with which Dr Orkbourne was opening his answer, was stopt short, by the eager manner in which Lynmere re-seized his bread with one hand, while, with the other, to the great discomposure of the exact Miss Margland, he stretched forth for the teapot, to pour out a bason of tea; not ceasing the libation till the saucer itself, overcharged, sent his beverage in trickling rills from the tablecloth to the floor.

The ladies all moved some paces from the table, to save their clothes; and Miss Margland reproachfully inquired if she had not made his tea to his liking.

'Don't mind it, I beg, my dear boy,' cried Sir Hugh; 'a little slop's soon wiped up; and we're all friends: so don't let that stop your Latin.'

Lynmere, noticing neither the Latin, the mischief, nor the consolation, finished his tea in one draft, and then said: 'Pray, sir, where do you keep your newspapers?'[47]

In this tracing of each person's progress towards breakfast is a sense of the force required to assemble the family around the table. Only Sir Hugh, whose house it is and who originated the arranged marriage and orchestrated this meeting, wants to be there and is ready to take a straightforward pleasure in the meal and the company. His very joviality can reasonably be read as sinister to the girls, since, with the best intentions, he is set to ruin their lives and there is little they feel able to do to oppose him. Indiana takes cynical pleasure in Eugenia's distress at being found wanting and in Lynmere's dismay at being expected to marry a disfigured and highly educated woman. Miss Margland is pleased by Camilla's happiness and looking forward to a demonstration of Indiana's social superiority to Eugenia, but the tyranny of breakfast is such that everyone must sit together and eat until it is over ('I beg nobody will go out of the room, for the sake of our enjoying it all together,' says Sir Hugh.) In this light, Lynmere's disruptive 'libation' seems more like a protest than an accident, and indeed there is no suggestion that there is anything involuntary or accidental about it ('noticing', here, means 'attending to' rather than 'perceiving'). Lynmere's gluttony means that his excess pouring may manifest his desire for more tea than will fit in the cup as well as bringing an end to an uncomfortable social occasion, but in either case it is a radically direct response to the situation and one that simultaneously negates the social dimension of the meal and highlights the violent possibilities of food.

There is a similar but more serious incident in *Cecilia* when Mr Meadows trips Morrice at the tea table in such a way that 'the tea pot and its contents were overturned immediately opposite to Cecilia':

47 Burney, *Camilla*, p. 567.

Young Delvile, who saw the impending evil, from an impetuous impulse to prevent her suffering by it, hastily drew her back, and bending down before her, secured her preservation by receiving himself the mischief with which she was threatened.

[…] Young Delvile, though a sufferer from his gallantry, the hot water having penetrated through his coat to his arm and shoulder, was at first insensible to his situation, from an apprehension that Cecilia had not wholly escaped; and his enquiries were so eager and so anxious, made with a look of such solicitude, and a voice of such alarm, that, equally astonished and gratified, she secretly blest the accident which had given birth to his uneasiness, however she grieved for its consequence to himself.[48]

Again, unexpectedly close encounters with food reveal emotional truths concealed in the name of propriety. Meals seem to function as nexuses of tension in Burney's fiction, and for good reasons; men and women and happy and unhappy families are obliged to come together and act normally several times a day, and these are also the times when any mistake or involuntary manifestation of emotion will be magnified and publicised by the food in the hand or on the plate or, worst of all, all over the floor.

Her dreaded hosts: eating and indigence in *The Wanderer*

The Wanderer displays a more specific and sustained interest in food than any of Burney's earlier novels. Beginning with the Admiral's insistence on buying breakfast for the starving Incognita (and his annoyance that she appears to have 'no longing to taste the food of her mother country again'), moving through Mr Tedman's provision of cakes and sweets ('Don't be so coy, my dear, don't be so coy. Young girls have appetites as well as old men') and 'a sensation nearly of famine' in the New Forest, and concluding at last with 'a hearty meal of good roast beef' hosted by the Admiral in honour of Juliet's restoration and her engagement to Harleigh, this is a novel that charts 'female difficulties' in food. Juliet watches peasants cooking coarse food to which she is unaccustomed, shrinks from the large quantities of plain bourgeois cooking offered by farming families and resents being denied her fair share of delicate French dishes at the tables of the aristocracy. She is driven to abandon the virtuous gentlewoman's stance of indifference to food by real want, and must

48 Burney, *Cecilia*, p. 289.

therefore try to negotiate the (temporary) separation of culinary and social identities. Juliet is surrounded alternately by men trying to make her eat things she considers alien and unpleasant and women trying to deny her need for the elite foodstuffs they regard as their birthright but not, erroneously, hers. Juliet's class, after all, is the part of her identity that is constantly questioned and contested, so it is not surprising that there is a strong sense in *The Wanderer* that class is biologically innate, hereditary on what we would now see as a genetic level that dictates not only food preferences but nutritional needs. Juliet's eating is different from Evelina's, Camilla's and Cecilia's in that she is not performing a stable identity but trying to feed her 'true' (aristocratic) self while keeping her social identity in constant flux. She finds it difficult to eat and thrive on the kinds of food appropriate to some of the stations in life that she briefly occupies and so once again, albeit in a very different way, food works as the location of hidden truths about identity.

The episode of Mr Tedman and the cakes dramatises many of the issues relating to food, class and the gendering of work. 'Ellis', as the Incognita is now known, has been compelled to attend a public concert by one of her pupils, Miss Bydel. However, Miss Bydel abandons Ellis on arrival at the 'New Rooms', leaving her 'to strive to parry the awkwardness of her situation [as an unprotected young woman at a public gathering], by an appearance of absorbed attention.'[49] Inevitably, this does not work and Ellis is harassed by a man with 'the air of a decided libertine' who offers to escort her home when everyone else forms groups for tea. She declines, but her pupils and acquaintances continue to ignore her, and presently the well-meaning but irredeemably vulgar Mr Tedman, the father of one of her pupils who sees piano lessons as a passport to social climbing, tries to come to her aid,

> with a good humoured smirk upon his countenance, to bring her a handful of cakes; he placed them, one by one, till he had counted half a dozen, upon the form by her side, saying, 'Don't be so coy, my dear, don't be so coy. Young girls have appetites as well as old men, for I don't find that tudeling [Tedman's nonce word for piano playing] does much for one's stomach; and, I promise you, this cold February morning has served me for as good a whet, as if I was an errand boy up to this moment.[50]

49 Frances Burney, *The Wanderer*, ed. Margaret Anne Doody *et al.* (Oxford: Oxford University Press, 1991) p. 242.
50 Burney, *Wanderer*, p. 244.

Mr Tedman goes on to regret that his daughter's desire to impress 'the quality' precludes his inviting Ellis to join them, and then, 'good humouredly nodding, begged her not to spare the cakes, and promising she should have more if she were hungry, returned to his daughter'. The libertine, Sir Lyell, 'in a tone the most familiar, enquired whether she wished for any refreshment'. An elderly gentleman bows to her, but

> Not knowing him, she let his salutation pass apparently disregarded; when, some of her cakes accidentally falling from the form, he eagerly picked them up, saying, as he grasped them in his hand, 'Faith, Madam, you had better have eaten them at once. You had, faith! few things are mended by delay. We are all at our best at first. These cakes are no more improved by being mottled with the dirt of the floor, than a pretty woman is with the small pox.[51]

Ellis recognises the man as Mr Riley, a fellow passenger on her boat from France, and begins to worry about being recognised when Mr Tedman returns and,

> gently pushing him aside, produced, with a self-pleased countenance, a small plate of bread and butter, saying, 'Look here, my dear, I've brought you a few nice slices; for I see the misfortune that befell my cakes, of their falling down; and I resolved you should not be the worse for it. But I advise you to eat this at once, for fear of accidents; only take care,' with a smile, 'that you don't grease your pretty fingers.'[52]

This somewhat surreal persecution with unwanted and unsolicited baked goods highlights all the anomalies of Ellis's position and constitutes a sustained attack on her gentility. Mr Tedman thinks to bring her cakes in the first place only because she is not receiving the attentions she deserves and expects from her (unwitting) equals, and his announcement of the similar physical needs of young girls and old men adds to his offence, especially when compounded by his reference to her paid work and its probable effect on her appetite. The comparison between the work of the errand boy and giving piano lessons elides the difference between physical labour and genteel expertise upon which Ellis's shaky and limited social acceptability depends, making the well-meant offer of cakes into a sign of degradation. In any case, Ellis is above the frivolous and immature femininity usually associated with a taste for cakes and tea. Mr Riley

51 Burney, *Wanderer*, p. 246.
52 Burney, *Wanderer*, p. 246.

and Mr Tedman exacerbate the situation by insisting on reading the dropping of the cakes in the most literal way, as a regrettable result of carelessness and a personal loss to Ellis rather than merely the end of some unwanted ephemera. Their assumption that the cakes matter to her constitutes a large part of their distressing misinterpretation of her position, although the comparison of sullied food to a woman with smallpox, with its echoes of *Camilla*, adds to the sense that Ellis is threatened by the men's underestimation of the importance of her subjectivity. They are both working on the basis of established and class-specific views of women's needs and desires without reference to Ellis's articulation of her own wishes, and part of Burney's art here to is leave Ellis's distress unspoken, silenced, and thus – presented with this barrage of unsolicited male advice and interpretation – shared by a reader. The assumption of common difficulties in managing the basic business of getting food from plate to mouth confirms Mr Tedman's conviction that Ellis's social status is determined by her current circumstances rather than her habitual demeanour, which he is not anyway equipped to read. It is a misunderstanding that is repeated when Mr Gooch, the farmer's son, tries to overcome Ellis's resistance to accepting his invitation to a party by promising her, 'a goose at top, and a turkey at bottom, and as fine a fat pig as ever [she] saw in [her] life in the middle; with as much ale, and mead, and punch, as [she could] desire to drink.'[53] In both instances, the men are treating Ellis as if she can be mollified, comforted or attracted by food itself, which is an underestimation of her noble character, and also as though particular kinds of food will appeal to her. Mr Tedman offers her treats for little or young girls, sweets and cakes strongly associated with children and flighty, immature women, while Mr Gooch tries to lure her with the plain, substantial foods of the rural bourgeoisie, dishes believed to be appropriate for successful labouring men and for wives and daughters intimately involved with the work of the farm (the much celebrated country women who find their fictional apotheosis much later in Hardy and Eliot). But Ellis is too gentle and too delicate for such things and, inasmuch as she attends to her physical needs at all, she craves aristocratic cooking. Working as a paid companion to the vile and snobbish Mrs Ireton, the lack of appropriate food is one of Ellis's reiterated grudges:

---

53 Burney, *Wanderer*, p. 414.

At meals, the humble companion was always helped last; even when there were gentlemen, even when there were children at the table; and always to what was worst; to what was rejected as ill-cooked, or left, as spoilt and bad. No question was ever asked of what she chose or what she disliked. Sometimes she was even utterly forgotten; and, as no-one ventured to remind Mrs Ireton of any omission, her helpless protégée, upon such occasions, rose half famished from the inhospitable board.[54]

This plaint makes clear how the rituals of eighteenth-century dining could intersect with issues of health and survival more directly than in the case of the Harrels, and how conventions of precedence could be used to humiliate diners as well as to reinforce the social status quo. The point seems to be both that being served last is demeaning in itself, constituting an attack on Ellis's social identity when she is defined as female but not feminine enough to be counted before men and children, and that it actually deprives her of sufficient and palatable food. In this instance, the ambiguous status of the paid companion, unable to define herself as worker or guest, means that she is denied both the ample fare of the servants' hall and the enjoyment of the mistress's table. However she is paid, the arrangement does not include any calculation of her bodily needs, and nothing can make her articulate these needs in the setting of the big house. The maintenance of gentility, for a working woman, appears to depend on the tacit denial of embodiment, and this is why the young ladies of the town are reluctant to pay Ellis's bills. It is left to one of her unsolicited mentors, Mr Giles, to try to collect the money:

> 'Goodness, Mr Giles!' cried Miss Bydel, 'why what are you thinking of? Why you are calling all the young ladies to account for not paying this young music mistress, just as if she were a butcher, or a baker; or some useful tradesman.'
>
> 'Well, so she is, Ma'am! so she is, Mrs. Bydel! For if she does not feed your stomachs, she feeds your fancies; which are all no better than starved when you are left to yourselves.'
>
> 'Nay, as to that, Mr Giles,' said Miss Bydel, ' ... I can't pretend to say I think she should be put on the same footing with eating and drinking. We can all live well enough without music, and painting, and those things, I hope; but I don't know how we are to live without bread and meat.'
>
> 'Nor she neither, Mrs Bydel! and that's the very reason that she wants to be paid.'[55]

54 Burney, *Wanderer*, p. 493.
55 Burney, *Wanderer*, p. 323.

There is a sense here that only those who provide food for money should require money for food and that Ellis's gentility should insulate her from the need to transact to survive. A Mr Scope implies that to pay Ellis for her services would be to 'encourage luxuries' at the cost of 'providing for necessities': 'Let me … ask, whether you opine, that the butcher, who gives us our richest nutriment, and the baker, to whom we owe the staff of life, as Solomon himself calls the loaf, should barely be put on a par with the artist of luxury, who can only turn a sonata, or figure a minuet, or daub a picture?' Part of the point of this discussion of the food value of music, written by an author who grew up in a household whose prosperity depended on her father's success as a musician and musicologist, is to illustrate the philistinism of Ellis's detractors. People who reckon art and music in terms of bread and beef cannot possibly esteem Ellis as they should, and yet this somewhat staged discussion also reiterates one of the central dilemmas of the lady who works. It is precisely because she is not 'on a par' with the butcher and the baker that Ellis must go hungry and ragged; her physical deprivation is a function of her social elevation. It is only when she turns from art to trade, from teaching music to sewing dresses, and from freelancing (with an aura of leisure) to employment by a tradeswoman, that Ellis can rely on being paid for her work. Until then, she must suffer being regarded as too posh to eat.

Nevertheless, Ellis's most worrying encounters with food come when she has finally fallen through the net protecting 'gentle' women from the physical hardships of real destitution. The possibility of this kind of fall is perhaps what underlies some of the panic about money in Burney's earlier novels, where the prospect of the total loss of status is an unvoiced but incessant fear. This briefly befalls Cecilia in her madness when she cannot find Delville and is turned away from all her friends, but she passes the days of lost identity and social standing in unconsciousness, recovering her senses only after she has been identified and supplied with appropriate employees, goods and services. Many novels for and about women in this period include an episode of absolute or relative poverty, but Ellis, or, as she has now been named, Juliet is unusual in experiencing open-ended indigence in which she does not know where the next meal is coming from. Hunted around Salisbury, Romney and the New Forest by persons still unknown and unexplained to the reader, Juliet survives by being rewarded for her kindnesses to children by meals and the occasional night's lodging. This eliminates money from the exchange of services for sustenance and, in removing the medium of exchange, also removes all of Juliet's control. She must eat, but is no longer able to exert any influence at all over what she eats or when and where she eats it. It is at this stage that *The Wanderer* moves into sequences of great detail about the exact nature, sources and preparation methods of Juliet's food. On her first day of homelessness, a gift of milk and water makes Juliet 'believe herself initiated in the knowledge of the flavour, and of all the occult qualities, of Nectar'.[56] In response to a homily from their grandmother, the children bring her 'half an apple ... a quarter of a pear ... a bunch of red currants; another, of white'. Feeling revived by this, Juliet, 'putting a shilling into one of their hands, requested to have a couple of eggs and a crust of bread'. For the first time in Burney's fiction, she describes the taste of something eaten by the heroine: 'The eggs were immediately baked in the cinders; the crust was cut from a loaf of sweet and fresh brown bread. And if her drink had seemed nectar, what was more substantial appeared to her to be ambrosia!'[57] No-one else is eating or drinking at this time, and Juliet is sitting in the grandmother's chair while the children move around the room and the grandmother sits in a 'smaller, and less commodious' chair from the kitchen. It seems that the absence of ritual, the status of the fruit, bread and eggs as food but not a meal, allows a sensual experience of eating. There can be no question of precedence or running from the table in distress when Juliet alone is eating what is available because she is very hungry, and this is a pattern which continues throughout Juliet's exile from her own class. Her next destination is 'a small hut; in which, though the whole dimensions might have stood in a corner of any large hall, without being in the way, she found a father, mother and seven young children at supper'. Juliet has to offer them money before being invited to join them:

> She felt mortified that so mercenary a spirit could have found entrance in a spot which seemed fitted to the virtuous innocence of our yet untainted first parents; or to the guileless hospitality of the poet's golden age. She was thankful, however, for their consent, and partook of their fare; which she found, with great surprise, required not either air or exercise to give it zest: it consisted of scraps of pheasant and partridge, which the children called chicky biddy; and slices of such fine-grained mutton, that she could with difficulty persuade herself that she was not eating venison.

56 Burney, *Wanderer*, p. 669.
57 Burney, *Wanderer*, p. 671.

All else that belonged to this rustic regale gave surprise of an entirely different nature; the nourishment was not more strikingly above, than the discourse and general commerce of her new hosts were below her expectations. They were rough to their children, and gross to each other; the woman looked all care and ill humour; the man, all moroseness and brutality.[58]

It is not obvious why this squalid and overcrowded hut should be reminiscent of Eden or a golden age, and perhaps part of the point of this episode is to educate Juliet in the grimness of poverty without (class-specific) virtue or gentility. Again, the combination of real hunger and a very casual dining arrangement seems to allow Juliet a full experience of the taste and texture of her food, but her apparent ignorance of the illegality of unlicensed game undermines her 'surprise' at her host's failure to meet her expectations. I think there is an assumption here that readers do know that it is illegal to kill game birds without a licence, and perhaps also that the chances are that a desperately poor and rather shifty peasant family who live in the middle of a famous deer forest and appear to be dining on venison have poached a deer. The children's name for their supper can be seen as marked because it implies that they have been taught to call the illegal pheasant and partridge something that sounds like a pet name for chicken, which was legal if, for families like this who did not keep hens, rare. In this case, Juliet's surprise at the good quality of her hosts' ingredients has the same source as her surprise at their rough behaviour, for both demonstrate a naivety – not shared by Burney or, implicitly, a reader – about what it might be like to raise seven children in a small hut in the forest.

This naivety leads to one of the strangest encounters with food in late eighteenth-century fiction, when Juliet's misinterpretation of poaching conflates eating, violence and class war. As the family retire to bed, Juliet overhears the couple debating in whispers whether the man will be able to leave the house while Juliet is asleep without waking her. Afraid, she tries to leave the house when everyone is in bed, but finds herself locked in and has to feign sleep as the man creeps past her. When he returns, the woman comes down to let him in and greet his companion and then Juliet 'heard something fall, or thrown down, from within, weighty, and bearing a lumpish sound that made her start with horrour'.[59] When the couple at last

---

58 Burney, *Wanderer*, p. 679.
59 Burney, *Wanderer*, p. 681.

retire, Juliet looks towards the door and 'espied, close to its edge, a large clot of blood. Struck with terrour, she started up; and then perceived that the passage from door to door was traced with bloody spots.' She freezes, 'wholly absorbed by the image which this sight presented to her fears, of some victim to murderous rapacity' and then 'determined upon making a new attempt to escape'.[60] The only unlocked door is the one to which the blood leads, so Juliet goes through it and finds 'a miserable outer-building, without casements'. Hesitating over whether to run away immediately, thus betraying her knowledge of the family's crimes, or whether to go back and pretend ignorance, she 'touched the handle of a large wicker-basket, and found that it was wet: she held out her hand to the light, and saw that it was besmeared with blood'.

> She turned sick; she nearly fainted; she shrunk from her hand with hor-rour; yet strove to recover her courage, by ejaculating a fervent prayer.
> To re-enter the house voluntarily, was now impossible; she shuddered at the idea of again encountering her dreaded hosts, and resolved upon a flight, at all risks, from so fearful a dwelling.[61]

Having left, Juliet wanders in the wood debating with herself whether she is obliged 'to denounce what she could not have detected, but from seeking, and finding, a personal asylum in distress'. On the other hand,

> who was she who must give such information? Anonymous accusation might be neglected as calumnious; yet how name herself as belonging to the noble family from which she sprung, but by which she was unac-knowledged? How, too, at a moment when concealment appeared to her to be existence, come forward, a volunteer to public notice?[62]

She abandons this as fruitless, and asks 'admittance and rest' at a cottage where an elderly couple are breakfasting 'upon a rasher of bacon'. She sits with them, 'unable to converse, and turning with disgust from the sight of food'.[63]

Juliet's inability to distinguish between poaching and murder echoes that of the English legal system, in which both were capital offences. Whether this constitutes a critique of Juliet or the legal system (or both) on Burney's part is hard to tell, but it does work

60 Burney, *Wanderer*, p. 682.
61 Burney, *Wanderer*, p. 684.
62 Burney, *Wanderer*, p. 684.
63 Burney, *Wanderer*, p. 685.

to situate Juliet firmly within the establishment and reiterates her cultural alienation from the poverty she shares. Like her hosts, she is accustomed to game and able to recognise it, but for the opposite reasons. She has eaten it because it is such exclusive food that privilege and hereditary right as well as money are required to buy it, while her unnamed hosts eat it because, since they have nothing to lose, it is free. Juliet's inability to imagine such indigence suggests that 'female difficulties' of powerlessness, however acute, are not endemic in the same way as poverty and the oppression of the labouring classes; she can and will be reinstated at tables where venison is legitimately present.

This episode also echoes Burney's perception of herself as the hunted object of a game in the dining room at Streatham. There is something comic about Juliet's confusion, but, like most of Burney's jokes, the comedy reveals a telling anxiety. In a more explicit rendition of Evelina's fear of the gourmet rakes and Camilla's fear of Lynmere, Juliet has mistaken herself for something to eat. She has fallen so far that she might become 'chicky biddy' or 'fine-grained mutton' if she does not run away. It is important that unlike the fairy-tales echoed in this tale of bloodshed in the tumbledown cottage in the woods this is not 'real' violence (or at least, is real violence only for the deer). Juliet's fears are unjustified in a way that Evelina's and Camilla's are not, as if the aristocracy is finally more threatening than the peasantry to the well-born young woman. It is her mysterious 'husband', not the poor poachers, who threatens to eat her up.

Seen in another light, this strangely visceral intrusion of the Gothic into Burney's feminine picaresque unites the tropes of spilling and violence. The dead deer is food out of place, dropped messily in a place that draws attention to the uncomfortably visceral nature of eating meat, but it is also, in several ways, evidence of the violence committed in the name of food. Juliet's worst suspicions are in fact true, not of her host but of the state, which will kill him as he kills the deer in response to his killing. He will kill to eat and the state will kill him for eating. I do not think there is any basis for suggesting that Burney felt any interest in vegetarianism or moral outrage at eating meat; the point is that for her, the dining table is a place of violence, and when the imperative to act normal is removed the blood runs free. Choking, spilling and, in the end, smearing blood across the house, food projects extremes that may bear little relation to the normal behaviour encoded by rituals of dining.

2

The maternal aliment
Feeding daughters in the works of Mary Wollstonecraft

But you have no petticoats to dangle in the snow. Poor Women how they are beset with plagues – within – and without.

> — Mary Wollstonecraft, housebound and newly pregnant, to William Godwin, January 12th, 1797

They [many pregnant women] think they ought to eat more, instead of less, in their new state; and torture their invention to find out something to conquer the squeamishness of their appetite. This is a very fruitful source of whims and fancies, the indulgence of which is almost always injurious.

> — William Buchan, *Advice to Mothers*

Motherhood, one might say, had once been an ascribed function. It was becoming an achieved status.

> —Judith Schneid Lewis, *In the Family Way*

Judith Schneid Lewis and, more recently, Toni Bowers, Susan Greenfield, Claudia Johnson and Barbara Charlesworth Gelphi have shown how, in the late eighteenth century, motherhood ceased to be exclusively defined by the physiological processes of child-bearing and became a social and emotional undertaking with a defining moral content.[1] In fiction, advice literature, sermons and

---

1 Judith Schneid Lewis, *In the Family Way: Childbearing in the British Aristocracy 1760–1860* (New Brunswick: Rutgers University Press, 1986); Toni Bowers, *The Politics of Mother-hood: British Writing and Culture 1680–1760* (Cambridge: Cambridge University Press, 1996); Susan Greenfield, *Mothering Daughters: Novels and the Politics of Family Romance, Frances Burney to Jane Austen* (Detroit: Wayne State University Press, 2002); Susan Green-

journalism if not in daily practice, becoming a mother depended on breastfeeding one's children rather than sending them to wet-nurses, taking responsibility for the more interesting parts of day-to-day childcare, and making it one's defining business to pass on the feminine virtues of piety, charity and modesty. (Boys, it was assumed, would be sent to school or to a tutor to learn the masculinities that would equip them to complement these characteristics in adult life.) William Buchan, one of the best-selling of several well known obstetricians whose books on pregnancy, breastfeeding and childcare became very popular in the second half of the eighteenth century, confirms that he writes both in response to and in support of this perceived cultural shift:

> But while I speak thus of the dignity of the female character, it must be understood, that by a mother I do not mean the woman who merely brings a child into the world, but her who faithfully discharges the duties of a parent – whose chief concern is the well-being of her infant, – and who feels all her cares amply repaid by its growth and activity.[2]

This shows precisely how the shift in the understanding of reproductive labour both produces and is produced by shifts in the literary marketplace. The mother is not merely the woman who has a baby but the woman who reads about how to have a baby, the woman who situates her body in relation to a print culture doubly concerned with her consumption (of pregnancy handbooks and the diet they advocate) and production (of babies and the 'duties of a parent'). Part of the excitement surrounding the rise of this 'new' maternity is the birth of a new genre and the implication of reproduction, like cooking, in the burgeoning economy of books.

Nevertheless, it seems likely that this, like most announcements of 'new' cultural phenomena, is something of an oversimplification and, as Wollstonecraft herself reminds us, it is necessary to suspect any neat distinction between the physiological and the social or the natural and the cultural. The fact that this quotation comes from the beginning of one of many contemporary pregnancy handbooks demonstrates that the focus on the 'achieved status' of mother-

field and Carol Barash (eds), *Inventing Maternity: Politics, Science and Literature, 1650–1865* (Lexington: University of Kentucky Press, 1999); Claudia Johnson, *Equivocal Beings: Politics, Gender and Sentimentality in the 1790s* (Chicago: University of Chicago Press, 1996); and Barbara Charlesworth Gelphi, *Shelley's Goddess: Maternity, Language, Subjectivity* (Oxford: Oxford University Press, 1992).

2 William Buchan, *Advice to Mothers* (London: T. Cadell and W. Davies, 1803), p. 3.

hood complicated rather than replaced the act of 'bringing a child into the world'. The conduct of pregnancy and childbirth was implicated in and not replaced by a more social than biological understanding of maternity; pregnancy, labour and delivery also became bases of 'achieved status' in which it was possible to perform well or badly. These physiological processes, which had received almost no textual attention outside very few specialist medical textbooks until the middle of the eighteenth century, quickly acquired an immense weight of discourse. In books that were rapidly reprinted and revised, members of the new profession of obstetrics instructed two generations of middle- and upper-class British women in how to be pregnant, and it is revealing to place this discourse in the context of the more general late eighteenth-century concern with the relationship between women's production and consumption.

Andrea Henderson, one of very few literary scholars to pay attention to these texts, argues that,

> the conceptualization of childbearing labor in mechanistic terms, in the context of the development of early industrial capitalism, threatened to align birth with commodity production. This threat prompted the reconception of the maternal body as a part of nature as it was soon to be defined in high Romantic art: the realm of the spontaneous and incalculable, a realm not governed by hard and fast laws.[3]

I will be suggesting in this chapter that this model of 'commodity production' versus 'nature' is complicated by the handbooks' interest in women's diet, and furthermore that, seen from a late eighteenth-century rather than a 'Romantic' point of view, it is less obvious that the identification of reproductive labour with commodity production is damaging to women. For all of the writers I study here, an economic understanding of women's productivity has some potential to liberate, and although this is complicated in relation to pregnancy, birth and breastfeeding, it is not necessarily contradicted.

The production of babies, then, like the production of books, is in some way dependent on the consumption of the producer. Some of the connections between maternity and food appear obvious. Mothers make milk. Mothers cook, or, more usually in the fiction of this period, instruct the cook. Mothers decide what there will be to eat, and when and by whom it will be eaten. The final failure

---

3 Andrea K. Henderson, *Romantic Identities: Varieties of Subjectivity* (Cambridge: Cambridge University Press, 1996), p. 6.

of motherhood is to be unable or unwilling to feed one's children; the basic mother–child relationship is gustatory, and since mothers cannot be mothers without children (although children can, of course, be children without mothers), it could be said that mothers exist primarily through food. Mothers produce and children consume, except that the acts of transubstantiation by which women make babies and milk out of their own flesh and blood are not miraculous. Mothers, like writers, must consume if they are to produce, and it is in relation to the anxiety surrounding women's consumption that it may be most fruitful to locate the rise of pregnancy and breastfeeding handbooks. This chapter, focusing primarily on Wollstonecraft as a writer for children who politicises maternity, concentrates on writing and reproduction and the ways in which discourses of writing and reproduction are phrased in terms of nutrition. The following chapter, concentrating on Maria Edgeworth's writing for children, considers the centrality of food in the cultural and social constitution of the child.

Much of the rich secondary literature on Wollstonecraft analyses images of maternity in her work, and this has been especially fruitful in relation to discourses of nationhood and the body politic. What I would like to offer here is a more basic reading, one grounded in the materiality of reproductive labour. In this context it is possible to situate Wollstonecraft with and against writers in a genre that critics do not in general read, although Wollstonecraft both read and planned to write pregnancy and breastfeeding handbooks. Here, it seems, we can see a deeply conservative Wollstonecraft, not the ambivalent and painfully divided figure who alternately proclaims women's right to sexual fulfilment and turns in disgust from the idea of sensual pleasure, delights in babies but condemns women who find physical satisfaction in motherhood, and defends women's need to eat while reviling their appetites. Angela Keane writes that, 'For Wollstonecraft, the fraught condition of mothers is intimately related to the objectified condition of women under the sign of the modern nation in which discourses of political economy determine the work of its subjects' participation.'[4] I will argue here that Wollstonecraft's disturbing accord with frequently misogynist handbooks suggests a much less ambivalent and critical stance than Keane finds in Wollstonecraft's later writing.

4 Angela Keane, *Women Writers and the English Nation in the 1790s* (Cambridge: Cambridge University Press, 2001), p. 87.

Wollstonecraft's conservative approach to class is well known. Like discussions of women's economic productivity – including Wollstonecraft's – this new concern about pregnancy is explicitly not directed at the labouring poor, who are said to have no choice about deportment in pregnancy because they must work inside and outside the home until contractions begin and from the moment after delivery. Several writers on pregnancy remark upon this as an instance of 'Nature's' powers of organisation. Cornwell writes of 'symptoms' which include foetal movement and an enlarged uterus:

> These symptoms are not all, however, to be expected in every pregnant woman; for many of the laborious part of the lower class of life, go through their whole time in the midst of fatigue and trouble, and that without any of these symptoms, so that they are in a great measure to be attributed to the course of life, not the course of nature, in the pregnant women of better fortunes. Those women are most subject to them who are of a tender and delicate frame, and those who are of a plethoric habit, an idle life, or given to intemperance, or subject to passions of various kinds, fear, anger, grief or the like.[5]

'A tender and delicate frame' sounds like an invitation to be cared for, but idleness, intemperance and subjection to passion are classic and even defining vices of aristocratic femininity across the political spectrum of writing for women. It seems that, in acknowledging a need for, buying and reading Cornwell's book, his reader has already made an admission of failure and guilt, for by definition the woman reading this has both 'symptoms' and the leisure to investigate them. This exclusion of the labouring poor from the discourse of pregnancy neatly side-steps the issue of the need for books on pregnancy and birth. The argument seems to be that pregnancy and childbirth must be 'natural' because those who cannot read about it give birth without difficulty. The handbook exists to teach readers how to give birth like women who do not buy or read handbooks. This is a parallel to the 'African woman' who stalks modern pregnancy books, pausing in her agricultural work to let slip a baby which she tucks in a hand-made sling before continuing with her

---

5 Bryan Cornwell, *The Domestic Physician, or, Guardian of Health* (London: J. Murray, 1784), p. 550. See also, for example, Buchan's *Advice*, p. 250ff, and, with regard to breastfeeding, William Cadogan, *An Essay Upon Nursing* (London: Robert Horsfield, 10th ed., 1772), p. 8: 'Health and Posterity are the Portion of the Poor, I mean the Laborious. The Want of Superfluity confines them more within the Limits of Nature: Hence they enjoy Blessings they feel not, and are ignorant of their Cause. The Mother who has only a few Rags to cover her Child loosely, and little more than her own Breast to feed it, sees it healthy and strong, and very soon able to shift for itself.'

real labours; in both cases there is a clear sense that productive physical labour displaces reproduction as the site of identity. Women whose lives are devoted to the production of material goods and services are exempt from definition by reproduction, and there is little or no concern for their conduct of pregnancy and childbirth. Then and now, this is a discourse for people with choices; we can relate the reading of pregnancy books to the diet they prescribe, for both are forms of consumption that also constitute a performance of discipline. Buy this; it will tell you how to control your consumption.

As this suggests, much of the advice is similar to, and shares the ideological problems of, modern handbooks. Both eighteenth-century and modern pregnancy books set out prescriptive regimes of diet, exercise, rest, medical attendance and even social and sexual activity, making pregnancy a time-consuming activity as well as a state of body, and requiring specialist knowledge for successful accomplishment. Women are also instructed that they must under all circumstances remain calm and relaxed. The central contradictions are the same. Alexander Hamilton informs his readers that 'In the greatest number of cases women are delivered without much difficulty or danger; such labours are therefore styled Natural.'[6] Under the chapter on 'Lingering Labours', we learn that 'The improper regulation of the passions of the mind very often interrupt and retard the progress of labour.'[7] Labour is natural as long as the 'passions of the mind' are 'properly regulated'. According to John Aitken, 'It is obvious, that parturition … is altogether a *natural* and *healthful* action … and that the Accoucheur ought not to consider the woman to be under disease, or that the interference of art is strictly necessary.'[8] He is also clear that labouring women should be encouraged to be mobile and that 'the less handling, the better'.[9] (This from a writer who advises students that a symptom of complete dilation is that 'The mother's cries at this crisis are exceedingly bitter, and mark the racking anguish.'[10]) *The Compleat Family Physician*, explicitly written for women, says,

6 Alexander Hamilton, *A Treatise on the Management of Female Complaints, and of Children in Early Infancy* (Edinburgh: Peter Hill, 4th ed., 1797), p. 177.

7 Hamilton, *Female Complaints*, p. 195

8 John Aitken, *Principles of Midwifery, or Puerperal Medicine* (London: J. Murray, 3rd ed., 1786) p. 61.

9 Aitken, *Principles of Midwifery*, p. 63.

10 Aitken, *Principles of Midwifery*, p. 59.

we are not to consider pregnancy as a disease, but a natural indisposition of the female body ... Temperance and regularity are of great importance to women in this condition, and they should be cautious in their choice of food, eating only such as is light of digestion ... to these precautions should be added, a free and mild air, and gentle exercise ... An attention ought equally to be paid to the passions of the mind; man, the natural protector of the female sex, should, at all times, guard them with care and treat them with tenderness; but at no time should these duties be performed with such exactness as in a state of pregnancy.[11]

The Closet Companion allows that women do sometimes suffer unpleasant side-effects of pregnancy, but continues,

Anger, grief, fear, and other passions of the mind, when they are too violent, may injure the health of the embryo, and often cause abortion in the beginning of pregnancy. Pregnant women should therefore cautiously restrain themselves, and avoid all occasions wherein they may possibly be too affected.[12]

Women who are naturally healthy and active, who labour, live moderately, and observe a proper regimen, experience but very little of these complaints. They are considerable only to women of a delicate constitution, who eat too much, observe no regulations with respect to diet, or who lead an inactive life.[13]

As modern pregnancy books warn women not to use their pregnancy as an excuse to eat chocolate and cake, so Buchan and his colleagues are keen that the increased need for energy in pregnancy should not be seen to legitimate women's appetites for such proscribed foods as spices, salt, red meat, sweetmeats and French cooking. Buchan writes:

In laying down rules of temperance, I do not wish to impose any restraint on the moderate use of good and wholesome food or drink: but under these heads we must not include spirituous liquors; relaxing and often-repeated draughts of hot coffee and tea; salted, smoke-dried, and highly-seasoned meats; salt fish; rich gravies; heavy sauces; almost indigestible pastry; and sour unripe fruits, of which women in general are immoderately fond. We pity the green-sick girl, whose longing for such trash is

---

11 Anon, *The Compleat Family Physician: Being a Perfect Compendium of Domestic Medicine* (Newcastle: Matthew Brown, 1801), p. 636.
12 Silvester Mahon, *Every Lady her own Physician, or, the Closet Companion* (London: M. Randall, 1788), p. 98.
13 Mahon, *Closet Companion*, p. 101.

one of the causes as well as one of the effects of her disease; but can any woman, capable of the least reflection, continue to gratify a perverse appetite by the use of the most pernicious crudities?[14]

Any extra food must be taken for the good of the foetus and not for the gratification of the mother, and in the case of doubt or possible overlap women should assume that their 'whims and fancies' are damaging to the foetus and therefore that their 'vitiated appetites' are leading them to misread their bodies' 'natural requirements'. It is interesting that Buchan's 'pernicious crudities' are all high-status foods with strongly gendered associations. Preserved meat and 'rich gravy', a reduction of meat essences, are seen as so masculine that some writers of conduct books recommend that parents keep a careful guard over daughters who have inflamed their appetites by consuming such things.[15] The 'heavy sauces' suggest French cuisine, which remained predictably controversial throughout the late eighteenth century, while the pastry and fruit are universally recognised as feminine tastes, sometimes harmless because not masculine, but often an example of women's inability to control unreasonable consumption. Appetite is problematised by the very words that claim to free it as the pregnancy handbook, inevitably, comes to stand between the reader and her body even as it tells her what her body really needs, rather than what she has been culturally conditioned to imagine it wants. It begins to seem clear that one can have a 'natural' – i.e., straightforward – pregnancy and labour either on condition of self-regulation, self-restraint, controlled appetites and physical exercise or as a result of a lifestyle in which these qualities are externally imposed. The repeated comparisons with poor or peasant women suggest several things: that this is a discourse aimed at the rich for whom there is the possibility of deliberate modifications of diet and exercise, and that this may be part of a broader concern about luxury and self-indulgence. If women are to produce, economically and/or biologically, it is clear that they must consume, but it appears that such consumption is legitimate only and to the extent that it serves the production.

This is one of the contexts in which we can see a professionalisation of pregnancy. Pregnant women must behave in ways that privilege their existence as producers above any subjective sense of needs and desires, and in this sense they must mimic the economic

14 Buchan, *Advice*, p. 13.
15 See, for example, Fordyce, *Sermons*, p. 76.

function of other labourers. Pregnancy does not entitle women to a surplus; in fact, it takes away any anterior entitlement they may have had. Women of low social status and meagre diet will do well because they have no alternative, and the more comfortably situated must abjure their customary status and diet for reproductive success.

If proof were needed, this insistence on the class specificity of the genre is evidence that the rise of the pregnancy handbook has no direct link to new ideas about physiology. To the extent that there has been critical work on these texts, the tendency has been to place them in relation to the history of medicine. They have been used to support both of the polarised arguments about childbirth in the late eighteenth century: either that men with metal instruments invaded the intimacy of the birthing chamber, replacing the traditional skills of gentle midwifery with clock-watching and dangerous intervention, or that research-based obstetrics came to save labouring women from the dirty hands of unlettered midwives. Even Henderson's nuanced account is influenced by this distinctively modern understanding of healthcare and authority, arguing that for man-midwives, 'the body of the mother itself is understood as a productive machine … the midwife is represented as a worker at the machine of the maternal body'.[16] While problematising both, Henderson places this 'mechanistic' understanding of reproductive work in contrast to the 'mythical nature figure' that determines the course of birth in later eighteenth-century female midwives' work. The problem with this is that, like less scholarly histories, it erases the economics of the birthing-chamber. Women's bodies were certainly damaged by early obstetric implements, and those who wielded them certainly display attitudes to the female body that we would not wish to find in modern healthcare, but in the absence of insurance companies and the welfare state, the labouring woman was also the consumer. Most women chose and paid their own attendants (although, as ever, poor women given these 'services' free were particularly vulnerable to abuse), and so the model of the powerful physician denying the subjectivity of the patient is complicated.

I would like rather to sidestep this debate and place pregnancy and breastfeeding handbooks beside cookbooks in relation to a professionalisation of domesticity which may go as far as the professionalisation of maternity, of the body as well as the hands.

16 Henderson, *Romantic Identities*, p. 18.

Wollstonecraft is famed for defending and explicating women's economic productivity; she is also known for her profound ambivalence about bodily needs and pleasures. The context of handbooks on pregnancy and breastfeeding may offer some ways of bringing together her thinking about consumption, production and reproduction, the economics and economies of the female body.

Wollstonecraft is notoriously ambivalent about the relationship between popular culture, feminism and the female body. She is keen to acknowledge women's sexuality but also anxious to present equality of opportunity as compatible with, and perhaps even productive of, some versions of conventional femininity. Alternately, if not simultaneously, Wollstonecraft argues against a sexual double standard and for the power of education to enhance women's 'natural' delicacy and reinforce their 'innate' chastity, while raging against conduct books that construct an interest in fashion and beauty as 'natural'. She exhorts mothers to encourage young girls to exercise and eat well but presents the private consumption of fruit and cakes as a sin on a level with lying and stealing: 'rational' bodily needs should be met, but physical self-gratification is criminal. There is no place for the inevitability of physical pleasure, and, even trying to disregard modern formulations of gender, sex and power and allowing for the historical specificity of bodily experiences, it is hard to imagine a world in which it is actually possible to distinguish need from pleasure as precisely as Wollstonecraft seems to require. Certain circumstances help to determine particular acts of consumption as 'necessary' or 'reasonable': commensality, the social setting of the table, is a precondition of eating that is both moral and feminine, but girls in her fiction do overeat or eat inappropriately at the family table. It is always wrong for women and children to eat sweetmeats or any but the plainest baked goods. Small quantities of fruit knowingly provided by a virtuous guardian and carefully shared out may be compatible with virtue, but in general fruit is associated with greed. This is a particularly conservative position for Wollstonecraft to occupy as, by the end of the eighteenth century, fruit was well on the way from its biblical associations with uncontrollable female greed towards its modern position as the ultimate 'light' and 'natural' food which men might scorn but women can consume with impunity. I can see no way of understanding Wollstonecraft's accounts of food that does not offer a direct contradiction to her project of liberating femininity from impossible demands. This has been said before with regard to Wollstonecraft's writing about sexuality, but I will argue here that her polemic and fictional writing about food and motherhood works to elide and discipline these most basic and inevitable forms of (re)production and consumption.

All of Mary Wollstonecraft's published work keeps maternity firmly at the centre of women's identities and offers it as the justification for women's education. This need not be a conservative position (although compared with Burney's it arguably is), but her argument that women should be educated so that mothers will be able to override their 'natural' tendency to over-indulge their children and so they will be capable of choosing the deferred gratification of 'natural' breastfeeding over the immediate pleasures of an independent social life, certainly undermines her traditional position on the radical/conservative axis of late eighteenth-century women writers. Ashley Tauchert, commenting on these inconsistencies, attributes them to 'a deep melancholic longing for an absent female body that is both desired and disclaimed in a repeated hysterical gesture'.[17] Angela Keane writes that Wollstonecraft 'tried and failed to resist the objectification of the maternal body in contemporary political economy'.[18] I find no such ambivalence in the early writings studied below. Wollstonecraft is clear and consistent that it is good to produce and bad to consume and appears, in this particular context, to be in absolute accord with the dictates and priorities of what Keane calls 'a commercial culture'. Need may excuse, but rarely justifies, consumption, and consumption beyond need is invariably shameful. (Re)production may be done well or badly, but it is invariably the ground upon which women stand or fall.

Wollstonecraft's writing for children, which has been analysed very little, explicitly elides the mother as the source of milk and provider (or withholder) of food and the mother as teacher and writer, so that the provision of text becomes confused with the provision of food. This is a familiar metaphor in the Romantic era, but Wollstonecraft's rendition is astonishingly literal. In all of her writing for children, the mother-figure who controls what children eat also controls what they read, and frequently generates knowledge as she generates milk. In her posthumous 'Lessons', the writer is also the mother, and the baby who depended on her mother's milk is now the child who depends on her mother's text. If Burney emphasises

---

17 Ashley Tauchert, 'Maternity, Castration and Mary Wollstonecraft's Historical and Moral View of the French Revolution', *Women's Writing*, 4:2 (1997), 173–203 p. 200.
18 Keane, *Women Writers and the English Nation*, p. 109.

eating as a way of wielding power, Wollstonecraft is acutely alive to the endlessly complicated manipulative and metaphorical potentials of feeding. The uneasy and unstable equations of writing and feeding, reading and eating, are similar.

The instability of Wollstonecraft's thinking about women's rights to consume and produce can be explored through her ambivalence about conduct literature, which she derides in *A Vindication of the Rights of Woman* and offers approvingly for girls' attention in *The Female Reader*. Her analyses encode an astutely suspicious view of gender, but her wholehearted endorsement of pregnancy and breastfeeding handbooks shows how the discourses surrounding physiological maternity can seem to offer a way of reconciling women's minds and bodies. This reconciliation is marked by words like 'nature' and 'reason', which, to quote Barbara Charlesworth Gelphi, 'flag the presence of ideology'.[19] Claudia Johnson argues that, 'Wollstonecraft's turn toward the female body, as that body is a daughter and/or mother, is a turn away from the political normativity of the male body in conservative and radical discourse.'[20] I will be suggesting rather that while Wollstonecraft's moral investment in the physiological processes of maternity participates in the inclusion of the female body in a gendered 'virtue', her insistence that the proper enactment of such processes requires women to overcome their innately 'indolent' and self-serving inclinations in fact reasserts normative masculinity. She suggests that women must assert a moral force clearly gendered as masculine and related to more regulated forms of labour in order to discipline their bodies to perform virtuous maternity. Good mothers must overcome their depraved femininity, which is associated with the amoral self-indulgence of the aristocracy, and bring to maternity the work ethic of the masculine middling sort.

Wollstonecraft, who shares the early Foucault's interest in textual forms of discipline, cannot, like him, be accused of 'constructing the body as a concrete, material entity' and/or as 'a notion ... which has no materiality outside the representation'.[21] She is articulately aware of the disciplinary processes of culture and of the subjective experience of inhabiting a sexual as well as gendered body, if rarely of both

19 Gelphi, *Shelley's Goddess*, p. 59.
20 Claudia L. Johnson, 'Mary Wollstonecraft, Styles of Radical Maternity', in Greenfield and Carol Barash (eds), *Inventing Maternity*, p. 87.
21 Joan Entwhistle, *The Fashioned Body: Fashion, Dress and Modern Social Theory* (Cambridge: Polity Press, 2000), p. 27.

at once, in relation to sexual behaviour, marriage, paid and unpaid work and the ownership and management of property. She offers a salutary account of 'nature', ideology and power, responding to Rousseau and John Gregory's preference for well-dressed women,

> He [Gregory] advises them to cultivate a fondness for dress, because a fondness for dress, he asserts, is natural to them. I am unable to comprehend what either he or Rousseau mean, when they frequently use this indefinite term. If they told us that in a pre-existent state the soul was fond of dress, and brought this inclination with it into a new body, I should listen to them with half a smile, as I often do when I hear a rant about innate elegance. – But if he only meant to say that the exercise of the faculties will produce this fondness – I deny it. It is not natural; but arises, like false ambition in men, from a love of power.[22]

The problem is that this critical awareness falls into abeyance before a pregnant belly, a loaded table and a hungry baby. Wollstonecraft was identified with the late eighteenth-century natural childbirth movement by nineteenth-century readers partly because Godwin's *Memoirs of the Author of the Rights of Woman* recounts her obstetric history in detail and attributes her death partly to her insistence on having a non-interventionist midwife rather than an obstetrician at the birth of the future Mary Shelley. Godwin writes of Wollstonecraft's preparations for childbirth:

> Influenced by ideas of decorum, which certainly ought to have no place, at least in cases of danger, she determined to have a woman to attend her in the capacity of a midwife. She was sensible that the proper business of a midwife, in the instance of a natural labour, is to sit by and wait for the operations of nature, which seldom, in these affairs, demand the interposition of art.[23]

But there are also definitive reasons for connecting Wollstonecraft with those who opposed the rise of obstetrics. Notes towards future works found after her death include a plan for a volume of 'Letters on the Management of Infants', to progress from 'Management of the Mother during pregnancy' through 'Lying-in' to the baby's second year; she clearly considers writing about pregnancy and breast-feeding to be part of her role as a literary critic and cultural analyst. Her own account of Fanny Imlay's birth strongly supports the view that "good" births are a matter of the mother's moral exertion and

---

22 Mary Wollstonecraft, *A Vindication of the Rights of Men, A Vindication of the Rights of Woman*, ed. Janet Todd (Oxford: Oxford University Press, 1999), p. 94.
23 William Godwin, *Memoirs of the Author of the Vindication of the Rights of Woman* (Harmondsworth: Penguin, 2000), p. 265.

not the training of the attendants, and also expresses considerable pride in the idea of her own labour as productive of commodities for the national good. Reproductive labour is unashamedly compared to commercial manufacture:

> Here I am, my Dear Friend, and so well, that were it not for the inundation of milk, which for the moment incommodes me, I could forget the pain I endured six days ago. – Yet nothing could be more easy and natural than my labour – still it is not smooth work – I dwell on these circumstances not only as I know it will give you pleasure; but to prove that this struggle of nature is rendered much more cruel by the ignorance and affectation of women. My nurse has been twenty years in this employment, and she tells me, she never knew a woman so well – adding, Frenchwoman like, that I ought to make children for the Republic, since I treat it so slightly … I feel great pleasure at being a mother – and the constant tenderness of my most affectionate companion makes me regard a fresh tie as a blessing.[24]

Wollstonecraft is ardent and imperative on the subject of maternal breastfeeding throughout her oeuvre, insisting that breastfeeding is a natural replacement for female sexuality, and it is interesting in this context that nearly all the breastfeeding infants in her writing are girls. She seems to be moving towards an understanding in which all the bodies that matter, consumers and producers, are female, gesturing towards a strange economy of food, babies and milk that nonetheless replicates the priorities and values of the marketplace. The anxieties engendered by women's need to eat in order to feed and by the recent and imperative interest in this female transubstantiation of food into milk and milk into growing baby once again seem to unite the politics of the body with those of the book trade. The project here is to begin to look at the vexed and jumbled ideologies of feeding daughters in Wollstonecraft's work.

Breast milk: the cement of family concord, or, what nature freely produces

It is conventionally said that breastfeeding became fashionable or more popular in the second half of the eighteenth century. Of course, in fact almost all babies were breastfed until the advent of domestic sterilisation in the early twentieth century. It is not that more breastfeeding happened after 1750 than before, but that there was an increased expectation that elite and aristocratic (literate and

24 Letter to Ruth Barlow, Havre, May 20th 1794 in Mary Wollstonecraft, *Collected Letters of Mary Wollstonecraft*, ed. Ralph M. Wardle (Ithaca: Cornell University Press, 1979), p. 255.

leisured) women would breastfeed their own children rather than sending them away immediately after birth to professional wet-nurses. It is very hard to tell how much effect this expectation had on women's behaviour, since, as Barbara Charlesworth Gelphi points out,

> If women were conforming totally to the model considered so desirable by those dominating the society's media of communication, what need would there be to continue spending resources – time, money, human energy – urging them to conform?[25]

Valerie Fildes writes that 'the impression gained over years of study is that the great majority of British infants were breastfed at home by their mothers until the twentieth century, and that only a tiny proportion of families ever used wet-nurses.'[26] It remains plausible that this tiny proportion exercised a disproportionate influence on print culture. Judith Schneid Lewis, whose study is limited to a small group of aristocratic women whose lives are intimately documented in letters and diaries, writes:

> While there may have been more women breastfeeding by the 1780s than in earlier generations, it had become by no means uniform practice … the women in our group who breastfed enjoyed the experience, and those who were against the idea usually did not feel compelled by custom to take up the practice against their own preferences. This is an area in which women exercised a high degree of autonomy.[27]

Although it is impossible to be categorical, then, it seems that there was a fashion for writing about breastfeeding which had some effect on what some women chose to do, but it may be analogous to the modern British fashion for writing about cooking, which seems to have an inverse relationship with the number of people starting with raw ingredients at home on a daily basis. The consumption of text can be a less alarming substitute for eating and feeding. This matters because one of the defining characteristics of childcare manuals and conduct literature, which Wollstonecraft wrote as well as analysed, is their relationship to the reader's body and their explicit constitution of their own power over that body, particularly in their capacity to raise anxiety which is said to undermine

25 Gelphi, *Shelley's Goddess*, p. 39.
26 Valerie Fildes, *Breasts, Bottles and Babies: A History of Infant Feeding* (Edinburgh: Edinburgh University Press, 1986) p. 98.
27 Lewis, *In the Family Way*, p. 209.

the quality and quantity of breastmilk. Unlike modern cookbooks, childcare manuals – including Wollstonecraft's – are vitriolic about those who do not conform to their requirements. If most readers were breastfeeding, then this indictment would have worked to affirm their sense of moral superiority. But if upper-class breast-feeding was a literary rather than a practical trend, then there is a serious disjunction between texts and readers, in which we find Wollstonecraft, despite her own difficult experience of breastfeeding, firmly on the side of the texts and supporting a rhetoric of feminine selflessness to which she is otherwise fluently opposed. One of the earliest and most articulate analysts of the role of conduct literature in constituting gender appears to contribute to the defining function of discourse rather than agency. The tendency to castigate women who do not conform is illustrated by the characteristically forthright William Buchan, who follows the bemusing assertion that, 'Not only the inhabitants of the howling wilderness, the she-wolf and the fell tigress, but even the monsters of the great deep, draw out the breast, and give suck to their young',[28] with a tirade concluding:

> Women, enervated by luxury, allured by a false taste for mistaken pleasures, and encouraged by shameless example, are eager to get rid of their children as soon as born, in order to spend the time thus gained from the discharge of their duty in dissipation or indolence. Let not husbands be deceived: let them not expect attachment from wives who, in neglecting to suckle their children, rend asunder the strongest ties in Nature. Neither conjugal love, fidelity, modesty, chastity, nor any other virtue, can take deep root in the breast of a female that is callous to the feelings of a mother.[29]

Maternity here is not merely a matter of practice as well as biology but a precondition of all other feminine virtue. The extent to which 'nature' has been co-opted into this account is particularly clear in the last sentence where the woman who does not breastfeed has become 'a female' (someone whose femininity is merely biological, sexual but not gendered) 'that' (not 'who', an object rather than a person) 'is callous to the feelings of a mother'. Mothers, then, have such generic and obvious feelings that the indefinite object suffices to indicate them and, crucially, the woman who has given birth but does not breastfeed places herself outside the category. It is these 'feelings', which can be demonstrated only by breastfeeding, that define a mother, and giving birth is (usually) necessary but never

28 Buchan, *Advice*, p. 215.
29 Buchan, *Advice*, p. 217.

sufficient. Breastfeeding thus becomes the public performance and guarantee of a woman's correct interiority or 'feelings', an interesting relationship in an era marked by a contradictory interest in and respect for an essentially private construction of gender and virtue. Buchan's coercion, which is only a particularly good example of the genre as a whole, works by collapsing feminine emotions and physiological performance. A mother's feelings equal breastfeeding. No milk in your (literal) breasts, no virtue in your (metaphorical) breast. A mother's mind (or at least her 'heart') and her body are one.

It is important to remember that this is not necessarily about the baby's physical well-being. The alternative to mother's milk was someone else's mother's milk, which was usually regarded as equally nutritious, although there were concerns, particularly later in the period, that wet-nurses might over-indulge or neglect their charges. The point is not whether babies get breastmilk but whether mothers breastfeed. It is the definition and practice of middling and elite maternity that is at stake, and these women are told both that they exist primarily as mothers and that, as mothers, there is not the slightest difference between 'hearts' and bodies. Maria, the heroine of Wollstonecraft's last novel, remains the definitive mother despite, or even because of, her forcible separation from her infant daughter. Her 'burning bosom' is 'bursting with nutriment' and she spends most of her time writing to her daughter in an attempt to generate a text that will stand for active maternity. 'Motherhood' in these terms requires the total biological performance of a total – and totally prescribed – psychic commitment. It is, in this context, disconcerting to find Wollstonecraft firmly reinscribing this monolithic form of maternal identity, particularly given her own ambivalent experience of maternity. The introduction to her rewriting of C.G. Salzmann's children's book *Elements of Morality*, which includes despairing comments on the moral inadequacy of most parents, adjures women,

> To you does the pleasing task belong of forming their tempers, and giving them habits of virtue; for as the sight of your breast is a hint to you that you were destined to suckle your children, so is the consciousness of your abilities, and the domestic ties, which so firmly attach your children to you, hints from God, that the first formation of their character belongs to you.[30]

30 *Elements of Morality* in Mary Wollstonecraft, *The Works of Mary Wollstonecraft*, ed. Janet Todd and Marilyn Butler (London: William Pickering, 1989), vol. 2, p. 11.

Wollstonecraft's readers are instructed to read their bodies, and specifically their breasts, analogically as 'hints from God'. To say that the maternal body's meanings are divinely ordained is to make them at least as incontestable as to say they are 'natural' or 'self-evident'. God wants you to breastfeed – in fact, God designed you in order to breastfeed, but breastfeeding is only the outward sign of your readiness to bring your children up properly, to 'form' their 'tempers' and 'characters' into 'habits of virtue' (which are self-evident). Breastfeeding is not only the performance and transparent language of virtuous (i.e., adequate) maternity, but a necessary model of cultural conformity to children. Wollstonecraft's Nonconformist background is perhaps relevant both to the analogical account of the body and to the unfashionably disciplinarian approach to childcare, in which the parents' job is to mould or 'form' an acceptable personality rather than, as the Rousseauvian and Wordsworthian tradition demands, nurturing and celebrating a pre-existent identity. There is a sermon on the moral effects of maternal breastfeeding on children later in the book, when George's mother has 'a bad breast':

> Dear play-fellows, said George, I never thought before how good it is of parents to be so anxious about their children. See now how much my mother endures with that little infant. As often as it sucks, it gives her as much pain as if a knife were stuck in her breast; and still she does not send it away. She puts it again to the breast, bears all the pain, rather than the poor infant should feel hunger.[31]

Again, breastfeeding is absolute evidence of proper maternal feeling, and code for the perfectibility of maternal women. Those who reject or fail in any aspect of this monolithic identity place themselves outside motherhood, among those whose interest or investment in other kinds of self-definition makes them 'unnatural'. Nevertheless – and it is important that there is, with Wollstonecraft, always a 'nevertheless' – this image of breastfeeding as a martyrdom also runs through her writing on maternity, especially when she is writing for children. The breast can be bad, not in the Kleinian sense, for the baby, but for the woman who is morally as well as physically bound, or in this case stabbed, by her biology. Breastfeeding here seems like one of the 'plagues' which 'beset women'.

There is another, equally disturbing example of this in the 'Lessons' which appear in Wollstonecraft's Posthumous Works.

31 Wollstonecraft, *Elements of Morality*, p. 162.

Probably written for Fanny Imlay in infancy, these are apparently designed, *pace* Edgeworth, to teach reading based on familiar domestic scenarios. By the fifth Lesson, the baby has been introduced: 'O here it comes. Look at him. How helpless he is. Four years ago you were as feeble as this very little boy ... He is forced to lie on his back, if his mamma do not turn him to the right or left side, he will soon begin to cry.'[32] There is something slightly menacing in this insistence on the baby's dependence, especially in the implication that the mother might not turn the baby. By the sixth Lesson, this menace is developing:

> Perhaps he is hungry. What shall we give him to eat? Poor fellow, he cannot eat. Look in his mouth, he has no teeth.
> How did you do when you were a baby like him? You cannot tell. Do you want to know? Look then at the dog, with her pretty puppy. You could not help yourself as well as the puppy. You could only open your mouth, when you were lying, like William, on my knee. So I put you to my breast, and you sucked, as the puppy sucks now, for there was milk enough for you.[33]

One is reminded of the puppies brought in to 'draw off' Wollstonecraft's poisonous milk as she lay dying from puerperal fever after the birth of Mary Godwin Shelley, and this image of the child as the mother's dog persists. In Lesson XIII, the child must pour milk for the dog because otherwise, 'He would cry for a day with hunger, without being able to get it'. She tells the child: 'The dog will love you for it, and run after you. I feed you and take care of you: you love me and follow me for it.' Milk here is both the substance of power and the substance of love, an unappetising cocktail used to equate the obedience of a dog to the appropriate behaviour of a loving child. The pounding emphasis on the children's helplessness and the mother's agency is disturbing, hammering home her power and their weakness in a way that becomes typically complicated in Lesson VII:

> When you were hungry, you began to cry, because you could not speak. You were seven months without teeth, always sucking. But after you got one, you began to gnaw a crust of bread ... At ten months you had four pretty white teeth, and you used to bite me. Poor mamma! Still I did not cry, because I am not a child, but you hurt me very much. So I said to papa, it is time the little girl should eat ... I have given her a crust of bread and I must look for some other milk.

32 Wollstonecraft, *Works*, vol. 4 p. 469.
33 Wollstonecraft, *Works*, vol. 4 p. 470.

... Yes, says papa ... Come to me, and I will teach you, my little dear, for you must not hurt poor mamma, who has given you her milk, when you could not take anything else.[34]

Power and agency are complicated here because the mother-as-writer, who is also the mother-as-milk-source, appears to be blaming the child-as-reader for her conduct as a breastfed baby. In consuming her mother's text, the daughter as reader must internalise her badness as a consumer of milk; writing here works as a kind of revenge for breastfeeding. The baby may hurt the breast but the text wields a similar power over its readers, especially when the mother who feeds is also the mother who writes the lessons, in some ways replicating the infant's dependence on the breast in the child's dependence on the text. The mother's power here inheres not in her past role as the baby's only food source but in her current ability to remember and represent the daughter as a consumer whose helplessness is here exploited. 'You' is both the sucking baby and the reading daughter, but also, of course the other readers for whom Wollstonecraft may or may not have intended this text. No reading, it seems, without breastfeeding.

Apart from maternal depravity and selfishness, one of the most common reasons given in fiction and conduct literature for not breastfeeding is that husbands forbid (as in *Pamela*) or discourage (as in several of Judith Schneid Lewis's families) their wives. In *Pamela* this becomes a technical issue about whether a woman who perceives a conflict between her husband's will and God's is obliged to obey her husband, as promised in the marriage service, or follow her own sense of God. By the end of the century, it is merely part of women's occupation of the moral high ground, in which men are presented as prioritising their own sexual pleasures over their children's morals. Both Valerie Fildes and Judith Schneid Lewis are clear that, for Protestant couples, there was no proscription against sex for nursing mothers, and even most of the books on wet-nursing suggest that the wet-nurse's milk is likely to be better if she is allowed occasional "conjugal visits" with her husband. As in modern breastfeeding books, the issue is about sexual aesthetics rather than access, and Wollstonecraft is predictably scornful:

34 Wollstonecraft, *Works*, vol. 4, p. 470.

> Cold would be the heart of the husband, were he not rendered unnatural
> by early debauchery, who did not feel more delight at seeing his child
> suckled by its mother, than the most artful wanton tricks could ever raise;
> yet this natural way of cementing the matrimonial tie, and twisting esteem
> with fonder recollections, wealth leads women to spurn.[35]

The sense here that suckling a child is an alternative to 'artful
wanton tricks' reinforces the crucial role of breastfeeding in defining
feminine identity. In Wollstonecraft's account, breastfeeding replaces
female sexuality and constitutes feminine maturity. There is no sense
that a husband might legitimately have his own emotional or sexual
interests which cannot be sublimated by watching breastfeeding,
and this insistence on the priority of 'esteem' and 'fond recollec-
tions', rather than love or sex, in 'cementing the matrimonial tie' is
typical of Wollstonecraft's sense that maternity must succeed sexuality. Wifehood itself is co-opted into maternity as she writes, 'The
wife, in the present state of things, who is faithful to her husband,
and neither suckles nor educates her children, scarcely deserves the
name of wife and has no right to that of citizen.'[36] Breastfeeding and
involved maternity replace, or at least – since the virtuous mother
is asexual and thus incapable of adultery – subsume, fidelity as the
basic qualification for socially acceptable wifehood. This is partly a
feminist point that a woman's body is hers to give to her child and
not her husband's to take for himself, but the insistence that right-
minded women will feel the need to do this, and that those who
continue to expect to find fulfilment in marriage after maternity are
immature and/or dirty-minded, is exactly the kind of hijacking of
'nature' and 'culture' that Wollstonecraft resents in Rousseau. This
is particularly clear at the end of the *Vindication*, where the present
tense – a mode we might call the 'medical present' – makes the
economy she describes seem both actual and immutable, and the
words 'providence' and 'natural' bear great weight:

> In the exercise of their maternal feelings Providence has furnished women
> with a natural substitute for love, when the lover becomes only a friend,
> and mutual confidence takes the place of overstrained admiration – a
> child then gently twists the relaxing cord, and a mutual care produces new
> mutual sympathy.[37]

35 Wollstonecraft, *Vindication*, p. 213.
36 Wollstonecraft, *Vindication*, p. 217.
37 Wollstonecraft, *Vindication*, p. 223.

The 'medical present' describes a succession of events in the present tense, emphasising progression and contingency while appearing to recount telescoped real-time observations. This mode leaves no opening for alternative possibilities – might some lovers remain lovers? are some relationships initiated by something other than 'overstrained admiration'? do some 'mutual cares' fail to produce 'mutual sympathy'? – but avoids sounding obviously didactic, theoretical or personal by using 'becomes', 'takes the place of', 'twists' and 'produces', as if these are invariable phenomena impersonally observed. Combined with 'providence's' provision of 'maternal feelings' to all women as a 'natural substitute' for love (which is itself, in Wollstonecraft, often more cultural than natural), this is coercive writing at its highly wrought and multi-layered best.

Wollstonecraft's construction of breastfeeding as an act that subsumes all other forms of female virtue, and the maternal relationship – specifically, the mother–daughter relationship – as the definitive consummation of a woman's life, reaches a disturbing apogee in a story in *The Female Reader*. Many of the extracts in this anthology of readings for girls are unsettling, particularly in conjunction, and the collection sometimes seems like a collage of contemporary femininities, but Wollstonecraft's version of the Caritas Romana is egregious:

> One of the Roman judges had given up to the Triumvir a woman of some rank, condemned for a capital crime, to be executed in the prison. He who had charge of the execution, in consideration of her birth, did not immediately put her to death: he even ventured to let her daughter have access to her in the prison, carefully searching her, however, as she went in, lest she should carry with her any sustenance; concluding that in a few days the mother must of course perish for want, and that the severity of putting a woman of quality to a violent death, by the hand of the executioner, might thus be avoided. Some days passing in this manner the Triumvir began to wonder that the daughter still came to visit her mother, and could by no means comprehend how the latter should live so long. Watching, therefore, carefully what passed in the interview between them, he found, to his great astonishment, that the life of the mother had been all this time supported by the milk of the daughter, who came to the prison every day to give her mother her breasts to suck. The strange contrivance between them was represented to the judges, and procured a pardon for the mother. Nor was it thought sufficient to give to so dutiful a daughter the forfeited life of her condemned mother; but they were both maintained afterwards by a pension settled on them for life; and the ground upon which the prison stood was consecrated, and a temple to Filial Piety built upon it.[38]

38 Wollstonecraft, *Works*, v. 4, p. 96

Wollstonecraft does not give a source for this, but it is a version of the story from Valerius Maximus' *Memorable Acts and Sayings of the Ancient Romans*, more famously explored by Madame de Staël in *Corinne* and Byron in Canto 4 of *Childe Harold's Pilgrimage*.[39] Caravaggio shows this subversive breastfeeding as one of the *Seven Works of Mercy*, while Rubens, Zoffany and Jean-Baptiste Greuze were also attracted by the subject. But what all of these depictions have in common is the shocking contrast between the smooth, round flesh of the young mother and the wizened face of her father. Wollstonecraft has replaced this difference with similarity, erasing masculinity for the fantasy of a bodily economy without men. This inverted filial relationship and the return of the maternal aliment to the mother seem like a psychological consummation, as if the good mother's final vindication is to produce a daughter whose mothering of her own mother knows no bounds, as if the last word on virtuously breastfeeding mothers and daughters is that the exchange of milk makes them interchangeable. This is cognate with fantasies of the return to the womb, in which the breastfeeding mother postpones or dissolves her separation from her daughter so effectively that she can become her daughter's daughter without ceasing to be her daughter's mother. In birth they are not divided. Also – and this is probably why it is disturbing to our era – it is a fantasy of a matrilineal replacement for sex, in which the mother and daughter achieve emotional fusion through the exchange of body fluids. The absence of any male relatives from this version of the story, the complete lack of interest in the mother's original crime and Wollstonecraft's decision to modify the story by having the pair redeemed and pensioned and the prison turned into a temple, attest to her intense investment in the vignette of the daughter breast-feeding her mother.

It is not surprising that Wollstonecraft differs from the obstetricians in presenting breastfeeding as a replacement for sexuality and sexual mothers as immature or depraved. However interesting this stance may be in the construction of gender, it is not likely to sell books to pregnant young women and their husbands. Buchan and his colleagues insist more straightforwardly that mothers who breast-feed will afford more satisfaction as wives than they would other-wise, although this is based on the assumption that their readership

39 For discussion of the Caritas Romana in Childe Harold, see Jane Stabler, 'Byron's World of Zest', in Morton (ed.), *Cultures of Taste*, p. 144.

regard childbearing and childcare as necessary, but not sufficient, to the good wife. The desirable wife of these books takes pleasure in providing her husband with plenty of strong sons and virtuous daughters. In addition to bringing up a child who, 'invigorated by his mother's milk, would, like the young Hercules, have force sufficient to strangle in his cradle any serpents that might assail him', this woman,

> thus also ensures the fulfilment of the promises made by the best writers on this subject – speedy recovery from childbed, the firm establishment of good health, the exquisite sense of wedded joys, the capacity of bearing more children, the steady attachment of her husband, the esteem and respect of the public, the warm returns of affection and gratitude from the objects of her tender care, and, after all, the satisfaction to see her daughters follow her example, and recommend it to others.[40]

It seems startling that such basic physical pleasure and well-being is made to hang upon 'the promises made by the best writers on the subject', as if it is the obstetricians' authority that makes breastfeeding a good thing to do, an almost explicit acknowledgement that part of the virtue of breastfeeding lies in the fact of obedience to cultural expectation. Again, 'the best writers' mediate between the reader and her body, affirming her alienation and subjection in the moment of announcing her physical gratification. The reader's recovery and future health, ability to give and receive sexual pleasure and her fertility, not to mention her public persona and her relationship with her children, are all presented as being in the gift of the experts and the authorities. Although eighteenth-century writers go to greater lengths than modern ones to avoid referring to babies as 'he', it is interesting that this is abandoned in the context of breastfeeding. Buchan's breastfed serpent-wrestler is male, and Alexander Hamilton warns that the previously ungendered child of a woman 'involved in the dissipations of high life' and 'confined to a crowded city' will find that 'the deficiencies of his mother's breast must be supplied by unnatural and hurtful food'.[41] Sons must be breastfed to guarantee their physical robustness, while daughters should merely be encouraged to breastfeed their own sons. The cautionary tales of children who die at the hands of wet-nurses or while being artificially fed all involve doting couples losing only or oldest sons, and it seems likely that, then as now, more boys were maternally breastfed

40 Buchan, *Advice*, p. 211.
41 Hamilton, *Female Complaints*, p. 409.

than girls. Mary Wollstonecraft's mother breastfed only the oldest son, which Wollstonecraft resented in later life, and in this context her insistence on the importance of breastfeeding girls at all may be seen as radical.

As the quotations from Buchan and Hamilton suggest, women who did not breastfeed were accused of sins that are recognisably those of the aristocracy in the plethora of conduct literature aimed at young girls of the middling ranks. These are essentially failures in domesticity and self-restraint, coupled with an excessive sense of women's aesthetic rather than functional importance. Only prostitutes and aristocrats are happy to be valued for their bodies, as for the self defined middling sort, 'It is a woman's participation in public spectacle that injures her, for as an object of display, she always loses value as a subject.'[42] The generic aristocrats of late eighteenth-century conduct manuals are dissipated and amoral women who devote themselves to appearing desirable and maximising their own base and physical pleasures, showing – or rather, seeking to hide – the passionate pursuit of money, sex and food. Since the first two, at least in the world of fiction and conduct literature, are controlled by men, and most (unworthy) men are assumed to be unable to choose a truly virtuous woman over a conventionally attractive one, then the caricature aristocrat must maximise her physical attractions in the acknowledged hope of maximising her personal power. These texts present aristocratic marriages as legal prostitution, some of the more daring even hinting at the alleged elite convention whereby a woman who has produced two legitimate sons may commit adultery with impunity, while showing the middle-class readership that their own marriages, founded on feelings and upheld by virtuous conduct, are far above such sordid negotiations. To quote Gary Kelly's useful definition of late eighteenth-century feminine virtue,

> 'Virtue' stood for professionalized affectivity, or 'sensibility' disciplined into a moral self capable of deferring immediate gratification for future benefits, declining material gratification for moral and intellectual benefits, and thus acting ethically according to 'truth' and 'justice' – code words for professional middle class ways of creating knowledge and evaluating individuals and their actions free from 'custom', 'tradition', or codes of value controlled by the upper classes or controlling the common people.[43]

42 Nancy Armstrong, *Desire and Domestic Fiction: A Political History of the Novel* (Oxford: Oxford University Press, 1987) p. 77.
43 Gary Kelly, *Women, Writing and Revolution, 1790–1827* (Oxford: Oxford University Press, 1993).

The contemporary construction of breastfeeding presents it as part of this class-specific as well as gendered definition of 'virtue', and it is interesting that several of the aristocratic women discussed by Judith Schneid Lewis who breastfed left London in order to live a more domestic and perhaps less markedly elite life in the country for a few months. Vanity is a vice of the aristocracy, and it destroys the physical as well as moral capacity for maternity. All the child-care manuals, including Wollstonecraft's, assume that women who choose not to breastfeed do so partly because they are unwilling always to be physically available to their children, but also because they both fear the damage breastfeeding may do to their appearance and find that their concern for their appearance makes them unable to breastfeed by damaging their breasts with tight corsets. This pref-erence for functioning as an 'object of display' (which could also be seen as defining oneself outside the arts of domesticity) rather than as a maternal subject attracts the obstetricians' wrath at least as much as the refusal to breastfeed in itself. William Cadogan, who is anxious about women's eating during pregnancy and while breast-feeding, couples this with another ideologically loaded accusation:

> The plain natural Plan I have laid down, is never followed; because most Mothers, of any Condition, either cannot, or will not undertake the troublesome Task of Suckling their own Children; which is troublesome only for want of a proper Method; were it rightly managed, there would be much Pleasure in it, to every Woman that can prevail upon herself to give up a little of the Beauty of her Breast to feed her Offspring; tho' this is a mistaken Notion, for the Breasts are not spoiled by giving suck but by growing fat.[44]

Cadogan's readers are demeaned at every turn here. They – we – will not follow a 'plain natural Plan' (so simple even a mother can under-stand it) because they cannot be bothered to breastfeed at all, but they imagine it would be a bother only because they will not follow the plan. If they would only 'prevail upon' themselves (a clear indi-cation that moral fibre and self-discipline are required) to sacrifice a little physical appeal, they might even find pleasure – an odd word in this context – but they are mistaken in believing that this effort of will, of which they are anyway incapable, is required, since it is self-indulgence and not breastfeeding that 'spoils' 'the Breasts'. Since Cadogan is also of the view that if a new mother does not intend to breastfeed her baby herself, 'The antient Custom of exposing them

44 Cadogan, *Essay Upon Nursing*, p. 28.

to wild Beasts, or drowning them, would certainly be a much quicker and more humane way of dispatching them', he presents women who do not breastfeed as irredeemably selfish and oblivious to their children's welfare in their own quest for beauty. Alexander Hamilton shares Cadogan's concern that women are unable to control their appetites and vanity, arguing that the phenomenon of pregnancy cravings is invented by pregnant women and the midwives who have traditionally cared for them as part of a female conspiracy to legitimise women's innate gluttony and manipulate husbands into providing expensive delicacies to which women would not usually have access. He advises that, 'Women often claim indulgence in their longings, by an argument which is well calculated to ensure success, the dangers which might happen to the child from their cravings being neglected.'[45] There had been a tradition in midwifery that a woman's cravings in pregnancy were actually those of the child, which might need unusual foods to develop properly (which is close to the modern explanation that they result from minor dietary deficiencies which become important during pregnancy), but this is an instance where Hamilton and his colleagues are keen to have something that had been thought 'natural' accepted as a cultural construction with implications for gender. Genteel maternity is no place for a woman's appetites, and virtue is a matter of disciplining the body for its own good. We have already seen how a woman 'involved in the dissipations of high life' 'cannot be supposed capable of furnishing milk in due quantity, or of a proper quality'. This is because, 'The luxuries which refinement has produced in the manner of living, although they do not prevent every woman from being a Mother, certainly render many very unfit for the office of Nurse.[46] The solution is moral reform:

> When, therefore, ladies of this description wish to suckle their own infants, they ought to retire to the country, where, remote from the impure air of crowded cities, and removed from the allurements of fashionable amusements, they should endeavour, by the most scrupulous attention to regularity in diet, and hours of rest, and to moderate exercise in the open air, to repair their constitutions, and to fulfil the duties which they owe to their offspring.[47]

---

45 Hamilton, *Female Complaints*, p. 190.
46 Hamilton, *Female Complaints*, p. 409.
47 Hamilton, *Female Complaints*, p. 410.

The vices of 'luxury', 'refinement' and 'the allurements of fashion-able amusements', as well as the implicitly irregular diet and rest and excessive or inadequate exercise are those of the urban elite which literary heroines from Pamela to Gwendolen Harcourt must learn to negotiate. The move from the city to the country reverses the harlot's progress which typifies eighteenth-century novels about women from *Fanny Hill* to *Evelina*, a moral journey which is echoed in the transition from 'impure air' to the fulfilment of duty. Whereas 'when … ladies of this description wish … ' seems to make far more allowance than middle-class women are granted for the possibility that many ladies will not choose to breastfeed, the closing invitation to 'repair their constitutions' and 'fulfil the duties which they owe their offspring' suggests that aristocratic women may be viewed as less likely to breastfeed but are not therefore exempt from the moral imperative to do so.

Wollstonecraft herself is clear that universal morality is defined by middle-class ideologies of gender, and that pretensions to or affectations of aristocratic licence destroy any claim to maternity. The draft fragments of *Letters on the Management of Infants* found after her death open by identifying the target readership: 'My advice will probably be found most useful to mothers in the middle class; and it is from them that the lower imperceptibly gains improvement. Custom, produced by reason in one, may safely be the effect of imitation in the other.'[48] In the opening pages of *Mary*, the hero-ine's mother Eliza, described as having been 'educated with the expectation of a large fortune, of course became a mere machine'. 'As she was sometimes obliged to be alone, or only with her French waiting-maid' she would send 'to the metropolis' for 'those most delightful substitutes for bodily dissipation, novels'. She has 'two most beautiful dogs', of which she is extremely fond, but her fond-ness 'proceeded from vanity' and 'gave her an opportunity of lisping out the prettiest French expressions of ecstatic fondness, in accents that had never been attuned by tenderness'. Needless to say, Eliza is not a good mother, and in fact dies a well-deserved death from lazi-ness in childbirth and her refusal to breastfeed:

> In due time she brought forth a son, a feeble babe; and the following year a daughter. After the mother's throes she felt very few sentiments of maternal tenderness; the children were given to nurses, and she played with her dogs. Want of exercise prevented the least chance of her recovering

48 Wollstonecraft, *Works*, vol. 4, p. 459.

strength; and two or three milk fevers brought on a consumption, to which her constitution tended. Her children all died in their infancy, except the two first, and she began to grow fond of the son, as he was remarkably handsome. For years she divided her time between the sofa, and the card-table. She thought not of death, though on the borders of the grave; nor did any of the duties of her station occur to her as necessary.[49]

This laconic summary of the effects of refusing post-natal exercise is almost funny in its brevity, but the point that self-indulgence in childbirth both causes and symbolises irredeemable frivolity of mind and dysfunctional wasting of the body is serious. There is no space here to separate behaviour during and after labour from life-long, and potentially fatal, moral tendencies. We know that Eliza is a bad woman and must die because she 'fails' in childbirth and breast-feeding, and she fails in childbirth and breastfeeding because she is a bad woman. In this version of maternity, the middle-class require-ment for a woman to be morally as well as biologically productive, to generate feelings and behaviour as well as bodies and beauty, would be salvific.

The final connection between failures in maternity and attitudes to the body presented as aristocratic, is the corset. Here again, it is important to emphasise that there is no particular evidence that waists diminished as social status rose, but rather that tight lacing is presented as a feminine vice in the same bundle as staying up too late dancing to the detriment of domestic and charitable projects during the day, conspicuous consumption, disregard for debt, sexual incontinence and a disorderly relationship with food, a stereotype that will be further investigated in relation to Susan Ferrier. Books on women's health and conduct commonly assume that such quali-ties are regarded with aspiration by foolish middle-class adolescents, often misguided by too much novel reading, and in this scheme corseting generates as much anxiety as debt and rather more than eating disorders. Wollstonecraft, interestingly, having dismissed the whole business of personal adornment as the gilding on the cage of the female body and the opiate of women, gives little attention to corsets outside her writing for children. It seems likely that she regarded the whole issue as beneath contempt, but she also wrote

---

49 Mary Wollstonecraft, *Mary* and *Maria* / Mary Shelley, *Matilda*, ed. Janet Todd (London: Penguin, 1991) p. 7.

most during the years in which British women were least likely to wear corsets, and least likely to lace them tightly, for several centuries. Nevertheless, the fluid meanings of the corset are well illustrated by the suggestion that Wollstonecraft continued to wear 'stays' while heavily pregnant in revolutionary France, presumably as a gesture of scorn for high fashion.[50] As Barbara Charlesworth Gelphi points out, there was a fashion in the early 1790s for a 'six month pad', a stuffed pad tied round the waist to simulate pregnancy, and 'fashions through the 1790s showed a high degree of consideration for the health and comfort of pregnant women'.[51] The flowing, high-waisted, low-necked gowns of the 1790s and early 1800s all look like maternity dresses to the modern eye, and, as the much reproduced Gillray print of 'The Fashionable Mama' demonstrates, they were well adapted for breastfeeding. Anyone might be pregnant and everyone has that air, so much so that many of the women in contemporary fashion plates look pregnant whether they are or not,[52] but one might question whether this fetishisation of pregnancy constitutes an ideological improvement on corsetry or not. After all, a woman's lung capacity is rather more impaired in late pregnancy than when wearing even a tightly laced corset, and the digestive tract and vital organs are similarly compressed. The assumption that maternity is so crucial to, and such an attractive part of, a woman's identity that both those who have delivered their children and those who have never been pregnant must assume the guise of a woman whose child is still part of her, but publicly so, is the *reductio ad absurdam* of the *fin de siècle* conflation of femininity and maternity. Heavily pregnant women in the twenty-first century tend to experience their strange double identity and liminal public presence as problematic, but a society in which all women are required at least to suggest such a state of being may be even more troubling. The denial of reproductive function implicit in the tiny waist and flat stomach may be liberating as well as oppressive. As Valerie Steele writes in *The Corset: A Cultural History*:

> Corsetry was not one monolithic, unchanging experience that all unfortunate women experienced before being liberated by feminism. It was a situated practice that meant different things to different people at different

50 See Janet Todd, *Mary Wollstonecraft: A Revolutionary Life* (London: Weidenfeld and Nicolson, 2000) p. 255.
51 Gelphi, *Shelley's Goddess*, p. 46.
52 See Aileen Ribeiro, *The Art of Dress: Fashion in England and France 1750–1820* (Newhaven: Yale University Press, 1995).

times. Some women did experience the corset as an assault on the body. But the corset also had many positive associations – of social status, self-discipline, artistry, respectability, beauty, youth and erotic allure.[53]

Nevertheless, Buchan and others describe the habit of tight-lacing before marriage as a vain attempt to ensnare a man who will only be disappointed when the wedding night reveals the true state of affairs, which also jeopardises a young woman's reproductive capacity. The 1803 edition of his *Advice* claims, remarkably, that corsets are responsible for 'a defect very prevalent among young women of the present day in London', 'the want of nipples'.[54] (Note the emphasis on this lack as a characteristic of urban life.) Alexander Hamilton announces that, 'Tight lacing, besides impeding the ascent of the womb, and hence inducing abortion, by compressing the breasts, often renders women unable to suckle their children.'[55] In this sense tight lacing appears as the opposite of breastfeeding, demonstrating duplicity, cupidity and the separation of female form and function.[56] The idea that tight lacing caused nipple damage as well as miscarriages, stillbirths and congenital abnormalities is repeated in Valerie Fildes' history of infant feeding and in Leigh Summers' *Bound to Please*, but the virulence of some of the anti-corset rhetoric, particularly in a context when all writers agree that most of their readers were not wearing corsets because it had ceased to be fashionable to do so, flags a strong ideological current.[57] Buchan, admittedly writing about swaddling, backboards and corsets for young children as well as adult women's 'stays', says that, 'tight and oppressive clothing … has really inflicted deeper wounds on population, than famine, pestilence and the sword'.[58] Such overkill suggests that something other than fashions in women's underwear is at stake here, and some interesting modern research on corsets bears this out. Valerie Steele's measurements of surviving eighteenth-century corsets indicated a minimum external measurement of 24 to 25 inches, exactly the smallest dress size normally stocked by

53 Valerie Steele, *The Corset: A Cultural History* (Newhaven: Yale University Press, 2001), p. 1.
54 Buchan, *Advice*, p. 19.
55 Hamilton, *Female Complaints*, p. 237.
56 Modern women are told not to wear underwired bras in pregnancy for similar reasons, although there is no medical evidence for this requirement. The prohibition of underwear associated with adult sexuality offers an interesting parallel to the ban on corsets.
57 Leigh Summers, *Bound to Please: A History of the Victorian Corset* (Oxford: Berg, 2001).
58 Buchan, *Advice*, p. 144.

modern British women's clothes shops, and she points out that they were rarely laced closed and were often open several inches at the back.[59] Steele also suggests that only a few of the youngest women of the urban elite actually abandoned stays altogether during the 1790s and early 1800s – a view shared by Aileen Ribeiro – and that almost all British women wore some kind of corset-shaped foundation garment from the seventeenth century until weight restriction and exercise replaced external shaping in the mid-twentieth century. In this reading, corsets or stays seem to have occupied roughly the same position in women's lives as the modern bra – a garment that nearly all women put on daily without thought, in the belief that it supports their bodies for their own greater comfort and 'decency'. Some women, mostly in the later nineteenth century, almost certainly did fasten their corsets so tightly that their bodies looked 'unnatural' to contemporaries used to the corseted silhouette and they probably made themselves uncomfortable (as well as possibly titillated) in the process, but it was a minority interest generally regarded at the time as a perverse fetish. There is no evidence for widespread self-destructive 'tight lacing' in the eighteenth century. It becomes clear that Buchan, Cadogan and Hamilton are at least as anxious about women's taking charge of their own sexuality as they are about reproductive health, and that the sexual assertiveness encoded in women's re-shaping their bodies is absolutely inimical to the definitive maternity encoded by breastfeeding. For the best-selling celebrity obstetricians of her era, as for Wollstonecraft herself, breastfeeding is a celebration of female function over form, which – like most constructions of gender – has at least as much potential for oppression as for liberation.

Preparing the dainties: eating women in Wollstonecraft

A moderate quantity of proper food recruits our exhausted spirits, and invigorates the animal function; but, if we exceed moderation, the mind will be oppressed, and soon become the slave of the body, or both grow listless and inactive. Employed various ways, families meet at meals, and there giving up to each other, learn in the most easy, pleasant way to govern their appetites. Pigs, you see, devour what they can get; but men, if they have any affections, love their fellow creatures, and wish for a return; nor will they, for the sake of a brutish gratification, lose the esteem of those

---

59 Steele, *The Corset*, p. 101.

they value. Besides, no one can be reckoned virtuous who has not learned to bear poverty: yet those who think much of gratifying their appetites, will at last act meanly in order to indulge them.[60]

While breastfeeding in Wollstonecraft's work is a sacramental act for both mother and child, feeding children is much more problematic. Unloved children, like Jemima in *Maria* are 'fed with the refuse of the table' while the over-indulged are 'pampered with cakes and fruit'.[61] Those who are properly and moderately loved and respected must be taught to manage naturally uncontrollable appetites, although girls must not be allowed to aspire to weakness and debility. There are several instances of adults who have never been taught gustatory self-discipline whose appetites bring them to moral and financial ruin, and there is a clear moral hierarchy of foods in which, in contrast to Wollstonecraft's critic Amelia Opie, fruit, sweets and cakes are signs of depravity and plainly cooked meat is a 'rational' thing to eat. Food should ideally be taken like medicine, with reference only to physical need and maximum health, although at the same time Wollstonecraft recognises and asserts its enormous symbolic and social value. An individual's interest in or 'weakness for' food is an exact index of his or her capacity for or vulnerability to sexual passion, and foolish women are described as literal prey to sexually hungry men. Too much food is stupefying and makes people bestial and incapable of intellectual activity (this is well illustrated by her frustration with long meals in Sweden), while not enough food, whether as a result of affectation or poverty, makes people too weak to function intellectually or politically.[62] Wollstonecraft struggles to divest food of any significance beyond the physiological while simultaneously using it as the definitive image of power over oneself and others.

This is most obvious in her deployment of men's appetites. Arguing for women's education in the *Vindication*, she writes,

> Women having then necessarily some duty to fulfil, more noble than to adorn their persons, would not contentedly be the slaves of casual lust; which is now the situation of a very considerable number who are, literally speaking, standing dishes to which every glutton may have access.[63]

60 Wollstonecraft, *Original Stories*, in *Complete Works*, vol. 4, p. 400.
61 Wollstonecraft, *Maria*, p. 81.
62 Mary Wollstonecraft, *A Short Residence in Sweden, Norway and Denmark*, ed. Richard Holmes, (London: Penguin, 1987).
63 Wollstonecraft, *Vindication*, p. 208.

'Standing dishes' are those that remain on the table and are available throughout a meal in addition to the regulated courses which come and go in a prescribed order, so this is an image of women who are both superfluous to normal requirements and arrested in sexual availability. The complete collapse of appetite for food and 'casual lust' is invariably gendered in Wollstonecraft's writing. Women's hunger is a dangerously accurate index of their sexuality, but men's voracity does not distinguish between women's bodies and things to eat. This indiscriminate hunger also appears as a shorthand for depraved masculinity in *Mary*, where Eliza's pursuit of languor and debility drives her husband into the arms of the local peasant women:

> He hunted in the morning, and after eating an immoderate dinner, generally fell asleep: this reasonable rest enabled him to digest the cumbrous load; he would then visit some of his pretty tenants; and when he compared their ruddy glow of health with his wife's countenance, which even rouge could not enliven, it is not necessary to say which a gourmand would give the preference to. Their vulgar dance of spirits were infinitely more agreeable to his fancy than her sickly, die-away languor. Her voice was but the shadow of a sound, and she had, to complete her delicacy, so relaxed her nerves, that she became a mere nothing.[64]

Eliza and the nameless husband, who becomes 'Mary's father' after Eliza's death, seem to deserve each other in Wollstonecraft's moral economy. His gluttony, which, as Burney shows, is a highly fashionable masculine vice, complements her equally fashionable assumed sickliness. He lives to serve his body with excesses of food, sleep and sex while she embarks on a deliberate path to mere nothingness. Pretentious self-deprivation and unselfconscious greed are mirror images, and both vices arise from a pernicious misapprehension of the body's importance. Eliza devotes her energies to offering herself on a plate while her husband only wants live prey, and it is no surprise when Mary's father dies of a fall from his horse while his 'blood was inflamed' by food and alcohol. Those who live by food, die by food. He exists only in relation to sensuality and a life lived in merely physical terms comes to its logical conclusion.

The gendering of gluttony as masculine makes women's appetites transgressive in a way that debility, which Wollstonecraft presents as merely stupid and ignorant, is not. This reinstitution of the sexual double standard at the table is particularly interesting in a writer who (sometimes) strives to reject it in bed. Her critique of the cultural institution of female fragility in no way mitigates her sense of individual women's culpability, but the sin of female gluttony is greater because there is no social trend to detract from the female eater's full knowledge and full consent. Foolish girls reading too many novels without the supervision of an enlightened and devoted mother might readily come to believe that anorexia (literally, lack of appetite) is attractive to men and, being uneducated and therefore unable to distinguish between discursive trends and best practice, might embark on self-attenuation as a result. Women who over-eat must do so because their commitment to their own physical pleasure is so great as to override all taboos and deny their very femininity:

> Men are certainly more under the influence of their appetites than women; and their appetites are more depraved by unbridled indulgence and the fastidious contrivances of satiety. Luxury has introduced a refinement in eating, that destroys the constitution; and, a degree of gluttony which is so beastly, that a perception of seemliness of behaviour must be worn out before one being could eat immoderately in the presence of another, and afterwards complain of the oppression that his intemperance naturally produced. Some women, particularly French women, have also lost a sense of decency in this respect; for they will talk very calmly of an indigestion. It were to be wished that idleness was not allowed to generate, on the rank soil of wealth, those swarms of summer insects that feed on putrefaction, we should not then be disgusted by the sight of such brutal excesses.[65]

If it were not already obvious, the image of wealthy women's eating as 'summer insects' feeding 'on putrefaction' to 'our' disgust would demonstrate a disproportionate interest in eating and its relation to gender. Wollstonecraft's strength of feeling here brings her into unholy communion with John Gregory, whose *Father's Legacy to His Daughters* remarks with a shudder,

> There is a species of refinement in luxury, just beginning to prevail among the gentlemen of this country, to which our ladies are as yet as great a strangers as any women upon earth; I hope, for the honour of the sex, they may ever continue so: I mean the luxury of eating. It is a despicable selfish vice in men, but in your sex it is beyond expression indelicate and disgusting.[66]

As we have seen, Wollstonecraft is an astute critic of Gregory in

---

65 Wollstonecraft, *Vindication*, p. 207.
66 John Gregory, *A Father's Legacy to his Daughters* (John Murray: London, 1801), p. 28.

particular and the genre of women's conduct literature in general. The combination of an awareness that gender is socially constructed with an unreconstructed revulsion at women's consumption makes for awkward reading, for it is hard to attribute Wollstonecraft's over-whelming dismay. The suspicion and dislike of the female body that runs through the *Vindication* can often be read as a potentially liberating drive towards androgyny, albeit one that subsequent feminisms have come to distrust in turn. Her longing for women to practice 'cleanliness, neatness and personal reserve' can readily be seen as a desire to distance the feminist body from the mess of reproductive biology and the feminist mind from the opiate of gossip, but in that case Wollstonecraft's insistence that gluttony is intrinsically masculine ought to make it a more, rather than less, bearable failing in women, especially since she is also sometimes ready to defy the double standard and defend women's sexual appetites. Instead, over-eating, partly because it is an entirely solitary vice unmitigated by any kind of coercion, figures as less redeemable than pre-marital sex and illegitimate pregnancy.

One of the most extreme examples of this is the servant in *Elements of Morality*, who loses her place because of her failure to control her eating disorder. This is discovered when the virtuous mother Mrs Jones asks Betty to serve preserved cherries in honour of a particular friend of Mr Jones. Betty first ignores the request and then pretends that there are no cherries, but Mrs Jones is too careful a housekeeper to forget the exact level of her stores and 'at last Betty owned she had eaten them'. Mrs Jones asks her, 'how could you be so inconsiderate and greedy, when you want for nothing?' Betty cries and explains,

> I have been a glutton from my infancy. Whenever I went to my mother's closet I took an apple or a pear, though she had just given me one, and if she sent me to buy any sweet things, I tasted them before I brought them to her. I became by degrees such a glutton, and so fond of nice things, that I used to eat them all up from my brothers and sisters, who never let me partake of their feasts, because I eat my own cakes alone. This habit has so grown upon me, that when I see any thing nice I cannot help eating it in a corner, and eat till I am sick – I eat so many of those cherries, that nurse thought I should have died with a pain in my stomach; she made me take two or three basons full of camomile tea, and I have hated the sight of preserved cherries ever since. – Pray forgive me, dear mistress, whilst I live I will never do it again![67]

---

67 Wollstonecraft, *Elements of Morality*, p. 87.

Mrs Jones, who is, it should be emphasised, the model of maternal and domestic virtue who otherwise forgives everyone everything, refuses on this occasion because, 'you have owned that, though it makes you sick, you cannot conquer this mean, selfish habit'. Betty continues to weep and begs again for pardon and help, but it is clearly even less a part of virtuous femininity to countenance overeating than premarital sex (which is forgiven elsewhere in the book). Mrs Jones tells her, 'Nay, the pimples on your face expose your gluttony; we should seldom look ugly, or be obliged to take nasty medicines, if we did not greedily overload our stomachs.' The little girl Mary is left to determine, as the family come to the table, 'not to eat more than her share of the plumb-pye, lest she should acquire a habit that would expose her to shame and ridicule, besides making her sick and ugly'.[68] Unusually, here gluttony appears as something recognisably like an illness, something that has taken over the woman's body without her volition and that causes her physical discomfort, but it is still treated as a moral rather than a physical disorder. Particularly in Mary's reflection, Wollstonecraft suggests that everyone's appetite could easily grow to 'gluttony', to disorder and excess, if it is not carefully guarded, and that 'nice things' are particularly dangerous to morality and threaten the mind's control of the body. In this account, eating is to gluttony as recreational drug use is to addiction, except that there is no alternative to eating and any attempt to eat less than a 'rational' quantity is also sinful. The requirements to eat enough and not to eat too much are similarly inexorable and at the same time as problematising appetite, she presents 'prudent' and 'reasonable' consumption as self-evident. The limits of Mary's 'share' of pie are obvious to Mary as the line between debility and excess is obvious to the other Mary, Eliza's daughter, so that Wollstonecraft simultaneously presents food as a powerful and dangerous substance and as mere fuel for physiological functions. In fact, of course, it is almost always both, but there are ideological incompatibilities in announcing that moral laxity leads to eating disorders and that food is without moral value to the virtuous.

Wollstonecraft's hierarchy of foods places anything sweet and particularly cake on a level with alcohol as substances that, having no place in a 'simple' or 'temperate' diet, can be consumed only for social or self-indulgent reasons. It is difficult to separate this explicitly moral objection to sugar from the modern view that it serves

68 Wollstonecraft, *Elements of Morality*, p. 88.

no nutritional purpose, adversely affects blood sugar levels and destroys teeth, and indeed from the shared concerns of the late eighteenth and early twenty-first centuries with sugar and fair trade, but it is important that Wollstonecraft articulates none of this. Just as women are to breastfeed for the sake of their own moral status rather than because their milk is thought especially conducive to good health in their babies, so women and children are to avoid sweets and cake because they are innately corrupting substances rather than because they are unhealthy or have adverse effects on others. In Wollstonecraft's account, only men drink alcohol and only children and women (usually wilfully) arrested in childhood eat sweets; this is a dilemma which the mature, maternal woman has solved, although whether this is a result of complete abstinence or entirely internalised 'moderation' is not specified. As in Betty's case, the consumption of cake and fruit outside authorised and parentally regulated situations is often attended by disproportionate disaster. Children eating cake on the sly do not just get stomach ache or find that they cannot eat their next meal. They are assailed by terrible pains while their parents, who might call the doctor, are away, or their houses burn down. In *The Young Grandison*, Emilia writes to her mother about her friends the Miss Wilsons, who used to 'treat with such disdain the neighbouring farmers' daughters, because they were their inferiors in birth and fortune':

> They had in the evening, without its being observed, lighted a fire in their play-room; and spread the coals on the hearth to bake privately some cakes. The fire must certainly have caught the boards; but they did not perceive it; as they were interrupted before the cakes were half baked, and obliged to go to their mother, who called for them. They swallowed hastily the unwholesome, and even unpalatable cakes, and shut the door without thinking any more about it. The flames did not burst out till the whole family had been some time fast asleep. There is not any thing saved. All the furniture, clothes and the stock of the farm were reduced to ashes. The poor girls escaped with only a single petticoat on; and Mrs Wilson was with difficulty rescued from the devouring flames, which consumed all her substance.[69]

Betty's binge on preserved cherries leads to her dismissal and disgrace and the Miss Wilsons' attempt at a little illicit baking results in the complete destruction of their parents' house and farm and the ruin of the family. The private eating is clearly somehow of a

---

69 Wollstonecraft, *Young Grandison*, in *Works*, vol. 2, p. 239.

part with the pride in wealth, perhaps because both demonstrate a hubristic conviction of one's own right to more than a fair share of resources. Certainly Mrs Wilson's 'substance' would support this merging of commercial and corporeal consumption, since it is not immediately clear that the 'substance' is the property on which her social standing is based rather than the more literal substance of her body. Eating, then, stands for the capitalist as well as sexual absorption of others' resources, and it is in this final, political reading of food in society that we may find Wollstonecraft at her most straightforward.

Her biographer Janet Todd writes of *Original Stories* that, 'the tie between higher and lower remains charity, and story after story which cries out for resolution in social reform is answered by personal benevolence'.[70] It could be argued that the requirement for the rich to moderate their consumption in order to leave more for the poor constitutes a gesture towards social reform, albeit one that falls short of the centralised redistribution of wealth. The virtuous Mrs Mason, who is in all but name indistinguishable from Mrs Jones of *Elements of Morality*, one afternoon gives her charges Caroline and Mary 'leave to amuse themselves'. 'A kind of listlessness' hung over them and, 'at a loss what to do, they seemed fatigued with doing nothing. They eat cakes though they had just dined, and did many foolish things merely because they were idle.'[71] Mrs Mason comes to their rescue with 'clothes, that a poor woman was in want of' to make and an improving story to read aloud, and then sends them to 'act, for once, like women' by taking the clothes to the woman and 'exercising their own judgement with respect to the immediate relief she stood in need of'. When the girls return, she makes quite sure that the moral is not lost:

> Observe now, said Mrs Mason, the advantages arising from employment; three hours ago you were uncomfortable, without being sensible of the cause, and knew not what to do with yourselves. Nay, you actually committed a sin; for you devoured cakes without feeling hunger, merely to kill time, whilst many poor people have not the means of satisfying their natural wants ... Recollect this in future when you are at a loss what to do with yourselves; and remember that idleness must always be intolerable, because it is only an irksome consciousness of existence.[72]

70 Janet Todd, *Revolutionary Life*, p. 128.
71 Wollstonecraft, *Original Stories*, in *Works*, vol. 4, p. 414.
72 Wollstonecraft, *Original Stories*, in *Works*, vol. 4, p. 414.

Again, idle wealth and the unregulated consumption of cake are ideologically similar. This is partly a well-founded political suspicion of luxury, but at the close of the eighteenth century it is only the broadest definition of luxury that could include cake. Even if the poorest had no access to ovens and could rarely afford sugar, the number of recipes in the least pretentious cookbooks suggests that most other people ate sweet things more or less as often as they wanted to. William and Dorothy Wordsworth in their poorest days at Dove Cottage had apple pie and gingerbread, so even if cake is the nursery equivalent of turtle, this is an engineered scarcity. It is not, in Wollstonecraft, engineered in the name of health or the campaign against slavery, but because eating for pleasure is both innately immoral and an insult to the hungry poor, and eating for gendered pleasure, transgressively or not, is depraved. The body must be tended because it houses the mind, but its voracity is dangerous and corrupting. Only in the act of breastfeeding, turning food to milk and feeding another with one's own body, can the body and the mind be reconciled. Wollstonecraft's daughters are weaned straight onto Eve's apple.

3

The bill of fare
The politics of food in Maria Edgeworth's children's fiction

I, however, appeal to those readers who are not gluttons, but epicures, in literature, whether they do not wish to see the bill of fare?

—Richard Lovell Edgeworth, Preface to *Popular Tales*.

Maria Edgeworth's interest in the politics of production and consumption is widely acknowledged, particularly in the context of her Anglo-Irish identity and colonial fictions. Catherine Gallagher notes in *Nobody's Story* that, 'This belief in the free market's ability to stimulate efficient production and hence promote the general good is fundamental to Edgeworth's works.'[1] Gallagher goes on to show how Edgeworth's fear of her own excessive literary productivity shapes her understanding of the literary marketplace and the relationship between profitability and moral value in women's writing. Julie Kipp offers a detailed analysis of wet-nursing and colonial discourses of production and consumption in *Ennui*, but it is noticeable that most of Edgeworth's writing for children seems distant from the Anglo-Irish identity politics which shape her better-known writing. As I will suggest later, part of the point may be that one size of moral child fits all. Her children's fiction, when it is read at all, is seen to inculcate the precepts of Malthus and Smith in the new generation, sometimes allowing the childless writer to 'metonymiz[e] the book (or, more precisely the pen) into the figurative breast'.[2] But, as recent

1 Catherine Gallagher, *Nobody's Story: The Vanishing Acts of Women Writers in the Market-place, 1670–1820* (Berkeley: University of California Press, 1994), p. 258.
2 Kipp, *Maternity and the Body Politic*, p. 121.

accounts of *Belinda* suggest, Edgeworth views the breast and indeed the rest of the maternal body with suspicion and ambivalence; what she offers in her writing for children is a self-consciously rational, unembodied bill of fare.

Edgeworth is unusual in writing about, and apparently for, people for whom hunger is more of a problem than appetite. Sandra Sherman's *Imagining Poverty* argues that 'the prehistory of the industrial novel is a congeries of texts that imagine the poor as one-dimensional consumers of food'.[3] This view is broadly convincing; one might think of the starving family in Austen's *Emma* or the shadowy figures of whom Mrs Norris speaks with such arrogance in *Mansfield Park*. As we have seen, Wollstonecraft's ideal of charity is to give the poor money so that they can buy food, and this is partic-ularly marked in her writing for children. Poor people in fiction are hungry where the rich have appetite, and this means, oddly, that the poor are justified in consuming, morally entitled to food, in a way that the rich are not. Entitlement, in this reading, is the oppo-site of possession; the hunger of the poor is not complicated. The cookbooks, essays on economics and sermons that form the basis of Sherman's book certainly confirm her view that across much late eighteenth-century print culture,

> The equation of repletion and happiness, reducing the poor to insensate eaters, subtends the attenuated happiness contrived by supporters of the status quo. Such happiness was the correlate of a cohort that eats to work, that lacks subjectivity except to hate hunger. 'Happiness' and 'hunger' were opposed coordinates of a rationale that denied the poor complex, indi-vidual realities, and hence denied the need for personally chosen foods.[4]

There are, of course, loci of resistance to this equation, although their existence probably confirms its general validity. In some ways Burney's *Cecilia* constitutes a critique of such a convention with its insistence that systemic responses to poverty encode greater virtue than the mere alleviation of hunger. Cecilia's response to a chance encounter with a starving family is to send for the bread-winner's widow and 'assure her that she was immediately ready to fulfil the engagement she had entered, of assisting her to undertake some better method of procuring a livelihood'.[5] One might contrast

3 Sandra Sherman, *Imagining Poverty: Quantification and the Decline of Paternalism* (Colum-bus: Ohio State University Press, 2001), p. 18.

4 Sherman, *Imagining Poverty*, p. 76.

5 Burney, *Cecilia*, p. 200.

this with Emma, whose 'charitable visit' may be characterised by 'personal attention and kindness' but whose solutions are limited to bread and broth. To the extent that Edgeworth's writing about food has been described at all, she has been seen as closer to Austen than Burney in this regard. Certainly the prevalence of food in her writing for children and the poor (a telltale category in itself) suggests an understanding of these conditions as dominated by the control and/ or gratification of hunger, but I would like here to explore the extent to which food encodes more sophisticated negotiations over need, entitlement and desert.

There are good reasons why food might be particularly important in writing for children. Children, at least in eighteenth-century fiction, have limited access to and control over money. For poor children this intensifies the importance of food because in some fictional understandings of poverty, food and money are interchangeable; money's only use to the poor is for food. Children may have access to food where they do not have access to money, and are therefore able to use food to demonstrate virtues (generosity, self-denial, love) and vices (greed, selfishness, insensitivity) where adults might use money. The other possibility is that poor children may decline the equation of food and money, choosing to go hungry in order to exchange the money for something else (medicine for a sick relative, charity, investment), thus demonstrating a subjectivity that can rise beyond poverty and think like the middling sort. Such thinking is invariably rewarded with social mobility, so that the basis of an escape from poverty is the ability to think – and eat – like a person who is not hungry. Because Edgeworth is so rare in writing about poor children in the first place, it is hard to find comparisons for her model of poverty, hunger and social worth.

There is a clear example of this in 'Lazy Lawrence' in *The Parent's Assistant*.[6] Jem's father is dead, and he and his mother are living in poverty, behind on the rent and dependent for food on Jem's exertions and the produce of their garden. Under pressure from the landlord, Jem's mother agrees to sell their horse, for which Jem has great affection. Jem determines to earn the money for the rent before the horse must be taken to market, and, having earned four shillings and sevenpence selling fossils and working as a gardener's boy, he encounters Lazy Lawrence, a boy from the same village. Lazy Lawrence asks Jem what he plans to do with his earnings, and

6 Maria Edgeworth, *The Parent's Assistant* (London: Macmillan, 1897).

continues, 'I know what I'd do with it if it was mine. First, I'd buy pocketfuls of gingerbread; then I'd buy ever so many apples and nuts. Don't you love nuts? I'd buy nuts enough to last me from this time to Christmas ... '[7] But Jem, whose industrious exertions and poverty mean that he is always hungry, has his mind on higher things. Rewarded for honesty and hard work by the patronage of 'a lady', he recovers his horse and is helped into profitable work while Lawrence, whose love of self-gratification has led him into bad company, ends in prison. As we shall see, animals occupy a complicated and contested place in children's fiction of this period, but the horse provides a convenient marriage of the object of affection and the means of production, allowing Jem and his mother to travel further to find work and to take their produce to more distant markets than would otherwise be possible. By saving the horse rather than buying food, Jem demonstrates industry, a capacity for deferred gratification, a measure of well-controlled sensibility (he is able to stop himself crying when it looks as if the horse must go after all) and a strong interest in investing in future profit. It is also important that he is not able to take the final step himself; when Lawrence steals the hard-earned two guineas, Jem requires, and is grateful for, the intervention of the lady to return to him the fruits of his own labour. The package of *petit-bourgeois* virtues is necessary but not sufficient for upward mobility. It must be, and invariably is, consummated by the reward of the gentry's patronage.

Food works in surprisingly similar ways for rich children, who may have access to more money but do not control it in the way that adults control money and children may control food. Late eighteenth-century children's literature is replete with scenes in which wealthy children choose between spending their pocket money on 'trifles' (which meant pleasing ephemeral objects before it came to mean a labour-intensive pudding), sweet snacks for themselves or wholesome fare for beggar children. Such scenes foreground food as the basis of a metonymic, child-size economy in which the disposable income of the rich figures as sweetmeats and cake while the poor long for bread in place of a living wage. Almost every writer for children in this period provides at least one example of this, as if money and sweets are equivalent for rich children as money and bread for the poor. Apart from in Edgeworth's most famous short story, 'The Purple Jar', there is rarely any sense that children's money

7 Edgeworth, *Parent's Assistant,* p. 36.

could be converted into anything other than (good) food for the poor or (morally but not physically) bad food for children. 'Arabella Argus' tells young readers of *The Juvenile Spectator* about Sophia Welmore, 'a girl who possesses some qualities rarely to be met with in those of her age':

> I have seen her parents present her with money, sometimes a guinea, at other times half that sum; and I have known her, uninfluenced by any advice whatever, devote it to the noblest purposes of humanity. She has, on a Saturday evening, sent a crown to a poor family, with whose troubles she made herself acquainted. She was accustomed to calculate what would purchase a loaf and a joint of meat ... Sophia Welmore, to my knowledge, never expends a penny in any eatable whatever for herself. She has been taught that the table prepared for her by order of her parents is to suffice. Thus, she has none of those Epicurean longings after good things which so frequently disgrace children.[8]

Food, here, figures as an economic unit, one cake being worth several loaves and joints of meat, but as Wollstonecraft's children's writing has already signalled, food can also speak for sexuality, another form of adult power and interaction from which children – or at least children's books – are debarred. In the context of Romantic-era children's fiction in general, Wollstonecraft's revulsion at girls' interest in food is not in the least idiosyncratic. Early in this work, Arabella Argus warns readers that 'it is so easy to acquire a taste for "nice things", as they are called' and that this taste 'is so capable of deforming the human character, that I know not how to mark my disapprobation of the fault, in language sufficiently strong'.[9] She is appalled by children 'so anxious to taste good things, that they descended to become thieves; in order to eat a spoonful of jelly, or pick a *corner* out of a cake'. Children expressing pleasure at the sight of a favourite dish 'betray themselves disgustingly'. She insists that there is no distinction between pleasure in food and uncontrollable gluttony, which is a debasement of the image of God in Man. The glutton is lost to humanity: 'an epicure is the most selfish of all animals'. Elsewhere, adults who give children treats deny the children's capacity for reason: 'Of all indulgencies, that of the palate is most disgraceful to reasonable creatures; and to make nice fruit, tarts or cakes, rewards to children who have performed their lessons well, is to level them with irrational animals.'[10] Dorothy Kilner in *The Life*

8 Bator and Cott (eds), *Masterworks*, vol. 4, p. 418.
9 Bator and Cott (eds), *Masterworks*, vol. 4, p. 371.
10 Bator and Cott (eds), *Masterworks*, vol. 4, p. 352.

and Perambulations of a Mouse takes an interest in food with similar gravity, as the mother tells her children about a childhood friend who was transported for stealing in early adulthood as a result of a devious and selfish nature evident in childhood:

> if at tea, or any other time, she got first to the plate of cake or bread, she would place the piece she liked best where she thought it would come to her turn to have it: or if at breakfast she saw her sisters' [sic] bason have the under crust in it, and they happened not to be by, or not to see her, she would take it out, and put her own, which she happened not to like so well, in the stead.[11]

Unsurprisingly, these writers make no direct reference to sex, but the fear that gluttony will make children unable to control and discipline their appetites and incapable of denying themselves physical gratification must connote sexuality as well as theft, which figures here as another form of out-of-control consumption.

Edgeworth is unique in this genre and period in denying that food has any innate moral content. It is, for her, much more like money than like sex, although the need to eat means that the body cannot be excluded from the children's economy. My interest here is in the relationship between poverty, childhood and food. If the poor are indeed defined by hunger, what possibilities does Edgeworth offer for subjectivity within or in resistance to this model? Does the education which may alleviate poverty teach a different relation to hunger?

To Kill a Pet Lamb: Labour Relations in *The Parent's Assistant*

The preface to *The Parent's Assistant* sends contradictory messages about the intended readership. It begins by referring to education as a 'science' requiring 'facts' about child development, a position which would seem to align the text with the professionalisation of domesticity in the print culture of the gentry and upper middling sort. Edgeworth goes on to map out what appears to be a conventionally conservative position:

> The question, whether society could exist without the distinction of ranks ... we leave to the politician and the legislator. At present it is necessary that the education of different ranks should, in some respects,

---

11 Bator and Cott (eds), *Masterworks*, vol. 4, p. 267.

be different. They have few ideas, few habits, in common; their peculiar vices and virtues do not arise from the same causes, and their ambition is to be directed to different objects. But justice, truth and humanity are to be confined to no particular rank, and should be enforced with equal care and energy on the minds of young people of every station; and it is hoped that these principles have never been forgotten in the following pages.[12]

The stories that follow begin with an account of indigent Irish orphans in a peasant community and end with the English rural poor, but along the way there is a son of the landed gentry living with a professional family and learning to control a love of ostentation that his own parents can readily afford to gratify, boys at a public school learning to resist peer pressure and a boy in service being rewarded for integrity by promotion. Unlike *Moral Tales* and *Popular Tales*, both of which situate most of the stories among the gentry and the middling sort, *The Parents' Assistant* is predominantly interested in the lives of the labouring poor with occasional excursions into professional life. Even if, as seems probable, most buyers and readers of the book expected and aspired to more than the stories can offer the peasant protagonists, the focus on the subjectivity and moral potential of poor children anticipates Dickens in its radical aspect. Food dominates these stories, and the invariable reward for virtue is to acquire a wealthy patron and be lifted from indigence to a precarious self-sufficiency, but nonetheless the heroes and heroines are children who self-consciously resist definition as 'machines who eat' and the villains are those who try to cage them in such a definition. There is no project of systematic social change here. Edgeworth accepts, and wants her wealthier readers to recognise, lives shaped by hunger and limited by the struggle to eat. But there is a requirement both that the reader identify with this plight and that the child in it insists on a moral identity which can and does challenge 'the distinction of ranks'.

'Simple Susan' is the most intricate and engaging example of this. This story begins 'in a retired hamlet on the borders of Wales' with the village children meeting 'at a hawthorn which stands in a little green nook, open on one side to a shady lane' to 'make up their nosegays for the morning and to choose their queen'. The pastoral is no sooner invoked than complicated, for across the 'thick sweetbrier and hawthorn hedge' is 'the garden of an attorney'; 'Such were

---

12 Edgeworth, *Parent's Assistant*, p. 2.

his litigious habits and his suspicious temper that he was constantly at variance with his simple and peaceable neighbours'.[13] Mr Case's abusive imposition of the letter of the law upon local custom has changed the landscape. 'The paths in his fields were at length unfrequented', and stiles and gates were blocked off to stop animals crossing his land. Mr Case has two children, 'to whose education he had not had time to attend, as his whole soul was intent upon accumulating for them a fortune'. Wishing to make them 'a little genteel' he has sent his son to school, hired a maid for Barbara and instructed her to avoid the village children. She is hiding in her garden and eavesdropping on the children praising the absent Susan for her kindness, modesty and hard work. The children choose Susan as their May Queen, but she cannot come out to play because her father has come home late and distressed, and her sick mother is too tired from baking bread to sell to make his supper. He 'could not be prevailed upon to eat any of the supper which had been prepared for him; however, with a faint smile, he told Susan that he thought he could eat one of her guinea-hen's eggs'. Susan thanks him, presumably for deigning to want something of hers, and goes out to find that the guinea-hen has strayed into the attorney's garden. Barbara catches it and demands a ransom, which Susan cannot pay. She pleads for one egg for her father, but Barbara replies, 'What's your father, or his supper, to us? Is he so nice that he can eat none but guinea-hen's eggs?'[14]

Back home, Susan's father explains that he had borrowed money from Mr Case to pay someone to join the militia as his substitute after he was conscripted. Mr Case took the lease of their cottage as security and found that it was invalid. He then called in the loan, obliging Susan's father to leave his family for the army, and refused to return the lease. The family face homelessness and indigence. The shock exacerbates Susan's mother's chronic illness, and Susan spends the following days caring for her mother. The village children give her their May Day money to redeem the guinea-fowl, but she saves it towards redeeming her father instead. The family who have recently inherited the local Abbey and all the surrounding land send out for bread, which Susan's mother is too weak to make. So Susan 'went to work with much prudent care, and when her bread the next morning came out of the oven, it was excellent'.[15] The ladies of

13 Edgeworth, *Parent's Assistant*, p. 79.
14 Edgeworth, *Parent's Assistant*, p. 84.
15 Edgeworth, *Parent's Assistant*, p. 94.

the Abbey, who are 'judiciously generous' and 'wish to diffuse happiness', send for Susan and arrange to visit her at home later in the day. Barbara hears of this and interrupts Susan, who is 'gathering some marigolds and some parsley for her mother's broth'. Barbara follows Susan into the house and watches her:

> Susan had now poured the broth into the basin, and as she strewed over it the bright orange marigolds, it looked very tempting. She tasted it, and added now a little salt, and now a little more, till she thought it was just to her mother's taste. 'Oh, I must taste it,' said Bab, taking up the basin greedily. 'Won't you take a spoon?' said Susan, trembling at the large mouthfuls which Barbara sucked up with a terrible noise. 'Take a spoonful, indeed!' exclaimed Barbara, setting down the basin in high anger ... And she flounced out of the house, repeating 'Take a spoon, pig, was what you meant to say.'[16]

The narrator steps in to explain that as a small child, Susan had shared a bowl of bread and milk with a pig and realised that, 'as she ate with a spoon and he with his large mouth ... he was likely to have more than his share; and in a simple tone of expostulation she said to him, 'Take a poon, pig.' The village children have since used this as a proverb 'whenever anyone claimed more than his share of anything good' and often to reprove Barbara for her 'unjust methods of division'.

I dwell in such detail on the guinea-hen and the broth because they work as a child's eye version of moral and political economy in this fable. For the grasping upstart lawyer's family and, in a different way, for the gentry at the Abbey, food is merely something to eat, but part of Susan's virtue seems to lie in a more complex understanding. Her guinea-hen is precious to her not because of its food value, or even its value as a producer of eggs, but because it is her 'favourite' and her 'pretty guinea-hen'. The care over the ingredients and seasoning of the broth demonstrates both expertise and love, and indeed the coming together of emotion and productivity which is a hallmark of Edgeworth's children's writing. Susan's sophisticated relation to food is central to Mr Case's final comeuppance which, inevitably, occurs when Sir Arthur Somers, the head of the new generation at the Abbey, hears of his iniquity and restores the traditional order. Food works as the currency of moral economy.

Sir Arthur Somers wants to make a new ride on his domain and finds that Mr Price's land blocks the route. Case tells him that because the Prices' lease is flawed, 'Price's whole land [is] at his

16 Edgeworth, *Parent's Assistant*, p. 98.

disposal.' Sir Arthur points out that to act on this would ruin the Price family, but agrees to inspect the lease. Case, who is hoping for a job as Sir Arthur's agent, decides to try to bribe him and remembers hearing the Abbey's housekeeper saying that 'Sir Arthur was remarkably fond of lamb, and that she wished she could get a quarter for him.'[17] Back home, Barbara says, 'I know of one … Susan Price has a pet lamb that's fat as fat can be.' Case finds Susan crying as she packs her father's case while her mother's illness worsens and asks what she would give to keep her father at home a week longer. Susan replies, 'Anything! – but I have nothing.'

> 'Yes, but you have a lamb,' said the hard-hearted attorney. 'My poor little lamb!' said Susan; 'but what can that do?' 'What good can any lamb do? Is not lamb good to eat? Why do you look so pale, girl? Are not sheep killed every day, and don't you eat mutton? Is your lamb better than anyone else's, think you?' 'I don't know,' said Susan, 'but I love it better.' 'More fool you,' said he. 'It feeds out of my hand, it follows me about; I have always taken care of it; my mother gave it to me.' 'Well, say no more about it, then,' he cynically observed; 'if you love your lamb better than both your father and your mother, keep it, and good morning to you.'[18]

At this, of course, Susan agrees to take her lamb to the butcher 'before nightfall'.

Against the background of Edgeworth's usual distrust of sensibility, there are several ways of reading this encounter. In some ways Case is obviously right; if Susan is content with meat-eating in general and the consumption of lamb in particular, there is no ideological reason why her emotional investment in the lamb should preclude its slaughter. In this case, Susan's capitulation may constitute a victory of sense over sensibility that contributes to her maturity and selflessness. She is distressed at the idea of her lamb's death and consumption, but she is able to override dismay with reason. Alternatively, particularly in the context of Edgeworth's dependence on enlightened self-interest as a guiding principle, perhaps it is Susan's staccato run of unconnected clauses that bears the truth here. 'It feeds out of my hand, it follows me about; I have always taken care of it; my mother gave it to me.' The lack of conjunctions in this sentence contrasts with Case's dispassioned reasoning. Susan has no counter-argument to this demonstration of the animal-loving carnivore's irrationality except, 'I love it better'. She cannot explain why the lamb should have taken on human behaviours in her mind.

17 Edgeworth, *Parent's Assistant*, p. 103.
18 Edgeworth, *Parent's Assistant*, p. 104.

She can only assert, haltingly, that it has. If this is an example of a little peasant who is more than a 'machine that eats', then it may be that the truth, here, lies in the semi-colons. It follows her about; she has always taken care of it; her mother gave it to her. This is not just meat.

This is a constant problem for children's writers who depend on kindness to and affection for animals as proof of children's benevolence and moral promise but decline to advocate anything so radical (and domestically inconvenient) as vegetarianism. Sarah Trimmer's *Fabulous Histories, or The Story of the Robins*, has a similar line to tread. As I suggested in the Introduction, any kind of animal suffering in this book meets with a horror and disbelief that is not so reliably offered to human distress. The frame narrative is provided by Mrs Benson, who is using the story to teach her children to live rightly and manage responsibly the resources they will inherit. It is wrong to hurt an animal, and children who do so grow into adults who hurt people and come to bad ends. Harriet and Frederick are told to imagine what animals, including wasps, might say to defend themselves against human aggression and to remember 'how excellently [animals] are informed and instructed by their great Creator, for the enjoyment of happiness in their different classes of existence, which happiness we have certainly no right wantonly to disturb'.[19] Nevertheless, we learn in Trimmer's final summing up, 'Some creatures have nothing to give us but their bodies; these have been expressly destined, by the supreme Creator, as food for mankind, and he has appointed an extraordinary increase of them for this very purpose; such an increase as would be very injurious to us if all were suffered to live.'[20] A queasy and unconvincing blend of Malthus and predestination.

Edgeworth may be resolving the same problem in a similar way, but the story's continuation suggests a more involved understanding of human, animal and dietary relations. The lamb's primary value is neither as sustenance, as Case suggests, nor because of any innate moral or emotional qualities, as Susan imagines. Like much of the food in this story, it carries a meaning beyond both nutrients and individual identity. It is the substance of the relationship between rich and poor, and indeed between adults and children.

After Case has left, Susan settles down to making out the bills for her bread; 'She was not, to be sure, particularly inclined to draw

19 Bator and Cott (eds), *Masterworks*, vol. 4, p. 330.
20 Bator and Cott (eds), *Masterworks*, vol. 4, p. 349.

out a long bill at this instant, but business must be done.' This sequence affirms Susan's consciousness of the need to put 'business' ahead of feeling and her constant awareness of the circular relationship between production and consumption. If the Prices are to eat, Susan must make bread for others, sell it and send out her bills. Then she must collect her little brothers from school, and when she gets home the Miss Somers have come to call. They take her to the draper's shop and tell her to 'choose herself a gown' because, 'you set an example of industry and good conduct, of which we wish to take public notice, for the benefit of others.' Susan is able to signal modestly that a new gown is not her first wish, and she is given the money, a guinea, instead. This in addition to the bread money and the children's May Day money makes her believe that, with the week's reprieve, she will be able to buy her father's freedom. Then she and her brothers have time to go to see the lamb. Case and the butcher are already there. The little boys beg for the lamb's life and then deck it with 'blue speedwell and yellow crows-foot'.[21] The village children follow the butcher and the lamb through the village and the butcher's son asks him to spare it. The butcher replies, 'I was thinking about it, boy, myself, […] it's a sin to kill a pet lamb, I'm thinking – any way, it's what I'm not used to and don't fancy doing.'[22] He bribes Case with 'a fine sweetbread' to accept another 'choice, tender lamb, fit to eat the next day' (Susan's lamb would require hanging).

Ignorant of her lamb's reprieve, Susan returns home, where her father tells everyone, 'by-and-by, she'll be worth her weight in gold.' He goes on, 'Tell us, child, how came you by all these riches? and how comes it that I don't go tomorrow? … speak on, child – first bringing us a bottle of the good mead you made last year from your own honey.'[23] Again, there is an emphasis on Susan's economic value, which seems to be conflated with her moral value. She is productive but also, it seems, potentially exchangeable, 'worth her weight in gold'. Susan is valuable because she is productive and productive because she is good. One effect of this goodness is to disclose the community's final priority of virtue over value (although they may, in most cases, be the same). It is the butcher, the man who is defined by his exchange and equivalence of money and animal life, who insists that Susan's lamb is outside ordinary trade

21 Edgeworth, *Parent's Assistant,* p. 117.
22 Edgeworth, *Parent's Assistant,* p. 117.
23 Edgeworth, *Parent's Assistant,* p. 119.

and this is explicitly because Susan, 'is a good girl, and always was, as well she may, being of a good breed and well reared from the first'. Particularly coming from the butcher, this reference to Susan's 'breed' and 'rearing' seems to conflate her with the animals who come to the slaughter. It is as if Susan herself, being a good girl, has an equivalency value. Susan is so much like the lamb that the lamb is like Susan, unsuitable for human consumption. She makes mead, bread, broth and cakes. She owns the means of production of honey, meat and eggs. But rather than make her powerful, all this productivity identifies her uncomfortably closely with the commodities she produces. It seems that part of the virtue of the good girl who produces is to invest herself so thoroughly in what she makes for others to consume that they are almost invited to partake of herself. Take, eat. This is my body, given for you.

In the end, of course, Case's machinations and Barbara's malice are exposed. Barbara invites a wealthy family to breakfast and then tries to snatch from Susan the honeycomb that Susan is removing from the hive for her mother's breakfast. Barbara is so badly stung by the bees that she has to cancel all social engagements and explain her behaviour to her father, who is beginning to fear Susan because she is in favour at the Abbey. Case's endeavours to have the Prices evicted fail when he accidentally sends in his own lease and Sir Arthur finds that it, too, is flawed. His malice, greed and lack of principle revealed, Case is evicted from the village and Sir Arthur asks Mr Price to work for him.

On the face of it, then, *Simple Susan* certainly offers the poor a subjectivity that is not defined by hunger. Susan is not a machine that eats. But her merit seems to depend almost entirely on her productivity, and its recognition depends entirely on the presence, interest and judgement of the Somers family. If there is escape from definition by hunger, there is no escape from definition by food. A social order in which virtue meets its just deserts relies on a bucolic idyll of benevolent aristocracy and dutiful peasants, in which there is no place for Attorney Case's pretensions of independence. The poor make food for the rich to eat and the rich give the poor money for food. Rich and poor feed on each other in a cycle of mutual alimentary dependence confined by the corporate and individual relation to food.

To some extent, it can of course be argued that food matters so much to the constitution of virtue and class in Edgeworth's fiction simply because food really does matter more than anything else, especially to the poor who may reasonably be haunted by the possibility of insufficiency. But even in *Simple Susan*, where the plot would lead us to expect destitution to be an issue, there is no reference to such fear, even in metaphor. The mother and children dread the loss of the husband and father, but the dread is expressed in exclusively affective terms. Love appears to obliterate the fear of hunger, and food here appears as the currency of virtue and affection rather than the condition of survival. The pure in heart are above hunger, and it is precisely this purity and its consequent lack of appetite that marks the potential for an individual to rise above the labouring poor.

This distinction between children who see food primarily as something to eat and those who recognise it as the currency of morality is marked elsewhere in *The Parent's Assistant*. In *The False Key*, the destitute orphan Franklin is given a month to compete with the cook's nephew Felix for a place as Mrs Churchill's domestic servant. He offends the other servants by refusing to lie to cover their clandestine absences and petty thefts and is soon forbidden to enter the butler's pantry where 'he [Franklin] could not avoid seeing Felix drinking a bumper of red liquor, which he could not help suspecting to be wine', as a result of which, 'he was involuntarily forced to suspect they were drinking his mistress's wine'. The alimentary distinction continues:

> Nor were the bumpers of port the only unlawful rewards which Felix received; his aunt, the cook, had occasion for his assistance, and she had many delicious douceurs in her gift. Many a handful of currants, many a half-custard, many a triangular remnant of pie, besides the choice of his own meal at breakfast, dinner and supper, fell to the share of the favourite Felix; whilst Franklin was neglected, though he took the utmost pains to please the cook in all honourable service, and, when she was hot, angry or hurried, he was always at hand to help her ... Yet when ... the hour of adversity had passed, the ungrateful cook would forget her benefactor, and, when it came to his supper time, would throw him, with a carelessness that touched him sensibly, anything which the other servants were too nice to eat. All this Franklin bore with fortitude, nor did he envy Felix the dainties which he ate, sometimes close beside him: 'For,' he said to himself, 'I have a clear conscience, and that is more than Felix can have.'[24]

The emphasis here is on Felix's greed and Franklin's emotions. Franklin has fortitude, honourable service and a clear conscience and knows that these are jewels beyond price compared to Felix's

24 Edgeworth, *Parent's Assistant*, p. 60.

currants, custard and pie. The contrast in their diets distresses Franklin because it demonstrates the cook's 'ingratitude' and 'carelessness' rather than because he would like to have more appetising meals. It is not precisely that one cannot eat one's cake and have a clear conscience; there is nothing intrinsically immoral about Felix's *douceurs*. But the backstairs economy which favours Felix is based on routine cheating and deception which poisons its fruits to the virtuous boy. The cook is angry with Felix because he reports having seen a missing joint of beef in a basket sent to her sister, and on the next page she is sacked when Mrs Churchill's lapdog pulls out of Felix's pocket half a turkey, which she has asked Felix in writing to take to her cousin. Meanwhile, Felix's readiness to lie about the butler's whereabouts when he was out drinking puts Corkscrew 'at liberty to indulge his favourite passion' until, '[h]is health was ruined. With a red, pimpled, bloated face, emaciated legs, and a swelled, diseased body, he appeared the victim of intoxication.'[25] At last, out of credit at the alehouse, Corkscrew meets 'a gang of housebreakers' who bribe him to give them the key to Mrs Churchill's house. The butler 'whose integrity ha[s] hitherto been proof against everything but his mistress's port' proves corruptible, demonstrating that 'a drunkard will sacrifice anything, everything, sooner than the pleasure of habitual intoxication'. Felix is persuaded to join him in exchange for some cravats. The narrator reflects: 'How much easier it is never to begin a bad custom than to break through it when once formed!'[26] By Franklin's intelligence, the plot is discovered. Corkscrew and Felix come to bad ends and Mrs Churchill settles an annuity on Franklin.

The plot and the moral of *The False Key* are predictable. Even on the humblest level, virtue will be perceived and rewarded and vice will be discovered and punished. Peer pressure and social expectation are no justification for dishonesty. The meek shall inherit the earth and the proud will be brought to dust. Drunkenness is a sin that ends in crime and punishment but is easily avoided. The emphasis on food is more interesting. The more food is understood as a symbol and the less its physical properties are regarded, the more likely the subject is to receive the aid and favour of the omniscient and omnipotent gentry. The way out of poverty is to regard food as a metaphor.

A final example from *The Parent's Assistant* confirms the compli-

25 Edgeworth, *Parent's Assistant*, p. 65.
26 Edgeworth, *Parent's Assistant*, p. 67.

cated relation between childhood, labour and food in these stories. *The Little Merchants* is set in Naples where 'the children are busied in various ways', selling fish, picking up chips of wood from carpenters and driftwood from the beach to sell to 'labourers, and the lower sort of citizens'.[27] Edgeworth informs us with apparent approval that, 'children of two or three years old, who can scarcely crawl along upon the ground, in company with boys of five or six, are employed in this petty trade'. There is also a closed children's economy at work: 'Others again endeavour to turn a few pence by buying a small matter of fruit, of pressed honey, cakes and comfits, and then, like little peddlers, offer and sell them to other children, always for no more profit than that they may have their share of them free of expense.'[28] With a typical elision of commerce and morality, Edgeworth explains how this benefits the children:

> The advantages of truth and honesty, and the value of a character for integrity, are very early felt amongst these little merchants in their daily intercourse with each other. The fair dealer is always sooner or later seen to prosper. The most cunning cheat is at last detected and disgraced.[29]

We are then introduced to Francisco, 'the son of an honest gardener' who 'in all his childish traffic … imitating his parents, was scrupulously honest' and Piedro, a fisherman's son, whose father has taught him 'that to make a good bargain was to deceive as to the value and price of whatever he wanted to dispose of; to get as much money as possible from customers by taking advantage of their ignorance or of their confidence.'[30] Piedro steals fruit from Francisco's father, but Piedro's father excuses him because, '*He is but a child* yet, and knows no better.' Edgeworth allows no concessions to childhood. Francisco's father replies, 'But if you don't teach him better now he is a child, how will he know when he is a man?'[31] In the wake of this conversation, Piedro's father sends him to Naples with instructions to sell some day-old fish as if it were fresh. 'Good judges of men and fish knew that what he said was false', but at last he passes the fish off on an English servant boy to whom Francisco refused to sell a melon because it was bruised. The boys discuss this on the way home, Francisco maintaining that honesty will pay off

27 Edgeworth, *Parent's Assistant*, p. 373.
28 Edgeworth, *Parent's Assistant*, pp. 373–4.
29 Edgeworth, *Parent's Assistant*, p. 374.
30 Edgeworth, *Parent's Assistant*, p. 375.
31 Edgeworth, *Parent's Assistant*, p. 375.

in the long run and Piedro preferring a short-term profit even if he eventually loses all his customers.[32] The mercantile terms are noticeable; the issue is not that one course is innately better than the other but that a sustained reputation for honesty is more profitable than cheating.

Like all of Edgeworth's stories apparently intended for labouring children, *The Little Merchants* insists on a happy elision of profit and virtue. Goodness leads unfailingly to wealth and badness to economic failure. There is no space to wonder what it might mean if the good failed to accumulate wealth and sharp practice paid off. Francisco, inevitably, acquires the patronage of an English nobleman by demonstrating honesty and fairness that make his servant 'take [him] for an Englishman, by [his] way of dealing'.[33] Francisco's parents share with him the fruits of his honour and success, while Piedro 'felt, as persons usually do, the natural consequences of his own actions'. Piedro's father's fortunes decline as customers avoid his son, and one day he finds Piedro 'at a little merchant's fruit-board, devouring a fine gourd with prodigious greediness'. Demanding, 'Where, glutton, do you find money to pay for these dainties?' Piedro's father finds that his son has been cheating him as well as the customers and beats him, saying 'I'll to teach you to fill your stomach with my money.'[34] The elision of food and the money used to purchase it is telling in a story where the villains exploit the slipperiness of the relationship between food and cash. By winter, father and son are short of food, obliged to witness 'the numerous advantages which Francisco's good character procured'. Francisco finds Piedro cold and starving on the beach and offers him half of Francisco's fruit to sell as the basis of a moral reformation.[35]

At first this succeeds. Piedro 'conducts himself with scrupulous honesty', and after a while 'his companions no longer watched him with suspicious eyes'. But 'in proportion to his credit, his opportunities of defrauding increased'. Piedro becomes impatient with Francisco's insistence that 'light gains and frequent, make a heavy purse' and decides to 'devise means of cheating without running the risk of detection'. He begins to sell sugar-plums to 'the younger part of the community', offering free 'burnt almonds' [caramel-

32 Edgeworth, *Parent's Assistant*, pp. 378–9.
33 Edgeworth, *Parent's Assistant*, p. 382.
34 Edgeworth, *Parent's Assistant*, p. 384.
35 Edgeworth, *Parent's Assistant*, p. 387.

ised almonds] as an incentive to buy.[36] He appears to have given generous measure, and 'Piedro's popularity continued longer even than he had expected.' But then one day, 'a boy of about ten years old passed carelessly by' and read Piedro's sign. The boy, Carlo, announces, 'Old as I am, and tall of my age, which makes the matter worse, I am still as fond of sugar plums as my little sister, who is five years younger than I.'[37] Piedro says he ran out of burnt almonds some time ago but remonstrates when Carlo removes them from his advertisement. Carlo insists, at least, on his sugar-plums, but he has brought his own box, and when Piedro pours from his measure into Carlo's box it is obvious that Piedro has been giving short measure. Carlo, a carpenter's son and apprentice, carries a carpenter's rule and finds that Piedro's box has a false bottom. He calls the children, who, 'forming themselves into a formidable phalanx' shout, 'The little Neapolitan merchants will have no knaves amongst them!' and break his board and his bench, incidentally giving Edgeworth the chance to explain the etymology of 'bankrupt', from '*banco rotto*', broken bench.'Piedro could never more show his face in the market.' Here the narrator steps in:

> If rogues would calculate, they would cease to be rogues; for they would certainly discover that it is most for their interest to be honest – setting aside the pleasure of being esteemed and beloved, of having a safe conscience, with perfect freedom from all the various embarrassments and terror to which knaves are subject. Is it not clear that our crafty hero would have gained rather more by a partnership with Francisco, and by a fair character, than he could possibly obtain through fraudulent dealings in comfits?[38]

Food and virtue both appear here as (interchangeable) economic functions. Even the uncommercial advantages of virtue are presented as a matter of self interest; it is simply more comfortable, more relaxing, to avoid 'the various embarrassments and terror to which knaves are subject'. There is no hint or implication that one should espouse honesty for its own sake, perhaps despite hardship or inconvenience. Virtue is not its own reward, but merely the most convenient and reliable source of income and comfort.

In predictable accordance with this, Francisco reaps unrealistic rewards from his honesty in the marketplace. Carlo and his father teach Francisco trigonometry and he begins to make architectural

36 Edgeworth, *Parent's Assistant*, p. 389.
37 Edgeworth, *Parent's Assistant*, p. 389.
38 Edgeworth, *Parent's Assistant*, p. 393.

drawings. The English nobleman's servant sees these and shows them to his master, who recognises great promise. The nobleman is involved in the excavation of Herculaneum, and he employs Francisco to draw the artefacts. While working on the site, Francisco recognises the early signs that Vesuvius is about to erupt and causes the evacuation of surrounding villages. A count accidentally leaves fireworks and gunpowder in his palace and Francisco goes back to retrieve them and save the palace. The count employs Francisco to guard his estate from looting. Piedro has joined a gang of armed robbers but betrays them in exchange for immunity from prosecution for stealing diamonds. The sbirri are in time to save Francisco from all but minor wounds in defence of the count's property, and when Francisco recovers he finds that the king has given his father a fine house and garden 'for having a good son' who has 'saved the lives and property of many of his subjects'.[39] At the same time the count gives Francisco money equal to the value of the property he has saved, which Francisco shares with his various patrons. The Englishman refuses money but accepts a drawing of fruit, saying, 'I like this very well ... but I should like this melon better if it were a little bruised. It is now three years since I was going to buy that bruised melon from you; you showed me your honest nature then ... A good beginning makes a good ending – an honest boy will make an honest man; and honesty is the best policy, as you have proved to all who wanted proof, I hope.'[40]

In both *The False Key* and *The Little Merchants*, children's moral worth and economic performance are identical and the currency of both is food. It is the mark of vice to separate or exploit the separation of money, virtue and food, to imagine that the economic value of food or goodness may be variable. The bruised melon is the image of Francisco's virtue, which consists in recognising absolute value. Fruit is not worth what the buyer is prepared to pay any more than sugar-plums are worth what the seller is able to ask. It is not the mark of an 'honest nature' to act on the basis of supply and demand. Francisco's 'goodness' is worth precisely the cost or value (the two concepts are elided) of the goods he preserves from evil-doers. There is no economy of need or desire and no space for unavailing effort or unfortunate virtue. The rich like the hand of God will reward the poor in exact proportion to their deserts. No impoverished virtue may blush unseen and no-one will get away with greed or covet-ousness, vices which destabilise an otherwise transparent and moral economy. These children are not machines that eat but they are machines, puppets of the *deus ex machina* that produce, consume and accept. There is no sense that Susan, Franklin or Francisco might be so modest or unassuming as to decline the gifts that seem dispropor-tionately lavish for mere generosity, and indeed disproportionate to the age and status of the children involved. Improbably empowered children are often a feature of children's literature – there is little narrative potential in a child who is told what to do and does it – but there is a clear and uncomfortable role reversal between Susan and Francisco and their parents, who eventually owe their homes and their livelihoods to the aristocracy's appreciation of their children. Despite Edgeworth's insistence in her preface that 'care has been taken to avoid inflaming the imagination, or exciting a restless spirit of adventure, by exhibiting false views of life, and creating hopes which, in the ordinary course of things, cannot be realised', the extent of the aristocracy's gifts clearly violates any straightforward interpretation of this.[41] Francisco's father receives a house and land, Susan's father is given a farm and a job, and Franklin has an annuity which will free him from paid work for life. If this is not 'exhibiting false views of life', it is working on a level much less 'in the ordinary course of things' than Edgeworth claims. The children accept their changed fortunes without comment or demur, and while there is the suggestion that those who were indifferent to poverty will not be overjoyed by wealth, there is a stronger sense that this is simply how the system works. The noble donors are not offering personal favours but fulfilling the requirements of an economy in which no slippage between financial and moral status can be tolerated.

Following the crowd to supper: learning to eat in *Moral Tales*

Moral Tales are implicitly aimed at a different readership and promote a different interpretation of food. The young people in these stories are learning to combine moral responsibility with lives of leisure. According to Edgeworth's conservative educational programme, this means accepting inequality and working towards a difficult combination of empathy, superiority and guiltlessness. In most of

41 Edgeworth, *Parent's Assistant*, p. 4.

the *Moral Tales*, the protagonists are bright and kind children who are instinctively generous to the poor and uninterested in their own privileges. The lesson they must learn is to control the generosity and accept privilege without abandoning an intelligent and sympathetic engagement with the world around them. However strong the sense of moral compulsion, neither quietism nor downward social mobility are possible. The same system that insists on rich rewards for the virtuous poor requires continuing wealth of the virtuous rich, compelling good and wealthy children to believe in the compatibility of wealth and virtue. A desirably observant child will notice the contrast between her own comfortable life and the hunger and hard labour of children on the street. A desirably altruistic child will wish to redress the balance. One of the aims of Edgeworth's didactic fiction is to prevent the logical conclusion while preserving the qualities that lead to it; the rich should use their power for good but they may not pass it to the poor.

Food is important here because it is one of the most obvious manifestations of wealth or poverty, particularly to children and even more particularly to children whose education and inclinations minimise their interest in other forms of consumption. The trope of the well-fed, well-clothed child interacting with the starving beggar on the street is standard from mid-eighteenth-century children's fiction through to Frances Hodgson Burnett and Edith Nesbitt. Some children can spend their pocket money on cake and it is in the course of things that there will be little beggars outside the bakery.

Moral Tales are for older children and Edgeworth's agenda is more subtle than the redistribution of bread and cake, but food remains central to the resolution of personal identity and social status. There are examples throughout the volume. In *The Good Aunt*, Oliver demonstrates his new resolution to refuse to be led astray by saving a 'jar of fine West India sweetmeats' sent by his aunt for the wise Mrs Howard; 'Mrs Howard too well understood the art of education, even in trifles, to deny to grateful and generous feelings their natural and necessary exercise.'[42] The West India connection establishes Oliver's social standing while the sweets work once again as the currency of childhood morality. In *The Good French Governess*, the bad servant Grace tries to undermine Madame Rosier's authority by giving 'queen-cakes' to Favoretta when the little girl has been sent to her room for arguing with her brother, and it is a sign of Favoretta's

42 Maria Edgeworth, *Moral Tales* (New York: AMS Press, Inc., 1967), p. 206.

moral progress that she returns the cake uneaten.[43] The following day, Herbert asks Madame Rosier for queen cakes from the baker: 'She complied, for she was glad to find that he always asked frankly for what he wanted.' There is 'a little boy … who looked extremely thin and hungry' outside, and Madame Rosier stops Herbert giving this child the queen cake, advising him 'to exchange it for something more substantial'.[44] This is a common vignette, but it establishes an exclusive hierarchy of foods. Queen cake is an acceptable treat for Hubert and Favoretta but wholly unsuitable for the thin and hungry boy. A recipe from the 1803 edition of Susannah Carter's *The Frugal Housewife* suggests the reason for this; in addition to the basic ingredients of butter, sugar, eggs and flour, queen cakes include rose water, dried fruit, and a labour-intensive icing.[45] Let them eat bread: to put it anachronistically, the cost per calorie of queen cake is high. It is interesting in this context that such a luxury remains an acceptable use of Hubert's money, for this suggests that Edgeworth can, unusually, endorse recreational eating for those whose nutritional needs are reliably met.

The two stories in which food figures in the most subtle and important ways confirm that the moral implications of eating are class-determined. In *Forrester* and *L'Amie inconnue*, the young protagonists espouse radical ideologies and leave wealthy homes in the belief that they are casting off false and extravagant lifestyles. The fall and the reform are both expressed in gastronomic terms. Forrester scorns the formality of bourgeois dining and Anne Warwick believes she can subsist in Romantic simplicity on peasant fare, but both adolescents learn in the end to accept their physical and social needs for fine dining in a refined setting.

Forrester was 'the son of an English gentleman', 'frank, brave and generous, but he had been taught to dislike politeness so much, that the common forms of society appeared to him either odious or ridiculous'.[46] 'His attention had been early fixed upon the follies and vices of the higher classes of people' so that 'he was disposed to choose his friends and companions from amongst his inferiors: the inequality between the rich and the poor shocked him'.[47] Forrester's

43 Edgeworth, *Moral Tales*, p. 317.
44 Edgeworth, *Moral Tales*, p. 317.
45 See the Feeding America website at
http://digital.lib.msu.edu/projects/cookbooks/display.cfm?TitleNo=2&PageNum=159
46 Edgeworth, *Moral Tales*, p. 1.
47 Edgeworth, *Moral Tales*, p. 1.

father dies when he is nineteen and Forrester is sent to live with his guardian, Dr Campbell, in Edinburgh. At first the footman is reluctant to admit him because he travels by carrier and not by coach, insists on carrying his own luggage and appears dirty and unkempt. These false signals being overridden, Forrester enters the drawing room and is 'much surprised by the effect which his singular appearance produced on the risible muscles of some of the company'. He is annoyed when dinner is announced,

> Not that Forrester was averse to eating, for he was at this instant ravenously hungry: but eating in company he always found equally repugnant to his habits and his principles. A table covered with a clean table-cloth; dishes in nice order; plates, knives and forks, laid at regular distances, appeared to our young Diogenes absurd superfluities, and he was ready to exclaim, 'How many things I do not want!' Sitting down to dinner, eating, drinking, and behaving like other people, appeared to him difficult and disagreeable ceremonies. He did not perceive that custom had rendered all these things perfectly easy to everyone else in company; and as soon as he had devoured his food his own way, he moralized in silence upon the good sense of Sancho Panza, who preferred eating an egg behind the door to feasting in public; and he recollected his favourite traveller Le Vaillant's enthusiastic account of his charming Hottentot dinners, and of the disgust that he afterwards felt, on comparison of European etiquette and African simplicity.[48]

The references to Don Quixote and Le Vaillant work to establish Forrester's underlying integrity and to suggest his inability to distinguish anthropology from every-day life. Educational books come naturally to Forrester in a way that Edgeworth invariably approves, but something is awry; he perceives superfluity and ceremony which he should be taking for granted and occupies the same position with regard to the family with whom he is to live and eat as the traveller does to 'Hottentots'. He is educated but alienated, and his dirtiness and uncouth eating suggest a courting of rejection and ostracism. Forrester may be Le Vaillant or he may be a Hottentot, but he is not comfortable at the table.

Forrester continues to make mistakes through an unwavering commitment to truth and morality at any cost. His principles are undiscriminating; 'He was always extravagant in his generosity; he would often give five guineas where five shillings would have been enough, and by these means he reduced himself to the

48 Edgeworth, *Moral Tales*, p. 3.

necessity sometimes of refusing assistance to deserving objects.'[49] Dr Campbell tries to teach Forrester by precept and example that virtue and social skills are compatible, but Forrester cannot countenance any attention to the inclinations of other people. He despises women, however intelligent and charitable, for attention to dress and conversation, and despises men, however upright, for any adaptation to company or situation. Compelled to accompany the family to a ball, Forrester is bad-tempered and resentful, arguing when Dr Campbell asks, 'Is it not as well, since we are here, to amuse ourselves with whatever can afford us any amusement, and to keep in good humour with all the world, especially with ourselves? – and had we not better follow the crowd to supper?'[50] Dr Campbell's daughter Flora serves him trifle and he comments, 'Some characters are like that trifle – flowers and light froth at the top, and solid, good sweetmeat, beneath.'[51] This is probably a reference to Flora herself, whom Forrester despises as frivolous, and he responds by 'pick[ing] the troublesome flowers out of his trifle, and [eating] a quantity of it sufficient for a Stoic'. 'Trifle' was a new name for a new dish in the mid-eighteenth century, and its original meaning of something light, insubstantial and insignificant ('a mere trifle') would have been more closely attached to the dish in the early nineteenth century than it is now. It was never intended to be consumed in large quantities, but Forrester cannot distinguish one foodstuff from another, nor recognise the social inflections of particular dishes. Later in the evening, he determines that 'his repose should not be disturbed by such mere trifles' as other people's scorn for his dirtiness. Forrester decides that he is unfit 'to live amongst idle gentlemen and ladies' and runs away to 'be a gardener and live with gardeners'.[52]

This is probably a deliberate echo – and critique – of Candide's conclusion that '*Il faut que chacun cultive son jardin*.' Some of Forrester's failings are those of Candide, and the earlier reference to Sancho Panza suggests that Forrester sees himself in the picaresque tradition. But Edgeworth, of course, is at odds with Voltaire; what Forrester needs to come of age is not a world without compromises but the ability to exist happily in the world as it is. The gardening scheme is a mistake. The day after running away, Forrester writes to Dr Campbell, 'Let those who have no virtuous indignation obey the

49 Edgeworth, *Moral Tales*, p. 13.
50 Edgeworth, *Moral Tales*, p. 31.
51 Edgeworth, *Moral Tales*, p. 31.
52 Edgeworth, *Moral Tales*, p. 36.

voice of fashion, and at her commands let her slaves eat the bread of idleness till it palls upon the sense!' He concludes, 'I mean to earn my own bread as a gardener; I have always preferred the agricultural to the commercial system.'[53] Dr Campbell replies by asking Forrester to 'return to dinner', saying, 'we will compare at our leisure the mercantile and the agricultural system'. If Forrester insists on his new scheme, Dr Campbell tells him: '[I will not] whilst you choose to live in a rank below your own, supply you with your customary allowance'. This is because, he continues, 'it is necessary that you should not deceive yourself by inadequate experiments: you cannot be rich and poor at the same time'. Similarly, Forrester is forbidden the company of Dr Campbell's son Henry: 'You cannot live among the vulgar (by the vulgar I mean the ill-educated, the ignorant, those who have neither noble sentiments nor agreeable manners), and at the same time enjoy the pleasures of cultivated society.'[54] Dr Campbell is the final authority in this story and he offers no sense of why a person with money cannot live without it or why it is impossible to move between 'the vulgar' and 'cultivated society'. Such hybridity is unthinkable, but Edgeworth's position here cannot but be contrived in the light of the cultivated poverty of most major writers of the period. Richard Lovell Edgeworth's friend Dr Johnson himself was famed for his unattractive personal habits, inability to tolerate fools and affection for the underclass, but the publication date of *Moral Tales* allows a wide range of targets for this attack on radical lifestyles.

Events, of course, prove Dr Campbell right: 'The gardener who had struck Forrester's fancy was a square, thick, obstinate-eyed, hard-working, ignorant, elderly man, whose soul was intent upon his petty daily gains, and whose honesty was of that "coarse-spun, vulgar sort," which alone can be expected from men of uncultivated minds.'[55] The accumulation of adjectives confirms the sense in Dr Campbell's absolute certainties that Edgeworth has lapsed into invective here. The gardener, Mr M'Evoy, understands the world only in terms of amassing capital: 'His views and ideas all centred in his own family; and his affection was accumulated and reserved for two individuals, his son and his daughter.'[56] The evident disapproval of the absolute commitment to family wealth is odd in the context of

53 Edgeworth, *Moral Tales*, p. 39.
54 Edgeworth, *Moral Tales*, p. 41.
55 Edgeworth, *Moral Tales*, p. 43.
56 Edgeworth, *Moral Tales*, p. 43.

The Parent's Assistant, but the difference may lie in ambition. Susan accumulates capital with the sentimental project of purchasing her father's freedom and Francisco works hard to please his father. These are contexts in which it is clear that the family, at least in the story, may act as a microcosm of the state or at least of the political status quo. Susan and Francisco labour in the name of the father, in happy subservience to benevolent patriarchy that precisely reflects Edgeworth's ideal of the relationship between the gentry and the labouring poor. These children do not imagine, much less aspire to, the rewards that change their fortunes; they refrain from envisaging their own worth. The M'Evoys, by contrast, are constantly assessing their monetary value. The daughter 'spent all the money she could either earn or save upon ribands and fine gowns, with which she fancied she could supply all the defects of her person'.[57] She has reckoned the amount by which 'her person' falls short and believes that money can supply the body's failings. (The nineteenth-century fictional marriage market would, of course, endorse this view, but Edgeworth's point is that money may mirror but cannot constitute essential value.) The son is 'ambitious of seeing something of the world', which is easier for him when his companions 'remember that he expected, when his father should die, *to be rich*'.[58] These children have Edgeworth's world turned upside down, looking to the father as the source of unearned income and not the recipient of labour's fruits.

The physical form of Forrester's unease with this situation is gustatory. The daughter 'squeezed all that could possibly be squeezed for her private use from the frugal household' and Forrester neglects to discover that 'the boy, whose place Forester thought himself so fortunate to supply, had left the gardener because he could not bear to work and be scolded without eating or drinking'.[59] His own more elevated discontents take the same shape:

> Forrester dug with all the energy of an enthusiast, and dined like a philosopher upon long kail; but long kail did not charm him so much the second day as it had done the first; and the third day it was yet less to his taste; besides, he began to notice the difference between oaten and wheaten bread. He, however, recollected that Cyrus lived, when he was a lad, upon water-cresses – the black broth of the Spartans he likewise remembered, and he would not complain. He thought, that he should soon accustom

57 Edgeworth, *Moral Tales,* p. 43.
58 Edgeworth, *Moral Tales,* p. 43.
59 Edgeworth, *Moral Tales,* p. 44.

himself to his scanty, homely fare ... The occupation of digging was laborious, but it afforded no exercise to his mind, and he felt most severely the
want of Henry's agreeable conversation; he had no-one to whom he could
now talk of the water-cresses of Cyrus, or the black broth of the Spartans;
he had no-one with whom he could dispute concerning the Stoic or the
Epicurean doctrines, the mercantile or the agricultural system.[60]

Forrester's problem here is that, while classical discourse might help
him to tolerate poor food by imagining himself as a Spartan and a
Stoic, he discovers that in fact such an interpretation depends upon
a reading community and is not sustainable in isolation. In the world
of Edgeworth's fiction, such a use of reading is impossible anyway
because the reading community is by definition wealthy and would
accompany the study of classical Greek with socially appropriate
food. No-one who reads Greek has any cause to eat black broth and
water cress. Those who are capable of theory are above practice.

It is a final incidence of this disparity that drives Forrester from
gardening. He was beginning to 'grow fond of the old gardener'
because 'there was nothing else near to him to which he could
attach himself, not even a dog or a cat'.[61] The gardener does not
return this affection; he 'rather wished to keep him in his service,
because he gave him less than the current wages' (a further example
of the absolute inability of the rich to function as poor; Forrester is
unable to estimate the value of his labour). Hoping that by 'applying
his understanding to the business of gardening, he might perhaps
make some discoveries, which should excite his master's everlasting
gratitude', Forrester exchanges some clothes for 'some volumes
upon gardening; and these, in spite of the ridicule of Colin and
Miss M'Evoy, he studied usually at his meals'. He remembers being
told that 'cherries were sometimes sold very high in Edinburgh'
and learns that the gardener 'wished, from the bottom of his heart,
that he had a thousand cherry-trees, but he possessed only one'.
Forrester suggests experiments based on his reading to increase
the productivity of this lucrative tree. 'But the gardener peremorpto-
rily forbade all such experiments, and, shutting Forrester's book,
bade him leave such nonsense and mind his business.'[62] Forrester is
discovering that gardener's boys have no right to books and theories
and that gardeners have no interest in writers and theorists. Infuri-
ated, he forgot 'his character of *servant boy*, and at length called his

60 Edgeworth, *Moral Tales*, p. 44.
61 Edgeworth, *Moral Tales*, p. 47.
62 Edgeworth, *Moral Tales*, p. 48.

master an obstinate fool'. Working as a servant boy has not changed his identity. Despite accepting wages for work, Forrester has been assuming a 'character' which is not his own, and it is this denial of the relationship between books and living that compels him back to his real identity as a reader.

Forrester proceeds to find work as a clerk in a brewery that he once visited with Dr Campbell. He is beginning to learn that 'separated from social intercourse, his mind, however enlarged, would afford him but a dreary kingdom', and he soon concludes that 'casting up and verifying accounts' is 'extremely injurious to the human understanding: "'All the higher faculties of my soul," said he to himself, "are absolutely useless at this work, and I am reduced to a mere machine."'[63] This alienation worsens when he learns that 'the business and duty of a brewer's clerk' are 'to assist his master in evading certain clauses in certain acts of parliament'. He protests, refusing to 'assist in evading the laws of his country' and is sacked.[64] He wanders out into the streets and is beaten up when he tries to prevent the master of dancing dogs from working them to exhaustion. A passer-by takes him into the nearest house, which belongs to a printer and bookseller, and Forrester is launched in his third career.

'Ashamed of his former versatility', he works hard and does well. Political radicals frequent the book shop and Forester conceives a 'blind, enthusiastic admiration' for a man known as Tom Random. Reading a biography of Benjamin Franklin goes some way to counter the idea that only immediate revolution can prevent apocalypse, and then Random laughs at Forrester for expressing opinions about some of the material he is printing. Forrester asks himself, 'Is this the man who would have equality amongst all his fellow creatures, and who calls a compositor a printer's devil?'[65] Returning, Tom Random knocks over the typeset for the evening newspaper and Forrester stays up most of the night to re-set it. Leaving the print-shop in the early hours, he passes Random persuading a mob 'who are continually, without knowing it, made the instruments of private malice, when they think they are acting in a public cause' to smash the windows of a confectioner whose daughter has rejected Random. Stopping to entreat that 'the poor man's windows might be spared', Forrester is caught up by the constables, who have often seen him in

63 Edgeworth, *Moral Tales*, p. 59.
64 Edgeworth, *Moral Tales*, p. 60.
65 Edgeworth, *Moral Tales*, p. 65.

Random's company. He is taken into custody, where a kindly French dancing master to whom he has previously been kind tells him that he is experiencing 'de grand inconvenience of concealing [his] rank and name': 'You, who are comme il faut, are confounded with the mob.' The Frenchman offers to assure the magistrate that he knows Forrester 'to be un homme comme il faut, above being guilty of an unbecoming action.'[66] Despite Edgeworth's later discussion of the English presumption of universal innocence until proven guilty, it is clear here that Forrester's rank would proclaim his innocence as his apparent status does not. Anyone who knew who he 'really' was would know the impossibility of his guilt, not because of his character but because of his class. It is as if Forrester has brought criminal proceedings on himself by seeking employment. Pasgrave tells the magistrate Forrester's identity, and he escapes further consequences. Back at work, he is able to supply a missing reference to Juvenal and the bookseller offers to 'advance [him], according to [his] merits, in the world', but only if he acquires 'a decent suit of clothes and a cleaner shirt.'[67]

Forrester buys new clothes, cuts his hair and begins to take dancing lessons. His career blooms until he is caught up in a dispute about a lost bank-note. The resolution of this leads to a general *éclaircissement* in which Dr Campbell is able to confound those who have behaved badly, reward the virtuous and take Forrester back into his house, remade as a gentleman and a fit husband for Flora. Food is not the means of Forrester's reform and restoration, but it is what forces him to begin the journey back up the social scale towards his proper position. Surrounded by plenty, he can imagine himself a Stoic and a Spartan, but it is the experience of an inadequate and unsuitable diet that compels him to recognise that the poor are physiologically, psychologically and morally different from old money. Edgeworth uses food here to claim a physical basis for her distinction between the gentry and the labouring poor.

The contexts and intertexts for *Forrester* range from *Don Quixote* and *Candide* through almost any radical or Romantic text to the high thinking and plain living of the Scottish Enlightenment. In general the cultural reference points are far more generic than specific, but there is a clear exception for Thomas Day's *Sandford and Merton*, which makes the opposite argument in similar terms. Thomas Day and Richard Lovell Edgeworth's friendship is well known, as is Day's

66 Edgeworth, *Moral Tales*, p. 70.
67 Edgeworth, *Moral Tales*, p. 75.

dislike and discouragement of women writers in general and Maria Edgeworth in particular.[68] Marilyn Butler writes of Day,

> While at Oxford Thomas read widely in the classics … from whom he imbibed an earnest passion for the pursuit of virtue and integrity. He admired the Stoic personal ideals, and looked back with veneration (…) to the simplicity and integrity of the early days of the Roman republic. At about this time, perhaps as a result of Edgeworth's influence, he discovered the modern primitivist Rousseau, and found his austerities so appealing that he became a disciple for the rest of his life.[69]

She continues, 'in general company he was either tongue-tied or severe, and both his clothes and his table manners gave real offence'. The connection is obvious, and in later life Edgeworth was clear that Day was the origin of Forrester. In itself, this is not necessarily important; most of Edgeworth's work contains characters who were recognised by readers of the day, including others in *Forrester*. But the purpose of *Forrester* is to show Forrester's misguidedness, which places the story in conversation with, or revision of, Day's own children's writing.

The History of Sandford and Merton relates the education – which is almost exclusively a moral education – of Tommy Merton and Harry Sandford. Tommy, the son of a plantation owner, lives in Jamaica until he is six, where 'he had several black servants to wait upon him, who were forbidden upon any account to contradict him'. His mother is 'excessively fond of him', and the result of this gendered and racially inflected indulgence is that,

> though Master Merton had everything he wanted, he became very fretful and unhappy. Sometimes he ate sweetmeats till he made himself sick, and then he suffered a great deal of pain because he would not take bitter physic to make him well … When any company came to dine at the house, he was always to be helped first, and to have the most delicate parts of the meat, otherwise he would make such a noise as disturbed the whole company. When his father and mother were sitting at the tea-table with their friends, instead of waiting till they were at leisure to attend him, he would scramble on the table, seize the cake and bread and butter, and frequently overset the tea-cups.[70]

---

68 Marilyn Butler, *Maria Edgeworth: A Literary Biography* (Oxford: Clarendon Press, 1972).
69 Butler, *Edgeworth*, p. 29.
70 Thomas Day, *The History of Sandford and Merton* (Philadelphia: Willis P. Hazard, 1857) pp. 3–4.

The Mertons relocate to England for Tommy's health, where 'near to Mr Merton's seat lived a plain, honest farmer, whose name was Sandford'. Sandford's son Harry was 'neither so fair, nor so delicately shaped as Master Merton; but he had an honest, good natured countenance, which made every body love him'.[71] This good-natured lovability is manifest in abstemiousness and kindness to animals (which as we have seen, are not unrelated in a meat-eating culture):

> If little Harry saw a poor wretch who wanted victuals while he was eating his dinner, he was sure to give him half and sometimes the whole; nay, so very good natured was he to every thing, that he would never go into the fields to take the eggs of the poor birds, or their young ones, nor practice any other kind of sport which gave pain to poor animals … In the winter time, when the ground was covered with frost and snow, and the poor little birds could get at no food, he would often go supperless to bed, that he might feed the robin-redbreasts.[72]

'These sentiments made little Harry a great favourite with every body', especially Mr Barlow, the vicar, who educates Harry out of affection and admiration for his virtues:

> And then you might believe Harry in everything he said; for though he could have gained a plumb-cake by telling an untruth, and was sure that speaking the truth would expose him to a severe whipping, he never hesitated in declaring it. Nor was he like many other children, who place their whole happiness in eating; for give him but a morsel of dry bread for his dinner, and he would be satisfied, though you placed sweetmeats and fruit, and every other nicety, in his way.[73]

The equation of an interest in animal welfare and childish goodness is common to children's fiction across the period, and certainly shared by Edgeworth. Children who, by definition, have little power over other people can demonstrate the capacity for kindness on animals. But the difference between Harry and Simple Susan is important here. Harry barely recognises the existential difference between 'poor wretches' and 'robin redbreasts', while his readiness to starve himself in order to feed the birds suggests a concept of humanity and selfhood which is the opposite of Susan's readiness to sacrifice her lamb and her guinea-fowl for her parents' well-being. Harry does not distinguish between food for boys and food for birds,

71 Day, *Sandford*, p. 4.
72 Day, *Sandford*, p. 5.
73 Day, *Sandford*, p. 5.

or between his need for food and animals' hunger, and this humility constitutes a significant part of his goodness. But Susan signals both her maturity and her readiness for social advancement by recognising that animals, however appealing, exist to feed people, either directly or as economic units. The pet lamb, the animal that is fed and does not feed, is an aberration that she must learn to give up, even if, as for Abraham, the fulfilment of the sacrifice is not finally required.

There is a similar comparison to be made between Harry's and Forrester's, and indeed Angelina's, preference for a dry crust over sweets and fruit. Forrester must learn that one of the inexorable obligations of wealth is visible consumption. Edgeworth rejects the association of plum cake and dishonesty; there are those whose role in life is to eat cake and those who, while aspiring to cake, must for the moment have bread. But she, via Forrester and then Angelina, ardently denies the innate virtue of the dinner of dry bread and bitter herbs. Some people get stalled ox and plum cake whether they like it or not.

Food works similarly in *Angelina*, which Edgeworth calls in her Preface a 'female Forester'. *Angelina* is Edgeworth's most gustatory story, prefiguring Susan Ferrier's fiction in the importance of food to both plot and character development. The story opens with Lady Diana Chillingworth, her sister Lady Frances Somerset and her companion Miss Burrage bewailing the elopement of Lady Diana's ward, Anne Warwick. The moral hierarchy is immediately established. Lady Diana is worried about her own reputation and anxious to vindicate her care for Anne's morals, Miss Burrage displays a sycophantic concern for the affect of anxiety on Lady Diana's health and Lady Frances calmly regrets that Anne was not better educated and hopes to find her 'before her reputation is injured'. Miss Burrage produces a letter 'found on the young lady's dressing-table, according to the usual custom of eloping heroines'.[74]

The letter addresses Anne as 'Angelina' and is signed 'Araminta'. Edgeworth offers an 'abridgement' which is characterised by hysteria and verges on the incoherent, a satire on sensibility in female friendship and an obvious attack on Wollstonecraft. It begins, 'Yes, my Angelina! Our hearts are formed for that higher species of friendship, of which common souls are inadequate to form an idea,

---

74 Edgeworth, *Moral Tales*, p. 223.

however their fashionable puerile lips may, in the intellectual inanity of their conversation, profane the term.' There follows a passage about reading Angelina's letters by moonlight, with raptures on 'The river silently meandering! – The rocks! – The woods! – Nature in all her majesty. Sublime confidante!'[75] Later it demands,

> The words ward and guardian appal my Angelina! but what are legal technical formalities, what are human institutions, to the view of shackle-scorning Reason! Oppressed, degraded, enslaved, must our unfortunate sex for ever submit to sacrifice their rights, their pleasures, their will, at the altar of public opinion; whilst the shouts of interested priests, and idle spectators, raise the senseless enthusiasm of the self-devoted victim, or drown her cries in the truth-extorting moment of agonizing nature! –You will not perfectly understand, perhaps, to what these last exclamations of your Araminta allude: – But, chosen friend of my heart! – when we meet – and oh, let that be quickly! – my cottage longs for the arrival of my unsophisticated Angelina! – when we meet you shall know all – your Araminta, too, has had her sorrows.[76]

Wollstonecraft's prose is of course more reasoned and more coherent than this, but as a thumbnail parody this letter is wickedly effective. The movement from staccato delight in nature to long rolling waves of rhetoric about freedom and oppression to broken exclamations of personal distress is typical of Wollstonecraft in form and content. The assertion that women are educated to collude in their own oppression is one of the cornerstones of the *Vindication of the Rights of Woman*. It is clear to the adult reader, and perhaps not to the girl for whom the story is intended, that Araminta is preparing Anne/Angelina to regard extra-marital sex and illegitimate motherhood as morally acceptable and politically desirable, for it is hard to imagine another interpretation of 'cries in the truth-extorting moment of agonizing nature'. (It was one of the duties of licensed midwives to require an unmarried woman in labour to tell the father's name before they would offer any assistance with the birth.) The implications of this are that the connections between poetic Romanticism, radical politics and sexual conduct are based on sloppy thinking and personal interest; that radicalism is an excuse for sexual misconduct and that, if Anne's running away is not the conventional elopement her relatives fear, it is nonetheless a form of seduction that endangers her integrity.

Edgeworth's account of Anne's reading this letter reinforces the

75 Edgeworth, *Moral Tales*, p. 225.
76 Edgeworth, *Moral Tales*, pp. 225–6.

reader's sense of Anne's vulnerability to false ideology. She was 'so charmed with the sound of it, that it made her totally forget to judge of her amiable Araminta's mode of reasoning'.[77] (Are we being warned against Romantic poetry?) Nevertheless, 'Miss Warwick, though she judged like a simpleton, was a young woman of considerable abilities: her want of what the world calls common sense arose from certain mistakes in her education.' Namely, her parents 'cultivated her literary taste but neglected to cultivate her judgment: her reading was confined to works of the imagination; and the conversation which she heard was not calculated to give her any knowledge of realities'.[78] As a result of this developed literary sensibility, Anne has been bored and disgusted by fashionable life in London and has consoled herself at a circulating library. After reading *The Woman of Genius*, she contacts the author and begins a correspondence which ends with the determination 'to accept of her unknown friend's invitation to Angelina Bower – a charming Romantic cottage in South Wales where, according to Araminta's description, she might pass her halcyon days in tranquil, elegant retirement'.[79]

In a phrase reminiscent of *Northanger Abbey*, Angelina (as Edgeworth now calls her) 'had the misfortune ... to meet with no difficulties or adventures, nothing interesting upon her journey'.[80] She reaches an inn at Cardiff, where the landlady offers her 'fine Tenby oysters' or 'a Welsh rabbit'. Angelina replies, 'Oh, detain me not in this cruel manner! – I want no Tenby oysters, I want no Welsh rabbits; only let me be gone – I am all impatience to see a dear friend. Oh, if you have any feeling, any humanity, detain me not!'[81] Her haste and anguish arouse the landlady's suspicions while the scorn for 'Mrs Hoel of Cardiff and her Tenby oysters, and her Welsh rabbit' antagonise Mrs Hoel into advertising Angelina's presence as a runaway 'in the public newspapers'. Her carriage arrives at last to take Angelina the last six miles, but the carriage road ends a quarter of a mile before the cottage and Angelina insists that the postilion leave her to walk alone by moonlight, refusing his offer to precede her and wake the inhabitants. She tries to wake Araminta by singing outside the cottage, but has to knock on the door, convincing the

77 Edgeworth, *Moral Tales*, p. 226.
78 Edgeworth, *Moral Tales*, p. 227.
79 Edgeworth, *Moral Tales*, p. 227.
80 Edgeworth, *Moral Tales*, p. 229.
81 Edgeworth, *Moral Tales*, p. 231.

servant girl that a ghost has come to call. After some by-play, the
postilion convinces the servant Betty Williams and 'an old slip-shod
beldam' that Angelina is 'a young lady come to visit their mistress'.
It turns out that Araminta, known to her servant as 'Miss Hodges'
has gone to Bristol for a few days. Anticipating 'elegant retirement',
Angelina resigns herself to a few days alone in the cottage but hits
her head on the low ceiling and lies awake all night with a head-
ache. In the morning she discovers that the cottage is small, damp,
smoky and badly furnished. Food is a problem:

> Coarse and ill-dressed was the food which Betty Williams with great bustle
> and awkwardness served up to her guest; but Angelina was no epicure.
> The first dinner which she ate on wooden trenchers delighted her; the
> second, third, fourth and fifth appeared less and less delectable; so that
> by the time she had boarded one week at her cottage, she was completely
> convinced that
> > A scrip with herbs and fruit supplied,
> > And water from the spring,
> though delightful to Goldsmith's Hermit, are not quite so satisfactory in
> actual practice as in poetic theory; at least to a young lady who had been
> habituated to all the luxuries of fashionable life. It was in vain that our
> heroine repeated
> > Man wants but little here below:
> she found that even the want of double-refined sugar, of green tea, and
> Mocha coffee, was sensibly felt.[82]

The texts by which Angelina lives come from polite literature for
ladies rather than the Greek and Roman canon of boys' education, and the commodities of which she feels the lack are similarly
gendered, but otherwise this is an obvious parallel to Forrester's experience in the gardener's house. It is not that food matters
particularly to Angelina. She is 'no epicure', but she is learning
that she has physical needs and that those needs are class-specific.
Whatever Goldsmith says, she cannot live comfortably without very
specific kinds of tea and coffee and the most expensive sugar. As the
many pamphlets agonising over the poor's insistence on spending
money on tea and coffee point out, these beverages have no nutritional content. Tea and coffee offer the experience of consumption
divorced from nutrition, beverages requiring ritual and expense
whose only physiological effect is the consumption of water which
could much more conveniently be drunk cold. The point is not that

82 Edgeworth, *Moral Tales*, pp. 235–6.

Angelina enjoys eating or even that her body requires nutrients in specific forms, but that the social content of what she ingests is missing.

When a neighbouring farmer sees Mrs Hoel's advertisement, Angelina decides to 'set out immediately in quest of her unknown friend at Bristol'.[83] Betty Williams accompanies her, but soon turns out to have no idea where Miss Hodges lives. Wandering the city at night, they pass Lady Diana buying lace and take refuge in a cheesemonger's shop. A child is minding the shop while his aunt has dinner, and he reports 'two women in some great distress – and astray and hungry'. The cheesemonger, a Quaker woman called Dinah Plait, offers them food and Betty eats eggs, bacon and toasted cheese 'like one half-famished'. Angelina refuses both food and money, despite Betty's entreaties that she 'eat a hegg, and a pit of bacon': '"I am in no want of food," cried she, rising: "happy they who have no conception of any but corporeal sufferings."'[84]

The next house they try is a girls' school, where Angelina discovers that she has lost her purse and the proprietor, who once knew Miss Hodges, tries to warn her that Miss Hodges' *whole* history' makes her an unsuitable companion for a 'very young lady' who is 'a stranger in Bristol'.[85] Unlike the unwashed Forrester, Angelina's real status is clearly still writ large on her person; both Dinah Plait and Mrs Porett recognise her as a misguided gentlewoman rather than making any more sinister interpretation of a pretty and unchaperoned young woman roaming a large city. Mrs Porett directs her to the house of a Mrs Bertrand, who keeps 'a large confectionary and fruit shop in Bristol', and it is against this background that Angelina at last meets Araminta. Meanwhile, Lady Diana Chillingworth and Lady Frances Somerset have seen Mrs Hoel's advertisement and are on Angelina's trail. In the shop, Angelina exclaims, 'Oh, my Araminta! How my heart beats!' Betty counters, '"How my mouth waters", 'looking round at the fruit and confectionaries'.[86] Mrs Bertrand takes the hint:

> 'Would you, ma'am, be pleased,' said Mrs Bertrand, 'to take a glass of ice this warm evening? cream-ice, or water-ice, ma'am? pine-apple or straw-berry ice?' As she spoke, Mrs Bertrand held a salver, covered with ices, to-ward Miss Warwick: but, apparently, she thought that it was not consistent

83 Edgeworth, *Moral Tales*, p. 239.
84 Edgeworth, *Moral Tales*, p. 249.
85 Edgeworth, *Moral Tales*, p. 254.
86 Edgeworth, *Moral Tales*, p. 262.

with the delicacy of friendship to think of eating or drinking when she was
thus upon the eve of her first interview with her Araminta. Betty Williams,
who was of a different nature from our heroine, saw the salver recede
with excessive surprise and regret; she stretched out her hand after it, and
seized a glass of raspberry-ice; but no sooner had she tasted it than she
made a frightful face, and let the glass fall, exclaiming –

'Pless us! 'tis not as good as gooseberry fool.'

Mrs Bertram next offered her a cheesecake, which Betty ate
voraciously.

'She's actually a female Sancho Panza!' thought Angelina: her own more
striking resemblance to the female Quixote never occurred to our heroine
– so blind are we to our own failings.[87]

This scene tells us that Angelina is out of place in several ways.
Most obviously, a confectionary shop is a place of trade and as such
not frequented by the gentry. In the wealthiest households, there
would have been no contact at all with purveyors of what, in the
case of ice-cream, must necessarily be street food, but even among
the middling sort who kept a 'plain cook' whose skills might not
extend to patisserie and sweetmeats, calling at the confectioner's
shop would have been part of the servant's job. The fact of being
in the shop at all attests to Angelina's social fall. It is clear from the
formality of her language that Mrs Bertrand recognises Angelina's
'quality'. Despite this sense of trespass, Edgeworth does not endorse
Angelina's disdain for the confectioner's goods; it is 'apparent'
(as opposed to taken for granted) that Angelina thinks eating 'not
consistent with the delicacy of friendship', a phrase straight from the
lexicon of sensibility. Betty is a figure of fun throughout the story, but
it may be that her greed here attracts no censure because it is simply
part of the peasant identity and it is Angelina who is mistaken in
expecting anything else of a Welsh servant girl. The reference to Don
Quixote strengthens the link with *Forrester* and also confirms that
Angelina is thinking in terms that are not useful because they are
not shared with anyone around her (and that, because of her defec-
tive education, her powers of analysis do not extend to herself).
Immediately after this, Mrs Bertrand mishears Angelina's soliloquy
of disbelief that Araminta could delay coming to 'her Angelina' as
a request for angelica, a plant whose stalk was candied and used
as a sweet and for cake decoration. The humour is not subtle, but
the confusion arising from the utterly incompatible discourses of
sensibility and the confectionery trade is pointed. Angelina needs to

87 Edgeworth, *Moral Tales*, p. 262.

recognise that there are people to whom the selling of angelica is more important that the posturing of Angelina, although she also needs to recognise that her proper place is not in such company.

When Angelina is at last ushered upstairs to meet Araminta, she finds 'a woman, with a face and figure which seemed to have been intended for a man' 'sitting cross-legged in an armchair at a tea-table, on which, beside the tea equipage, was a medley of things of which no prudent tongue or pen would undertake to give an inventory'. Miss Hodges is 'a slattern', fussily making tea while drinking brandy and receiving the attentions of a 'thin, subdued, simple-looking Quaker'.[88] Miss Hodges responds to Angelina with 'the tone and action of a bad actress who is rehearsing an embrace' and the process of disillusion is well under way when the group is interrupted by a constable accusing Betty Williams of stealing lace. Betty accuses Angelina, who is in the act of being carried off when Lady Diana and Lady Frances catch up with her. Lady Diana wants no more to do with Angelina than is essential to protect her reputation (she would not like it to be thought that her ward had misbehaved so seriously as to forfeit her recognition), but the practical and sympathetic Lady Frances takes Angelina into her own protection and soon, 'under the friendly and judicious care of Lady Frances Somerset', Angelina proves that 'it is possible for a young lady of sixteen to cure herself of the affectation of sensibility and the folly of romance'.[89] She has learnt, at last, to eat like somebody rich.

In conclusion, then, food in Edgeworth's fiction works as a currency, showing the enmeshing of money and morals in her didactic project and perhaps in Romantic-era children's fiction more generally. Those who are good with food are also both good and good with money, and the reverse is also true. The inevitability of eating means that liars are revealed at the table or, more usually, snacking secretly in the nursery or closet. Food does not lie, here as in Burney, because the wealthy body cannot tolerate poor food, and this position insists that a biological basis for social inequality is inseparable from the 'truths' of the free market. Food and money are so linked that capitalism will promote the wise eater, while the body and the self are so linked that the wise eater is also the good person. There is no space in Edgeworth's work to separate consumption, production and morality.

88 Edgeworth, *Moral Tales*, p. 264.
89 Edgeworth, *Moral Tales*, p. 282.

4

Eating for Britain
Food, family and national identity in Susan Ferrier's fiction

Romantic-period women writers developed the particular form of reading relations that made the postulate of depth possible and necessary. They had the forms for interiority.[1]

—Deirdre Lynch, *The Economy of Character*

What is at stake in the Scottish novel, however, is not simply a mode of reading but the future of British literary culture and cross-cultural understanding, for the romanticised vision of Scotland portrayed by Scott and his contemporaries actually retards the process of intellectual union it claims to make possible.[2]

—Katie Trumpener, *Bardic Nationalism*

Ferrier develops the relationship between maternity, feeding and the body politic established in earlier women's fiction in the context of early nineteenth century Scottishness. Declining to associate subjugated women with the subjugated nation, Ferrier argues instead for colonialism as the basis of female liberation, depicting the replacement of Scottish with British rule as the replacement of the stifling father for the (unusually generous) step-mother. Ferrier's work is explicitly anti-Romantic, anticipating in several ways Katie Trumpener's critique of Celtic Romanticism, and unusually opposed to the logic of the fairy tale. The step-mother's regime in these novels

---

1 Deirdre Lynch, *The Economy of Character: Novels, Market Culture and the Business of Inner Meaning* (Chicago: University of Chicago Press, 1998), p. 37.
2 Katie Trumpener, *Bardic Nationalism: The Romantic Novel and the British Empire* (Princeton: Princeton University Press, 1997), p. 18.

is both benevolent and wise, and the repeated elision or invalidation of the biological mother is often welcome. Mary in *Marriage* has Alicia as her mother-figure; *Destiny*'s heroine Edith, after moving to England, finds Lady Arabella Conway; and Gertrude's repentance and moral restoration in *Inheritance* are guided by another aunt. The birth mother is dead or morally inadequate, and in relation to Ferrier's interest in the need to remake heredity, to forge a new nationhood and, in a very modulated way, to reimagine gender, the eagerness to dispossess biological parents is telling.

These are novels about the decapitation and remaking of the family and nation state, dramas in which the inadequacy or absence of biological parents is taken for granted. Ruth Perry writes in *Novel Relations* that '[t]he "aunt", being simultaneously both mother and other, solves both the problem of separation and that of identification for the female protagonist'.[3] The aunt as mother figure offers precisely the kind of belonging-at-a-remove, the mixture of consanguinuity and elective affinity, that Ferrier promotes as the future for national identity. Wollstonecraft and, in a very different way, Edgeworth see themselves 'mothering the nation' in writing didactic fiction for women and children, but Ferrier is profoundly distrustful of maternity. Biological lineages within national bounds are not functional in her work, and the step-parenting that replaces such lineages clearly mimics the English occupation of the Scottish throne. This is a revision of the early modern metaphor of the king as the nation's father, but Ferrier's concern with the (philosophical) subjectivity of the feminine (political) subject means that bloodless patricide is not necessarily a bad thing. As in much nineteenth-century children's fiction, the removal or reinvention of familial structures (an act that is necessarily, on some level, violent) opens the way for daughters' self-invention. If patricide as the precondition of the woman writer's utopia seems to anticipate some of the narratives of feminist psychoanalysis, one should be wary. Ferrier's fictions are finally interesting because they use food and domesticity to explore colonialism as the basis of women's liberation.

Food, in these novels, is the only aspect of culture which retains an absolutely 'Scottish' identity. Ferrier's actually or practically orphaned heroines pride themselves on reading and discussing English and

---

3 Ruth Perry, *Novel Relations: The Transformation of Kinship in English Literature and Culture, 1748–1818* (Cambridge: Cambridge University Press, 2004), p. 368.

French literature, objectify the 'Highland dress' of the local peasants while dressing in modified metropolitan fashions themselves, speak in standard English (and are observed to do so on visits to London) and attend Episcopal churches. They are fictional subjectivities of the conventional kind, issued with a pan-British novel-reading identity which can, and, implicitly, should, be emulated and with which it is easy for the novel-reader to identify. Those who cling to apparently unadulterated Scottish proceedings in these regards are 'flat' characters, stereotypes whom the protagonists treat as navigation hazards in the way of the path to wedded bliss. Ferrier's emphasis on the flatness of these Scottish characters can make her fiction difficult to negotiate, for it is hard to know exactly where to suspend disbelief when the normally plausible heroine converses with an 'Admiral Yellowchops' who likes to eat turtle or dines with a 'Mr Gawffaw' who laughs at inappropriate moments. Interiority is reserved for those whose cultural identity blurs their national identity – that is, those who regard themselves as 'British' rather than English or Scottish and move confidently between the two countries. The worst characters – both the most malevolent actors in the plot and those whose characterisation is least developed – are men who make (false) claim to a colonial identity, insisting, primarily at the table, that their first affiliation is to post-Revolutionary France, independent America or colonial India.

It is illuminating, in this context, to consider Deirdre Lynch's suggestion that 'the first really round character in literature (or the first to get his due in the eighteenth century) was William Shakespeare's fat knight'.[4] Lynch goes on to play with the connection between a 'fully rounded character' (one in whose interiority the Romantic-era reader is able to believe) and the rotund bodies of Hamlet and Falstaff. This is not a connection that works in relation to Ferrier: fatness, here as elsewhere in contemporary fiction, is characteristic of the 'flat' character whose outward appearance accurately represents both moral value and function in relation to the plot, but the idea remains useful. As demonstrated in my reading of Wollstonecraft, the fat in Romantic-era prose are those with an exaggerated sense of entitlement, those interested enough in their own experience of being in the world to feel that the world owes them a good living. For Ferrier this is more complicated than it is for Wollstonecraft because issues of national entitlement interact

4 Lynch, *Economy*, p. 133.

with those of class and gender (although it is important that both writers endorse the self-consciously moderate consumption of the bourgeoisie), but the connection between entitlement and interiority remains important. As Penny Fielding writes, 'Scotland's construction of a national identity in the nineteenth century is inextricably bound up in the means of its own transmission.'[5] The forms of Ferrier's fiction, the flatness and roundness of her characters, her dependence on quotation and intertextuality and the formulaic nature of her settings, are not separable from her Scottish nationalism. Food's omnipresence in Ferrier's fiction makes it hard to tease out precise implications, but my project here is to consider the complex interactions between interiority, gender and nationhood enacted in the kitchen, at the table and in the mouths of Ferrier's fictions.

The Englishwoman at the castle

All three of Ferrier's novels begin with the arrival in Scotland of a woman who is either not Scottish or absolutely alienated from her Scottish roots, constructing the cultural conflict which the novel then takes three volumes to resolve. At the beginning of *Marriage* (1818), we meet Lady Juliana, a seventeen-year-old 'educated for the sole purpose of forming a brilliant establishment' in whom 'a fashionable mother and an obsequious governess' have fostered 'the forward petulance of childhood' until 'selfishness and caprice … formed the prominent features of her character'.[6] Lady Juliana's father, the Earl of Courtland, is determined to marry her to a rich, old and ugly peer, but she is persuaded to elope to Scotland by her young, handsome lover, and the end of chapter one finds the couple two months into their marriage, running out of money, and becoming bored with each other. 'There now remained but one course to pursue'; Douglas and Lady Juliana make for his father's Highland castle, where Juliana anticipates 'wander[ing] through long galleries' and 'lov[ing]' old pictures, and armour, and tapestry'. Juliana's name, her father's name, his obsession with 'political interest' and 'the advancement of the family' and the location of his 'magnificent mansion' in 'D__shire'

---

5 Penny Fielding, *Writing and Orality: Nationality, Culture and Nineteenth Century Scottish Fiction* (Oxford: Clarendon Press, 1996), p. 19.

6 Susan Ferrier, *Marriage*, ed. Herbert Foltinek (Oxford: Oxford University Press, 2001), pp. 4–5.

suggest some comparison with Lady Georgiana Spencer, but in any case the one-chapter summary of a conventional sentimental novel plot is typical of Ferrier's off-handed approach to novelistic convention. We all know the story – the lapdogs, the Earl's name and the indulgent governess can perfectly well substitute for the plot.

Ferrier's second novel, *The Inheritance* (1824), opens with an epigraph from *All's Well that Ends Well*, followed by the sage assertion that, 'It is a truth universally acknowledged, that there is no passion so deeply rooted in human nature as that of pride.'[7] By the end of chapter one, this pride, 'cherished time immemorial by the noble race of Rossville' (sic) has been wounded by the younger son's marriage to 'Miss Sarah Black, a beautiful girl of obscure origin and no fortune'. 'The usual consequences' have followed, 'viz. the displeasure of friends, the want of fortune, the world's dread laugh, and, in short, all the thousand natural ills that flesh is heir to when it fails in its allegiance to blood'.[8] 'The unfortunate pair, thus doomed to unwilling exile, retired to France' where 'the natural wish for a child' remains ungratified for many years. At last Mrs St Clair 'announced herself in the way of becoming a mother' and the couple undertake a flight into Scotland, interrupted 'at an obscure village' by a premature labour resulting in 'a remarkably fine thriving baby' for whom a wet-nurse provides 'that abundant stock of love and tenderness, which those dealers in the milk of human kindness always have so freely to bestow on their nursling for the time'.[9] The plan to adjourn to Scotland is postponed until Mr St Clair has suffered 'a palsy' and taken several years to die, at which point Lord Rossville commands the presence of Mrs and Miss St Clair and they 'hastened to exchange the gay vineyards, and bright suns of France, for the bleak hills and frowning skies of Scotland'.[10] The dominance of such general terms as 'universally', 'usual' and 'always' joins with Ferrier's gathering use of quotation here to suggest that this tale is more hackneyed than is in fact the case (the marriage may be a standby of sentimental fiction, and the birth story clearly gestures towards the trope of the nurse who is not what she seems, but the combination of these stories, the setting and the weak husband are not particularly conventional). It is as if Ferrier needs to set out a

7 Susan Ferrier, *The Inheritance* (Edinburgh: William Blackwood, 1824), vol. 1, p. 1.
8 Ferrier, *Inheritance*, vol. 1, p. 2.
9 Ferrier, *Inheritance*, vol. 1, p. 6.
10 Ferrier, *Inheritance*, vol. 1, p. 8.
11 Ferrier, *Inheritance*, vol. 1, p. 10–11.

puppet show, to provide a literary location for her own version of Scotland, before the 'round' characters can come in; it is only in the second chapter that we learn that Mrs St Clair has learnt to be 'captivating; but the change was merely outward', that she has come to distrust appearances since discovering her husband's looks and breeding to 'add no more to real distinction than a flaming sign does to an ill-kept inn' and, most importantly, that she has failed to 'render her daughter as great an adept in dissimulation as she was herself' so that 'Miss St Clair remained pretty much as nature had formed her.'[11]

The beginning of *Destiny*, published in 1831 and (not noticeably) 'respectfully dedicated' to Walter Scott, works similarly, the opening lines reminding us wearily that,

> All the world knows that there is nothing on earth to be compared to a Highland Chief. He has his loch and his islands, his mountains and his castle, his piper and his tartan, his thousand acres of untrodden heath, and his tens of thousands of black-faced sheep, and his clans of bonneted clansmen, with claymores, and Gaelic, and hot blood, and dirks.[12]

This increasingly jumbled list, coupled with cheerful elision of the pre- and post-Clearance landscapes of the Highlands (sheep and 'untrodden heath' replaced the 'bands of bonneted clansmen' who had previously inhabited the heath) establishes the centrality of Ferrier's anti-Romanticism and particularly her satire on Walter Scott and his reader's expectations. Nevertheless, the Chief of Glenroy is a victim of – or at least defined by – his own publicity, for 'The inward man was much what the outward man denoted. He was proud, prejudiced and profuse; he piqued himself upon the antiquity of his family, the heroic deeds of his ancestors, the extent of his estates, the number of his followers, their physical strength, their devoted attachment.'[13] The inward man is much what the outward denotes; we are not expected to devote interpretative energies to Glenroy. He marries 'a merely pretty girl of neither family nor fortune' who remains nameless ('he could derive no consequence from his wife; his wife must owe all her dignity to him') and, having produced two children, dies at the beginning of the next paragraph.[14] This opens the way for Lady Elizabeth Waldegrave, the wicked stepmother, whom Glenroy meets on a rare visit to London, and who is 'such an

12 Susan Ferrier, *Destiny* (William Blackwood: Edinburgh, 1831), vol. 1, p. 1.
13 Ferrier, *Destiny*, vol. 1, p. 5.
14 Ferrier, *Destiny*, vol. 1, p. 6.

enthusiastic admirer of tartan, and Highland bonnets, and Highland scenery, that Glenroy was captivated'. Again, by the beginning of the second chapter at least three plots have been written off. The next event, in all three novels, is a meal, and it is over food that Ferrier's novels come to life. Lady Juliana becomes hysterical when she sees that the castle of her novel-fuelled dreams is cold, cheerless and badly furnished. Her husband's aunts, who become models for a certain kind of Scottish femininity, press upon her 'a huge bowl of coarse Scotch broth, swimming with leeks, greens and grease. Lady Juliana attempted to taste it; but her delicate palate revolted at the homely fare; and she gave up the attempt, in spite of Miss Nicky's earnest entreaties to take a few more of this excellent family broth.'[15] Miss Nicky's dialect here merges with her cuisine to emphasise Lady Juliana's, and perhaps by extension the reader's, alienation from this anti-Romantic Highland scene. This merging of food and speech is repeated over and again in this context; at breakfast a few days later, Lady Juliana threatens to faint at the sight of a herring and Miss Grizzy inquires, 'Was it the sight or the smell of the beast that shocked you so much, my dear Lady Juliana?', necessitating a footnote from Ferrier to point out that 'In Scotland, everything that flies or swims, ranks in the bestial tribe.'[16] The reader is again aligned with Lady Juliana, English novel-readers both. In place of the herring, the aunts offer 'charming barley meal scones', 'tempting pease bannocks' and 'oatcakes! I'm sure your Ladyship never saw such cakes.' Lady Juliana 'can't eat any of those things' and requests 'muffins and chocolate', neither of which are available. When toast is also impossible ('we happen to be quite out of loaf bread ... but we've sent to Drymsine for some'), Lady Juliana offers to ingest 'some grouse, or a beef steak, if it was very nicely done'. These are procured only to avoid the aunts' guilt if 'the child was to resemble a moor-fowl' or 'have a face like a raw beef steak,' a moment which constitutes Ferrier's announcement to the reader of Lady Juliana's pregnancy.[17] London whims may be indulged in the name of a Scottish heir and the selfish aristocrat's appetite gratified at great expense for the sake of her unborn child, but it is not Lady Juliana whom the aunts intend to feed. The request for muffins and toast in place of the barley, pease and oat-based cakes and biscuits dramatises one of the major differences between English and Scot-

15 Ferrier, *Marriage*, p. 16.
16 Ferrier, *Marriage*, p. 30.
17 Ferrier, *Marriage*, p. 33.

tish cuisine between the seventeenth and nineteenth centuries; wheat remained rare outside Glasgow and Edinburgh long after it had become the staple of almost all English diets. Ferrier's authentic Scotland may be indigestible, obscure and unattractive to metropolitan visitors, although it is also clear that metropolitan visitors' failings are thrown into relief by their response to the real place.

There is a very similar gustatory representation of the English female aristocracy's failings in *Destiny*. To summarise a rarely available novel, the two children born in the first chapter grow up as Edith, the heroine, and her brother Norman. Their cousin Reginald comes to live with them because his father holds an important post in India (more of this later). The marriage between Glenroy and Lady Waldegrave breaks down while the children are young and she leaves with her daughter Florinda. A romance develops between Edith and Reginald, which is still flourishing when Reginald departs on his Grand Tour, where he meets again the adult and beautiful Florinda. After Norman's death, brought on partly by over-indulgence, Lady Waldegrave re-establishes contact and arranges a visit of reconciliation to the now decrepit and grieving Glenroy. Again, Ferrier relies heavily on the provision and consumption of food to portray the selfishness of the bad and the selflessness of the good.

Florinda, accompanied by her French governess (another stock villain of the genre), arrives at the grief-stricken castle before her mother. Florinda is well-mannered and pleasant, but her speech works against her eating to modify her moral status. Despite protestations of enduring affection, she fails to note her host's absence until she has impressed everyone else with her beauty and sweet demeanour. Edith explains that Glenroy is ill: '"How sorry I am!" said Lady Waldegrave, in a tone beautifully modulated to pity; then, in a moment changing it to one of delight,"Come, dear Fido!"as Sir Reginald's dog entered the room, and flew to her with demonstrations of joy.'[18] Dogs, in Ferrier, have no infallible instinct, and it is the kind of variations in Florinda's voice that show her to be her mother's daughter. She can modulate her tones to give the appearance of sensibility, but it is the beauty of the representation that reveals its falsity. The implication is that genuine pity would be less beautiful as well as less transient, but when dinner is served the reader sees that education is, as usual, at the root of all evil. Edith asks Florinda if she has dined:

18 Ferrier, *Destiny*, vol. 2, p. 131.

'Were I to answer you myself, I should say I had dined,' replied Lady Waldegrave. 'As I really don't mind dinner so much as many people do, and we had some not very bad chops at the last stage – only they did taste a little of peats and whisky,' she added, laughing. 'But if you ask Madame Latour, she will tell you she has not dined since she left London.'[19]

The comparison between herself and 'many people' makes it apparent that Florinda is still at least as concerned to appear well as to consult her appetite, but her joke about different interpretations of the idea of 'dining' alerts us to Madame Latour's real failings. 'To dine' in the context of Edith's question is simply to eat an appropriate dish at an appropriate moment, as modified by other priorities such as journeys and location, which Madame Latour has certainly done during her days of travelling. But the other meaning is to dine well, to consume a menu that confirms the diner's sense of her own social value in a setting similar to her habitual environment. For Madame Latour, the first kind of eating does not count, but there may be hope for Florinda. Rather than requiring a dinner, Florinda sees the remains of the dessert laid out on the table and gives Reginald his third or fourth opportunity to show Edith and the reader that she and he have an unhappy but unexplained history:

> 'I think I might be prevailed upon to eat some of these Alpine strawberries,' said Lady Waldegrave, as she seated herself at table. A slight bend of the head was the only reply Sir Reginald vouchsafed as he helped the strawberries without once looking towards his beautiful guest.[20]

Florinda is baiting Reginald here, making a request which requires him to interact with her when she knows that he is trying to escape her presence, and incidentally demonstrating to Edith her power over Edith's lover. The strawberries are currency not fuel, although a currency more flexible and multivalent than anything in any mint.

Sir Reginald escapes, and Madame Latour reveals her true colours, remarking to Florinda, 'How extrêmement Saar Ragenall est changé' and telling Edith that "he was si joli, si charmant, vat you call pleesante."[21] Edith still – and for most of this volume – has no idea where or under what circumstances Florinda and Reginald knew each other and came to such a coldness, and Madame Latour has no intention of telling her. The references to a shared past are intended to disturb Edith, and if Madame Latour speaks with a forked tongue

19 Ferrier, *Destiny*, vol. 2, p. 132.
20 Ferrier, *Destiny*, vol. 2, p. 133.
21 Ferrier, *Destiny*, vol. 2, p. 133.

she eats like a vampire. 'A repast from the *debris* of the dinner had been quickly got up at the other end of the room, and no sooner was it arranged than Madame Latour started up with great alacrity and repaired to it':

> 'Cette grosse est excellente, excellente,' said Madame Latour, after she had helped herself to the back and breast of a moorfowl … She flew like a butterfly or bee, from dish to dish, extracting the very heart and soul from each as she skimmed along, while at the same time she kept calling for every species of sauce and condiment that ever had been heard of, which she contrived to mix with the most admirable dexterity.[22]

Ferrier's use of the French (and italicised) *debris* in this context is interesting. Madame Latour's dependence on French is repeatedly called 'bad English' and the lack of italics in her speech makes it appear more jumbled, more of a pidgin, than it is. It is as if the narrator knows how to use language, or languages, properly, each marked off from the other, while Madame Latour's epicurism applies as much to what comes out of her mouth as what goes in. She feeds and speaks selfishly, taking the best bits without thought for the integrity of the whole. In some ways, as we will see, this is typical of expatriates in Ferrier's fiction, but here it serves partly to establish Florinda's relative integrity. Florinda may be beautiful and 'polished' by foreign travel, able to control her surface in a way that Edith, who has spent her life at the castle, cannot, but here the complexity of her relationship with food works to construct interiority. Food is a currency for her, a means of communicating what cannot or should not be said, and to this extent it constitutes one of the 'forms of interiority' where Madame Latour's naked greed confirms her flatness, her puppet-like role as the raddled but vain French villainess.

Later in the evening, Florinda's mother arrives and behaves similarly, requiring Edith as the mistress of the house to provide a third dinner:

> 'This soup is very good – it is very good,' – sending away her plate after taking two spoonfuls. 'I know you don't recommend salmon to me, Dr Price, but that looks so particularly well, I will just taste it.' Then, having taken a little of it, it was also sent off. 'Pray, send me a pâté, Dr Price – ah, chicken pâté, very well seasoned, though?' – putting down the knife and fork, after the first mouthful. 'Yes, I will try the fricandeau,' and so on with game, tarts, jellies and dessert, in a manner enough to have raised the ghost of Lycurgus, or Dr Gregory.[23]

22 Ferrier, *Destiny*, vol. 2, p. 135.
23 Ferrier, *Destiny*, vol. 2, p. 163.

This kind of disorderly eating is strongly inflected by both gender and class. Lady Elizabeth and Madame Latour consume excessively, assuredly responding to appetite and not hunger, but it is a qualitative and not a quantitative excess. Their absolute disregard for the domestic inconvenience of producing a sequence of dinners for a sequence of late guests shows an aristocratic disdain for the work of housekeeping, while their behaviour at the table makes great show of highly refined palates without the coarseness of hunger. In some ways, this is recreational eating at its worst, an abuse of resources, of Edith's produce, without even the justification of pleasure, much less need. The point is to show off what one can afford to waste, especially when what is wasted belongs to someone else.

Sins in eating are mirrored in speech. Lady Elizabeth's many French words and phrases are italicised, but when the women withdraw to the drawing room she revels in Florinda 'pouring forth the full tide of song in strains of perfect melody'.[24] In a trope repeated across Ferrier's work, the polished aristocrat delights the company with exquisite renditions of French and Italian opera while the Anglo-Scottish heroine stumbles through simple but pretty Scottish folk songs (usually from the fake folk tradition born of the growing Romantic-era metropolitan interest in Scotland), hampered by her inability fully to conceal her emotions. Tourism and cultural miscegenation beyond the British Isles are invariably associated with a particular kind of cherry-picking greed, and this works partly to distinguish those who feel themselves part of the newly united kingdom from those who take an omnivorous approach to nationhood. It is all right, or indeed right and necessary, for Scottish women to take a post-nationalist approach to Scotland, singing Scottish songs in the forms created for and popularised by English Romanticism, of whose colonial aspects Ferrier is entirely aware. But this is qualitatively different from the failure to engage with nationhood displayed in the appetite of the touring aristocrat or the foreigner with a taste for luxury. In ways endlessly complicated by class and gender, the Waldegraves, like Lady Juliana in *Marriage* and Mrs St Clair in *The Inheritance*, are expatriated by wealth or travel, tourists at the table without sufficient allegiance even to finish what's on their plates.

---

24 Ferrier, *Destiny*, vol. 2, p.167.

The British woman at home

What, then, is the alternative to this model of alienated and selfconscious consumption? Does Ferrier, unlike any of the other novelists studied here, offer her readers an unproblematic, or at least unproblematised, way of eating and cooking – a diet for the new Britain; and if so, how might these forms of production and consumption relate to her interest in the formulation of national identity?

The answer, at least initially, appears to be that there is no way of eating without complications. Lady Juliana cannot understand much of her aunts' and cousins' speech and regards their warm, waterproof homemade clothes with horror, but she is even more alienated from their compulsive interest in cooking and the lines of supply of food. When the first 'round' character appears, she shares Lady Juliana's distaste for the minutiae of domestic life while pitying and despising her selfishness and hysteria. Alicia Douglas, Lady Juliana's new sister-in-law, lost her English mother at birth and her Scottish father shortly afterwards. She was brought up by an elegant and wealthy English aunt on condition that there should be no contact with her Scottish family, but, in contrast to Lady Juliana, 'her governess, a woman of a strong understanding and enlarged mind, early instilled into her a deep and strong sense of religion' as a result of which, at seventeen when she was 'produced in the world, she was a rational, cheerful, and sweet tempered girl, with a fine formed person, and a countenance in which was … clearly painted the sunshine of her breast'.[25] 'Her open natural manner, blending the frankness of the Scotch with the polished reserve of the English woman, her total exemption from vanity, were calculated alike to please others, and maintain her own cheerfulness undimmed by a single cloud.'[26] Alicia has her own history, a sentimental drama in which circumstances have obliged her to make the best of her second choice of husband, and she is partly here as the exemplar of the virtuous woman who has achieved maturity through novelistic emotional drama. It is a virtue marked by a competent but disdainful approach to domestic labour and especially food.

As with Gertrude in *The Inheritance* and Edith in *Destiny*, to have one Scottish and one English parent seems to be a necessary but no means sufficient condition of both interiority and virtue.

25 Ferrier, *Destiny*, vol. 2, p. 74.
26 Ferrier, *Destiny*, vol. 2, p. 75.

Ferrier's Englishwomen are always caricatures, either lazy aristocrats or shopkeepers' wives, while the Scottish women are – joyfully or complainingly – mired in domesticity and living too close to the land for intellectual or spiritual activity. The next scene in which Alicia plays a role exemplifies these alternatives in a way reminiscent of a psychological experiment.

Lady Juliana gives birth, producing, 'not, alas! the ardently desired heir to its ancient consequence, but twin-daughters, who could only be regarded as additional burdens on its poverty'.[27] The substitution of not one but two daughters for the 'ardently desired heir' speaks again to Ferrier's interest in disrupted lineages. It is important that Ferrier does not identify women with the colonised subject; it is not that subaltern girls take the place of the boy ruler, but rather that the multiplication of babies opens up both narrative and subjective possibilities. The girls, partly because they are girls and because there are two of them, are deracinated from birth. Unable to represent 'ancient consequence', their potential is unconfined by tradition, although inevitably the way Ferrier fulfils this potential is deeply conservative. Lady Juliana, herself morally and geographically adrift, 'turns from them in disgust', requiring the nurse to take them away and bring her lapdogs instead:

> At the pressing solicitations of her husband, the fashionable mother was prevailed upon to attempt nursing one of her poor starving infants; but the first trial proved also the last, as she declared nothing upon earth should ever induce her to perform so odious an office … A wet-nurse was therefore procured; but as she refused to undertake both children, and the old gentleman would not hear of having two such incumbrances in his family, it was settled, to the unspeakable delight of the maiden sisters, that the youngest should be entrusted entirely to their management, and brought up by hand.[28]

So there is a twin study, one brought up by the paid lackeys of the English aristocracy and one entrusted to the over-weaning ambition of provincial Scottish housewives. The results for the younger girl are realistic: 'The child, who was naturally weak and delicate at its birth, daily lost a portion of its little strength, while its continued cries declared the intensity of its sufferings' while the nurse 'by her fawning and flattery … succeeded in exciting a degree of interest,

---

27 Ferrier, *Destiny*, vol. 2, p. 116.
28 Ferrier, *Destiny*, vol. 2, p. 118.

which nature had not secured for it in the mother's breast'.[29] Nevertheless, the dwindling baby survives a regime of home-made medicines and bread and water for three weeks, when Alicia arrives for
a visit and comments wistfully in response to Lady Juliana's wish
that someone would gag the baby, 'Alas! what would I give to hear
the blessed sound of a living child!'[30] The deal is soon done, and we
hear little more of Alicia and her adopted daughter for some years.

There is an extent to which Mary's aunts, and all the Scottish
housewives in Ferrier's fiction who resemble them, constitute a
rather vicious parody of some of Walter Scott's 'gudewife' characters. It is a comparison which verges on the explicit at the end of
volume one of *The Inheritance*, when Gertrude goes to stay with
her maternal cousins the Blacks, to assist at the oldest daughter
Bell's wedding. Mrs Black is entirely absorbed by domestic cares
and concerned only that her children should be as prosperous as
possible, and Gertrude is shocked to see at close hand the work and
disruption of leisure required to produce a meal inferior to those she
eats daily at Rossville Castle. The day before the wedding,

> during the whole day, the steam of soups, pies, pastries, &c. &c. which
> issued from Mrs Black's kitchen, and penetrated to the very interior of
> the drawing room, might (as some one has parodied it) have created a
> stomach beneath the ribs of death. To Gertrude, the commotion caused
> by what is called giving a dinner, was something new. The total *bouleverse-
> ment* of all orders of the community, where much was to be done without
> the proper means – where a sumptuous banquet was to be prepared by
> the common drudges of the kitchen, and where every servant had double
> their usual portion of work to perform, besides being thrown out of their
> own natural sphere of action.[31]

One of the functions of the word '*bouleversement*' here is to promote
a reader's identification with Gertrude, whose reported interior
monologue this implicitly is, rather than her cousins, whose less
novelistic and more ordinary lifestyle would be more familiar to the
majority of readers. But the cousins, absorbed in the minutiae of the
daily life of the ambitious middling sort (mostly clothes, gossip and
flirting) do not understand French. What is wrong here is the Blacks'
inability to raise their eyes to higher aspirations. The dinner is 'about
three times as large and as elaborate as was necessary' and it is this
over-reaching of necessity that constitutes an inappropriate use of

29 Ferrier, *Destiny*, vol. 2, p. 119.
30 Ferrier, *Destiny*, vol. 2, p. 120.
31 Ferrier, *Inheritance*, vol. 1, p. 330.

time and energy: 'Mrs Black was chiefly emulous of a character for her dinners, and probably laboured infinitely harder to stuff a dozen dull bodies, than the author of Waverley does to amuse the whole world.'[32] This sentence, like the moments when Ferrier introduces us to Mr and Mrs Fairbairn, the parents obsessed with indulging their children, or Mr Gawffaw who laughs enthusiastically when there is no laughing matter, constitutes a knowing lapse in the pretence of fiction. There are two ways of stuffing dull bodies and 'the author of Waverley' engages in at least one of them, not literally feeding the boring (although there would be a metaphorical case for that too), but filling out literary characters, trying to make the flat round in order to amuse the world. There may also be an implication that Walter Scott's labours are similarly redundant, an attempt to dress up the mechanics of daily life in inauthentic glory akin to Mrs Black's conspicuous cooking.

If so, an obvious focus for this is the contrast between Ferrier's images of Scottish domesticity and Walter Scott's. Both Mrs Black and Mary's aunts can be read in relation to such stock Scott characters as Mrs Dinmont in *Guy Mannering* and Lady Margaret in *The Tale of Old Mortality*, both of whom devote much of their time to food preparation in a way which is certainly objectified in relation to both gender and national identity, but also presented as attractive and engaging. Ailie Dinmont welcomes her returning husband and his guest with great affection and then retreats to the kitchen:

> The active bustle of the mistress (so she was called in the kitchen, and the gudewife in the parlour) had already signed the fate of a couple of fowls, which, for want of time to dress them otherwise, soon appeared reeking from the gridiron – or brander, as Mrs. Dinmont denominated it. A huge piece of cold beef-ham, eggs, butter, cakes, and barley-meal bannocks in plenty, made up the entertainment, which was to be diluted with home-brewed ale of excellent quality, and a case-bottle of brandy.[33]

'Brander' is not, so far as I can tell, a Scottish dialect word; it appears in cookbooks published in London rather more often than 'gridiron', so this gloss works to estrange Mrs Dinmont from Scott's readership rather than to introduce a new word. The 'want of time' for

---

32 Ferrier, *Inheritance*, vol. 1, p. 330.
33 Walter Scott, *Guy Mannering*, ed. P.D. Garside (Edinburgh: Edinburgh University Press, 1999) p. 165.

more elaborate ways of cooking suggests the immediacy of Mrs Dinmont's response to her husband. This is not a wealthy household in which celebratory viands can be commanded instantly, but the cooking of the chickens here demonstrates skill and affection which, in the English guest's view, make up for any lack of grace. The preoccupations which Scott presents as one of the more charming Scottish peculiarities of 'thirty years since' are those which Ferrier depicts as ultimately malign. Scott, according to Ferrier, is labouring to stuff dull bodies, producing a result three times as elaborate as it needs to be. For Ferrier, this kind of easy, benevolent domesticity is a myth. Those who devote themselves to production and consumption sacrifice interiority and turn away from what really matters. One could read this in the light of Julie Kipp's observation that 'the overtly sympathetic mother becomes emblematic of the dangers associated with narrow allegiances or highly localized loyalties' so that '[a]n obsessive concern for things local provides a distraction from duty to nation'.[34] Excessive domesticity works against good citizenship, and in this context the incompatibility of biological and moral parenting in Ferrier's work makes sense. There is little room for compromise; both the English aristocrats who consume without producing and the Scottish housewives who produce without consuming are denied the illusion of interiority and the prospect of salvation. It is only the English–Scottish heroine, following the model of a woman who is never her biological parent, who can aspire to the finely modulated relation with production and consumption that allows for the development of 'real' character and real morals.

The results of the twin study, then, are as one would expect – Mary grows up to be the heroine of the last two volumes of *Marriage*, exemplary in faith, virtue and properly controlled sensibility while Adelaide, brought up in her uncle's stately home after her father has despaired of Lady Juliana's debts and gone to India, is selfish, beautiful and cold. But the terms of the experiment, merging nutriment and nationhood, are telling. Lady Juliana's refusal to breastfeed works as an apparently adequate synecdoche for the English aristocracy's absolute lack of productivity and failure to take responsibility for the results of its conduct, a theme insistently re-echoed in Henry and Lady Juliana's return to London and descent into debt. It is important, however, that the answer is not, as it might

34 Kipp, *Romanticism*, p. 14.

be in most Scottish Romantic texts, that the native Scots family can nurture its own. Left to the care of her aunts, Mary will die; their local and national identities are characterised by an obsessively narrow-minded dependence on out-of-date ideas and an inability to contemplate freeing themselves from a pastiche of feudal loyalty to the appalling Lady Maclaughlan. It is the bicultural English–Scottish woman who has chosen to leave London high society for the peaceful domesticity of remote mountains who can offer, by proxy, proper sustenance to the growing girl.

The way that family relations and national politics come together in these novels is exemplified by Alicia's gardening and interior design, for what we are invited to admire in her domestic arrangements is a kind of colonisation. Showing Henry and Lady Juliana her house and garden, she says,

> 'had our little embellishments been productive of much expense, or tending solely to my gratification, I should never have suggested them. When we first took possession of this spot, it was a perfect wilderness, with a dirty farm-house on it: nothing but mud about the doors, nothing but wood, and briers, and brambles beyond it; and the village presented a still more melancholy scene of rank luxuriance, in its swarms of dirty idle girls, and mischievous boys.'[35]

So Alicia and Douglas solve two problems at once, 'engaging these ill-directed children, by trifling rewards, to apply their lively energies in improving instead of destroying the works of nature'. The taming and planting of the wilderness, especially coupled with the mission to bring civilisation to the natives, is a classic trope in settler narratives from *Robinson Crusoe* to the journals of late nineteenth-century emigrants to Canada and Australia. This 'improved' landscape stands in contrast to the muddy yard and farm buildings scattered around the ancestral castle, a corner of a Scottish hill that is forever Britain and a blueprint for a united kingdom where girls can come to maturity away from both the fleshpots of London and the mind-numbing provincialism of Highland femininity. This is where Mary grows up, and it is from this prototypical home that she emerges sixteen years later to promote an alternative to the dichotomy of English and Scottish femininities.

This consumption-based model of national identity is sustained across Ferrier's oeuvre, and it is clearly in part a critique or parody

35 Ferrier, *Marriage*, p. 97.

of more romanticised accounts, and especially Walter Scott's. *The Inheritance*'s version of the food-obsessed Scottish aunt found in all Ferrier's novels is Miss Pratt, a busybody maiden aunt who cannot keep out of the kitchen at the castle and, like Mary's aunts in *Marriage*, greets every challenge or distress with advice to eat more or differently, and almost invariably to eat in a more 'Scottish' way. From the beginning of the first volume, Miss Pratt hurries everyone to the table where she discourses knowledgeably about the composition and comparative aesthetic and nutritional benefits of each dish, causing irritation and dismay to her socially ambitious companions. Gertrude has 'no taste for poking into pantries, and chimneys, and cellars, or of hearing any of the inelegant minutiae of life detailed', and Miss Pratt serves as an insistent reminder of the mundane.[36] The path of virtue, however, is more complicated here than in *Marriage*; Gertrude is a flawed heroine who must learn humility before she becomes fit to marry and live happily ever after, and much of this learning revolves around consumption. Miss Pratt is a figure of fun, but we are not invited to dismiss her as irrelevant in the way that the aunts, with their parodic names, are irrelevant to the plot of *Marriage*.

This becomes particularly clear in volume two, when this darker novel gathers pace. Lord Rossville has died (of apoplexy, usually associated with too much rich food and a tendency to anger) and Gertrude has inherited the estate. She has persuaded her Uncle Adam, a wealthy miser who likes Gertrude partly because he discerns the goodness that underlies her beauty and fickleness and partly because she bears a startling resemblance to a woman he loved in his youth, to come for a visit. Settled by Gertrude in a warm, quiet room with the latest newspapers, Uncle Adam is interrupted by Miss Pratt, who opens civilities by 'hop[ing] he had taken something since he came – it wanted a long while to dinner yet'. Uncle Adam declines, 'adding, that he never took anything between breakfast and dinner'.[37]

> 'And an excellent rule it is,' said Miss Pratt, in her most emphatic tone, 'for them who can keep it; for I really think there's a great deal too much eating and drinking goes on in the present day, especially amongst young people … I really think poor Lord Rossville hurt himself very much by his manner of eating – not but what he was a moderate man in the main – but

36 Ferrier, *Inheritance*, vol. 1, p. 88.
37 Ferrier, *Inheritance*, vol. 2, p. 228.

to tell the truth – God knows! but I never can help thinking he dealt a deal too deep in a fine fat venison pasty that was at dinner, the very last day he sat at his own table, poor man!'

'I dinna doot it,' said Mr Ramsay, secure that he would never come to an untimely end by any such means.

'I've given our young Countess a hint about that,' resumed Miss Pratt; 'for I really think there's need for a little reform in the kitchen here. It was just yesterday I was saying to her that, for all the cooks she had, and for all the grand things they sent up, I didn't believe she had one that could make a drop good plain barley broth, or knew how to guide a sheep's head and trotters. – She laughed, and desired Philips, the maitre d'hotel, to be sure to have one Scotch dish on the table every day; but I've no great brew of any Scotch dish that'll ever come out of the hands of a French cook.'[38]

This exchange is in many ways a more articulate version of much that Mary's aunts have to say about her upbringing – that she has been allowed too much variety in her diet, that tea and coffee are unwarranted indulgences for young girls, that she has not been fed enough porridge – except that Mary's aunts are undeveloped characters, there to represent a particular false ideology of gender and nationhood, and Miss Pratt, whose views are supported by Uncle Adam, is to some extent right. Gertrude's reluctance to contemplate 'the mechanisms by which life is supported' coupled with her lack of commitment to anywhere in particular, her lack of roots, leads her into excess consumption which is clearly and consistently associated with a lack of local or national identity. Unlike Ferrier's other heroines, Gertrude has spent formative years in continental Europe, and unlike them, she has no moral exemplar to replace or supplement her inadequate 'mother' (who subsequently turns out not to be her biological mother). *Inheritance* shows the limits of deracination as a route to liberation, especially as Gertrude's uncertainty about her parentage and her nationality gathers strength.

Gertrude's spending spirals as her beliefs about her own past come under question. In the next volume she moves to London, rents an expensive house where we find her eating from a 'magnificent breakfast service of richly chased antique plate and Sevres china'[39] which she buys instead of building a school for the children living near Rossville, surrounded by 'a litter of new publications,

38 Ferrier, *Inheritance*, vol. 2, p. 289–90.
39 Ferrier, *Inheritance*, vol. 3, p. 91.

and music, and expensive toys'.[40] Unhappy in love, she 'squander[s] money in dissipating thought'.[41] Returning at last to Rossville at the end of the season,

> Her conscience smote her as she passed some old cottages which she had planned pulling down, and building new and more commodious ones in their place. 'Half of what my opera box cost me would have done that,' sighed she; 'and that bridge!' as she caught a glimpse of one, half-finished; 'the poor people must still go two miles about, till my diamond necklace is paid;' and tears of contrition dropped from her eyes.[42]

Ferrier is adamant that self-indulgent metropolitan expenditure and meeting a landowner's responsibilities are incompatible alternatives. Half an opera box or new cottages, a bridge or a diamond necklace: false equivalences made by incompatible currencies. Gertrude returns to the castle itself to find her Italian garden and new theatre complete in an image that offers the opposite of Alicia's remodelling of her new Scottish home. Alicia's new Scotland is based on job creation and public amenities, while Gertrude's exacerbates the rich/poor divide by bringing more alien and inaccessible wealth into an impoverished community. It is noticeable here that the French-born Gertrude's expenditure promotes precisely the kind of pan-European identity that characterises Florinda and Lady Elizabeth Waldegrave. She buys French china, attends Italian opera, commands an Italian garden on the banks of a Scottish river and employs a French chef to feed her household on foreign food. It is not clear if it is the individual nations that attract Ferrier's disapproval or a sense that this kind of cultural fusion is fundamentally inauthentic, a trivialisation of the serious issue of national belonging. If it is the latter, this serves in part to contrast with the authentic and moral marriage of England and Scotland and the children of that marriage who are uniformly pure, lovely and of good report.

Men eating turtles

There are very few characters in Ferrier's novels whose relationship with food is not disordered to a greater or lesser extent, but it is noticeable that those with the most extreme forms of disorder are

40 Ferrier, *Inheritance*, vol. 3, p. 96.
41 Ferrier, *Inheritance*, vol. 3, p. 125.
42 Ferrier, *Inheritance*, vol. 3, p. 153.

men and boys. Women might approach food in a wasteful, exhibi-
tionist or punitive way, but they do not eat too much. Men's greed
is often dangerous in Ferrier's fiction, the mark of a man with more
entitlement than he is able to use constructively. Gluttons take too
much and give nothing, a rapacity inseparable from a certain kind of
masculinity that menaces Ferrier's young heroines. By contrast, ultimately marriageable men can be spotted at the beginning of their
trajectory to moral heroism by minimal appetite and well-controlled
hunger. This is particularly clear in *Destiny*, which follows the main
characters from infancy to marriage or death. Norman, Glenroy's
only son, for whom the family are in mourning when Florinda and
her mother arrive, is marked from childhood by an unattractive
interest in what he eats, which is repeatedly contrasted to the more
abstemious habits of the eventually triumphant hero Ronald.

Men's consumption is always a reliable guide to their moral
standing, but it also offers a more complicated guide to the relationship between the individual and the nation. After her father the
Laird's death, Edith finds herself cast out into the world and obliged
to seek refuge with 'a half sister of her mother's' whose antecedents
are carefully traced to show that, although a blood relation of Edith,
Mrs Ribley has no Scottish blood and has always lived in London.
Mr Ribley has made his money in trade, as 'a sleeping partner in the
old-established house of Rudge, Ribley and Company' so the childless couple are rich but devoid of grace or elegance.[43] Mrs Ribley's
only previous attention to Edith has been to send her Fordyce's
sermons (also frequently recommended to Mary by her Scottish
aunts) and when she writes to invite Edith to stay, 'it was evident
from this letter that Mrs Ribley was at least fifty years behind the
rest of the world in her ideas'.[44] Like Mary's aunts in *Marriage* and
Mrs Black in *The Inheritance*, Mrs Ribley is marketing an out-of-
date and nationally specific kind of femininity which it will be the
heroine's painful duty to reject.

 Edith travels to London with her old nurse, Mrs Macauley, and
the husband of her mother-figure aunt, Captain Malcolm. They are
greeted by Mr Ribley, whose welcome revolves around the offer
of food: first 'a rump-steak – London rump-steak? – a great delicacy to Scotch people!' and then, 'a sandwich – nice ham sandwich?
– Westphalia ham in the house at this moment – beautiful ham! –

43 Ferrier, *Destiny*, vol. 3, p. 69.
44 Ferrier, *Destiny*, vol. 3, p. 51.

bought it myself! – the flesh as red as a rose, fat as white as a lily!'[45] The steak clearly represents Mr Ribley's local affiliations, but it also inaugurates the theme of urban isolation or insulation from the land. It cannot really be a 'London rump-steak' because, especially so far into the nineteenth century, there were no beef cows in London. The association is about dining habits and butchery, not the provenance of the cows, and this contrasts with Edith's father's great interest in precisely where on his estate each animal consumed at his table was reared and killed. The imported ham, bought where all the meat in Edith's previous experience was farmed or hunted by and for those who intended to eat it, emphasises the point, and also sets up a new kind of commercial masculinity which revolves around shops rather than farming and hunting.

At breakfast the next morning, Mr Ribley descants on 'the charming location of our square' based on its proximity to Cheapside, 'the India House' and Lloyds, and continues,

> 'Now here comes the muffin – must take it while it's hot – sure you never tasted such a muffin; from the very first muffin-maker in the world – Moggs' muffins celebrated all over London. – Now only think how lucky it is you came to us before we left town – couldn't have given you Mogg's muffins in the country – hot rolls there – hot rolls more rural than muffins – An't they, Kitty, my dear? – only think, made three hundred thousand pounds by his muffins – white as snow, soft as down, are Mogg's muffins – An't they, Kitty, my dear?'[46]

Moggs' muffins acquire further significance later when Edith finds herself viewed as the rival of Moggs' heiress, but Mr Ribley continues to advocate new kinds of food for Edith. When Mrs Ribley tries to divert the conversation to plans for the day, Mr Ribley asks what dinner is planned and then turns to Edith,

> 'Pray, Miss ... did you ever taste Birch's turtle soup?'
>   Edith replied in the negative.
>   'Never tasted Birch's turtle soup!' exclaimed he, in astonishment; 'why Birch's turtle soup goes all over the universe – East and West Indies, China, America – Scotland is sadly out of the way, to be sure. Why, if you never tasted Birch's turtle-soup, you have tasted nothing. – Kitty, my dear, let us have Birch's turtle-soup today – three quarts for a party of six, eh?'[47]

45 Ferrier, *Destiny*, vol. 3, pp. 66–7.
46 Ferrier, *Destiny*, vol. 3, p. 77.
47 Ferrier, *Destiny*, vol. 3, p. 79.

Mr Ribley suggests taking Edith to see the lions at the Tower of London,'– no lions in Scotland, eh? – Lions won't eat porridge, eh?', and then reverts to Miss Mogg, her education 'at the first boarding school in town – finished off at Paris' and the contrast to Edith's poverty:'– suppose you haven't brought much money from Scotland – not much comes from it – not much goes to it – Kitty, my dear, you'll get everything that's proper for Miss your niece?'[48]

This sense of food as the currency of political and economic as well as domestic and corporal power is at the heart of Ferrier's almost obsessive interest in cooking, eating and buying things to eat. It is through food that issues of nationhood and issues of personhood come together most compellingly; if not much comes into Scotland and not much goes out, is Edith not much? If Edith has never been served Birch's turtle soup, does that mean Scotland is less part of the empire, or even 'the universe' than China and the East and West Indies? Ribley uses the brand name here as an instrument of empire, the turtle soup functioning as a kind of early nineteenth century Coca-Cola, a food so intensively processed that it has lost all discernable connection with any recognisable organic ingredients, and whose constituent parts are anyway exotic to the culture whose tool or weapon it has become. Moggs' muffins stand for a new, masculinised food chain, in which men in cities trade food whose commodity value is determined by brand more than by intrinsic merit, a far cry from the hand-made bannocks and oatcakes served for breakfast in the Highland castles of Ferrier's fiction. Birch's turtle soup takes this a step further, promoting a global menu of tinned and branded food that is not served in Scotland. The later rivalry between Miss Mogg and Edith, the classic pitting of new money against authentic virtue as shown by good taste, implicates women in this trade, glancing towards another moment in which Romantic-era women's writing seems to accept the edibility of the female subject. Virtue turns out to be worth more than muffins, but it is a quantitative difference.

It is clear from Mr Ribley's diction that the pleasure in edible imperialism is not Ferrier's. As much as the lairds' and the Scottish aunts' use of dialect contrasts with the standard English used by the heroines and their mother-figures to emphasise the dialect speakers' representative function and lack of interiority, so Mr Ribley's tele-graphic omission of subjects and jerky succession of unrelated clauses bespeaks his commercial background. Like Austen, Ferrier posits a direct relation between graceful use of language and moral integrity. Mr Ribley, and perhaps London in general, represents a kind of Englishness which is no more the shape of the future than the kind of Scottishness symbolised by Edith's father. He stands for profoundly alienated forms of production and consumption and an industrialised version of national identity which must perforce exclude Scotland. He speaks, and eats, for England and not for Britain.

Mr Ribley is different from the other eating men in Ferrier's fiction because his interest is, tellingly, in buying food at least as much as in eating it. His understanding of food as economic currency more than the stuff of life is, according to Ferrier, false consciousness, but it seems morally preferable to the straightforward self-indulgence of the other gluttons, whose voracity can also be read in gendered and political terms. The first of these, Dr Redgill in *Marriage*, also has a taste for turtles.

Mary encounters Dr Redgill when she arrives at her mother's establishment in England after manifesting signs of a decline while living with the Douglases. Her cousin, Lady Emily, describes Dr Redgill as 'a sort of medical aide-de-camp of papa's ... who, for the sake of good living, has got himself completely domesticated here.'[49] On her first morning, Mary enters the breakfast salon with Lady Emily to find Dr Redgill 'at the winding up of a solitary but voluminous meal'. He greets the young ladies with 'a feint of half-rising from his chair' and then sits 'without stirring hand or foot' while Lady Emily rings the bell herself. He speaks of having 'rode [sic] from [his] friend Admiral Yellowchops this morning' and, asked if he had a pleasant time there, replies 'So-so – very so-so.'

> 'Only so, so and a turtle in the case!' exclaimed Lady Emily.
> 'Phoo – as to that, the turtle was neither here nor there. I value turtle as little as any man. You may be sure it wasn't for that I went to see my old friend Yellowchops. It happened, indeed, that there was a turtle, and a very well dressed one too; but where five and thirty people (one half of them ladies, who, of course, are always helped first,) sit down to dinner, there's an end of all rational happiness in my opinion.'
> 'But at a turtle feast you have surely something much better. You know you may have rational happiness any day over a beef-steak.'
> 'I beg your pardon – that's not such an easy matter. I can assure you it is a work of no small skill to dress a beef-steak handsomely; and moreover,

49 Ferrier, *Marriage*, p. 234.

to eat it in perfection, a man must eat it by himself. If you once exchange words over it, it is useless ... The fact is, a beef-steak is like a woman's reputation, if once it is breathed upon it's good for nothing!'[50]

It is clear here that Dr Redgill's misogyny is somehow of a part with his gluttony. He begrudges women's food because the convention that they be served first delays his gratification, and there is a sense in the comparison of beefsteak and a woman's reputation that they are similarly available for consumption and similarly appetising. The dysfunction that views rational happiness as coterminous with unimpeded access to a well-dressed turtle also regards women as in some sense edible. Dr Redgill also thinks of Scotland – although not, interestingly, England – as something to eat. When Lady Juliana comes late to breakfast, she asks Dr Redgill to pronounce on Mary's health, suggesting that 'she should be confined to her own apartment during the winter, that she may get quite well and strong against the spring'. Dr Redgill replies that since Mary's appetite is good, nothing can be wrong with her, especially since she has managed to 'cut so good a figure after the delicious meals you have been accustomed to in the north: you must find it miserable picking here'.[51] Lady Juliana interjects, 'I thought the breakfasts like everything else in Scotland, extremely disgusting.' Dr Redgill responds:

> 'Ha! well, that really amazes me. – The people, I give up – they are dirty and greedy – the country, too, is a perfect mass of rubbish – and the dinners not fit for dogs – the cookery, I mean; as to the materials, they are admirable – But the breakfasts! That's what redeems the land – and every county has its own peculiar excellence. In Argyleshire you have the Lochfine herring, fat, luscious and delicious, just out of the water, falling to pieces with its own richness – melting away like butter in your mouth. In Aberdeenshire, you have the Finnan haddo'with a flavour all its own, vastly relishing – just salt enough to be piquant ... In other places, you have the exquisite mutton of the country made into hams of a most delicate flavour; flour scones, soft and white; oatcakes, thin and crisp; marmalade and jams of every description; and – But I beg pardon – your ladyship was upon the subject of this young lady's health. – 'Pon my honour! I can see little the matter – We were just going to look over the bill together when your Ladyship entered.'[52]

50 Ferrier, *Marriage*, p. 233.
51 Ferrier, *Marriage*, p. 236.
52 Ferrier, *Marriage*, p. 237.

Again, there is the collocation of eating and women's bodies, this time in conjunction with a kind of eater's guide to Scotland which explicitly dismisses everything which is not edible, as if Scotland exists and has value only to the extent that it produces what can be consumed. The people are 'given up' and the land itself thrown out as 'rubbish'; the raw materials of nationhood – which are not readily consumed or easily digested – discarded in favour of this shockingly lingering catalogue of ingestion that mimics the erotic in sensual detail. Dr Redgill has little power, except over the poor of the district, whom he refuses to treat, and no apparent interest in anything beyond his own comfort, so it would be hard to argue that he speaks for England in any significant way. It is also clear that he is disturbingly emasculated and desexualised by greed, having allowed one kind of hunger to absorb, perhaps even digest, all others, so if he does represent any type of masculinity it is in a deeply perverted way. He is a flat character with a one-track mind, but he is not a trivial presence. It is as if Dr Redgill's appetite, his single and omni-present metaphor, threatens everything that is below him in the supply chain from Mary to Scotland itself, as if he cannot distin-guish between the food chain and the supply chain and is in danger of ingesting the land along with Mary's health, the poor woman who tries to summon him from his breakfast and anything else that might interfere with or even be tangential to gustatory pleasure. As a simple organism, a man who eats, Dr Redgill is laughable – and indeed Lady Emily finds some amusement in laughing at him – but as a man who eats everything and a man who does nothing but eat, he is a more sinister being, a figure of pure consumption that recognises no limit. This malign purity is hard to interpret in relation to national identity. The desire to eat Scotland sounds English, but Dr. Redgill is so disempowered that he is markedly not an imperial figure. The devotion to physical pleasure is a parody of aristocratic vice, but he is resolutely dependent. The constant references to sex and gender suggest that a reading in these terms may be more fruitful. Less redirected forms of sexuality than Dr Redgill's, after all, involve productivity in some form, most obviously for men. To subli-mate any kind of active male sexuality into eating, as Dr Redgill so explicitly does, displaces production and the possibility of fruitful-ness with consumption and the certainty of depletion. Greed is a monomania that renders him entirely parasitical, and he stands as a distinctly creepy monitory figure. Unregulated, appetite can eat you.

This is also, in a more complicated and politicised way, the lesson of Ferrier's final novel, where the glutton is more straightforwardly, and therefore less disturbingly, malevolent. Once again to summarise the convoluted plot of a novel which is hard to access, Gertrude, as the only issue of Lord Rossville's only fruitful son, inherits the Rossville estate on his death. Intoxicated by wealth and egged on by the rich cousin who hopes to marry her (thereby securing the means of paying off debts of which she is ignorant), she leaves Scotland for London where she embarks on a career of excessive expenditure, much to the displeasure of the virtuous poorer cousin with whom she is secretly in love. When, as we saw, she returns to Rossville, the concerns of the estate and the dilatory absence of the rich cousin incline her towards more laudable concerns, but before these can develop Jacob Lewiston reappears. Lewiston, the husband of Gertrude's wet-nurse, is a figure who has pursued Gertrude's mother throughout the novel, appearing from behind bushes and round corners to exert a strange power over Mrs St Clair and leading to several scenes of hysteria in which Gertrude's mother compels her to do as the mysterious stranger demands, often in contravention of propriety and frequently in ways that undermine Gertrude's moral standing in the eyes of the cousin she secretly loves. (The shades of both Evelina and Camilla come to mind.) Usually this merely involves remaining in Lewiston's presence while he behaves abruptly and without ceremony, but Gertrude has also been compelled to hand over all her jewels on pain of 'destroying' her mother's life in unspecified and apparently unspeakable ways. Earlier in the novel, Gertrude and Mrs St Clair became convinced from a newspaper report that Lewiston had drowned crossing the Atlantic after being bribed to leave England, but half way through the third volume he returns, forcing his way into the drawing room at Rossville to announce that this would be his 'home for some time'.[53] Gertrude rings the bell to have Lewiston thrown out, but her mother sends the servants away. Gertrude tries to leave the house herself but her mother kneels at her feet to beg 'for [her] life – for [her] fame – at [Gertrude's] hands.'[54] Still no explanations ensue. Mrs St Clair tells Gertrude, 'It is in vain that you would seek to penetrate the mysterious tie which links my fate with that of Lewiston, and which extends even to you – and it will be no less vain to

---

53 Ferrier, *Inheritance*, vol. 3, p. 183.
54 Ferrier, *Inheritance*, vol. 3, p. 187.

attempt to free yourself from his power.'[55] Gertrude is unconvinced, and Mrs St Clair threatens to leave the house alone and barefoot and never return. Gertrude gives up but sits 'in passive endurance, and as if scarcely conscious of the caresses lavished upon her'.[56] 'The hour of dinner' finds Gertrude still 'extended upon a couch', so her mother persuades her to come to the table:

> 'Gertrude, my dearest – you will come to dinner – I have had a long conversation with Lewiston – he has promised not to offend you with the bluntness of his American manners; but you ought to make allowance for them – he is an independent citizen of a republican state, where all, you know, is liberty and equality – but he means no offence, and will endeavour to adapt himself more to our notions of propriety.'[57]

Gertrude accedes, but Lewiston makes no such endeavour, and the meal that ensues is theatrical. Mrs St Clair leads Gertrude to the table, assuring her, 'We shall not expect you to talk, my love, but do eat something – the soup is very good – I think Brumeau has even surpassed himself today.' Lewiston, echoing Miss Pratt and Uncle Adam, demands, 'You keep a French cook?...that's a confounded expense, is it not?' The servants titter, and Lewiston requires Gertrude to serve him more soup: 'You may give me two spoonfuls – there – that's it – now, will you do me the favour to drink a glass of wine?' Gertrude will not. '[S]he still sat immoveable, with her eyes bent on her plate, though without even attempting to taste what Mrs St Clair had put upon it.' Lewiston begins to uncover the dishes on the table, asking 'What have we got here?' as he 'looked at it as at something he had never seen before'. He mimics the French chef's answer and tries to serve Gertrude, whom Mrs St Clair excuses with the words, 'You seldom eat, I think, my love, till the second course. I hope there is something coming that you like.'[58] Gertrude evinces complete disinterest in food:

> Meanwhile, Lewiston was eating and drinking with all the ardour of a hungry man, and the manners of a vulgar one. – He tasted of everything, evidently from curiosity; and, though it was apparent that the style was something he had not been accustomed to, yet he maintained the same forward ease, as though he were quite at home.
> 'Well, that may do for once,' said he, after having finished; 'but, in

55 Ferrier, *Inheritance*, vol. 3, p. 187.
56 Ferrier, *Inheritance*, vol. 3, p. 189.
57 Ferrier, *Inheritance*, vol. 3, p. 192.
58 Ferrier, *Inheritance*, vol. 3, p. 195.

America, we should scarcely call this a dinner – eh, Trudge?' to his dog.
'Why, another such as myself would have looked silly here – I like to see
a good joint or two.'

Mrs St Clair tried to laugh, but she coloured again, as she said – 'Lady
Rossville and I make such poor figures by ourselves, at anything of a substantial repast, that our dinners have, indeed, dwindled away into very
fairy-like entertainments; but, Jourdain, you will remember to let us have
something more solid tomorrow.'

'What do you think, for instance, of a fine, jolly, juicy, thirty pound
round of well-corned beef and parsnips; or a handsome leg of pork and
pease-pudding, and a couple of fat geese well stuffed with sage and on-
ions, swimming in apple-sauce? – Ah! these are the dishes for me!' and he
rubbed his hands with horrid glee.[59]

Much of Lewiston's offence here is in seeming at home when he
should not. It is as if he cannot recognise or acknowledge foreignness, as if the American must make everywhere in America's image,
or at least pretend to do so. It is a metaphorical as well as literal
gluttony that wants to eat up everything and incorporate and erase
all foreign substances. Lewiston eats everything, but he wants something 'more solid'. He wants to eat things that look like animals, to
ingest the subjectivity of other beings in the way that typifies male
greed in these novels. It is also here explicitly American greed, the
appetite of 'an independent citizen of a republican state where all is
liberty and equality'. Lewiston eats for America and Ferrier's disdain
is palpable.

Further explication of this disdain occupies the closing pages
of the novel. Lewiston eventually tells Gertrude that he is her
father and the woman she believes to be her wet-nurse is her
mother. Lyndsay, who is both Gertrude's guardian and her suitor,
disbelieves this and compels Lewiston to admit that he has taken
his dead cousin's identity in the hope of profiting from the riches
of the Countess of Rossville. In any case, it is now obvious that
Gertrude is not the Countess of Rossville, and Uncle Adam offers
her a mansion to live in while Lyndsay goes to America to discover
the true story. Like Edgeworth's *Ennui*, to which it bears many similarities, *Inheritance* becomes a story about mistaken identity and lost
roots, in which the Scottish uncle is able to offer an authentic and
appropriate refuge in contrast to the unjustified luxury of Rossville
Castle and the howling wilderness of New Jersey, where the false

59 Ferrier, *Inheritance*, vol. 3, p. 196.

father hopes to sell Gertrude on the marriage market. Lewiston's table manners encode a larger greed for everything to which he is not entitled, making him a figure of all that this period fears about democracy and republicanism. Gertrude is doubly orphaned, but the answer to her abandonment is not independence, liberty and equality but a reinscribed subjugation to benign patriarchy.

Dispossessed from Rossville, humbled by her sudden fall but nurtured and sustained by Uncle Adam, Gertrude's true story puts her back where she belongs. The wet nurse in France was the daughter of Lizzie Lundy, Uncle Adam's childhood sweetheart, and he takes in Gertrude for her sake. In the end, then, the Scottish lineage saves the heroine from the disgraceful greed of the New World as well as from the tempting luxuries of the English aristocracy. Her fall from aristocracy to indigence is arrested by the miserly Scottish uncle, whose care succeeds where both real and false parents have failed in their most basic duties. The tenuous nature of the connection between Gertrude and Adam Ramsay is important. There is no blood relationship, only one of sentiment, and that sentiment pertains to a grandmother whom Gertrude resembles but never met. As promised in the opening chapters, Gertrude's final identity is written on her face, in her resemblance to Lizzie Lundy. As throughout Ferrier, the body tells the truth. Mrs St Clair, exposed as a fraud, takes an overdose of laudanum. Delmour comes into the earldom on Gertrude's exposure, and renounces his love for her in order to marry a duchess whose capital will pay off the estate's debts. But the duchess, as duchesses will, betrays him, and when Delmour dies in the resulting duel the title comes to Lyndsay, whose true virtues have become apparent to Gertrude in her dispossession. She marries him, and thereby returns to Rossville as the Earl's wife and not the Countess in her own right.

Gertrude, then, has been consuming not only beyond necessity but beyond entitlement. Only when she has lost everything and accepted that she has, by birth, no entitlement at all, can she be restored to the fold by the courtesy of a reconstructed patriarchy whose authority rests on the shaky ground of sentiment and self-denial. Lyndsay returns Gertrude to Rossville, but on the condition of limited appetite and faithful productivity:

> The bewildering glare of romantic passion no longer shed its fair but perishable lustre on the horizon of her existence; but the calm radiance of piety and virtue rose with steady ray, and brightened the future course of a

happy and useful life; and Gertrude, as the wife of Edward Lyndsay, lived
to bless the day that had deprived her of her earthly Inheritance.[60]

And with 'usefulness', the novel falls silent. The calm radiance
of piety and virtue is no light by which to read fiction, for, however
moral the story, reading is consumption. In all three of Ferrier's
novels, the stories are literally and metaphorically fuelled by
consumption, measured out in barley bannocks and wheaten bread,
breast-milk and pap, turtles and branded muffins.

In reading fiction we consume consumption, evincing a double
appetite which may be, in the end, the source of the anxiety which
bedevils the genre well into the nineteenth century. Even if there
are good novels – novels which make morality seem attractive as
well as modelling good writing and good thinking – fiction is still,
to return to Mary Brunton, a sweetmeat for vitiated appetites. There
is no need for fiction and therefore no entitlement and no hunger.
Reading novels is inescapably a form of recreational consumption,
divorced from any kind of 'usefulness' or productivity. Fiction is a
luxury. It may promote, but cannot enact, cannot produce, virtue,
and it is silenced by the practices it claims to recommend. Women
reading novels are feeding on Eve's apple and the final injunction
here, fittingly, is to go forth and produce.

Afterword

As I make what I fondly imagine (again) to be final revisions to *Spilling the Beans*, one of the things that distract me from scholarly productivity is the consumption of on-line newspapers. And one of today's headlines, under an investigation into the 'exploitation of migrant workers picking vegetables for supermarkets', beside 'Fatal e-coli case probe continues' and an advertisement for a job as a dietician specialising in obesity prevention, is 'Eating for two puts unborn child at risk of junk addiction'. I resist, for now, the compulsion to click 'more on food issues', and learn that 'pregnant and breast-feeding rats' fed on 'processed food such as doughnuts, muffins, biscuits, crisps and sweets' produced 'young with a greater preference for junk food' who 'also had a propensity to overeat and put on more weight'.[1] I do not know much about rats, but I do not think they have breasts. 'Lactating' would be a more conventional way of describing the state of a mother rat feeding its young, but 'breast-feeding' serves to forge a closer connection between women who snack in pregnancy and rats. We have not come far from Romantic-era comparisons between breastfeeding women who consult their own appetites and wild animals, and in a time and place which claims awareness of and even vigilance over sexual politics it seems to me, as a mother, an employee and a consumer, that much eighteenth-century vituperation of women's appetites and produce is mild by comparison to what I wrestle with on a daily basis.

Another recent article by which I allowed myself to be distracted

1 www.guardian.co.uk/science/2007/aug/15/sciencenews.foodanddrink accessed on 15 August 2007.

from the production of accurate footnotes reported research finding that 'middle class mothers who work long hours increase the risk of their offspring being overweight or obese'. The writers clarify that 'No link was found between the hours worked by the father or partner and weight problems' and include a warning from the chairman of the National Obesity Forum that 'If women are going back to work early after having children they are unlikely to be breastfeeding up to the recommended six months and the babies will go onto formula milk. If women are working there will be less time for food preparation and more resorting to convenience food. The types of food children are snacking on are going to be energy-dense and there will be more sedentary hours than activity hours.'[2] It was also clear that women working long hours for low wages do not have fat children. In this reading it is not maternal absence but professional success that promotes gratuitous consumption on the part of children, as if the mother's surplus income runs down the child's gullet. The implication is that women who take more – more status, more independence, more money – than mothers are entitled to will produce children who cannot recognise sufficiency. The economic and social greed of the mothers will be visited on the bodies of their – our – children.

Economic productivity, then, for women and not for men, works against domestic and biological productivity. Virtue inheres in the latter and the damnation of bad motherhood in the former. Women are answerable not only for their own consumption but that of their children, which women have in any case produced by their own recreational eating. If we met need and not inclination in pregnancy, if we ate for one (the baby), and then stayed at home producing milk by consuming minimally (for the baby) and cooking (for the children), we would produce a new generation of good citizens, i.e., people who consume and produce for the maximum health of the body politic. Nothing, it seems, has changed. I will now stop writing (having finished the chocolate I have been eating while writing this), go home, and cook.

2 news.independent.co.uk/health/article2790964.ece accessed on 15 August 2007.

Bibliography

Adams, Carol J., *The Sexual Politics of Meat: A Feminist-Vegetarian Critical Theory* (New York: Continuum, 1998).

Aitken, John, *Principles of Midwifery, or Puerperal Medicine* (London: J. Murray, 3rd edn, 1786).

Anon, *The Compleat Family Physician: Being a Perfect Compendium of Domestic Medicine* (Newcastle: Matthew Brown, 1801).

[Anon] 'A Mother', *The Polite Lady, or A Course in Female Education* (London: 1769).

Anon, *The Tryal of Lady Allurea Luxury* (London: F. Noble, 1757).

Armstrong, Nancy, *Desire and Domestic Fiction: A Political History of the Novel* (Oxford: Oxford University Press, 1987).

Arney, William Ray, *Power and the Profession of Obstetrics* (Chicago: University of Chicago Press, 1982).

Attfield, Judy, *Wild Things: The Material Culture of Everyday Life* (Oxford: Berg, 2000).

Austen, Jane, 'The Watsons', in *Northanger Abbey, Lady Susan, The Watsons and Sanditon*, ed. John Davie (Oxford: Oxford University Press, 1990).

Bailey, Rebecca, 'Clothes Encounters of the Gynecological Kind', in Ruth Barnes and Joanne B. Eichner (eds), *Dress and Gender: Making and Meaning in Cultural Contexts*, Berg, New York, 1992.

Barker, Hannah, and Elaine Chalus (eds), *Gender in Eighteenth-Century England – Roles, Representations and Responsibilities* (London: Longman, 1997).

Batchelor, Jennie, and Cora Kaplan (eds), *Women and Material Culture, 1660–1830* (Basingstoke: Palgrave Macmillan, 2007).

Bayne-Powell, Rosamond, *Housekeeping in the Eighteenth Century* (London: John Murray, 1956).

Bell, Vikki (ed.), *Performativity and Belonging* (Sage Publications, London, 1999).

Benedict, Barbara M., 'The Spirit of Things', in Mark Blackwell (ed.), *The Secret Life of Things: Animals, Objects and It-Narratives in Eighteenth-Century*

England (Lewisburg: Bucknell University Press, 2007).

Berg, Maxine, *Luxury and Pleasure in Eighteenth-Century Britain* (Oxford: Oxford University Press, 2005).

Berg, Maxine, and Helen Clifford (eds), *Consumers and Luxury: Consumer Culture in Europe 1650–1850* (Manchester: Manchester University Press, 1999).

Bergen Brophy, Elizabeth, *Women's Lives and the eighteenth-century English Novel* (Tampa: University of South Florida Press, 1991).

Bettelheim, Bruno, *The Uses of Enchantment: The Meaning and Importance of Fairy Tales* (Harmondsworth: Penguin, 1978).

Bilger, Audrey, *Laughing Feminism: Subversive Comedy in Frances Burney, Maria Edgeworth and Jane Austen* (Detroit: Wayne State University Press, 1998).

Blackwell, Mark (ed.), *The Secret Life of Things: Animals, Objects and It-Narratives in Eighteenth-Century England* (Lewisburg: Bucknell University Press, 2007).

Bordo, Susan, 'Reading the Slender Body', in Mary Jacobus, Evelyn Fox Keller and Sally Shuttleworth (eds), *Body/Politics: Women and the Discourses of Science* (New York and London: Routledge, 1990).

Bower, Anne (ed), *Recipes for Reading: Community Cookbooks, Stories, Histories* (Amherst: University of Massachusetts Press, 1997).

Bowers, Toni, *The Politics of Motherhood: British Writing and Culture 1680–1760* (Cambridge: Cambridge University Press, 1996).

Brumberg, Joan Jacobs, *Fasting Girls: The Emergence of Anorexia Nervosa as a Modern Disease* (Cambridge, Mass.: Harvard University Press, 1988).

Brunton, Mary, *Self-Control*, ed. Sara Maitland (London: Pandora, 1986).

Buchan, William, *Advice to Mothers* (London: T. Cadell and W. Davies, 1803).

Burney, Frances, *Camilla*, ed. Edward A. Bloom and Lillian D. Bloom (Oxford: Oxford University Press, 1972).

Burney, Frances, *Cecilia*, ed. Peter Sabor and Margaret Anne Doody (Oxford: Oxford University Press, 1988).

Burney, Frances, *The Early Journals and Letters of Frances Burney*, ed. Lars E. Troide and Steward J. Cook (Oxford: Clarendon Press, 1994).

Burney, Frances, *Evelina*, ed. Margaret Anne Doody (Harmondsworth: Penguin, 1994).

Burney, Frances, *The Journals and Letters of Frances Burney*, ed. Joyce Hemlow (Oxford: Clarendon Press, 1972).

Burney, Frances, *The Wanderer*, ed. Margaret Anne Doody *et al.* (Oxford: Oxford University Press, 1991).

Busby, Sian, *A Wonderful Little Girl: Starving for Fame* (London: Short Books, 2004).

Butler, Judith, *Gender Trouble: Feminism and the Subversion of Identity* (London: Routledge, 1990, new edn 1999).

Butler, Marilyn, *Maria Edgeworth: A Literary Biography* (Oxford: Clarendon Press, 1972).

Cadogan, William, *An Essay Upon Nursing* (London: Robert Horsfield, 10th ed., 1772).

Caplan, Pat (ed), *Food, Health and Identity* (London: Routledge, 1997).

Carol, H., 'The Story of the Pineapple: Sentimental Abolitionism and Moral Motherhood in Amelia Opie's *Adeline Mowbray*', in *Studies in the Novel*, 30:3.

Carter, Jenny, and Duriez, Thérèse, *With Child: Birth through the Ages* (Edinburgh: Mainstream Publishing, 1986).

Carter, Pam, *Feminism, Breasts and Breastfeeding* (London: Macmillan, 1995).

Cassidy, Tina, *Birth: A History* (London: Chatto and Windus, 2007).

Caton, Donald, *What a Blessing She Had Chloroform: The Medical and Social Response to the Pain of Childbirth from 1800 to the Present* (Newhaven and London: Yale University Press, 1999).

Clarkson, L.A., and E. Margaret Crawford, *Feast and Famine: A History of Food and Nutrition in Ireland 1500–1920* (Oxford: Oxford University Press, 2001).

Copeland, Edward, *Women Writing about Money* (Cambridge: Cambridge University Press, 1995).

Cornwell, Bryan, *The Domestic Physician, or, Guardian of Health* (London: J. Murray, 1784).

Cosslett, Tess, *Women Writing Childbirth* (Manchester: Manchester University Press, 1994).

Coveney, John, *Food, Morals and Meaning: The Pleasure and Anxiety of Eating* (London: Routledge, 2000).

Cunnington, Phillis, and C. Willet, *The History of Underclothes* (London: Michael Joseph, 1951).

Cutting-Gray, Joanne, *Woman as 'Nobody' and the Novels of Fanny Burney* (Gainsville: University of Florida Press, 1992).

David, Elizabeth, *Harvest of the Cold Months: The Social History of Ice and Ices* (Harmondsworth, Penguin, 1994).

Day, Thomas, *The History of Sandford and Merton* (Philadelphia: Willis P. Hazard, 1857).

Derrida, Jacques, '"Il faut bien manger" ou le calcul du sujet', in *Points de suspension: entretiens* (Paris: Editions Galilée, 1992).

Devine, T.M., *The Great Highland Famine: Hunger, Emigration and the Scottish Highlands in the Nineteenth Century* (Edinburgh: John Donaldson Publishers, 1988).

Donnison, Jean, *Midwives and Medical Men: A History of Inter-professional Rivalries and Women's Rights* (London: Heinemann, 1977).

Doody, Margaret Anne, *Frances Burney: The Life in the Works* (Cambridge: Cambridge University Press, 1988).

Douglas, Mary, *Implicit Meanings: Essays in Anthropology* (London: Routledge and Kegan Paul, 1975).

Douglas, Mary, and Baron Isherwood, *The World of Goods: Towards an Anthropology of Consumption* (London: Routledge, 1979, rev. edn 1996).

Duden, Barbara, *Disembodying Women: Perspectives on Pregnancy and the Unborn* (Cambridge, Mass: Harvard University Press, 1993).

Eberle, Roxanne, *Chastity and Transgression in Women's Writing 1792–1897: Interrupting the Harlot's Progress* (New York: Palgrave, 2002).

Edgeworth, Maria, *Moral Tales* (New York: AMS Press, Inc., 1967).

Edgeworth, Maria, *The Parent's Assistant* (London: Macmillan, 1897).

Edgeworth, Maria, and Richard Lovell Edgeworth, *Practical Education* (London: J. Johnson, 1801).

Eger, Elizabeth *et al.* (eds), *Women, Writing and the Public Sphere* (Cambridge: Cambridge University Press, 2001).

Ellis, Markman, *The Coffee House: A Cultural History* (London: Weidenfeld and Nicholson, 2004).

Ellmann, Maud, *The Hunger Artist: Starving, Writing and Imprisonment* (London: Virago, 1993).

Entwhistle, Joan, *The Fashioned Body: Fashion, Dress and Modern Social Theory* (Cambridge: Polity Press, 2000).

Epstein, Julia, *The Iron Pen: Frances Burney and the Politics of Women's Writing* (Bristol: Bristol Classical Press, 1989).

Farrar Thaddeus, Janet, *Frances Burney, a Literary Life* (London: Macmillan, 2000).

Fasick, Laura, *Vessels of Meaning: Women's Bodies, Gender Norms and Class Bias from Richardson to Laurence* (De Kalb: Northern Illinois University Press, 1997).

Ferrier, Susan, *Destiny* (William Blackwood: Edinburgh, 1831).

Ferrier, Susan, *The Inheritance* (Edinburgh: William Blackwood, 1824).

Ferrier, Susan, *Marriage*, ed. Herbert Foltinek (Oxford: Oxford University Press, 2001).

Fielding, Penny, *Writing and Orality: Nationality, Culture and Nineteenth Century Scottish Fiction* (Oxford: Clarendon Press, 1996).

Fildes, Valerie, *Breasts, Bottles and Babies: A History of Infant Feeding* (Edinburgh: Edinburgh University Press, 1986).

Floyd, Janet, and Laurel Forster (eds), *The Recipe Reader: Narratives–Context–Traditions* (Aldershot: Ashgate, 2003).

Fordyce, James, *The Character and Conduct of the Female Sex* (London: 1776).

Fordyce, James, *Sermons to Young Ladies* (Edinburgh: rev. edn, 1775).

Forth, Christopher, and Ana Carden-Coyne (eds), *Cultures of the Abdomen* (Basingstoke: Palgrave Macmillan, 2005).

Freud, Sigmund, *The Interpretation of Dreams*, in *The Standard Edition of the Complete Psychological Works of Sigmund Freud* (trans. James Strachey *et al.*), vol. iv (London: Hogarth Press, 1958).

Furst, Lilian R., and Peter W. Graham (eds), *Disorderly Eaters: Texts in Self-Empowerment* (Philadelphia: Pennsylvania State University Press, 1992).

Gallagher, Catherine, *Nobody's Story: The Vanishing Acts of Women Writers in the Marketplace, 1670–1820* (Berkeley: University of California Press, 1994).

Gelphi, Barbara Charlesworth, *Shelley's Goddess: Maternity, Language, Subjectivity* (Oxford: Oxford University Press, 1992).

Gigante, Denise, *Taste: A literary History* (Newhaven: Yale University Press, 2005).

Glasse, Hannah, *The Art of Cookery Made Plain and Easy* (London: printed for the author, 1774).

Glenny, Allie, *Ravenous Identity: Eating and Eating Distress in the Life and Work of Virginia Woolf* (London: Macmillan, 1999).

Godwin, William, *Memoirs of the Author of the Vindication of the Rights of Woman* (Harmondsworth: Penguin, 2000).

Gonda, Caroline, *Reading Daughters' Fictions 1709–1834: Novels and Society from Manley to Edgeworth* (Cambridge: Cambridge University Press, 1996).

Goody, Jack, *Cooking, Cuisine and Class: A Study in Comparative Sociology* (Cambridge: Cambridge University Press, 1982).

Goody, Jack, *Food and Love: A Cultural History of East and West* (London: Verso, 1998).

Greenfield, Susan, *Mothering Daughters: Novels and the Politics of Family Romance, Frances Burney to Jane Austen* (Detroit: Wayne State University Press, 2002).

Greenfield, Susan, and Carol Barash (eds), *Inventing Maternity: Politics, Science and Literature, 1650–1865* (Lexington: University of Kentucky Press, 1999).

Gregory, John, *A Father's Legacy to His Daughters* (London: John Murray, 1801).

Guerrini, Anita, *Obesity and Depression in the Enlightenment: The Life and Times of George Cheyne* (Oklahoma, University of Oklahoma Press, 2000).

Guest, Harriet, *Small Change: Women, Learning, Patriotism, 1750–1810* (Chicago: University of Chicago Press, 2000).

Gutierrez, Nancy A., *Shall She Famish Then? Female Food Refusal in Early Modern England* (London: Ashgate, 2003).

Hamilton, Alexander, *A Treatise on the Management of Female Complaints, and of Children in Early Infancy* (Edinburgh: Peter Hill, 4th edn, 1797).

Hammerton, James A., *Cruelty and Companionship: Conflict in Nineteenth-Century Married Life* (London: Routledge, 1992).

Hanson, Clare, *A Cultural History of Pregnancy* (Basingstoke: Palgrave Macmillan, 2004).

Hanway, Jonas, *A Plan for Establishing a Charity-House or Charity-Houses, for the Reception of Repenting Prostitutes, to Be Called the Magdalen Charity* (London: 1758).

Harcstark Myers, Sylvia, *The Bluestocking Circle: Women, Friendship and the Life of the Mind in Eighteenth-Century England* (Oxford: Clarendon Press, 1990).

Henderson, Andrea K., *Romantic Identities: Varieties of Subjectivity* (Cambridge: Cambridge University Press, 1996).

Heywood, Leslie, *Dedication to Culture: The Anorexic Aesthetic in Modern Culture* (Berkeley: University of California Press, 1997).

Hollander, Anne, *Seeing through Clothes* (Berkeley: University of California Press, 1975).

Humble, Nicola, *Culinary Pleasures: Cook Books and the Transformation of British Food* (London: Faber, 2005).

Hyde, Mary, *The Thrales of Streatham Park* (Cambridge, Mass.: Harvard University Press, 1977).

Innes, Sherrie, *Dinner Roles: American Women and Culinary Culture* (Iowa City: University of Iowa Press, 2001).

Johnson, Claudia, *Equivocal Beings: Politics, Gender and Sentimentality in the 1790s* (Chicago: University of Chicago Press, 1996).

Keane, Angela, *Women Writers and the English Nation in the 1790s* (Cambridge: Cambridge University Press, 2001).

Kelly, Gary, *Revolutionary Feminism: The Mind and Career of Mary Wollstonecraft* (London: Macmillan, 1992).

Kelly, Gary, *Women, Writing and Revolution, 1790–1827* (Oxford: Clarendon, 1993).

Kilner, Dorothy, 'The Life and Perambulation of a Mouse', in Robert Bator and Jonathan Cott (eds), *Masterworks of Children's Literature*, vol. 3 (New York: Stonehill Publishing, 1983).

King, Helen, *The Disease of Virgins: Green-sickness, Chlorosis and the Problems of Puberty* London: Routledge, 2003).

Kipp, Julie, *Romanticism, Maternity and the Body Politic* (Cambridge: Cambridge University Press, 2003).

Kowaleski Wallace, Elizabeth, *Consuming Subjects: Women, Shopping and Business in the Eighteenth Century* (New York: Columbia University Press, 1997).

Krugovoy Silver, Anna, *Victorian Literature and the Anorexic Body* (Cambridge: Cambridge University Press, 2002).

Lamb, Charles and Mary, 'Tales of Mrs Leicester's School', in Robert Bator and Jonathan Cott (eds), *Masterworks of Children's Literature*, vol. 4 (New York: Stonehill Publishing, 1984).

Lane, Maggie, *Jane Austen and Food* (London: Hambledon Press, 1995).

Lehmann, Gilly, *The British Housewife: Cookery Books, Cooking and Society in 18th-century Britain* (Totnes: Prospect Books, 2003).

Levi-Strauss, Claude, *The Origin of Table Manners: Introduction to a Science of Mythology*, vol. 3 (London: Jonathan Cape, 1978).

Lewis, Judith Schneid, *In the Family Way: Childbearing in the British Aristocracy 1760–1860* (New Brunswick: Rutgers University Press, 1986).

Locke, John, *Two Treatises of Government*, ed. C.B. McPherson (Indianapolis and Cambridge: Hackett Publishing, 1980).

London, April, *Women and Property in the Eighteenth Century English Novel* (Cambridge: Cambridge University Press, 1999).

Lynch, Deirdre, *The Economy of Character: Novels, Market Culture and the Busi-*

ness of Inner Meaning (Chicago: University of Chicago Press, 1998).

McKeon, Michael, *The Secret History of Domesticity: Public, Private and the Division of Knowledge* (Baltimore: Johns Hopkins University Press, 2005).

McMaster, Juliet, *Reading the Body in the Eighteenth Century Novel* (Basingstoke: Palgrave Macmillan, 2004).

Mahon, Silvester, *Every Lady her Own Physician, or, the Closet Companion* (London: M. Randall, 1788).

Malthus, Thomas, *An Essay on the Principle of Population* (Harmondsworth: Penguin, 1985).

Marland, Hilary and Anne Marie Rafferty (eds), *Midwives, Society and Childbirth: Debates and Controversies in the Modern Period* (London: Routledge, 1997).

Mead, Margaret (ed.), *Cultural Patterns and Technical Change* (New York: UNESCO, 1955).

Mintz, Sidney, *Sweetness and Power: The Place of Sugar in Modern History* (Harmondsworth: Penguin, 1985).

More, Hannah, *Strictures on Female Education* (Oxford: Woodstock Books, 1995).

Morton, Timothy, *The Poetics of Spice: Romantic Consumerism and the Exotic* (Cambridge University Press, Cambridge, 2000).

Morton, Timothy (ed.), *Cultures of Taste/Theories of Appetite: Eating Romanticism* (New York and Basingstoke: Palgrave Macmillan, 2004).

Murphy-Lawless, Jo, *Reading Birth and Death: A History of Obstetric Thinking* (Bloomington: Indiana University Press, 1998).

Opie, Amelia, *Adeline Mowbray, or, the Mother and Daughter*, ed. Shelley King and John B. Pierce (Oxford: Oxford University Press, 1999).

Parkins, Wendy (ed), *Fashioning the Body Politic* (Oxford: Berg, 2002).

Pearson, Jacqueline, *Women's Reading in England 1750–1835: A Dangerous Recreation* (Cambridge: Cambridge University Press, 1999).

Perry, Ruth, *Novel Relations: The Transformation of Kinship in English Literature and Culture, 1748–1818* (Cambridge: Cambridge University Press, 2004).

Porter, Roy, *Flesh in the Age of Reason* (London: Penguin, 2003).

Porter, Roy, and Lesley Hall, *The Creation of Sexual Knowledge in Britain, 1650–1950* (Newhaven: Yale University Press, 1995).

Probyn, Elspeth, *Carnal Appetites: FoodSexIdentities* (London: Routledge, 2000).

Raffald, Elizabeth, *The Experienced English House-Keeper* (Manchester: Printed for the author, 1769).

Ribeiro, Aileen, *The Art of Dress: Fashion in England and France 1750–1820* (Newhaven: Yale University Press, 1995).

Ribeiro, Aileen, *Dress and Morality* (London: Batsford, 1986).

Rich, Adrienne, *Of Woman Born: Motherhood as Experience and Institution* (London: Virago, 1977).

Richards, Eric, *The Highland Clearances* (Edinburgh: Birlinn, 2005).

Rogers, Pat, 'Fat Is a Fictional Issue: The Novel and the Rise of Weight-Watching', in Marie Mulvey Roberts and Roy Porter (eds), *Literature and Medicine During the Eighteenth Century*, Wellcome Institute Series in the History of Medicine (London: Routledge, 1993).

Sarti, Raffaella, *Europe at Home: Family and Material Culture 1500–1800* (Newhaven: Yale University Press, 2002).

Sceats, Sarah, *Food, Consumption and the Body in Contemporary Women's Fiction* (Cambridge: Cambridge University Press, 2000) .

Scott, Walter, *Guy Mannering*, ed. P. D. Garside (Edinburgh: Edinburgh University Press, 1999).

Scholliers, Peter, *Food, Drink and Identity: Cooking, Eating and Drinking in Europe since the Middle Ages* (Oxford: Berg, 2001).

Sen, Amartya, *Poverty and Famines: An Essay on Entitlement and Deprivation* (Oxford: Oxford University Press, revised edn, 1982).

Sherman, Sandra, *Imagining Poverty: Quantification and the Decline of Paternalism* (Columbus: Ohio State University Press, 2001).

Sherman, Sandra, '"The Whole Art and Mystery of Cooking": What Cookbooks Taught Readers in the Eighteenth Century', *Eighteenth-Century Life*, 28:1 (2004), 115–35.

Sherwood, Martha, 'The History of Little Henry and His Bearer', in Robert Bator and Jonathan Cott (eds), *Masterworks of Children's Literature*, vol. 4 (New York: Stonehill Publishing, 1984).

Smith, Mrs E., *The Compleat Housewife, or Accomplish'd Gentlewoman's Companion* (London: printed for the author, 15th edn, 1758).

Sontag, Susan, *Illness as Metaphor* (London: Allen Lane, 1979).

Spang, Rebecca, *The Invention of the Restaurant: Paris and Modern Gastronomic Culture* (Cambridge, Mass.: Harvard University Press, 2000).

Stearns, Peter, *Fat History: Bodies and Beauty in the Modern West* (New York: New York University Press, 2001).

Steele, Valerie, *The Corset: A Cultural History* (Newhaven: Yale University Press, 2001).

Stone, Laurence, *Uncertain Unions and Broken Lives: Marriage and Divorce in England 1660–1857* (Oxford: Oxford University Press, 1995).

Straub, Kristina, *Divided Fictions: Fanny Burney and Female Strategy* (Lexington: University Press of Kentucky, 1987).

Strong, Roy, *Feast: A History of Grand Eating* (London: Jonathan Cape, 2002).

Summers, Leigh, *Bound to Please: A History of the Victorian Corset* (Oxford: Berg, 2001).

Sussman, Charlotte, *Consuming Anxieties: Consumer Protest, Gender and British Slavery, 1713–1833* (Stanford: Stanford University Press, 2000).

Sweeney, Morag, *Anorexic Bodies: A Feminist and Sociological Perspective on Anorexia Nervosa* (London: Routledge, 1993).

Tauchert, Ashley, 'Maternity, Castration and Mary Wollstonecraft's Historical and Moral View of the French Revolution', *Women's Writing*, 4:2 (1997).

Tavor Bannet, Eve, *The Domestic Revolution: Enlightenment Feminisms and the Novel* (Baltimore: Johns Hopkins University Press, 2000).

Thirsk, Joan, *Food in Early Modern England* (London: Hambledon Continuum, 2006).

Todd, Janet, *Mary Wollstonecraft: A Revolutionary Life* (London: Weidenfeld and Nicolson, 2000).

Trimmer, Sarah, 'Fabulous Histories, or The Story of the Robins', in Robert Bator and Jonathan Cott (eds) *Masterworks of Children's Literature*, vol. 3 (New York: Stonehill Publishing, 1983).

Trumpener, Katie, *Bardic Nationalism: The Romantic Novel and the British Empire* (Princeton: Princeton University Press, 1997).

Trusler, John, *The Honours of the Table* (London: 1791).

Vandereycken, Walter, *From Fasting Saints to Anorexic Girls* (New York: New York University Press, 1994).

Vickery, Amanda, *The Gentleman's Daughter: Women's Lives in Georgian England* (Newhaven: Yale University Press, 1998).

Walker Bynum, Caroline, *Holy Feast and Holy Fast: The Religious Significance of Food to Medieval Women* (Berkeley: University of California Press, 1987).

Weatherill, Lorna, *Consumer Behaviour and Material Culture in Britain, 1660–1760* (London: Routledge, 1988) .

West, Jane, *Letters to a Young Lady* (London: Longman, Hurst, Rees, Orme and Brown, 1811).

Wilson, Adrian, *The Making of Man-Midwifery: Childbirth in England 1660–1770* (London: University College London Press, 1995).

Wollstonecraft, Mary, *Collected Letters of Mary Wollstonecraft*, ed. Ralph M. Wardle (Ithaca: Cornell University Press, 1979).

Wollstonecraft, Mary, *Mary* and *Maria* / Mary Shelley, *Matilda*, ed. Janet Todd (London: Penguin, 1991).

Wollstonecraft, Mary, *A Short Residence in Sweden, Norway and Denmark*, ed. Richard Holmes (London: Penguin, 1987).

Wollstonecraft, Mary, *A Vindication of the Rights of Men, A Vindication of the Rights of Woman*, ed. Janet Todd (Oxford: Oxford University Press, 1999).

Wollstonecraft, Mary, *The Works of Mary Wollstonecraft*, ed. Janet Todd and Marilyn Butler (London: William Pickering, 1989).

Wordsworth, Dorothy, *The Grasmere Journals*, ed. Pamela Woof (Oxford: Oxford University Press, 1991).

Yeazell, Ruth Bernard, *Fictions of Modesty: Women and Courtship in the English Novel* (University of Chicago Press, Chicago, 1991).

Zonitch, Barbara, *Familiar Violence: Gender and Social Upheaval in the Novels of Frances Burney* (Newark: University of Delaware Press, 1997).

Index

animals
  birds 26–7, 152
  deer 79–81
  dogs 100, 109, 136, 149, 164,
    167
  guinea hen 129
  horses 124–5
  pigs 130
  sheep, lambs 131–3, 165
  see also meat-eating 22, 25–8
anorexia nervosa 36
Austen, Jane
  Emma 123, 124
  Mansfield Park 19, 123
  Pride and Prejudice 13
  The Watsons 12–13

Benedict, Barbara 5
Berg, Maxine
  Luxury and Pleasure 33
bread 4, 11, 24, 39, 74, 78, 129,
  132–3, 166
breastfeeding 2, 18, 23–4, 42,
  59–60, 84–5, 95–108, 164,
  172, 175
Brunton, Mary
  Self Control 17–18, 37–42
Buchan, William
  Advice to Mothers 82, 83,
    88–9, 97, 105, 112–13

Cadogan, William
  Essay upon Nursing 86,
    107–8, 113
cake 22, 23, 26, 50, 73–4, 114,
  117, 119, 120, 125, 142–3,
  153
Caritas Romana 103–4
cheese 19, 24
chocolate 39, 192
Cornwell, Bryan
  The Domestic Physician 86
corsets 110–13

Day, Thomas 151–2
  Sandford and Merton 152–3
fat, fatness 18–19, 37, 41, 162
Fielding, Penny
  Writing and Orality 163
Fordyce, James
  Sermons to Young Ladies
    15–16
French cuisine 7, 33–5, 63, 72,
  89, 178
Freud, Sigmund
  The Interpretation of Dreams
    2, 4

fruit 3–4, 8, 21–2, 28, 30–1, 35,
  48, 78, 91, 114, 117, 138,
  140, 148, 168

Glasse, Hannah
  The Art of Cookery 34
gluttony 117–21
Godwin, William
  *Memoirs of the Author of the
    Vindication of the Rights of
    Woman* 94
Gregory, John
  *A Father's Legacy to his
    Daughters* 116

Hamilton, Alexander
  *Treatise on the Management of
    Female Complaints* 87, 105,
    108, 112–13
Henderson, Andrea
  *Romantic Identities: Varieties
    of Subjectivity* 84, 90

ice cream 65, 67–8, 157–8

Johnson, Samuel 37, 47, 48–51,
  58

Keane, Angela
  *Women Writers and the
    English Nation in the 1790s*
    85, 92
Kilner, Dorothy
  *Life and Perambulations of a
    Mouse* 22–3, 127
Kipp, Julie
  Maternity and the Body Politic
    23, 35, 122, 175

Lehmann, Gilly
  *The British Housewife:
    Cookery Books, Cooking
    and Society in 18th Century
    Britain* 7, 12–15
Locke, John
  Two Treatises of Government 3,
    4
Lynch, Deirdre
  The Economy of Character 160

meat-eating 15, 25–7, 67,
  79–81, 114, 126, 131–4,
  152, 181, 184
Morton, Timothy
  and Denise Gigante, *Cultures
    of Taste/Theories of Appetite*
    1, 3, 6, 8

Opie, Amelia
  Adeline Mowbray 28–33

Perry, Ruth
  Novel Relations 161
pregnancy 24, 32, 83–91, 111,
  154, 166
prostitution 24

Raffald, Elizabeth
  *The Experienced English
    Housekeeper* 34

Scott, Walter 165, 173, 177
  Guy Mannering 174
seafood 19, 66–7
Sherman, Sandra
  Imagining Poverty 123
Smith, Elizabeth
  Compleat Housewife 34–5
starvation 10–11, 77, 123, 142
self-starvation 32, 36–7, 38–42,
  47, 51–9
Steele, Valerie
  The Corset: A Cultural History
    112–13
Sussman, Charlotte
  Consuming Anxieties 1
sweetness, sweets 14, 17–18,
  20–2, 24, 32, 91, 119, 125,
  126, 138–9, 142, 145, 158,
  191

tea 56, 70–1, 156
thing theory 4, 5
Thrale, Hester 48–51, 54, 58–9
Trimmer, Sarah
  *Fabulous Histories, or, the
    History of the Robins* 26–7,
    132
Trumpener, Katie
  Bardic Nationalism 160
Trusler, John
  The Honours of the Table
    14–15
  *The Tryal of Lady Allurea
    Luxury*, 33–4
turtle 162, 181, 182, 183–4

vegetarianism *see* meat-eating

West, Jane
  Letters to a Young Lady 27–8
Wordsworth, Dorothy 8–9, 37

Youngquist, Paul 3, 9

Lightning Source UK Ltd.
Milton Keynes UK
UKHW020211280420
362405UK00007B/387